What readers are saying about
the Hunter Rayne highway mysteries:

"A great take to bed read for anyone who loves crime fiction in a
traditional fashion."

"Those were the best mysteries I've read in a long time!! As soon as I
finished the first one I bought the second and felt empty when I
finished it! The characters were awesome and so there that I
somehow think they are in my life ..."

"This is a great read for anyone who likes mystery, intrigue and those
that are looking for good reads from up and coming Canadian
authors."

"Great trucking detail, hardboiled characters, no-nonsense dialogue
...."

"... this book caught my attention from the very first pages and it
only got better. I recommend this book to anyone who has a love for
a good mystery."

" ... Hunter Rayne would make a great TV detective, driving around
the country in his rig visiting different states and helping to solve
crimes. He is that interesting of a character."

Also by R.E. Donald

SLOW CURVE ON THE COQUIHALLA

ICE ON THE GRAPEVINE

a Hunter Rayne highway mystery

R.E. Donald

PROUD HORSE

PUBLISHING

First print edition 2012 by
Proud Horse Publishing,
British Columbia, Canada
ProudHorsePublishing@gmail.com

First digital edition published September 2011

PUBLISHER'S NOTE:
This is a work of fiction. Names, characters, places and incidents either are the product of the author's imagination or used fictitiously and any resemblance to actual persons, business establishments, events or locales is entirely coincidental. This story is set in the year 1996.

PRINTED IN THE UNITED STATES OF AMERICA

To Jim, my inspiration,
and to my friend, Barbara, who has always believed I could.

Who longs in solitude to live,
Ah! soon his wish will gain;
Men hope and love, men get and give,
And leave him to his pain.

Johann Wolfgang von Goethe

CHANGE ── ── ── ── ──
CHAPTER
ONE

Every morning felt like Christmas now that he had a wife.

The sun had not yet mounted the ragged hills, but the sky behind the San Gabriels was that washed out yellow that signaled another hot July day in L.A. County as California Highway Patrol officer Lucas Triggs neared the end of his graveyard shift. Lucas could hardly wait to get home; home where his sweet little wife was waiting for him with a good morning kiss, a soft cuddle and maybe more if there was time before she left for work. She'd make him a fine breakfast of eggs and sausages and a slab of ham. Mmmm, mmh. The thought of Sylvana made him grin like a fool as he cruised his assigned stretch of Interstate 5, elbow out the window, uphill now between dry slopes dotted with scrub grasses and sage. He wished he could crank up KZLA and sing along but there was too much static this far north, so instead he hummed the chorus of "Standing Outside the Fire" over and over as he kept half an ear on the police band.

Lucas Triggs was forty-three years old and there'd been few women in his life. Oh sure, there were the ones he'd paid for when he sailed with the navy, but that wasn't like having your own girl. Let's face it, with his hare lip he wasn't the world's best looking guy. The day he'd stopped to help Sylvana and her mother with a flat tire near the Kern County line he now counted as the luckiest day of his life. Eight months later, here he was, a married man with a family on

1

the way. He'd never known it would feel this good, having someone to welcome you home and kiss you good bye and warm your back with her sweet breath as you slept. He'd never imagined how fine it was to sit in front of the TV with your woman in your lap, your hands cupped over her taut round belly and her own hands resting like baby birds on yours. "I get to hug you and Junior all at once," he'd told her, and she giggled like a little girl.

The Chev's radio crackled to life. A code 10-54, possible dead body at the brake check north of the Templin turn off. "Trucker called it in," said the dispatcher. "He's standing by on the emergency channel if you need specifics."

Lucas replied that he was on his way, and flipped to Channel 9 on his CB. The trucker wasn't hard to raise, but the signal was poor. "... a cop, so I know better than to touch a dead body, you know what I mean? Where you..."

Lucas powered up his window for a closer listen. "Come again," he radioed.

The signal cleared. "CHP, you want to get your ass over here PDQ. I just pulled into the brake check north of Valencia, got out to take a piss, and almost tripped over some poor bastard all curled up like a pretzel."

"Dead?" asked Lucas.

"I think so, but I sure as hell ain't gonna touch him. My brother-in-law's a cop and I know the drill. You touch him if you want to, but I got the hell outa there soon as I saw him, and I ain't gonna let nobody else near him either."

Lucas turned on his flashers and depressed the pedal. The Chevy growled and sprinted toward Gorman, where he turned around and headed south. Minutes later, he pulled off the I-5 into the brake check area, a paved level clearing about the size of two football fields, where he was hailed by a big man in blue jeans and suspenders, his gray tee shirt darkened by sweat rings beneath the armpits. He had a black beard and a barrel shaped torso that reminded Lucas of Bluto. Lucas nosed the Chevy in beside the man's big Kenworth and got out. Another big rig was stopped near the far end of the brake check, and a VW bus that had seen better days was perched half on and half

2

off the asphalt nearby, its side door open. As Lucas watched, a skinny man with an equally skinny ponytail and a Hawaiian shirt that fluttered around his bony frame like a weather beaten flag, hopped out holding an enormous plastic mug.

"I never touched the guy, and I never let those bozos..." Bluto nodded in the direction of the VW. "... near him either. My brother-in-law's with Houston PD, so I know the drill. He tells me about some of the shit he's seen go down." He started walking toward the back end of his rig and Lucas followed at his shoulder. "No way I'm gonna mess up a crime scene, and I didn't let those other bozos even come close."

They rounded a pile of dirt, one of several that ringed the brake check, and Lucas saw a patch of color against the sandy soil. It was a man, or the body of a man, with his legs tucked up and hugged tight to his chest, his neck angled forward as if he were resting his head on his knees. He wore blue jeans, Nikes, and a polo shirt of green and white and blue. Lucas couldn't see his face. They stopped and stood about five yards away, Bluto with his thumbs hooked behind his suspenders.

"See? I told you he was all curled up," said Bluto, nodding emphatically as if Lucas had disputed it. "Damn strange, the way he's lyin' there, ain't it?"

Lucas had to agree. It wasn't so much that the man's fetal position was awkward or unusual, it was that he was lying on his right side, and so stiff that his head and feet didn't touch the ground.

"Hey! Far out."

The voice belonged to the skinny man from the VW bus, who had caught up to them and now stood beside Lucas, sipping at the contents of his plastic mug. "Kinda looks like that little guy from Laugh-In, huh? You remember that? You know, the little guy in the raincoat who used to fall over on his tricycle and just lie there?'

"Step back, sir," said Lucas. "You'll have to keep clear of this area."

Bluto turned around and glared at the skinny man, started shooing him away with both hands. "Some assholes are like vultures, feeding off other people's misery," he said in a low voice to Lucas, then louder, "This ain't no picnic, Buddy. Get out of here and don't touch nothin'."

Lucas motioned Bluto to stay put, then approached the hunched up figure, watching carefully where he placed his feet so as not to obscure any tracks, and making note of where his own footprints lay. He suspected that he was going to have to call the county coroner, but he'd never seen a corpse that looked quite like this before. Proper procedure was to first determine if there was any sign of life. If the poor bastard was alive and having some bizarre seizure or something, there'd be hell to pay if he didn't call an ambulance first. When he reached the body, Lucas squatted, elbows resting on his thighs, to examine the man more closely.

At the nape of his neck, the man's dark hair fell in loose curls, parting to reveal the knobs of his upper spine. His forearms were thin but muscular, his hands clenched into fists. Folded up the way he was, it was hard to judge his height. Average, Lucas guessed. His skin was white. Very white. Lucas reached out to place two fingers against the man's neck, intending to feel for a pulse in the carotid artery. His hand jerked away as if he'd been burned, and he was so surprised that he stumbled backwards, barely able to keep from falling flat on his butt in the dirt.

"Holy shit!" he said. "This stiff's a fuckin' block of ice!"

4

CHAPTER _ _ _ _ _
TWO

Hunter Rayne had already picked up the receiver of the payphone before the kid in the black jeans stepped out of the men's room. Hunter punched in his dispatcher's 800 number, and reported that the trailer load of rice cakes he'd picked up in Vancouver three days ago had been delivered to the customer's warehouse in Orange, California, and that he was clear to pick up his return load. The dispatcher, Elspeth Watson, informed him that she didn't have a return load scheduled for him yet. Any load. "I've got to get out of here," he said.

"I thought you liked southern California."

"I said that during the winter, El. And that's beside the point. If I've got to lay over, this is a better place than some to pass the time, but I'd still rather be on the road." The kid in the black jeans stood five feet away, smoking a cigarette. When Hunter offered a smile, the kid scowled at his watch, then turned away. "I've got bills to pay. What about that load of nacho sauce or whatever it was you were talking about before I left? Isn't it supposed to be ready tomorrow morning?"

"You've got bills to pay!? You think I don't?" El said.

Hunter clenched his jaw and took a deep breath. It was already the seventeenth of July and he still had to run another four thousand miles this month just to break even, to meet the bank payment on his six-year-old truck and cover fuel and maintenance costs. Over and above that, he had personal expenses to cover. Rent on the one bedroom basement suite in North Vancouver that he called home, and monthly checks for his two teenaged daughters. If business didn't pick up, he'd start falling behind.

"What happened to that nacho sauce?" he asked again.

"Well, it's just... oh yeah, your daughter's been lookin' for you. Janice." Hunter heard another line ringing in the background, and El said, "Hold on, sweetcheeks."

"No, El! Don't put me on hold." But it was too late. Hunter sighed and tucked the phone between his ear and shoulder as he adjusted the rolled up sleeves of his shirt, leaning briefly against the aluminum frame of the phone booth. Hot. Too hot. The kid was standing about thirty feet away, smoking and watching the attendants fuel up an immaculate red Peterbilt.

While he waited through the Vancouver weather forecast and two verses of "Why not me?" by the Judds, Hunter looked up at the afternoon sky, blue with a slight haze, the air around him full of highway sounds and the smell of diesel. He'd paid for a shower at the truck stop in Buttonwillow the previous night, but already he felt rimed in dust, felt it clinging to his face and forearms the way it clung to the navy blue flanks of his Freightliner. Every time he moved he felt his sweat dampened jeans grabbing at his legs. El came back on the line. "Now, where were we?" she said.

"The nacho sauce?"

"Right." She cleared her throat. "The nacho sauce."

The kid in black jeans was back. He threw down his cigarette and ground it into the dirt with the toe of his boot. "Fuckin' hurry it up," he said. Hunter glanced at him, without a smile this time.

"I gave that to Ray Nillson," said El.

Hunter swore silently.

"I said fuckin' hurry it up," said the kid, stepping closer. He had about four inches and thirty pounds on Hunter, but Hunter had twenty-four years experience in the police force on the kid.

"Ray called this morning, said he and Sharon had to get back to Vancouver ASAP. I'm sorry, Hunter. He said it was urgent. I'll get on the blower and scare something up for you as soon as I can."

6

The kid stepped into Hunter's space, squaring his shoulders and shifting his sunglasses from his nose to the crown of his head. Slowly Hunter removed his own sunglasses and tucked them in his shirt pocket, then lowered his head slightly, staring upwards into the kid's eyes, sizing up the kid's courage. He had no intention of taking the kid on, but the kid didn't have to know that. The kid backed up a couple of steps, said, "Fuck it," and turned away, kicking a stone across the asphalt.

El was still talking. "You just park The Blue Knight under a palm tree somewhere and make yourself comfy. Where you gonna be?" Hunter heard the phone ring again. "Oh, never mind," she said. "Call me first thing in the morning, will ya. "

He heard her yell, "I got it, Wally!" just before the receiver clicked in his ear.

"It's all yours, chief," Hunter told the kid with a nod.

The kid grunted, maybe it was thanks and maybe it wasn't, and stepped wide of Hunter on the way by.

Hunter eased The Blue Knight through rush hour traffic up the 57 and out the I-10 toward the big truck stop in Ontario. Even with an empty trailer, the big Freightliner whined in complaint at the continual speeding up and slowing down. He couldn't help but think about the fuel he was burning just to cross L.A., and the fact that time was money, and it could be days before El found a load to pay his way home to Vancouver.

A black BMW cut in front of him and he had to brake. The radio station was playing an old Waylon tuned that he liked, so he turned up the volume, took a deep breath and worked his shoulders in an effort to relax. "So she gave the nacho sauce to Ray and Sharon," he muttered, trying to sic his mind onto a new subject. He'd run into Ray and Sharon Nillson at a truck stop restaurant in Yoncalla, Oregon, on the way down. He'd walked in just as they were finishing up, and they'd invited him to share their table.

"Come meet Peaches when you're done," Sharon had said in that loud, throaty voice of hers, tapping her cigarette on the edge of the ashtray. "We're not in a hurry, are we Ray?"

Ray shook his head. Ray didn't talk much. He was a big man with a full round face topped by a wavy shock of hair that looked fake, but wasn't. He had a tendency to let his jaw fall slack, pulling his mouth open. He made Hunter think of the big shy kid in school, the one the other boys made fun of because he wasn't cool, because he looked dumb, because he was nice even to those very boys who made his life hell. "Sure, Hunter," said Ray. "We're going to take the dog for a walk before we hit the road again, anyhow."

"I can do that by myself, hon', if you want to stay and talk to Hunter 'til he's done," said Sharon. She butted her cigarette, then tossed her hair behind her shoulders with a flick of her index finger. Her hair was long and blond, with dark roots, and locks of it were pulled back from her temples and fastened behind her head with a gold-colored clip. A trio of glittering discs dangled from each ear.

Ray frowned and shook his head. "I don't want you walking around out behind the lot by yourself. I'll come with you."

"It's still broad daylight, for Pete's sake!"

"I'll come with you," he repeated.

"Afraid me and Peaches will get kidnapped?" she asked, with a flirty lift of one eyebrow. Then she turned to Hunter and said, "Ray says it took him thirty years to find me, and he sure as hell doesn't intend to lose me." She laughed, tossing her hair back again and setting the earrings swinging with soft clinks. It occurred to Hunter there were lots of things Ray said privately to his wife that no one else could ever imagine the big, quiet man saying. Hunter knew that had been true of himself, too, in the early years of his marriage to Chris, but it seemed a lifetime ago. Long before she asked for the divorce.

Sharon reached over and stroked her husband's hand, her geranium pink nails dwarfed by his thick knuckles. Ray ducked his head shyly and started to blush, but looked more pleased than annoyed. Newlyweds. They wore their hearts on their sleeves, as the saying goes, and it made Hunter uncomfortable, as if he were a voyeur. Or was it that they flaunted their being together in front of his being alone. Just then his meal had arrived, and he'd tucked into it, saying he might come out to their truck when he was finished, or he might not.

8

He didn't.

The traffic had started to ease off by the time Hunter reached the Ontario East truck stop in San Bernardino County. He waited until after dinner to call his daughter. He never could keep track of the girls' hours, but evening seemed a better bet than afternoon. The sun was setting, its rays scattering in a golden arc above the horizon, highlighting specs of dust and smears of dirt on the truck stop restaurant's dirty window. He watched the molten circle sink, then punched in his calling card number, wondering who would answer. Janice, the eldest, Lesley, the youngest, or his ex-wife, Christine. He hoped it wouldn't be Chris.

It was Lesley. "Hi, Dad. Where are you?" she said. Then he heard, "Janice, it's Dad. Want to get it in the other room?" She lowered her voice. "Hang on a sec, we don't want Mom to hear." Hunter smiled. The kids were always plotting surprises. He'd been on the receiving end more than once.

"Dad, are you going to be home by Sunday?"

"I sure hope so." What was Sunday? July the… "Your mom's birthday?" he asked.

"It's next Wednesday," said Janice. "But we're going to have a barbecue and cake and stuff on Sunday. We thought it would be nice if you could drop by. Totally casual. Nothing fancy."

Hunter hesitated. He briefly wondered whether the girls were trying to get their parents back together. It had happened several times during the first year of separation, but never since. Their attempts had created some very awkward moments, usually evolving into heated recriminations and slammed doors from Chris, or clenched teeth and swift, silent departures on his own part. He didn't miss those scenes.

"We hardly ever see you anymore, Dad. You're always out of town," said Lesley.

It had been a few California trips ago, well over a month, since he'd seen either one of them. He'd tried to call several times, but he always hung up if he didn't get them on the phone. He didn't feel comfortable leaving messages for Lesley and Janice on their mother's answering machine.

"The only way we can make sure we see you," added Janice, "is to plan ahead. Come on, Dad. Come, okay?"

"Okay," he said. He winced at the thought, but added, "I miss you kids. It'll be good to see you all." And it would make a nice change from the usual restaurant dinner, with the girls always in a hurry to go somewhere afterwards, often leaving him to finish his coffee alone and pay the bill. He agreed to be there on Sunday at six.

He hung up the phone, stood there staring at it with his hands in his pockets for a minute, then sighed and headed for the driver lounge.

A movie was playing on a big screen TV, volume loud enough so he could hear the sounds of a car chase: squealing tires, thunks and clunks of speeding vehicles hitting curbs and flying across medians, terse dialogue and screamed epithets. Two men were watching the TV, another three sat at a table near the bar drinking long necks and talking. One of those men, a middle aged guy who drooped everywhere – moustache, jowls, belly and belt – looked up at Hunter and nodded, then turned his attention back to his companions. Hunter leaned against the wall by the door, his arms folded across his chest, and watched until the car chase ended in a hail of automatic gunfire, then wandered back outside.

The warm evening air lay across the parking lot like a wool blanket, no hint of a breeze. Hunter, alert to sounds and shadows, threaded his way back toward The Blue Knight through a maze of tractor-trailers. This truck stop wasn't as bad as some, but drivers and their loads were always a target for crime. The hum of refrigeration units on reefers surged and ebbed in several directions as he made his way alternately beneath the glare of security lights and the shadows of the big rigs. Occasionally he'd hear voices, or the sound of a television, or throbbing base rhythms coming from behind the closed doors of air-conditioned sleeper units. He exchanged a gruff hello with a young man wearing a cowboy hat who was leaning against the fender of a custom painted Kenworth, smoking a cigarette. Behind the Kenworth's partly open door, a white high-

10

heeled shoe appeared on the end of a naked female leg, then another, then a denim skirt that barely covered the woman's crotch. Hunter looked away.

Parked beside The Blue Knight was a cream-colored Ford, its interior lights on and a muffled male voice coming from inside. As Hunter unlocked his own door, the door to the Ford swung open and a big man climbed out, supporting himself on the grab bar with his right arm, and clutching something to his broad chest in his left.

"There you go, Scrappy," the man growled as he bent down to the ground. He straightened up with a grunt. Curious, Hunter paused with one foot on the lowest of the steps leading up to his cab to watch. The man had deposited a white miniature poodle with a sharp little face and glittery black eyes. It sniffed the Ford's front tire, then began to follow its nose in circles along the ground. As soon as it stopped sniffing long enough to look up, which was a matter of only a few seconds, it saw Hunter, planted its front paws and began to bark fiercely. The big man, who had remained standing with his back to Hunter, swung around.

"Mercy!" he said. "Where'd you come from alla sudden?"

Hunter looked down at the poodle, which had settled down to a growl that sounded like tiny ball bearings rolling across cement, punctuated here and there by two or three sharp yaps. "Hey, Killer," said Hunter. "Easy now. I'm not going to bite you." He crouched down and held his hand out toward the dog, glancing from the big man to the dog and back again. "Scrappy his name?" he asked.

The big man broke into a wide grin, the white of his teeth almost neon against the black of his skin. "Not *his* name, friend. Scrappy here's a little bitch, can't you tell? Always gots to be the center of attention, see?"

Hunter scratched the dog's back, just above its quivering tail, but the dog saw or heard something interesting on the other side of the Ford and scrambled across the gravel, tugging on its leash.

"Come back here, you l'il scamp" said the driver. He pulled the dog out from under the truck and tucked it under his arm. "They got a grassy patch out back," he said to Hunter, playing with the poodle's ears as it tried to climb his massive chest to lick his face.

Hunter nodded and smiled. "Goodnight," he said, and climbed up into his cab as the big man walked into the shadows. Hunter heard him talking to the dog again as he rounded the corner of the Ford's forty-eight foot trailer.

Maybe talking to a poodle was better than talking to yourself. He wondered sometimes if he had become a long-haul trucker in order to avoid human entanglements, rather than because he enjoyed the sense of freedom, as he liked to believe. His ex-wife had accused him of running away, and that thought made him uncomfortable. Running away was linked, in his mind, to cowardice, and he did not consider himself afraid. Cautious, perhaps, but not afraid.

He'd only had time to switch on the light in his sleeper when he heard the crunch of footsteps on gravel and then a knock on his door. He killed the light and looked out the window. A young girl with a ponytail and dangling earrings was looking up at him, smiling broadly. She motioned for him to come down, but he just rolled down the window. He could tell she wore nothing under her thin pink tank top, and he recognized the skimpy denim skirt and white high heels. "Hey, cowboy!" she said. "Want some company?" She winked and ran her tongue around her lips.

Hunter smiled at her, but shook his head. "Go home, little girl," he said. "Go home." She gave him the finger.

He rolled up the window, double checked his door locks, and clambered into his bunk. He glanced at the paperback beside his pillow, but decided against it. He had all day tomorrow to read.

Lonesome had hit him like a Mack truck, and sleep was the best antidote for now.

This was Sharon's first time at the Fontana lot. Whichever truck stop they settled at, for safety's sake, Ray always insisted on parking as close to the lot's security lights as he could. It hadn't taken long for Sharon to grow used to it, the soft blue of artificial light coming in through the tinted upper windows of the sleeper unit, like moonglow. They'd made love tonight, then he'd snugged up behind her, like spoons, and he'd fallen asleep right away. He always did. She pulled

12

herself gently out from under his heavy arm, giving his hand a kiss as she placed it on his pillow, then she propped her head on her arm, watching him. His breathing was deep and smooth - the sleep of the innocent - and his breath, still faintly hinting of peppermint mouthwash, puffed softly across her cheek.

A year ago, if you told her she'd be married to a trucker and driving the truck half the time herself, she would have laughed in your face. When Ray came along, he was just one more lonely long-distance trucker, a homely one at that, chatting up the barmaid while she stood waiting for him to pay for his beer. It was maybe the third or fourth time she'd seen him there that they'd started talking about dogs, she couldn't remember why. She told him how when she was a little girl, the neighbors had a Pomeranian and she thought it was the most perfect little animal, but her father wouldn't let her have one.

"Why don't you get one now?" Ray had asked.

She couldn't get one, she said, because she'd never had a dog and she wouldn't know how to take care of it properly. Ray had looked at her with those hound dog eyes of his and said, as if it were the simplest thing in the world, "Don't worry. If you truly love it, keeping care of it will come naturally." And that was one of those moments when it seems like God is speaking directly to you through someone else's mouth. It was like a light clicked on in her brain, and she realized that all those goddamn skunks she'd been crazy about through the years, those bastards who'd treated her like dirt, that they never really loved her at all. It got her thinking about how it would feel if somebody really did love her like that, somebody she could trust to treat her the way she would treat a little dog that she loved and who trusted her. If you loved somebody like that, you'd never want to cause them pain. That night she'd cried herself to sleep, fearing she was doomed never to be loved that way. Never in her life.

She didn't love Ray then, of course. But he'd got her thinking. Whenever he was in town, he'd spend long hours in the bar nursing one or two pints of beer, and he made no secret that he was there because of her. So when he finally said, "I love you", she was primed for it. She was ready. And she began to love him for loving her that way, that was how it started. And then they just kind of started getting used to each other. He was sweet and kind and so serious, but she could make him laugh. It got so that she was like one of those monkeys they do experiments with. She tried to say funny things to him, and when she pushed the right button and a laugh spilled out, it was like a fix for her. It gave her a warm feeling in her chest, and a bit of a tickly feeling at the base of her skull. So then she loved him for letting her make him laugh, too.

She never expected anybody to love her like this. She never thought she would be so precious to anybody. These last few weeks on the road with him had been like paradise. Fear circled her breastbone like a cold hand. Was it to end so soon?

She reached out and gently pushed the hair back from his forehead, and he stirred softly. His brow was smooth, untroubled. Perhaps he was in denial, she thought. She knew enough about denial from the treatment center. If there's something about your life you don't think you can deal with, you just pretend it doesn't exist. It wasn't just that Ray refused to talk about this morning, it was as if he refused to even acknowledge it. Except for driving all the way to the truck stop in Fontana, and being in a hurry to get out of California, he was acting as if nothing had happened, as if nothing had changed. He must be as afraid as she was of losing this beautiful life they had together. At the foot of the bed, Peaches got up and turned in a circle, then lay down again with a sigh.

"I love you both," Sharon whispered and lay back on her pillow.

There was nothing to see in the blue glow on the ceiling of the sleeper, but she could not close her eyes.

14

CHAPTER

THREE

Russell Kupka's partner was a pig. He dressed like a pig, he snorted like a pig, and his theories were often hogwash, so Russell thought it most appropriate that one of Merv Campbell's irritating affectations was wearing that stinking pork pie hat. Russell was counting the hours until Merv's vacation, which was due to begin at the end of the week. Ever since he'd started with the L.A. County Sheriff's Department, Russell had been itching for a chance to prove himself by working a good case alone, without Merv's help and questionable advice, and he couldn't contain a flutter of excitement in his gut. He was almost certain that this case would be the one.

Russell leaned back in his chair and rolled his tongue inside his cheek. "So, Merv," he said. "You think the Iceman was involved in some kind of gang initiation rite?"

Merv nodded, pushing his lips out so they looked like a snout. He'd just finished a fast food breakfast and had grease in the corner of his mouth. "I'm leaning that way. The way I picture it," he said, "is that some bonehead gang bangers decided that spending time in a freezer was a good test of manhood, but they were too fuckin' stupid to realize that a guy would freeze to death in - what did the doc say? - couple or three hours? They probably left the poor stiff in a meat locker overnight and panicked when he had turned into a popsicle before they let him out. Poor stiff. Ha, ha! Poor frozen stiff!"

"The Iceman looks a little old for a gang initiation, don't you think?" Russell suspected Merv was just looking for a reason to pass the case on to another department. It had happened often enough before.

"You never know these days, Cupcake," said Merv with a wink.

Russell gritted his teeth at Merv's use of that goddamn nickname. In his childhood, he'd bloodied at least a dozen noses in the school playground over that very name, and the thought of the ones he had to let get away with using it still rankled. There was always some kid who was bigger and tougher than he was, but Russell had never learned to back down gracefully.

Merv continued. "It's my opinion that a guy has to be crazy to get sucked into a gang, and crazies, as you should know by now, come in all shapes and sizes, ages and colors."

"Okay, Merv." Russell squinted at his partner out of the corner of one eye. "So it's a gang initiation gone wrong. If they were so panicked about their mistake, why'd they drop the corpse where it would get found so fast? And just where do you suppose these gang bangers live? An inner city neighborhood like Pyramid Lake? Fort Tejon? Otherwise, how the hell did they transport the body to the middle of nowhere so fast that it was still an ice cube when we got the call?" They'd spent all yesterday morning at the crime scene. When they'd loaded the curled up corpse in the coroner's van, the legs were still too frozen to lay him flat.

"They hitched a ride with the Good Humor man?" Merv laughed like an idiot.

"So how do you suggest we proceed with our investigation?" Russell asked, lifting an eyebrow in irony. Yes, he'd been partnered with an experienced detective. He was actually supposed to be learning the job from Merv. What a joke! All he'd learned from Merv, aside from how to fill in the paperwork and where the blank forms were kept, was where to pass which buck whenever possible.

"Well…" Merv actually looked as if he believed that what he was about to say had some kind of value to Russell. "Since the morgue doesn't have a microwave big enough to defrost the poor fucker, I'd say we wait 'til he thaws out enough to get at his pockets. If there's

16

no ID on the body, we run his prints. Once we know who he is, it'll give us more to go on. Maybe circulate his picture, see if the Missing Persons Unit has anything on him. I keep tellin' you, Cupcake," Merv said, suddenly leaning forward and pointing a finger, "you're gonna ruin them nice ties your girlfriend buys you if you keep running your oily fingers over them like that."

Russell almost bit his tongue. This from a guy who wore the same grimy sport jacket five days a week. "I've talked to the coroner. There was nothing in his pockets." He worked his jaw, then deliberately resumed stroking his tie between his thumb and forefinger. "So you wouldn't follow up on the barcode label?"

"What? Chase all over a foreign country looking for something that may or may not have anything to do with the stiff? Waste of time. Shot in the dark." Merv grabbed a business card off Russell's desk and started picking his teeth with it. "You'll just get yourself all frustrated, kid. Like trying to find a needle in a haystack."

The phone rang, and Russell dove for it. "Homicide."

"Detective Kupka?" said a crisp female voice Russell recognized as belonging to a U.S. customs clerk he'd spoken to less than an hour earlier.

"Cory! I appreciate you calling back so quickly. As I mentioned, time is of the essence in this investigation, since we're probably looking at a mobile crime scene. Did you turn anything up?" he asked her. He glanced up at Merv, hoping he would take the hint and leave, but Merv yawned, stretched, and continued picking his teeth. Russell hunched himself around the phone receiver.

"Yes. There haven't been many meat shipments coming across the border from Canada in the last few days, so it wasn't hard to track it down. The number you quoted belongs to a shipment of frozen beef that crossed the border Friday night at Blaine, Washington. I have photocopies of the 7533 and the commercial invoice right in front of me," she said.

"Seventy-five thirty-three?"

"The inward cargo manifest," she said without apology. "You want the shipper's name?"

"Perfect, Cory. Shoot." Russell took down the information, his ballpoint pen moving in broad, sure strokes across the yellow legal pad he always kept on his desk. The customs clerk gave him the name and address, not only of the shipper, but also of the consignee in Fullerton. "According to the 7533, the shipping company is Watson Transportation in Delta, British Columbia, Canada," she added. "If you're trying to track down the truck like you said, your best bet is to call them."

"Thank you, thank you, thank you," he told her. "You've gone above and beyond the call of duty. You're a treasure, Cory. An absolute treasure."

As he hung up the phone, he couldn't suppress a grin. "Shot in the dark, huh, Merv?"

Forget that Merv was his senior, in more ways than one. This was Russell's case, his first real chance to show what he could do. The case had his name on it, he could feel that right from the start. The techs would've found it eventually, but yesterday morning Russell had even been the first to see the label stuck on the bottom of the Iceman's Nike. "What's that?" he had asked one of the crime scene techs as they were waiting for the county coroner to arrive. "That white thing on the bottom of his shoe."

The tech - a tall, gangly redhead they called Stretch - bent down and practically put his ear in the dirt to take a close look. "It's some kind of self-adhesive label," he said. "A barcode label. Amanda!" he called to the young female tech with the camera who was photographing footprints a few yards away. "Come get a picture of this." Amanda walked over and took a look, then frowned, eyeing the ground warily. "Here," said Stretch, holding out his hand. "Give me the camera and I'll take it." He stretched out on the dirt on his belly, took a couple of close-up pictures of the bottom of the shoe, and handed the camera back to her. Then he carefully peeled the label off the shoe and held it up by a corner for Russell to see. Russell could tell that Stretch was just barely containing some kind of reaction. A gag? A cough?

"No shit," said Russell in wonderment. He met Stretch's eyes and they both burst out laughing. Amanda looked over from where

18

she had gone back to photographing footprints and frowned with disapproval, but neither Stretch nor Russell could stop. The label read Canada Grade A Beef.

Merv looked as blankly at Russell now as he had then. "Needle in a haystack, huh, Merv?" Russell said, picking up the phone again. "Well, let's just follow the thread attached to this little needle and see what's at the other end."

At the other end was a trucking company in British Columbia, Canada.

"Watson!" El barked into the receiver. She'd just hung up on some pinhead of a driver who had asked if it was okay to park a load for a couple of days to attend his brother's wedding in Boise, Idaho. "You were supposed to deliver that load in Chicago today," she'd told him. "Where the hell are you at now?"

"Boise," he'd said. "The wedding was Saturday, and I got just too shitfaced to drive until now."

"Well, get the fuck out of there!" she'd bellowed at him. "Now!"

Needless to say, she wasn't feeling too charitable toward drivers at the moment. She was glad when the caller identified himself as a policeman from L.A.

"L.A.P.D.?" she asked, intrigued.

"L.A. County Sheriff's Department," he said. "And I'm hoping you'll be able to help me track down one of your drivers. It's very important that we find him, as he may hold the key to an important investigation we're conducting."

"Oh yeah?" El never used to like cops, since her experience had been mostly limited to receiving citations and fines for traffic violations, but since she'd gotten to know Hunter Rayne, a driver who used to be a Mountie, she'd gained a lot more respect for them. Of course, detectives wouldn't all be like Hunter, but this guy sounded like he had a good head on his shoulders, and seemed cheerful and easygoing, just like Hunter was, most of the time. "I'll help if I can. What do you need?"

The cop explained that they had reason to believe one of Watson Transportation's drivers had been a witness to something the cop wasn't at liberty to divulge at this point and that it was imperative they locate him, "for his sake as well as ours."

"Your cooperation could save a life, Miss...?"

"Elspeth Watson," said El. "But call me El. Miss sounds downright prissy and Ms. makes me feel like a dyke."

He laughed.

"I'll take your word for it, Detective... what did you say your name was?"

"Kupka. But call me Russell."

El wrote his name down, and his phone number, just in case. "What do you need?" she repeated.

"One of your drivers was hauling a shipment of Canada Grade A beef from a shipper in Burnaby, British Columbia to Fullerton, California. He crossed the border on Friday."

"They," said El.

"They?"

"Ray and Sharon Nillson. They drive as a team. Just got married a month or so ago, made a detour to Las Vegas on their very first run."

"Really?" said the cop. "A couple? You're sure that's the shipment I'm talking about?"

"Sure. The Hanratty load. It's the only meat shipment I had out of here on Friday."

"Looks like I really lucked out, El, getting hold of you. I wonder if you'd be able to estimate where this Ray and Sharon Nillson would be about now, maybe tell me what their truck looks like, the license plate number, that sort of thing?"

"I can go one better," El said. "Ray's truck has all the bells and whistles on it, including a satellite pager and a cell phone. I'll get them on the blower and find out exactly where they are." She had her finger on the hold button when she heard the cop say, "Wait!"

"What?"

"It might be best not to let them know we're looking for them. Some drivers are a little nervous about the police, if you know what I mean."

Was the cop sounding a little nervous himself? El considered this silently for a few seconds, wondering if she'd been too quick to accept this guy for a cop, too quick to cooperate.

"What I mean, El," he continued, "is that I'd hate to upset them, make them worry and wonder about why the police want to talk to them, until we've had a chance to explain it to them fully." He sounded so relaxed that her doubts vanished. "I wish I could divulge more to you, right now, at this very instant, but that's just not possible. Once we've discussed it with them - Ray and Sharon - of course, we'll give them the okay to talk to you about it. In confidence, mind you, and only to you. It's never a good idea to spread information about active cases, except to the most senior and trustworthy people, if you know what I mean."

"Of course," said El, deciding that she'd have to talk to Hunter about this. Any information would be safe with him, and the L.A. cop couldn't have any objection to her discussing it with a former RCMP officer, could he? "Of course," she repeated, reaching for the hold button. "I'll just make it sound routine."

"Yes!" said Russell, pushing back his chair and punching the air with a happy fist. "Yes!"

"What?" asked Merv. Somewhere during Russell's conversation with the butch trucker in Canada Merv had wandered off to the can and now he was back, hitching up his pants. There were a few dark spots among the usual grease stains on Merv's khaki slacks, and Russell, momentarily and with distaste, wondered if they were water, or not.

"Let's go," said Russell, snatching up his jacket.

"Go where?" Merv was fiddling with his pant legs near his crotch, probably trying to straighten out his boxer shorts, as he reached for his pork pie hat with his other hand.

"To pick up our suspects for questioning." *My* suspects, he corrected himself mentally. *My* suspects.

"What suspects?"

"Mr. and Mrs. Ray and Sharon Nillson," said Russell over his shoulder, barely able to suppress a grin. Yes! This was his case. Things were clicking into place so beautifully it almost made him giddy.

"Where?" asked Merv, falling further behind.

"Hurry up," said Russell. "If we step on it, we can pull them over this side of the Ventura Freeway."

"Shit, Cupcake! I'm supposed to give evidence in the Cutter case in an hour."

"So do it then," said Russell, waving over his shoulder. "I've sent a couple of black and whites out to locate them and sit on their tail until I get there, so I won't be alone. Go to court, Merv. I can manage this on my own." He heard Merv's footsteps stop.

"Yes," said Russell, as the door closed between him and his partner. "Thanks for the help, Merv, you old porker, but I can manage this case quite well on my own."

Ray had volunteered to drive the Kenworth through the L.A. traffic, but Sharon told him she had to learn to do it sometime. Right at the start, they had decided that it would work best if she did most of the day driving and he did most of the night driving, but unless they had a real tight schedule, they'd pull over for at least a few hours in bed together during the night. They were practically still on their honeymoon, after all. So after picking up the load in Anaheim, Sharon took the wheel and Ray was relaxing in the passenger seat, trying to get forty winks so he'd be able to drive most of the night. She couldn't see his eyes behind his dark glasses, but from the tilt of his head and slack of his face, she thought he must have dozed off. Peaches slept curled up on his lap. The sleep of the innocent, she thought for the hundredth time.

She'd be glad to get out of California. Ray said that if El could find them a load from Vancouver to the Midwest, he had a few contacts that could give them loads out of Chicago, maybe just short hauls for starters, although she wouldn't officially be able to drive when they were moving loads from one place to another in the U.S., at least, not until she had her green card. Yes, that could really happen, she reminded herself.

Sharon tried to picture things way in the future. Her with her green card, being able to drive anywhere in the United States. The two of them spending time at that lakefront cottage Ray owned in Minnesota, having his brother and their family over for barbecues sometimes. She'd never met Ray's brother and his wife, but she'd seen pictures. She imagined herself and her sister-in-law working together in the kitchen while the two brothers were out on the porch discussing the day's catch. She pictured herself sharing confidences with her sister-in-law as they scrubbed potatoes and tore up lettuce for a salad, throwing a few funny remarks out at the men from time to time and laughing, just like a real family, like she'd always wished her own family had been. It felt good to think about the future. As the hours had gone by, what had happened Monday morning slipped farther and farther away, until it now felt more than ever like just a bad dream. They might forget about it completely, with time. It seemed to Sharon that they had made an unspoken agreement to do just that.

When she saw the first police car pass her, she felt a twinge of fear in her stomach, but it disappeared when he settled into the stream of rush hour traffic one lane over just ahead of her. She couldn't spend the rest of her life freaking out every time she saw a cop car on the road, for Pete's sake. It had been there for ten or fifteen minutes when she saw the second one come up beside her, staying level with the cab of the truck. One cop car nearby in traffic, that she could handle. But two sticking close by? She caught the cop in the passenger seat looking up at her with that unreadable expression cops have, and her stomach lurched. She wondered if she should wake Ray.

Get a grip on yourself, girl. She managed a tight little smile, then decided to try an experiment, taking her foot off the gas and letting the gap between her and the car in front widen. The cop car beside her nosed ahead at first, then slowed to keep pace. Sharon felt a wave of heat rise up her face and it occurred to her that she might faint. She took a deep breath. This can't be happening, she told herself. This has to be another bad dream. Just then the flashers on both police cars went on, and the cop beside her, looking right at her, pointed at the exit up ahead. Sharon suddenly turned cold and just as suddenly hot again. Could she just pretend she didn't see them? that she didn't understand? She fought the urge to put the pedal to the floor. There was nowhere to go, and if this was just a traffic stop, trying to run would only make things worse. A traffic stop. Maybe it was just a traffic stop.

Sharon eased the truck down the exit ramp, and pulled over on the shoulder just behind the first police car. Ray's hands had started moving, adjusting Peaches on his lap, so she knew he was awake. She tried to speak but her mouth and throat were so dry, she had to suck on her tongue and swallow before any sound came out. "Police," she said. "They've been following us a long time, Ray." She could see her own worried face reflected in his glasses, tried a smile, but it wouldn't take. "It's not a normal traffic stop, is it, Ray?"

Ray looked as stern and strong as she'd ever seen him, and part of her stopped worrying long enough to marvel at how handsome it made him look, as if she were watching this happen in a movie.

"Don't say a word," he said in a low voice. "You hear me? Not one word to any of them, ever. Nothing!" She'd never heard him talk that way before, with such force and anger.

"But, Ray. I don't know..."

"No, Sharon. When I say not one word, I mean it. You don't know how these guys can twist things around on you. Don't say nothing! Remember, you got a right to remain silent, whatever they tell you. Don't say a word."

"I can tell them I don't know anything, Ray." She couldn't keep her voice from shaking. She looked down at her hands and they were shaking, too. Shaking as bad as they'd ever shook when she was in withdrawal.

24

"Promise me, Sharon," said Ray, grabbing her hands and pressing them together, holding them still. "Promise me that you won't say a word."

And then a man's voice yelled, "Get out of the truck! Keep your hands where I can see them, and get out of the truck!" Sharon looked around her. There were six of them, now. Six cops standing at intervals around the cab, and every single one of them pointed straight at her and Ray, with a gun.

CHAPTER
FOUR

Hunter awoke to the gray light of dawn spilling in through the tiny window of his sleeper. He lay on top of the bedding wearing nothing but his watch and yesterday's jockey shorts, but even so his skin was clammy with sweat. This was his fifth night in the sleeper since he'd left Vancouver, the second one in L.A. waiting for a load. Sleeping in a tin box was starting to wear pretty thin. He would have sprung for an air-conditioned hotel room if work hadn't been so slow. His first thought was to call El. It would sure improve his mood if he knew there was a load for him to pick up today, that he'd be back on the road and getting his rig to pay its keep. He looked at his watch. If she wasn't in the office yet, she would be soon. He knuckled the sleep out of his eyes, and reached for his cell phone. This time of day was free.

"It's about fuckin' time!" said El.

Hunter checked his watch again. It wasn't even six o'clock. "This mean you've got a load for me?" he asked, his mood brightening.

El sighed, almost growled. "Yeah, you could say that."

"What is it?"

"Nacho sauce."

"Nacho sauce? You mean, Ray and Sharon didn't get the nacho sauce?"

"They got it all right." Her voice was grim. "But not any more."

"Stop tap dancing around, El." He reached over and unlocked the sleeper's little door, punched it wide open to the morning air.

"Ray and Sharon have been... uh... detained by the L.A. County Sheriff's department. I don't know what the hell is going on, except that Ray called me late yesterday and said they'd been arrested."

"Why? What have they done?" Hunter arched his back to stretch it, then reached for his blue jeans which he'd folded and placed at the foot of the bunk.

"Nothing."

He waited for her to continue. There had to be more.

"According to Ray, nothing," she said. "Getting an explanation out of Ray was like pulling teeth. He said they were being held for questioning, so I asked how long before they'd be back on the road, and he said he didn't know, but it might be a good idea if I lined up someone else to retrieve the load." She paused for another sigh. "I think it's serious, Hunter. I talked to the asshole cop who arrested them." Her voice was briefly vehement. "He wouldn't tell me anything either, but he did say not to count on them going back to work, that he expected Ray and Sharon to be arraigned tomorrow on suspicion of murder."

Hunter's jaw dropped. "Murder? This is Ray and Sharon Nillson you're talking about?"

"Murder," El repeated. "I'll give you the asshole's name and number, and maybe you can talk to him, cop to cop."

"I'm not a cop any more. He'll just tell me it's none of my business, and rightly so."

"But it is your business."

"It's not my business," Hunter said firmly.

"Ray's expecting you. I told him you'd straighten things out, get them lined up with a good lawyer, that sort of thing."

"Me?"

"Who better? You're there, and you know all about how cops work."

It was Hunter's turn to sigh. He ran his hand over his face. It needed the sweat scrubbed off and a good shave.

"Hunter? You still there?"

"Yes," he said.

"Something else," she said, then cleared her throat.

Hunter waited, knowing it was something he didn't want to hear.

"I also promised Ray we'd take care of Peaches."

The first thing Sharon saw when she opened her eyes was her left hand. It lay on a coarse sheet inches from her nose, and her fingers were bare. Her rings!? Where was her wedding ring? She was about to cry out for Ray when she remembered where she was, and the sharp edge of panic was replaced by a cold wave of fear and a churning in her gut. She was surprised she'd finally been able to sleep, and now she wished she hadn't awakened. The oblivion of exhausted sleep was better than this nightmare. She moaned, squeezing her eyes and lips tight to stifle a sob.

"Whatsa matter, girlie? You need a fix?" The woman in the cell with her could have been forty, or she could have been sixty. Skinny as a rake. Her face was badly weathered and she had no front teeth. "What you whimpering for? Ain't nobody here gonna feel sorry for you, precious. Them bitches just love to see you cry."

Sharon shot her a shut-up glare and buried her face in the pillow. She missed Ray something awful. It was like an anvil hanging from her heart, some kind of lead weight pulling at her insides.

A bell clanged, and a black woman in uniform strolled by, hollering for everyone to get up, wash up for breakfast. Sharon rolled over and swung her legs off the bunk, pushed herself halfway to her feet. "Wait!" she called to the back of the uniform. "Wait! I need to talk to somebody. Where did they take my dog?"

The woman in the uniform didn't even turn around.

Her cellmate laughed, an ugly raucous laugh. "What you think they want to talk to you for? You think they give a shit 'bout your dog?" she said. "Who you think you are? Princess Di?"

Sharon ignored her. She needed to talk to Ray. It wasn't fair to keep them separated like this. Goddammit. Why hadn't they talked before, when there was time? She needed desperately to talk to Ray.

28

Sharon walked the few steps over to the small sink, splashed some water on her face and tried to straighten her hair. Her fingers ran through it easily. Sometimes after she and Ray made love it would be so tangled that there'd be knotted clumps of it on her comb. Ray always apologized, like it was his fault. He loved her so much. Was that a crime?

"Aren't you so special," the skinny woman sneered, mincing around near the cell door, one bony hand flipped up at shoulder level, the other propped against her hip. "Aren't you just a glamour puss, painted nails and Farrah Fawcett hairdo and all."

"Shut the fuck up!" said Sharon. "Just shut the fuck up!"

Teresa Jagpal stepped out of the shower and pulled a towel off the rack, then bent at the waist to let her hair fall in dripping dark ropes, almost to her toes, before wrapping the towel around her head. She grabbed a second towel and scrubbed its rough surface against her skin, starting with her arms and working downwards, shoulders to breasts to hips, until she reached her feet, a daily routine performed on auto pilot, for her mind was occupied with something else.

This was Wednesday. Greg hadn't been home since Friday, and she didn't know what she should do. Saturday night she called the hotel in Chilliwack, and the man told her Greg hadn't shown up for his weekend gig. Chilliwack was east of Abbotsford, where she had grown up on her father's farm. Where her parents still lived with her two older brothers.

"Please, can you tell me? Did he call?" she had asked the man at the hotel.

"No, he didn't fuckin' call." The man snorted, then said, "He's a fuckin' low-life musician. Why the fuck would he call?" and abruptly hung up.

The first thing she'd done after setting down the phone was to go to Hellen's room and open the door. She saw a pair of blue jeans crumpled at the foot of the bed and resisted the impulse to check if they were Greg's. Hellen wasn't home.

On Sunday morning, she and Hellen had coffee together, then shared a plate of fresh fruit at the picnic table beneath the plum tree in the back yard. The little gray cat chased imaginary mice in and out of the abandoned wooden doghouse beside the fence. Moss dripped across its roof shingles like green lava, and the edges of the carpet scrap on its floor were black with mildew. Hellen sliced open a peach, offered one half to Teresa, then pried the stone out of the remaining piece with a green finger nail, its metallic paint half chipped away. Teresa could never understand why Hellen didn't treat those skilled hands of hers with more respect.

"Greg working out of town?" Hellen had asked casually, nodding toward the empty driveway where his car should have been. Too casually? She tossed the peach stone into the rhododendron bush, wiped her fingers on her cut-off jeans.

Teresa's own fingers, brown skinned and slender, picked up a strawberry, held it to her mouth, then put it back down. She couldn't confide in Hellen. Not anymore. "Chilliwack," she answered, nodding. But Chilliwack was only an hour's drive away. She turned at the sound of the little cat sharpening its claws on the doghouse carpet. "He's been busy at the studio," she had added, wishing that were enough to explain his absence.

But according to the other band members, Greg hadn't been to the studio either. And now Teresa didn't know whether to call the police and report him missing, or perhaps to call his brother Chad. She tried not to think about what could have happened. Had her own brothers found out about him? Who should she talk to? What would be the proper thing to do?

Teresa applied her underarm deodorant, then slipped on a silk robe, tying the belt in a bow to keep it from sliding undone while she dried her hair. She tried to imagine herself calling Chad. What would she say to a man whose hate for her smoldered in his eyes?

"Hello, Chad. Your brother has disappeared."

Or, "Good morning, Chad. Have you heard from Greg lately?"

Or, "Chad, this is Teresa. Did Greg tell you he was leaving me?" After all, someone who had moved into her bed with so little ceremony could easily have moved out with even less. The thought

30

of what Greg's brother might say and how he would speak to her made her stomach flutter. No, she couldn't call Chad. And she couldn't call her parents' home.

Teresa decided to wait. Maybe she was worrying for nothing. Maybe Greg would be here tonight, when she got home from work, and life would be back to normal. He'd only been gone since Friday, after all. If she hadn't heard from him by tomorrow, well... perhaps then it would be time to phone the police.

Hunter stepped up to the reception counter in front of one of the desk sergeants, a swarthy man with a heavy fringe of dark hair above his ears but only a few wisps of it on top of his head, visible as he bent over his paperwork. The other desk sergeant was in heated conversation with a young black man, who gestured wildly, a set of car keys dangling from the pinkie finger of one hand. "I'm here to see Detective Russell Kupka," Hunter said, leaning forward to be heard above the din. "He's expecting me." The sergeant asked Hunter's name and wrote it down, then told Hunter to take a seat.

He sat on one of the benches, between a large elderly woman who wheezed with every breath and a middle-aged man in a shiny brown suit that smelled faintly of mothballs. The young black man stalked away from the reception counter, dropped his keys on the floor, scooped them up with a "Shiiiit!", and yanked open the door. Hunter leaned forward with his elbows on his knees and sighed. He wondered, not for the first time, if Ray and Sharon had inadvertently run somebody down, or caused a fatal accident, or if it was a case of mistaken identity. Why else would someone like Ray be connected with a homicide? He tried to recall if there was anything the least bit abnormal about their behavior at Yoncalla, and he could think of nothing. Not a damn thing.

"Rayne? Is there a Hunter Rayne here?"

A young man in a loose-fitting fawn colored suit stood at the door, a piece of paper in his hand. His eyes scanned the room, settled on Hunter as he got to his feet. "You Rayne?' he asked. The man was tanned and fit, his brown hair long and smooth on top, curling slightly at the edges like a mushroom cap, and neatly trimmed around his ears and neck. He looked more like a stockbroker or a lawyer than a cop.

Hunter nodded. "Detective Kupka?"

The man looked Hunter up and down, making Hunter aware of the contrast made by his own conservatively barbered hair, work shirt and jeans, and steel toed running shoes. Hunter offered his hand, but the man ignored it, instead directing Hunter down a hallway to the left of the reception area. He opened a door and said, "Wait in there." It was a small interview room furnished with a table and four chairs. Hunter remained standing, facing the door.

"So. What can I do for you?" said the man when he entered about five minutes later. He sounded older than he looked, and Hunter guessed him to be in his mid-thirties.

Hunter extended his hand again, keeping his eyes on the detective's face, and this time, with only a few seconds of hesitation, the man took it. After a firm and abrupt handshake, the detective's hands went directly into the pockets of his slacks. "As I told you over the phone," Hunter began, "I work for Watson Transportation. I'm here for two reasons. The first is to look after the company's interests by picking up the load Ray and Sharon Nillson were hauling for Watson at the time they were detained, unless, of course, you're expecting to release them within the next twenty four hours...?"

Russell Kupka shook his head. He was tapping the toe of a camel colored loafer on the linoleum and jingling change in his pocket, as if Hunter were wasting his time.

"Second," continued Hunter, irritated but managing to keep his voice from showing it, "as a friend and coworker, I intend to line up a good lawyer for the Nillsons and do what I can to help them." He paused here, waiting for a reaction. The detective just looked at his watch. Hunter offered a wry smile. "And you," he added.

The detective showed surprise. "Me? You think you can help me?"

Hunter shrugged. "I'll do what I can. If the Nillsons are innocent, I'd like to see them out of here as soon as possible, and what better way than to help you come to the same conclusion?"

32

"And if they're not?" He continued to play with the change in his pocket, a habit Hunter found extremely annoying.

"If it's clear that they're guilty, I'll be just as interested in seeing justice served as you are. I'd appreciate it if you could tell me why they're under suspicion, so I can make that call."

The detective stopped short of rolling his eyes, but his demeanor indicated he wasn't taking Hunter seriously. Hunter hesitated. He wasn't sure whether identifying himself as a former law enforcement officer would work for or against him with this detective. It wasn't something he liked to disclose to anyone, if he could help it.

"I spent twenty four years behind a badge, for what it's worth," he finally said.

The jingling stopped. "Yeah? Where?" There was a hint of suspicion in the detective's voice.

"Royal Canadian Mounted Police. At the time I left, I was a Sergeant investigating serious crimes, including homicide, at the detachment in Burnaby, British Columbia. Vancouver, more or less."

"Why did you leave?"

Hunter shrugged. "Time for a change," he said. He had no intention of sharing anything personal with this man.

"Well," said the detective, "I'm sure we could chat about that all day, but there's somewhere I've got to be." He reached for the door handle. "If I think of anything you can do to help, I'll be in touch through your lady boss. She sounds like one tough mother trucker, by the way."

"Before you go," said Hunter, moving closer to the detective. "What about the Nillson's rig? Where can I go to pick up the load of freight?"

"I'll have to see if the crime scene techs are through with it. Call me at two." He opened the door and turned away.

"Hold on there, chief. Any suggestions about where to find a decent lawyer?" Hunter asked, raising his voice and no longer trying to hide his irritation at the detective's bad manners. Being polite hadn't won him any cooperation so far, anyway.

"That's an oxymoron, isn't it? Decent lawyer?" The detective snorted wryly. "Try the yellow pages. There's no shortage of lawyers in this town. You can practically hail them in the street, like cabbies."

Hunter followed him out of the room, back down the hall. Another young man, blond, wearing an olive green suit, and carrying a briefcase, but otherwise with an overall appearance similar to the detective's, walked in through the front door just as they emerged into the reception area. The blond man nodded to the detective. "Hi, Russell. How's it going?" he said with a smile.

"Catch any ambulances lately?" the detective shot over his shoulder as he pushed past, looking pointedly at his watch, perhaps to give the impression that he was in too much of a hurry to even say hello. Hunter shook his head at the detective's behavior, then smiled at the man with the briefcase.

"Is the detective a friend of yours?" he asked.

The young man shrugged. "Former classmate." He hesitated a second, then grinned. "He flunked out of law school, and I didn't. He's held it against me ever since."

"That's good to know," said Hunter. "Have you got a few minutes to talk?"

Russell leaned back and turned up the fan on the car's air conditioning. He was a little ticked at the way things had turned out so far this morning, that he'd been too rushed to think things through properly. If he hadn't been in such a rush to get to the coroner's office for the post mortem on the Iceman, maybe he could have used that cowboy trucker to his advantage. So far, lawyer or no lawyer, neither of the Nillsons had talked. Their tongues could have been cut out, for all he knew. Maybe he should have thrown the cowboy in with Ray Nillson to see if Nillson would say something - anything - that would point Russell in the right direction before a lawyer entered the picture. At least the trucker would be back. Before Russell let him pick up the load in the Nillsons' trailer, Russell would pump him for information about the Nillsons first. At this point, he knew he was relying too heavily on the Iceman's corpse.

34

When the corpse had finally thawed enough to get the clothes off the body to look for clues to the man's identity, there was nothing in the pockets. No wallet, no credit card receipt, no sales receipt or movie ticket, nothing that would give the Iceman a home and ultimately a name.

Russell caught himself absently running his fingers down his tie as he waited out a red light. He draped the tie over the steering wheel, admiring its plum and ochre whorls, and shook his head at fate. He had a suspicion that the Iceman's home would turn out to be in Vancouver, where the meat was from, and that's where Jennifer had bought the tie. Chinese silk. She was there again now, doing whatever a production assistant on the pilot for a new television series does. They'd only spent one night together on her last trip home. She said she was under a lot of pressure in her new job, trying to make a good impression. What a pair. Both of them with unpredictable hours, sometimes fifteen and sixteen hour days. Both of them with promising careers. He didn't take that thought any further. He had never asked her what kind of a salary she made, but she gave him better gifts than he gave her, and she leased a new BMW, left it parked weeks at a time while she was away. The light turned green, and he cranked his thoughts back to the Iceman.

Even without an autopsy, the coroner had been pretty sure that the victim froze to death. Russell had come to the same conclusion himself. It didn't take a genius. The Iceman's curled up position indicated that he was doing his damnedest to try to keep warm, and wherever he had been, it wasn't enough. He sure as hell didn't freeze solid anywhere in the Tehachapi Mountains. It wasn't even cold enough for that in most of Alaska at this time of year. It had to be a freezer, and given the location, most logically, a mobile freezer, like the Nillsons' trailer loaded with frozen meat. They'd lifted numerous prints and fibers from the inside of the trailer. Russell planned to pick up the prints from the corpse's thawed fingers and personally deliver them to the lab for a comparison. He had no doubt that many of the prints from the Nillsons' trailer would belong to the Iceman. Whoever he was.

When he stepped out of the elevator at the morgue, Merv was already standing outside the door, covered in a protective gown with a mask hanging under his double chin. Russell cursed under his breath. "I thought you were in court again today," he said aloud.

"Cutter copped a plea."

"I figured that would happen. His lawyer likes to cancel court dates. Gives him more time for booze. They got him out on the table?" Russell asked as he checked in and picked up his own mask and gown.

Merv nodded. "The doc's just finishing up a floater. Don't smell too nice in there right now."

"When does it?" Russell adjusted the gown to make sure it covered every inch of his suit sleeves and shirt collar. "You seen those shoe things?"

"Cupcake needs some booties!" hollered Merv.

Russell stiffened, tried to keep his breathing under control. What he wouldn't give to be able to drive Merv's teeth down his throat and into his voice box. Just then a morgue assistant opened the door to the autopsy room and leaned out.

"Hey, Merv. Your Iceman's on the table."

My Iceman, Russell said to himself, gritting his teeth. He elbowed his way past Merv and was first inside.

"Cupcake! You forgot your booties."

The corpse's torso was still partly frozen inside, so the coroner decided not to do a complete autopsy, which was fine with Russell. During autopsies, he usually spent most of the time studying the line where the ceiling met the wall. Today's post mortem revealed only a couple of pieces of information that Russell felt were of value. There was some bruising on the Iceman's neck, which the coroner suggested could mean he'd been held in an armlock and possibly choked unconscious before being placed in the trailer, but the cause of death remained the same: hypothermia, which seemed pretty much of an understatement. And the Iceman had been a musician, probably a guitarist. The tips of the fingers of his left hand were padded with calluses.

36

Russell left the morgue with a manila envelope containing the Iceman's photograph and fingerprints. Maybe the photograph would loosen the Nillsons' tongues, if he could get another crack at them before they'd been muzzled for good by lawyers. He left in a hurry, before Merv could fetch his pork pie hat and ask for a ride.

CHAPTER
FIVE

Sharon hung her head, kept her eyes on her toes, trying to hold her hands so she wouldn't feel the cold steel of the handcuffs against her wrists. Two women in uniform walked beside her, one on each side. Sharon herself wasn't a short person - she was five foot eight, not fat, but far from skinny - yet these women made her feel tiny. She didn't want to see the other prisoners gawking at her, didn't want to feel like part of their afternoon entertainment, so she didn't look up until she was out of the corridor.

She was ushered into a room with a small barred window. She recognized the two people already inside as the same ones who'd come to talk to her yesterday. An attractive dark haired policewoman in street clothes was seated at the table, and the yuppie detective who'd been there when she and Ray were arrested was pacing up and down, his hands in his pockets. He had the uniformed women remove the handcuffs and sent them away, then pulled out a chair and motioned Sharon to sit down in it. She sat.

The detective paced a little more, just as he'd done yesterday. Sharon could feel him looking at her, but kept her eyes down, trying to get used to the look of her ringless hands, stretching her fingers apart and examining her pink nails, badly chipped now. She held her hands below the table, where the others couldn't see them. The laminate along the edge of the table was chipped, too, as if someone had been picking at it.

The policewoman turned on a tape recorder and gave a little speech with the date and time and place. She identified herself as Detective Tina Salcedo and the yuppie detective as Russell Kupka, then spoke to Sharon. "You have the right to remain silent. If you give up the right to remain silent, anything you say can and will be used against you in a court of law. You have the right to an attorney, and to have that attorney present during questioning. Do you understand these rights?"

Sharon nodded, glancing up at the woman and then back down at her lap. A lawyer had called her less than an hour ago to say she'd be coming to visit after five o'clock this afternoon. The lawyer had said the same thing, that Sharon didn't have to talk to the police, and that she should insist on having her lawyer present if they wanted to interrogate her again.

"Do you waive and give up those rights?"

Sharon pressed her lips together and thought about it. She had said nothing yesterday and she didn't intend to say anything today, so what did it matter if there was a lawyer with her or not? If she said nothing - not one word - like Ray had warned her to, there'd be nothing on the tape to incriminate her. She nodded again, but Detective Salcedo asked her to answer out loud. "Yeah," she whispered, then cleared her throat. Why was she acting so timid? Timid was totally out of character for her. Don't be such a wimp! "Yeah," she repeated, loud and clear, looking the yuppie detective right in the eye.

Detective Kupka came and stood beside her, then flicked his hand at Detective Salcedo. She tipped up a manila envelope and shook it until something slid out - a stiff blank page that looked like the back side of an enlarged photograph - and she passed it across the table to him. He pulled a chair up right beside Sharon, sat very close, staring into her face. "Look at this," he said, and flipped the photograph over on the table in front of her.

Sharon closed her eyes and took a deep breath. She suspected what the photograph might be, and she wanted to be sure she was prepared for it. Then she opened her eyes and looked right at it. She turned to the detective. "So?" she said, keeping her eyes on his without blinking for so long that her eyes started to burn.

"Do you know this man?" he asked.

She looked at the photograph again. It was a shot of a man's head and shoulders. His eyes were closed and his skin color was odd, but there was nothing horrible about it, nothing scary. She shook her head, and the detective pointed at the tape recorder. Sharon hesitated, remembering Ray's warning. Not one word, he'd said. Perhaps she shouldn't have even shook her head, but it was too late now. "No," she said in a loud clear voice.

The yuppie detective smiled. "I'm going to give you another chance," he said. "You know we'll get the truth, sooner or later. Things will go easier for you if you aren't caught in a lie."

Sharon looked away from him, pressed her lips together.

"Do you know this man?" he repeated.

She said nothing, closed her eyes and tried to shut him out. She shouldn't have said anything, not one word.

"Do you know this man?" he repeated loudly, right into her ear. She could smell coffee on his breath.

"I'm finished." She turned to face him again, scowled at him until he pulled his head back. "I don't want to talk to you anymore."

"What was his body doing in your trailer?"

Sharon pinched her lips together and crossed her arms over her chest. The detective pushed back his chair, stood up and looked down at her. "We know he was in your trailer. What was he doing there?" he said. Sharon didn't answer. The detective's jaw was working, and he began to breathe harder. She'd seen that same look on men's faces before, just before they hit her. Involuntarily, she cringed, and immediately was disgusted that she had let him intimidate her. She was the wife of a good man now. She didn't have to live in fear.

Detective Salcedo cleared her throat. "Let me talk to her, Russell." The woman smiled at her, as if she were sympathetic and a friend. Sharon knew what they were trying to do. Bad cop, good cop. Everybody had seen that on TV at one time or another. Sharon looked away.

40

"You know," continued Detective Kupka, going back to his pacing, "it's going to look pretty funny, you saying one thing and your husband saying something else."

"You're lying! Ray didn't say anything," she blurted out before she could stop herself, then got clumsily to her feet. "If you aren't going to let me and Ray go, then take me back to jail. Right now." At the thought of returning to her cell, she shuddered, and added, "But can't you move me? That woman I'm with won't shut up. She's crazy, and she's making me crazy, too."

Detective Kupka shrugged. "Maybe if you'd cooperate...," he said.

"Don't push it, Russell," said the woman, then turned to Sharon. "We'll see what we can do."

Hunter was in a Denny's, seated at a window table with a cup of coffee and a day-old newspaper on the table in front of him, and a Denver omelette on the way, when his cell phone rang. It was Jeff Feldman, Ray's lawyer.

"Your buddy's not talking," he said.

"If he's innocent, maybe he hasn't got much to tell you," said Hunter.

"No. I mean, he's literally not talking. When I introduced myself, he grunted. That was all I got out of him until I mentioned your name."

"My name?"

"Right. When I said you were the one who'd sent me, he said, I want to talk to Hunter, and then clammed up again."

The waitress arrived with Hunter's omelet and a pot of coffee, set the plate in front of him, refilled his cup and was on her way again in less than three seconds. "Would that be possible?"

"I've talked to Russell Kupka, and he'll let me take you in this afternoon but he has a stipulation. He wants to be there. He says it can be off the record, but he'll use the information to further his investigation any way he can."

"What do you think of that?"

"I can't represent a client who won't communicate with me. I don't even know whether he's prepared to acknowledge that he has a lawyer. So I think it's worth the risk."

They set a time, then Hunter put the phone down and tucked into his omelet. He hadn't had anything but coffee since dinner at the truck stop the night before, so he ate quickly and with enthusiasm, although his mind wasn't on the food. He liked Jeff Feldman, but there was a niggling discomfort about his motives for taking on Ray as a client. The first thing he'd said when Hunter described the situation was, "The Iceman's killer, huh? Should be a pretty high profile case."

"You've heard of him?" Hunter had asked. They were still standing in front of the Sheriff's Department reception desk.

"You think a frozen corpse just south of the Grapevine Pass isn't going to make a good hook for the evening news? The public likes a good murder mystery, Mr. Rayne. This will stay in the news. Hey. The Black Dahlia still makes the news after thirty or forty years." He'd grinned then, and shook Hunter's hand. "Sure, I'll take your friend on as a client."

"My friends, you mean," Hunter had reminded him. "Ray and his wife were both arrested."

"No. In a case like this, I can't represent both husband and wife at the same time. Not ethical. I'm not saying it's true in this case, but it's quite possible there's a conflict of interest. She'll need her own lawyer."

Hunter had asked Jeff if he could recommend another lawyer for Sharon, and he'd fished a business card out of his pocket. "Here. Try Alora Magee. I just ran into her this morning and she gave me this card to give my wife. They're old friends or something. No, don't worry about it. Take it. I'll know where to reach her."

Hunter had called Alora Magee from a payphone, and she agreed over the phone to take on Sharon as a client, given Sharon was willing, although she warned him she would be tied up in court most of the day, and wouldn't have a chance to meet with her new client until late in the afternoon. It was a pretty haphazard way of arranging for lawyers, but Hunter felt he didn't have any other options, given

42

the circumstances and time constraints. Besides, he was nothing more than a matchmaker. It was up to Ray and Sharon from here on.

Detective Kupka was standing at the front door of the building when Hunter arrived, and stepped forward to greet him, offering a handshake. "I was hoping you'd be a little early. I'm sorry I wasn't able to talk to you longer this morning, but I was pressed for time."

Hunter smiled faintly to acknowledge the apology, although he didn't buy it. The detective held the door open for him, and Hunter nodded his thanks as he entered the building.

"You're a good friend of Ray's then," said Kupka. "How long have you known him?"

"Just a friend," Hunter corrected him. "I've only known him for a couple of years."

"What can you tell me about the man?" Kupka said over his shoulder as he led Hunter down a hallway toward an elevator.

"Those of us who've worked with him," said Hunter, realizing that his knowledge of Ray's working habits came mostly from what El had told him, and not from personal experience, "know him to be responsible, a hard worker, honest..."

"Honest?" The detective snorted softly. "You mean, you think he's never lied to you? How the hell would you ever know?"

"He's the kind of man who'd give you the shirt off his back..."

"The Hell's Angels say that about one another all the time."

Hunter's jaw stiffened and he took a deep breath. "What exactly is it you want to know?"

"Sorry. Go on." The elevator door opened and Kupka motioned Hunter inside.

Hunter stood where he was and crossed his arms over his chest. "Look, let me make something clear here. These people are my friends. I worked in law enforcement for over twenty years, and I know as well as you do that people are not always good judges of what their friends are capable of. I'm not going to swear that the Nillsons are innocent, because you've told me nothing about the case and I have no way of knowing one way or the other, but if they are

43

innocent, I want to help them. Why not make this a two-way street? It will save us both a lot of time if you'd tell me why you think they're guilty."

Kupka considered for a moment.

"What linked the victim to Ray and Sharon's trailer in the first place?" Hunter prompted. He still knew nothing more than what he'd read in the paper at Denny's, which wasn't much more than that a frozen body was found beside the I-5 in the mountains north of Los Angeles. He followed Kupka into the elevator.

The detective waited until the door closed before he spoke. "We found physical evidence that places the victim in the Nillsons' trailer."

"What evidence?"

"A label. A black and white, barcoded, numbered and dated shipping label that belonged to the load on their trailer. Specific enough for you?"

Hunter nodded. It was hard to dispute. A frozen corpse beside the route Ray and Sharon had driven hauling a refrigerated trailer, found close to the time they passed by, bearing a label that was unique to their load. He couldn't help but draw the same conclusion Russell Kupka had. "It's still possible they didn't know the body was there."

Kupka made a wry face. "Yeah, sure. I'd buy that if the body had been discovered when the load was delivered, or even if they'd phoned the police to report it as soon as they found it. But neither of them will even admit to seeing the body."

"What do they say?"

Kupka smiled, almost wistfully. "What do they say?" he repeated softly, then shrugged. "Zip. Nada. Zilch. Zero."

"Hunh," Hunter said, chewing on his lower lip.

"Right," said Kupka. "If they won't admit to seeing the body, or even offer an explanation of how it got from their trailer to where it was found, what else are they hiding? So, you figure your buddy's never lied to you, huh? Let's just see if he's about to start." The elevator door opened and they stepped out, walked down another corridor. "You did agree to see him, didn't you? I assume Feldman told you the drill. Your buddy's been told that I'll be watching and listening from the business side of a one way window. You ready? I'll have him brought down."

"What about Jeff?" Hunter said.

"Feldman? He said he'd be here. He's late, that's his problem."

"It's only ten to three."

Kupka shrugged. "Ask your buddy if he even wants his lawyer. It's his call. I don't think he was too impressed."

"I won't talk to him unless Jeff's here," said Hunter.

"Whatever," Kupka said, with a disgusted frown. He glanced up and down the corridor, tapped the toe of his loafer on the linoleum and started to play with the change in his pockets. Then he looked at Hunter speculatively and asked, "So, what's your theory? If your buddy didn't put this guy in his trailer, how did he get in there?"

Hunter leaned against the wall, arms crossed on his chest. "I wouldn't jump to any conclusions about how the man got inside. Could be he walked in himself. Any idea who he is or where he's from?"

The detective shook his head. "No I.D. on him. They're running his prints as we speak. Want to tell me how an unconscious man walks into a trailer by himself?"

Hunter felt his jaw muscles tighten. There was no point in reminding Kupka of the obvious, that Hunter hadn't been given all the facts. "How do you know he was unconscious?" The newspaper article had said the corpse was frozen in the position of a man trying desperately to keep warm.

"Technically, I don't. Let's just say it's probable."

"So let me answer your question, then. I see several possibilities. He could have climbed in the trailer himself, either to hide from someone or to steal something. He could have been accidentally locked inside either at the loading dock or somewhere along the way, or someone could have placed him inside the trailer without Ray's knowledge..."

Kupka waved his hand for Hunter to stop. "Whoa! If your buddy didn't know the guy was in there, then why wasn't the body still on the truck when he pulled up to unload the trailer?"

"He probably stopped to check his load. I do it all the time, especially when I've had to come to a fast stop somewhere along the route, or if the road's been bad, lots of hills and curves."

"Why?"

"Nothing more embarrassing than having freight fall out of the back when you open the trailer at the customer's loading dock." The elevator doors opened and they both turned to look. It was Jeff Feldman.

"Nothing?" asked the detective.

Hunter let the hint of a smile play over his lips. "Okay. You got me there. I'd rather have the whole damn load fall out than a frozen corpse."

When Jeff Feldman and Hunter entered the interrogation room, Ray had already been let in and his handcuffs had been removed. He had his arms folded on the table, his chair pushed back so he could rest his chin on his arms. He didn't smile when he saw Hunter, he just stared up at him with a hound dog face.

"Did they read you your rights?" Hunter asked him.

Ray nodded.

"And you know that you're being observed by the police through there." He indicated the dark mirrored surface of the window.

Ray nodded again. "He told me," he said, emphasizing the *he* and jerking his thumb at the lawyer.

Hunter and Jeff exchanged glances. "Jeff is your lawyer, Ray," said Hunter. "Why wouldn't you talk to him this morning?"

"I needed to talk to somebody I could trust "

"You can trust Jeff. He's on your side."

"I've never heard a lawyer being on anybody's side but his own," said Ray. "Bloodsuckers," he added.

"I'm just doing a job, Mr. Nillson, same as you do," said Jeff. "If I failed to act on my clients' behalf, I wouldn't be in business very long, would I?"

"Look, Ray," said Hunter. "You're in an ugly mess here. Like it or not, you need a lawyer to help you get out of it. Jeff's a good one, but he can't help you unless you cooperate with him. You don't have to tell him everything right now..." Hunter glanced meaningfully at

46

the window. "... but your best bet is to be straight with him, you understand?"

Ray said nothing, just rubbed his forehead, wincing as if he had a headache. "Right now I don't much care if I get out of jail. What I want is for you to get Sharon out of here. She doesn't belong in prison, Hunter. Would it help if I confessed?"

Jeff was writing something on a legal pad, but his head shot up and he looked at Ray in alarm. Hunter motioned him not to interrupt.

"Confessed to what?" Hunter asked. Jeff put up a cautioning hand.

"You know. They think we killed that frozen guy they found beside the highway."

"If you killed him, then you should confess," Hunter said firmly, ignoring Feldman's grimace. "If you didn't, then confessing would be stupid, and you're not stupid, Ray."

Ray put his forehead back down on his arms and said nothing.

"The justice system isn't perfect, but most of the time it works. And you've got a smart lawyer. Just tell him the truth, in confidence, and he'll know how to handle your case to your advantage."

Ray looked up at Hunter, his chin still on his arms. "What about Sharon's advantage? He has to handle it to Sharon's advantage. That's my point. That's what I have to be sure of, don't you understand?"

"Sharon has her own lawyer. She's got a good lawyer, too."

Ray sat bolt upright. "What?! We don't have the same lawyer?"

Jeff took a deep breath, then said gently, "That's not possible, Mr. Nillson. It wouldn't be ethical."

Ray got to his feet, and a guard who had been watching from a small window in the rear door pushed the door open. "It's okay," Hunter said to the guard. "We're okay in here. Ray, you'd better sit down."

"What's not ethical," said Ray, barely letting his thighs rest on the edge of his chair, "is trying to play a husband against his wife and a wife against her husband."

"I know you want to take care of Sharon..."

"Sharon had nothing to do with anything! Sharon's completely innocent and they should never have arrested her. Let her go, you hear me?!" he shouted at the mirrored glass, on his feet again. "She didn't do anything and she doesn't know anything. Let her go!" Then he turned to Hunter. "That's why I gotta know," he said. "Would it help her if I confessed?"

"Sit down, Ray," said Hunter, and waited for Ray to sit. "Listen to me. This isn't something to play around with. I can't give you legal advice, because I'm not a lawyer and the law's too complicated for ordinary guys like you and me to understand. You leave that to Jeff, here. But I can give you probably the most important advice you'll ever get." He paused until Ray looked him full in the eye. "You say you and Sharon are innocent. If that's true, then you deserve a life together, you and Sharon. You confess to something you didn't do, and you'll pull the rug out from under both of you, you understand? I've never figured you as the kind of man who'd give up without a fight, and I'm sure Sharon hasn't either. You and Sharon both deserve a chance, and Jeff is here to give you that chance. If you turn down his help and confess to something you didn't do out of some crazy idea that you'll be a hero to your wife, then you're too stupid to deserve her. Give Sharon some credit. You've both worked and waited a long time for what you've got. Don't throw away your marriage and your future by doing something stupid, Ray. You understand me?"

Ray dropped his eyes and nodded, his jaw slack, like a scolded child.

"So you'll tell Jeff everything you know so he can help you?"

Ray didn't look up, but he closed his mouth and worked his jaw.

"Think about it, Ray. This is no game. There's a lot at stake here." When Ray still said nothing, Hunter repeated, "Think about it. I'm heading back to Vancouver soon - tonight, I hope - but if there's anything I can do to help, anything you need me for, you talk to Jeff, okay?"

"I'll be back tomorrow, Ray," said Jeff. "I'll help you all I can."

A guard opened the door and Ray stood up, held his hands out for the cuffs. On his way out the door, he turned his hound dog face to Hunter and said, "El said she'd look after Sharon's dog. Could you...?"

Hunter half smiled, nodded.

"Thanks, Hunter." Ray came close to smiling for the first time since Hunter had arrived. "It would break Sharon's heart..." His voice trailed off, and the door closed behind him.

CHAPTER ___ ___ ___ ___ ___ ___
SIX

Merv wandered into the darkened observation room while Russell was watching the suspect and his trucker buddy dance around the truth on the other side of the window.

"I see you took my advice," said Merv, taking off his hat and scratching his scalp.

Russell didn't know what the hell Merv was talking about, so he ignored him. He was watching intently, still trying to figure that Rayne guy out. Cool as a cucumber, the guy had invited Nillson to confess. Russell wondered if that had been a calculated risk on Rayne's part, for Russell's benefit. Like he was saying, See? My friend wants to confess but he can't, because he didn't do it. Why his interest in this case? And why had the suspect been so anxious to talk to him?

"Where's that guy from, anyway?" said Merv. "Outa state? The FeeBee's?"

"Huh?" Russell frowned. So that's what Merv meant: he'd assumed that Russell had solicited help from another department. "That's Feldman, the scumbag lawyer who wants to get some free advertising from being part of the Iceman story."

"Not him. The cop. Who's the cop?" Merv said.

"That's no cop. He's a trucker, some buddy of the perp's." Russell buzzed the guard, letting him know the interrogation was

50

over, that he could take Nillson back to his cell. He watched the guard come in and put Nillson's handcuffs back on. Nillson was talking about his dog.

"If he's not a cop, then what the fuck are you letting him talk to the suspect for?" Merv blubbered. "What on earth are you thinking, Cupcake? Maybe I should cancel my vacation. I leave you alone for a couple hours and come back to find you running amok."

"Don't piss yourself, Merv. The guy's an ex-cop. I talked to his old department and they said he's straight. Besides, it was Feldman's idea. I promised Feldman I wouldn't take any of this down, but it gave me a chance to hear Nillson talk that I wouldn't otherwise have had. You'd rather Feldman had his client zip his mouth up and leave us to work without any kind of statement from the suspect at all?" Russell paused with his hand on the doorknob.

Merv shrugged. "Where's his old department?"

"Coincidentally …" and Russell wondered just how coincidental it was, "he's from the same place the load came from. Town called Burnaby. It's a suburb of Vancouver."

"Canada, eh? He a Mountie?"

"Was a Mountie," Russell said. "Looks like we'll need the RCMP's cooperation. If we don't get a match on the Iceman's prints here, I'll send his prints and photo to Burnaby. Since that's where the trailer was loaded, there's a good chance that's where the victim's from."

"Good," said Merv.

Russell opened the door and stepped out into the corridor. Rayne and Feldman were already at the elevators, deep in conversation. "Good?"

"It's as plain as your nose, Cupcake," said Merv, stabbing a pudgy finger toward Russell's nose. Russell turned away and started toward the elevators. Merv, following at his coat tails, raised his voice. "We've got a case where the vic's an import, the perps are imports, and there was interstate transportation … hell! international transportation involved. What more do you need? Hand it off to the Feds, or ship the whole damn lot back to Canada and save a few bucks for the L.A. County taxpayer."

Russell wheeled around so fast Merv's pink forehead almost ran into Russell's chin. "You'd like that, wouldn't you, Merv? One more case handed off to another department, one more buck passed, one less job for Merv Campbell to do." He shook his head in disgust. "Well, that's one thing I refuse to let you teach me. I don't work that way, Merv. I take pride in finishing what I start. I take pride in my job..." He looked down at Merv's good suit, his courtroom suit, which needed cleaning and pressing, or better yet, incineration. "And in myself," he added, again starting toward the elevator. Rayne and Feldman had disappeared.

"No need to get personal, Cupcake," said Merv with a scowl.

Russell turned on him again, keeping his voice low but almost shaking with the effort of it. "Don't you ever call me that again," he said, his index finger so close to his partner's nose that it made Merv's eyes go crossed, "or I'll fuckin' make you eat that fuckin' ugly hat."

"Shit. My hat," said Merv, and rushed back down the corridor.

Russell didn't hold the elevator for him.

Feldman was gone, but the trucker was waiting for Russell as he stepped off the elevator. "Well? Your pal's honest, is he?" Russell said, making no effort to conceal a smirk.

"I'll grant you that he's not telling what he knows," said Rayne, rubbing his chin, "but I don't think he did it."

Russell noticed that Rayne needed a shave, and that the stubble on his chin contained more gray than his hair. He figured the guy to be in his mid-forties, maybe older. "Then why won't he talk?"

"Isn't that obvious?"

"You think he's protecting his wife," said Russell. "Does that mean you also think she's a killer?"

"No," said the trucker. "I ran into them at a diner in Oregon on their way down here, and I'm sure they had no idea there was anyone in their trailer. I'd put money on it. My guess is that they found the body, panicked, and now they're afraid that if they admit to seeing it, they'll incriminate themselves for something they didn't do. He's more afraid for her than for himself."

"You sound awfully sure about something you can't prove. You couldn't have been much of a cop." That brought a look to the

52

trucker's face that was almost spooky. Russell couldn't put his finger on the change, but it was in the eyes, gray-blue and intense. "Just kidding, of course," he added, quickly. "Don't get me wrong, Rayne. I respect hunches, but I need more than that to work with."

The look was gone as quickly as it came, but the temperature had dropped a couple of degrees. The trucker nodded. "Call me Hunter," he said. "You said I could pick up the load that was on the Nillsons' trailer. When?"

"I'll find out if the lab is happy with the stuff we got off the trailer. If they don't need the load any more, it's all yours."

Alora Magee's first instinct had been to refuse. I'm too busy, she could have said, although she wasn't. I'm not qualified, she could have said, although she knew that she would probably do a better job than most. I'm scared, would have been the truth. She'd read about the case in the papers, heard about the arrest on the radio, and knew there'd be public interest in the trial, and that's why she was scared. Over the last ten years, she'd gotten restraining orders and alarm systems, tried apartments with security guards and even bought a German Shepherd.

She'd moved fifteen times. She'd changed her name twice and cut her long hair and taken to wearing mannish clothes. Although she'd heard nothing from her ex-husband for four long years, and she hoped he'd finally forgotten her, or at least lost interest in her, she still didn't feel completely safe from him. She wanted to remain hard to find because she knew she would fear him as long as he was alive.

It was the man on the phone who made her change her mind.

"Jeff Feldman gave me your name," he'd begun. "He's representing a friend of mine and suggested you might be willing to represent my friend's wife." He'd gone on to describe the situation, and Alora recognized it immediately from the news reports. She'd hesitated, trying to figure out which excuse to use to turn him down.

"I don't know for sure that they didn't do it," he'd said then, "but what I do know is that they're decent people and they deserve a chance." His voice was sure and sincere, with a faint accent that Alora couldn't identify.

"Guilty or innocent," she reminded him, "as a lawyer, it's my job to represent them all."

"Yes, that's the theory. Innocent until proven guilty. I always assume, until I find out otherwise, that other people feel the same way I do about murder, though," he said. "If I were a lawyer and I knew a client to be guilty but he refused to plead guilty, I'd have to drop him. Otherwise I'd blow the case. I guess I wouldn't make much of a lawyer."

"But you'd make a good judge," she joked.

"No. I make a good truck driver."

She was surprised at that, and surprisingly intrigued. From his voice, she'd pictured him in a business suit, maybe wearing glasses, definitely well educated and successful. She tried to match the voice to her image of a truck driver, hair a little unkempt, belly hanging over his belt buckle, maybe a tattoo on his forearm and cowboy boots. "Okay," she agreed, curious to know more. Maybe she could keep her face out of the news. This wasn't the O.J. trial, after all. "I'll meet your friend," she told the truck driver, but the one she really wanted to meet was him.

The woman in front of her wasn't exactly her idea of a truck driver either. She had nice features, although her skin had more lines than her age warranted. Alora guessed she was a smoker, or had been. "I guess my first question has to be, do you want me as your lawyer?" she said, smiling at Sharon Nillson.

"You said on the phone that Hunter picked you," Sharon said. "Then I guess you must be good." Her voice was husky, like a smoker's.

"Mr. Rayne's the one who called me." Alora shrugged. "I don't know if he picked me, exactly. He was given my name by your husband's lawyer, if that means anything."

"Why can't we have the same lawyer, me and Ray?" Sharon was fidgeting, rocking back and forth in her chair and moving her hands underneath the table. Alora could hear papery noises, as if her new client were rubbing skin against skin.

54

"Conflict of interest," she answered. "Would you like a cigarette?" Alora didn't smoke herself, but usually had a pack in her briefcase for nervous clients.

"Conflict of interest? What do you mean?" Sharon seemed to shudder. She swept her hair back off her face, then hugged her elbows, holding her breath.

"Well, what may be in the best interest of one party – yourself, in this case – may not be in the best interest of the other party – your husband." Alora slid a pack of Camels across the table and Sharon glanced at it but didn't move to pick it up. "That means a single lawyer couldn't do what was best for you without harming your husband, or vice versa, which would create an ethical dilemma, but if you each have your own…" She realized immediately that she should have put more emphasis on the word 'may', and she was about to correct herself.

"That's bullshit! We're husband and wife. We're a team. Ray loves me and he wouldn't do anything to hurt me. Ever! And I wouldn't hurt him for the world! We're not guilty, either of us. Why are you doing this?"

Alora sucked her breath in through her teeth, trying to think of the best way to answer. She could feel the woman's desperation. "It's not that we think one of you is guilty, necessarily…"

"Whatever you do has to be in both our interests. You have to get us both out of jail. This isn't right!"

"Mrs. Nillson. Sharon." Alora made calming motions with open hands. "It's not like that, it's all right. Just … let me explain it to you further."

Sharon sat with her lips pinched together. She eyed the cigarettes, but didn't reach for them. Instead, she hugged her elbows tighter, as if she were cold.

"It's a standard legal practice, that's all. It doesn't mean that you and your husband are adversaries in any way. It doesn't mean that either Mr. Feldman or myself thinks one or both of you are guilty, it's just a way to maximize your individual chances for a successful plea bargain or trial."

"Plea bargain? That would mean saying we're guilty, right? Noooo…" Sharon shook her head. "No way. Ray didn't do anything wrong, and you can't make me say he did. No." She kept shaking her head. "No. You can't turn us against each other. It isn't right."

Eventually Alora calmed her down, explained it again until she seemed to understand. She got her new client to accept a cigarette, although she admitted to not liking American cigarettes, but she couldn't get her to talk about the case. "I need to think about it," Sharon said. She begged to be allowed to talk to her husband, but all Alora could offer was to get a verbal message to him via his own lawyer.

"Tell him we're still the best damn team on the road," she said, as silent tears ran down her cheeks and fell to the laminated table top. Each tear formed a tiny helpless puddle.

Alora had to blink hard herself.

The Nillsons' tractor and trailer were being held at a secure compound not far from the county lock up. Russell Kupka, much to Hunter's surprise, volunteered to lead the way, and make sure the load was released to Hunter without a problem.

"What about the dog?" Hunter remembered to ask as they walked toward the parking lot.

Russell snorted. "Wasn't much of a dog." When Hunter didn't react, he continued, "Don't worry. I'm sure the K-9 unit's been taking good care of it. I'll have them drop it off at the compound. Where's your truck?"

"The closest spot I could find was about five blocks away. Unfortunately, seventy foot parking spaces are hard to come by," Hunter said drily. "I'd appreciate a lift."

Russell's car was parked in full sun. The detective opened the windows and turned up the air conditioning before easing the car out of the parking lot. "What made you choose to become a truck driver?" he asked without looking at Hunter.

"It's a living," replied Hunter, trying to direct the air conditioning vent directly at his face and neck. "You know whether the load's been kept refrigerated?" He was aware that he hadn't answered Russell's question. He didn't intend to.

"Yeah, I know. There's cheese in the sauce. Your boss said she'd come down here and break some heads if we didn't keep it cool." The detective shrugged. "We did our best. It's an air conditioned warehouse." He stopped at a red light. "You didn't answer my question."

"Yes. I did." Hunter studied the woman in the car next to them. She was very, very blond, wore oversized dark glasses, and was chewing gum. When he realized she was staring back, he turned away. "It's very important that I have the paperwork that came with the load," he said to Russell. "For customs. You any idea where it is?"

Turned out it was still in Ray and Sharon's tractor. Hunter backed his own rig up to a loading door, and a young man on a forklift started ferrying skids loaded with cartons of nacho sauce from the warehouse floor into Hunter's trailer. From the small window of the adjacent door, Hunter could see Ray Nillson's rig parked along the fence. It was dusty, but otherwise the same proud, russet colored machine he'd seen in Yoncalla just three days ago. Russell showed up beside him waving a set of keys. "Let's go see what we can find," he said.

The cab of the Kenworth was suffocatingly hot, so they left the door wide open. It was just as beautiful a rig on the inside as on the outside, but cluttered by the digging of the forensic team. The bunks were down, their blankets crumpled in one corner, untidy piles of clothing and personal effects littered the mattresses. Grey and black smudges marred the smooth surfaces where they had been dusted for prints, no doubt in the hope of placing the victim inside the vehicle. The sleeper had all the amenities of a well-equipped R.V., including microwave, television and a small fridge. On top of a mound of towels was a photograph of Ray and Sharon, smiling broadly, obviously on their wedding day. Hunter felt uncomfortable being there, as if he were violating the privacy of his friends. Russell stood back, and with a sweeping gesture invited Hunter to look for the paperwork, but watched him closely.

Hunter started with the obvious places, and found a clipboard tucked between the driver's seat and the console. On it was the bill of lading for the nacho sauce, plus an envelope with the name of a broker scrawled across it. "Here it is," he said.

"Isn't much like your truck, is it?" said Russell, making no move to leave.

"This is a Kenworth. Mine's a Freightliner. Older, too."

"Yours just looks like a truck with a blue sardine can tacked on the back of it." The detective was caressing his tie between a thumb and forefinger. "Can't be too comfortable."

"It's adequate," said Hunter. He was tempted to ask the detective why he cared, but instead he asked, "When is the dog supposed to get here?"

Russell looked at his watch, but didn't answer. Hunter decided to take the lead, and headed out the door.

"You like being a truck driver?" Russell asked.

"Not at the moment." Hunter stepped down from the cab, saying over his shoulder, "But you like being a detective."

"Yes," said Russell. "Indeed I do." He made sure the Nillsons' truck was locked, then turned to Hunter with a faint wry smile. "And I've got to believe that any man who would give up being a detective for a job whose greatest challenge involved staying between the lines on the Interstate must have had a good reason." He tossed the keys in the air and caught them again.

Hunter said nothing.

"The dog should be here soon." Russell slipped the keys into his pocket and headed back to his car. "Have a nice trip," he called out as Hunter watched him drive away.

A few minutes after Hunter had pulled his tractor-trailer away from the loading dock and fastened the trailer's doors with a padlock, an L.A. County Sheriff's car pulled up. An attractive, big boned African-American woman in uniform stepped out. She opened the car's back door and stooped inside. When she turned around, cradled inside her arms was a mop of golden hair with two little black eyes,

58

attentive ears and a glistening nose. The policewoman cuddled the little bundle, bending over it and making very unpolicewomanly kissing sounds. A tiny quick tongue shot out and licked her chin. "My little sweetheart," she crooned. "Does that bad man want to take you away from me? Huh?"

"So, just what do we have here?" asked Hunter, stepping forward.

The woman pretended to pull Peaches away, then swung back and offered the bundle up to Hunter with a smile that lit up her face like a halogen beam. "You take good care of this little punkin'," she said, and deposited the dog in Hunter's arms.

The mop of golden hair felt as light as a kitten. Hunter held it at arm's length so he could see what it was. "A Pomeranian?" he asked the woman.

She shrugged. "Whatever he is, he's a little cutie. Aren't you, sweetie pie?"

"Is there a cage?" asked Hunter.

The woman shook her head, then reached inside her car. "Just this stuff," she said, holding open an Albertson's bag. They both peered inside. It contained a retractable leash, a brush, a cardboard folder with the name and address of a veterinarian on it, a double dog food dish, and a small bag of kibble. "And this." She handed the bag to Hunter, and retrieved a folded blanket from the back seat. "Where you takin' the little guy?"

"Vancouver," said Hunter. "He's going to stay with a friend of his owners' for a while. She's got a Pomeranian herself," said Hunter with a frown, "or whatever. This dog's a lot smaller than hers unless maybe he's just a puppy." He turned Peaches this way and that until the dog began to squirm. "He doesn't have a puppy face, though, does he?"

The woman shook her head. "He looks all growed up to me," she said, tickling the dog under the chin. "You're a big little dog, aren't you, sweetie? Yes, you are."

"I wonder if he's ... uh ... done his business lately?" Hunter looked hopefully at the policewoman. She just smiled and shrugged. "I guess I'll take him for a walk before we leave then," said Hunter, rummaging in the Albertson's bag for the leash.

"You got to scoop it here," warned the policewoman. "It's the law," she added with her beautiful smile.

"Right," said Hunter. He could hardly wait.

Russell Kupka had been right when he called Hunter's sleeper unit a blue sardine can. It was a basic economy model, just a tin box with a sofa-sized bunk and some storage space, bolted to the rear wall of the Freightliner's cab as an afterthought. He could access the sleeper from his cab, but there was a heavy curtain with snaps that could seal that entrance, and a small outside door in the wall of the box. It wasn't fancy, but it served his needs.

Peaches didn't like it.

For safety's sake, Hunter had decided that the best place for Peaches was in the sleeper box. He fastened the snaps to seal the entrance to the cab, put some water – hopefully not enough to spill – and kibble in Peaches' dish on the floor, and arranged his doggie blanket on the bunk, near the foot of the mattress. Then he sat on the bunk and patted the blanket. "Here, boy. Here, Peaches," he called, encouraging the dog with a few little kissing sounds. "Here, boy." The little eyes glittered up at him from the blond mop as it circled a spot on the floor for a few excited seconds, then Peaches jumped. Ignoring the blanket, the dog perched itself on Hunter's thighs and tried to lick his face.

"Good boy," said Hunter. At least the dog could jump as high as the bunk. He lifted the dog off his lap and placed it squarely in the center of the blanket. "There you go. Lie down." He patted the blanket again. "Lie down."

Peaches wagged his tail, then scampered off the blanket and into Hunter's lap, its pink tongue connecting with Hunter's lips. Hunter turned his face away and wiped his lips with the back of his hand, then grabbed the dog again. "Stay," he said, plunking the wriggling body back onto the blanket. "Lie down." This time he applied some gentle pressure on the dog's back, until the rear legs folded underneath the mop and the dog was in a sitting position. "Stay," repeated Hunter, releasing the pressure. It didn't work. As Peaches

60

scampered for his lap again, Hunter leaped to his feet, banging his head in the process. "Ouch," he said, rubbing his skull. This wasn't going to work.

He finally had to resort to slamming the sleeper door in the dog's face. That was followed by frantic yapping and a flurry of scrabbling at the door panel. Hunter winced, but decided to leave it at that. The dog will calm down, he thought to himself. Once they were underway, the dog would be lulled to sleep by the motion of the truck.

This was not the case. Although the little dog gave up scratching and whining at the heavy curtain after about half an hour, on opening the door a few hours later at Buttonwillow when he stopped for dinner, Hunter discovered the sleeper was a shambles. Kibble and water were spread across the floor, with Hunter's clean clothes and pillow strewn on top of the mess. Hunter sighed, and clipped the leash to the dog's collar. "Let's go, Peaches," he said, and took the dog for a walk in the semi-darkness around the perimeter of the truck stop parking lot.

After a late dinner, and after cleaning up the mess in his sleeper, Hunter decided to take a chance on keeping Peaches in the cab. The little dog gave the inside of the cab a once over with his nose, then leapt lightly to the passenger seat and perched there with his ears pricked forward and his nose in the air. He looked over at Hunter once or twice as if to say, What're you waiting for? Let's get this rig on the road!

"I'll be damned," said Hunter.

Once they were back on the highway and moving at a steady speed, the dog stood up, tags clinking, made two or three tight circles, and curled up on the passenger seat with his nose to his tail, keeping one black eye on the driver. Hunter smiled. So tonight he had company, a fluffy hump dimly illuminated by the dashboard dials. Would that help to curb the nocturnal wanderings of his mind?

"What do you say, Peaches? Where'll we stop for the night? Santa Nella?" Hunter figured on driving until one o'clock or so, then bedding down for about seven hours and starting the day with a shower and a good breakfast before he got back on the road. By law, he was allowed no more than ten hours of driving at a time, alternating with a minimum of eight hours off duty. Whenever possible, he preferred to do most of his driving during daylight hours, in spite of the fact that traffic was better at night. Hunter's nights on the highway were haunted.

Regrets. What ifs. Memories of the missed and the lost and the restless dead. In the darkened interior of the cab, unwanted thoughts swirled around his mind like hornets, relentless and indestructible. Nothing outside to see but headlights, taillights, and the white lines that guided his wheels, themselves not distractions but instead, reproachful and resentful eyes, incessant pinpricks of guilt. Thinking black thoughts had become an impossible habit to break, but maybe tonight...

Maybe tonight he wouldn't dwell on the death of the best friend he'd ever had, and could ever hope to have. Maybe tonight he wouldn't dwell on the failure of his marriage, and the estrangement that seemed to be growing between himself and his daughters, in spite of his efforts to be closer to them. Maybe tonight he wouldn't dwell on the shame he still felt for having to leave his chosen career. He tried to steer his mind in other directions.

Ray and Sharon Nillson. Why wouldn't they admit to finding the frozen corpse on their trailer? The two of them sincerely loved each other, there was no doubt in Hunter's mind. He wondered when he and his ex-wife Christine had lost that closeness, that feeling their lives fit so closely together they were almost one life. It had dwindled gradually over the years, he guessed. The kids. His job. The arguments about his long hours, and the time he spent with Ken in the bar after work, trying to talk Ken out of his depressions. It had dwindled away until it was gone, that closeness between him and Christine, and she had asked him to leave. Hunter had thrown himself into his work then, withdrawn even from Ken, his best friend, his soul mate in the police force. So he hadn't been there for Ken, when Ken needed a friend most.

Hunter realized that he was doing it again. "Damn!" he slammed the steering wheel with his fist, then reached for his radio. He'd find a news show, talk show, anything. "Damn it, chief!" he said to

62

Peaches. "Why don't you say something? Why don't you tell me who that man was, the one that froze to death in Ray and Sharon's trailer?'

Hunter reached over and tousled its furry head, but the little dog only sighed.

CHAPTER
SEVEN

Teresa Jagpal called her supervisor at work, said she'd be late. Last night, after drinking two glasses of wine for courage, she had finally phoned the police and told them she wanted to report someone missing. "You'll have to come down and make the report in person," the man on the phone had said. Teresa had another glass of wine then, and resolved to do it in the morning. She couldn't leave it another day. Another day, and Greg would have been gone a week.

Teresa drove her Tercel into the parking lot behind the RCMP building. She pulled into a parking spot marked Visitors, let her car idle for about fifteen seconds, then backed out again. She exited the parking lot, turning left onto Deer Lake Avenue, and pulled into the nearly empty lot at the Shadboldt Theatre, where she found an isolated parking spot and turned off the ignition. What if Greg had just come home? What if he had just left a message on her answering machine? What if all this had just been a bad dream?

She locked her car and walked across the parking lot, her shoulder bag flapping against her hipbone. Inside the building she found a pay phone and dropped in her quarter. On the third ring, the phone was picked up. Teresa's breath stuck in her throat.

"Yeah?" It was Hellen's voice, thick with sleep.

Teresa hesitated. Since Hellen had moved back in, they didn't see each other much during the week, she and Hellen. Hellen's hours were more like Greg's. Hellen worked afternoon shift, often stayed up late after she got home, working on her sketches with her earphones on.

"Hello?" said Hellen. "Greg?"

At the mention of Greg's name, Teresa's stomach did a flip-flop. "No, Hellen. It's me."

"Jesus, Jag! Why didn't you say something?!"

Teresa could still think of nothing to say. She rolled the phone cord between her fingers, debated whether to just hang up.

"Jag? Are you all right?"

"Do you know where Greg is?" Teresa finally said. "Have you talked to him?"

There were a few seconds of silence. "Jag? Are you all right? Why are you asking me about Greg? You'd know where he is better than I would."

Teresa took a deep breath. Maybe telling Hellen about it would make it easier to talk to the police. "I haven't seen Greg since last Friday morning. I haven't seen him and he hasn't called. I don't know what to do." An old woman in a jogging suit, carrying a book bag, walked past, and Teresa lowered her voice, moved in closer to the phone. "I'm... I'm going to go see the police." Her voice shivered like a bad connection.

"What about the studio? Have you called the studio?" asked Hellen.

Of course she'd called the studio. "I talked to Max. Greg hasn't been to the studio since Friday either."

"But the police? Why the police? Do you think something's happened to Greg?" Hellen sounded sharper now, wide awake.

"I don't know what to think. I just know that he hasn't come home and he hasn't called. What else can I do?" It was a relief, such a relief, to finally talk to someone else about it, that Teresa was overcome by a confused rush of emotion and started to sob. "Where could he be, Hellen?"

"Look, Jag. There's no need to think the worst. Maybe he just needed some space. Maybe he got started one night and couldn't stop, you know?"

Teresa shook her head, got her voice under control. "No, I don't know." Teresa was the first one to admit that she was as naive as a six year old compared to Greg and Hellen and their friends. There were some things that she just didn't have in common with them.

"A binge. You know what a binge is, don't you?" Hellen's voice sounded almost exasperated and Teresa wondered why she had ever considered this woman her best friend.

"Greg's never been on a binge," Teresa said, now impatient to get off the phone.

"There's always a first time," said Hellen.

"But almost a week, Hellen? Last time I saw him was Friday morning, when I left for work." She paused briefly, then said, "When did you see him last? Hellen? When did you see him last?"

"I'm trying to think." There was a short pause, and a light thumping sound, as if Hellen were tapping the phone with her finger. "Before that," she said. "Maybe it was Thursday night, after he got home from his gig."

Teresa swallowed hard. "What... what did you talk about?" she asked.

"I don't know." Hellen's breath whooshed into the phone, as if she'd yawned. "I don't remember. Nothing. You know, maybe I made him a sandwich or something. He probably talked about his gig."

"Did he talk about..." Teresa took a deep breath, let it out again. "Did he talk about leaving me?"

"Jag. What the hell has gotten into you?" said Hellen, but that didn't answer Teresa's question.

"I gotta go," said Teresa, and hung up the phone.

Twenty-five minutes later, she was sitting across the desk from a uniformed policeman in a little office at the Burnaby RCMP detachment. He'd asked her all kinds of questions about Greg, like how long they'd been together, whether they fought much, whether he'd ever gone away without telling her before. "My friend says he might be on a binge," said Teresa, twisting her fingers in the strap of her purse.

"Has he ever done that before?" The RCMP officer's name was Tom Fong, but he looked only half Oriental. He didn't look any older than Teresa, maybe twenty-five or twenty-six.

Teresa shook her head.

"Is your husband a heavy drinker? Does he take drugs, that you know of?" The officer tapped his pencil on the paper, full of nervous energy, like Greg usually was.

"My husband? Greg and I aren't married." She'd called him her boyfriend.

Officer Fong glanced down at the form in front of him. "Sorry, Ms. Jagpal, if that made you uncomfortable. You do realize, though, that since you've lived together for more than two years, that makes you man and wife, by common law."

Teresa blinked in surprise, then nodded slowly. Her mother and father would be upset if they found out, her brothers angry. "We were only roommates," she would have to say, and hope that they would believe her. Being roommates with a man was bad enough.

"Does he drink?" repeated the officer, studying the photograph she'd given him. It was one of Greg's eight by ten glossies, the ones they put up in bars when he did a solo gig. She thought he looked like a rock star, resting his cheek against the neck of his guitar and gazing downwards and a little to the right, so his long dark eyelashes stood out against his skin.

"Greg drinks beer sometimes, and sometimes he does drugs, I guess. But not very much. I've only seen him get drunk, really, once or twice, at parties." And just a few weeks ago, she thought, he and Hellen got into a bottle of ouzo after Greg got back from his gig. For hours, Teresa lay in bed listening to them talk and laugh, although she couldn't make out the words, and decided that she and Greg should find a new place to live now that Hellen had moved back in. Greg finally crawled into Teresa's bed at three in the morning, stinking of licorice and wanting to make love. No. Not make love. He'd said, I want to fuck you. Fuck me, baby. And Teresa just lay there while he grunted on top of her, grunted and sweated and bruised her arms with his clumsiness. The tears had run down her cheeks and into her ears, but he'd been too drunk to know, or maybe to care.

"Anything else?" asked the officer. "Anything else you want to add that might help us to locate him?"

Teresa shook her head. Greg had secrets that he didn't share with her. She thought maybe one day he would, but so far that day hadn't come. She got up to leave, hiking her purse strap over her shoulder.

"Wait here just a minute, please, Ms. Jagpal. I'll just run through our recent John Doe files and be right back." He took the form and the photo and left the room.

Teresa sat back down, pressed her legs together and hugged herself. The soft click of computers and busy sounds of office machines and voices came in through the open door. John Doe files? Files of unknown dead people? She pushed that idea from her mind, and thought again about Hellen.

When Teresa was looking for a place to live in Burnaby, she'd answered Hellen's ad on the student bulletin board for a roommate. Hellen was renting a two bedroom basement suite in her aunt's house at a very cheap price, and was looking for someone to share it with. They'd both been students at BCIT, and although Hellen was a couple of years older, they got along very well. Teresa was shy, and Hellen quite outgoing, a lot wilder than any friend Teresa had before. Living with Hellen taught Teresa so much about life, things she would never have learned in her parents' house. Their arrangement went on quite comfortably for almost two years, and then Hellen met a drummer named Max and started spending a lot of nights with him. Max introduced Teresa to his guitar player, Greg. It wasn't long before Hellen moved in with Max, and Greg moved in with Teresa, and that was how it had been for two and a half years. Then Max and Hellen broke up, Teresa didn't know exactly why, and Hellen moved back to her old room. Teresa couldn't say no. The house belonged to Hellen's aunt, after all.

Teresa closed her eyes and nodded to herself. Yes, she'd have to find a new place for her and Greg to live. It didn't work, living with Hellen. Teresa just wasn't... what? Modern? Progressive? Western?

In any case, Teresa wasn't comfortable with it. What did they call it? A menage a trois? No. Three was a crowd.

Officer Tom Fong closed the door softly behind him and walked back to the desk, but he didn't sit down. When she looked into his eyes, Teresa's stomach dropped like a stone inside her body, and her mouth went dry.

"I'm sorry to have to tell you this, Ms. Jagpal," he said.

Russell Kupka switched the phone from one ear to the other, held it in the crook of his neck as he massaged his left arm. He'd been through his spiel half a dozen times already this morning, been put on hold, asked to repeat himself, transferred without warning, and cut off, and he had long ago lost all patience with the buck-passing pencil pushers in the U.S. Customs and Immigration bureaucracy. A voice came on the line again, at long last, and he switched the phone back to his left side, picking up his pen with the right. "Who am I speaking to?" he asked. He wanted names, so that he could map his trail in case he got lost again.

"Donohue, U.S. Customs Inspector at Pacific Highway border crossing. And you are... ?"

"Detective Russell Kupka of the L.A. County Sheriff's Office, Homicide Division."

"Okay, Detective Kupka. My colleague has briefly described your problem, but would you be kind enough to go over it again so I can be sure I understand it correctly?" The man's voice was brisk and businesslike, so much so that Russell dared to hope that his quest was over.

"I'm investigating a possible homicide. For purposes of that investigation, I have to know whether or not a given trailer was opened and the load examined by U.S. Customs and Immigration at Pacific Highway on the night of July 14th of this year. If records are kept, I would like to have copies of those records. I would also like to interview the customs officer who handled the clearance, to see if he can provide any information about the trailer and its contents, or the drivers who crossed the border with the load. Can you help me?" Russell held his breath.

"I'm your man," said Donohue. Russell grinned with relief. "I've got the records right here. Now give me just a couple of minutes to read through the paperwork, see if I can refresh my memory. This is a pretty busy border crossing, and it's not easy to remember one load out of hundreds."

"Take your time," said Russell. He put his hand over the mouthpiece and whispered, "Yes!" Yesterday the trucker had mentioned the possibility of a man stowing away in the Nillson's trailer without their knowledge, either when it was loaded or perhaps at the border, so Russell had decided to follow up on that possibility. He'd already talked to the shipper in Burnaby, and all of their employees were present and accounted for. He drew a little truck on his notepad as he waited, listening to the dry shuffle and crinkle of papers over the line.

Less than a minute later, the customs inspector's crisp voice said, "I won't be of much help, I'm afraid. Looks like it was pretty routine. Meat's got to be reported to Agriculture, but the paperwork was all in order, and I guess there was nothing suspicious about the load or the drivers, and it didn't come up on the computer as a random check, so there'd be no reason to examine the freight closely. The examination wouldn't have been much more than a rubber stamp, if you know what I mean. Friday's a busy night, so we don't spend much time on routine loads if we can help it."

"But the trailer was opened?"

"Uh. The paperwork says it was." The customs inspector sighed. "Off the record, Detective, let me put it like this. It's supposed to have been, but I wouldn't swear to it that it was."

"What are the chances someone could have entered the trailer without you and the drivers seeing it."

'Anything's possible but it's a secure area. I'd have to say highly unlikely."

Russell nodded at the phone line. "Good. Fine. That's what I needed to know. You remember anything about the drivers? Anything suspicious?"

"I'm sorry..."

"A husband and wife. The woman's blond, forties, brassy, if you know what I mean. The husband's a big guy, kind of dopey looking. They had a little dog with them. Does that help?"

"A dog? A husband and wife team with a little dog? You know," continued the customs officer, his voice thoughtful, "I think I do remember the drivers. Not that there was anything suspicious about them, but maybe I do remember them."

"Yeah?"

"Yes. Yes, I do," he said more emphatically. "There are getting to be more and more husband and wife teams, so that doesn't particularly grab my attention anymore, but what was interesting about this couple is that the husband is an American citizen and his wife is a Canadian, still maintains her Canadian address. I wasn't sure if I should let her through. Had to send her into the immigration office. There's a rule - I don't know if you're familiar with it - that says a foreign driver can't haul freight between American points. It's called cabotage. Same thing applies in Canada. That means the wife can't haul a load from, say, Seattle to Los Angeles, and the husband can't haul a load from, say, Vancouver to Toronto. We talked about that, how they're stuck with hauling loads to and from Canada." There were a few seconds of silence. "She said she's applying for her green card," he added.

"Anything about them strike you as suspicious? Did they seem nervous?" asked Russell.

"No. Like I said, if they'd acted suspicious, I would've made a close inspection of the load. As far as I can recall, they seemed pretty normal. Friendly." The agent paused again. "She was the more talkative of the two. He seemed pretty quiet."

"That's them all right. Thanks, you've been a great help. If you think of anything they might've said or done that was out of the ordinary, might point to them being nervous or paranoid, worried about something, could you give me a call?"

"Mind telling me what's going on?"

Russell paused. The guy had been so cooperative, he hated not to reciprocate. "They're suspects in a homicide," he said. "So far, the evidence is pretty circumstantial. We haven't uncovered a motive yet."

"I see. Yeah. Sure, I'll give you a call if I think of anything."

Russell spelled his name for the customs agent, and gave him his telephone number, then hung up with a smile on his face. Merv, who was out picking up donuts for himself and a bran muffin for Russell, had only one more day to interfere before he left on vacation, and then Russell was on his own. The Iceman case would make his reputation, he had no doubt about it. Now he had one more piece of the puzzle to work with. He might not know where it fit yet, but if that little lady was applying for her green card, that meant she had something to lose, didn't it? The way everything had been falling into place for him in this case, it wouldn't be long...

"Detecting. I love it!" he said, grinning at the foxy young clerk he ran into at the coffee machine. She looked impressed, gave him a once over and a slow smile that told him she liked what she saw. He did, too. She had skin the color of coffee ice cream - his favorite flavor - and legs worthy of a statue by Michelangelo. Russell wondered how long Jennifer was going to be away this time. "How long you been working here?" he asked the clerk. "Got any plans for the future?" His question was ambiguous, and he intended it that way.

"Future? Like, ten years from now or did you maybe mean this weekend?" she asked coyly, then ran her tongue along the rim of her coffee cup. Ooooh, she was good. Very good.

Before Russell could answer, he heard his phone start to ring. "Catch you later," he said, touching her lightly on the arm. He sure liked the way she smiled. But by the time he got to his desk, Merv had picked up the phone, a brown paper bag with a grease spot in one corner hanging from his other hand.

"Yeah. Uh-huh. Just a sec." Merv dropped the bag on Russell's desk and scrabbled around with both hands for pen and paper, the receiver almost swallowed up by his chins. As he juggled the phone and a notepad, his hat fell off, hit the edge of the desk, and landed upside down on the floor. Russell didn't volunteer to pick it up. "Okay, go ahead," said Merv. "Yeah. Uh-huh."

Russell waited impatiently, came just short of snatching the phone out of his partner's hand. "What?" he mouthed, but Merv waved at him to be quiet. Russell took a careless sip of coffee and burned the roof of his mouth. "Shit," he said, grinding his teeth.

"Great. Thanks for the information. We'll be in touch." Merv finished making a few notes after he hung up the phone, then turned to Russell with a smug look on his face. "We've got an I.D. on our Iceman," he said.

My Iceman, you asshole! Russell wanted to correct him. Instead he asked "Who was that on the phone?" through clenched teeth.

"Your RCMP buddies from Burny... Burno..."

"Burnaby," said Russell, not hiding his impatience. He reached for the note pad - his note pad - that Merv was holding. When Merv wouldn't let go, Russell snatched it out of his hand.

"Seems like our Iceman is some kind of musician. A guy named Greg Williams, just reported missing this morning by his common-law wife." Merv rushed to say it aloud before Russell could read it, as if that gave him some kind of Brownie points. "The vic's from there, all right. He's from Canada."

Russell glared at him, but it didn't stop Merv from saying what he said next.

"Like I told you, Cupcake, this isn't our case. The Mounties already admit they'll have to do a lot of the legwork on it. If you're smart, you'll ship the whole file off to Canada and save the L.A. County taxpayers some money."

Russell smiled grimly, and poured what was left of his coffee into his partner's pork pie hat.

"Bullshit!" El planted her fists on either side of her thick waist and glared.

The square faced man in front of her scratched his belly and looked at the floor, then rubbed his jaw with grubby knuckles. He was trying to explain to her why he'd been late for an appointment delivery at a major grocery warehouse.

"I was there in plenty of time, I tell you," he repeated, just inches short of a whine. "They're the ones screwed up, taking a long goddamn coffee break so they ran out of time. They're trying to blame it on me."

"Give it up, Dunc. They called me right at two to find out where you were." She looked him up and down, taking in the grease stains on his pants, the mud caked on the seams of his steel toed boots, and the scraggle of chest hairs exposed above the top button of his work shirt. She wondered if he ever dressed up for his wife.

The driver's eyes were skittering around the warehouse, trying to avoid hers. He readjusted his Mack Trucks cap and took a deep breath, as if he were about to try again.

"Don't fuck with me, Dunc. Don't ever fuck with my loads like that again. If you're running late, you get on the horn to me, right away. You make sure I know it before the customer does. Understand?" When he didn't answer, she lowered her head and deepened her scowl. "Understand?"

"Yeah," he muttered.

"Now you're gonna have to wait til Monday to get outa here. Your goof-up just cost you that load for San Fran. It's got to go tonight, and I'm not gonna let you leave town until you've kept your end of the bargain on this load, and there's no way we're gonna get another appointment until Monday morning."

"Fuck."

"Yeah, fuck," she said. "I'm sure as hell not gonna absorb the cost of another delivery just because you fucked up. Where were you? Stuffing your fat face at Arby's again?" The man pissed her off. He ate like a pig but wasn't really fat, just an average sized beer gut. He wasn't a small man, but she weighed more than he did.

The driver muttered something unintelligible just as the phone began to ring. El waved him away in disgust and headed toward her office. "Call me this afternoon and I'll tell you what time you're rescheduled for. And this time, Dunc, BE THERE!" she bellowed over her shoulder as she yanked open the door.

The call was from the grocery warehouse. They needed Dunc's load for next week's sale, so they had made a switch and could accept

74

it at two this afternoon. El dropped the phone and was heading out to tell Dunc the news when she heard a rig gear down to turn into the yard. She looked out the window and there was Hunter Rayne's navy blue Freightliner. "All right! The Blue Knight!" she said, then rushed out to the warehouse to grab Dunc before he had time to leave.

She was back on the phone listening to a driver bitch about his schedule when Hunter walked in the office door with the little bundle she'd been waiting for. "Yeah, yeah," she said into the mouthpiece. "I'll see what I can do." She nodded at Hunter and rolled her eyes. "Leave it with me, Jack. I'll try to get you back in time gotta go now bye. Hi, Skookums!" She threw down the receiver and held out her arms.

Hunter's eyebrows rose and he drew back, feigning shock. "Skookums?"

"Not you, you idiot. How's my little princess?" She took the dog from under Hunter's arm and gave it a brief cuddle, then held it at arm's length. "Awfully tiny, isn't she?"

Hunter nodded. "It's a she? Here I've been having man-to-man talks with it all the way from Buttonwillow."

"Of course, she's a she. What do you think, with a name like Peaches?"

Hunter shrugged.

El turned the dog this way and that way, frowning. "Awfully small, compared to Peterbilt, eh?"

"That's what I thought."

They both regarded the dog intently for a few seconds, then Hunter seemed to lose interest.

"Have you heard anything more from California?" he asked.

"Not from California, but one of Her Majesty's finest was here this morning. He said he knows you. Left a card." She rested the dog on one pillowy hip as she rummaged around in the paperwork on her desk and found a business card. "Kowalski. Ring any bells?"

"Al Kowalski? Sure."

"Good. Maybe you can get him to give you the inside poop."

"What did he want to know?"

"He showed me a picture of the dead guy, to see if I knew him."

"Did you?"

"No." El stroked the dog's ears and looked down into its glittery black eyes. After having volunteered too much information to that American cop, she hadn't been sure how much to say to the Mountie and had decided to err on the side of caution, so two or three times she'd just told him sorry, she couldn't answer his question. "Other than that, I pretty much just gave him the facts about the shipment, gave him copies of the paperwork and stuff. But I told him I didn't think Ray could hurt a flea. Are you going to be able to get them out of jail?"

"It's not up to me," said Hunter.

As useful as it was when there was a problem to solve, Hunter's calm pragmatism could be infuriating. "But you can do something, can't you?" she said. His expression told her she should know better, but she wasn't prepared to buy that. "Well? Can't you?"

With a faint smile and narrowed eyes he asked, "What makes you think Ray couldn't have done it?"

El frowned, taken aback. "You can't think he did it."

"I didn't say that I thought he did it. I just don't know him well enough to bet my reputation that he didn't. Do you?"

El's frown deepened and she thrust out her jaw. Hunter did that a lot, put things in a new perspective, and it always took her by surprise. "Yeah, I guess that's what the neighbors always say about serial killers, isn't it? Old Wayne was such a quiet pleasant guy, yadda, yadda, that kind of shit." She eased into her captain's chair, the little dog squirming until she'd settled it comfortably on her belly. She scratched under its chin and it closed its eyes, looked like it was damn near grinning with pleasure. "Aw, look. Look at her smiling. Isn't she cute as a bug? But, goddamn it! Ray IS a nice guy. We had a couple of heart to hearts, me and him, before he met Sharon."

Hunter leaned his elbows back against the counter, looked her in the eyes like he was waiting for more.

"You know how shy he is, eh? Especially with women," she continued. "I'd almost bet he was a forty-year-old virgin before he met Sharon, wouldn't you?"

Hunter shrugged. "Does that make him harmless?"

76

"I guess not. Maybe it makes him a nut. What do you think?"

"I don't think it makes him a nut. I've only met Sharon a couple of times, but she seems nice enough. Pleasant enough."

"Yeah, she does. You always worry, though, with a guy like Ray. He's such a mark, you know? It'd be so easy for a woman to take advantage of him." The dog squirmed, tried to scramble up her chest. She let it go and the dog was immediately in her face. "Oh, you're such a cutie! That's your mom we're talking about, isn't it? How could she be a bad lady if she's your mom, eh, Peaches?" said El, swinging her head from one side to the other in a hopeless effort to dodge the quick tongue. "You're such a cutie, aren't you, you little mugwump?"

"How well do you know her?"

"Same as you. I only met her a few times before they got married."

"You see her more now that she's teaming with him, I guess."

El shook her head, finally pulled the little dog away from her face. "Not much. Ray does all the business, sometimes doesn't even pick her up 'til after he's through here. She seems okay, though. A bit rough around the edges, maybe."

"Unlike yourself, you mean," said Hunter, deadpan.

"Fuck off," she said.

But she had to laugh.

CHAPTER
EIGHT

At one thirty, Hunter was sitting in Corporal Al Kowalski's unmarked car, heading for the Burnaby home of Greg Williams, whose thawed corpse was still in the L.A. County morgue. He had dropped by the Burnaby detachment on his way home from Watson Transportation, and been shown to Al's office.

"What took you so long?" Al had said with a crooked smile. "Kupka said you'd been in his face like a dirty shirt. Civilian or not, you can't seem to stay clear of homicide investigations, can you?" He put down his pen and leaned back in his chair. His hairline had receded some and he was a little thicker around the waist, but otherwise Al looked just as he did the day Hunter left the force four years earlier.

Hunter grunted. "I don't go looking for them, if that's what you're trying to say."

Al stuck out his jaw, nodded, then said, "I made it clear to Kupka that you could be trusted. Even told him I might call you in as a consultant, given your inside knowledge of the trucking business."

Hunter studied Al's face, trying to understand his meaning and whether he had just said that for Kupka's benefit, or was this some kind of proposition?

"Unpaid, of course," said Al.

"I'm not sure I follow. Are you asking me...?"

"Since you seem to have some kind of stake in this anyway, I'm asking you to donate a few hours of your time to help me out, answer a few questions."

As soon as Hunter had agreed, Al said, "Good. Let's go," and hooked his jacket off the back of his chair. "I'm due to interview the victim's wife in fifteen minutes. I talked to her briefly yesterday, but she was too shook up to answer questions. We can talk on the way."

They drove east, then south, on Canada Way toward New Westminster. It was a summer Friday afternoon, and traffic heading out of the city was already heavy. "He's got no record," said Al.

"What do you know about him?"

"Almost zip. Just what his wife told us when she reported him missing." Kowalski turned right onto Edmonds. "The guy was a musician, played pubs and lounges, him and his band in a box."

"Synthesizer."

"Right. The wife works for the telephone company. She goes off to work at her usual time Friday morning, leaves the guy in bed, as usual. Gets home that night, goes to bed alone, gets up the next morning. No sign of her squeeze. He works nights, sometimes parties a bit afterwards, like all good citizens he doesn't drink and drive, so at that point she still wasn't too worried, she says. So the day goes by and she doesn't hear from him, so she phones the club he was working at. Turns out he never made it to his gig on Friday night. Nobody heard from him. That's when she starts calling around."

"You talk to his employer yet?"

Al grunted. "Some employer. I say, Do you know him? and the bar manager says to me, The fucker never showed up for a Friday night gig. He'll never fuckin' work here again. Right, I say. He's dead. Then get his fuckin' equipment offa my stage, he says."

Hunter shook his head. "Sensitive guy. What bar is this?"

"Place called Fraser's Dock, at the Shores Hotel in Chilliwack."

"Long way from home."

"Buyers' market. As a musician, this Williams guy wasn't exactly beating clients off with a stick."

They'd headed back west on Kingsway, turned off just before the Middlegate Mall, and pulled up outside a three story house that had seen better days. Al led the way to a side door.

The woman who answered the door was in her early thirties, maybe younger. Her hair was short and dark with a harsh red sheen to it, and stuck up in shiny spikes like licked fur. Her nose was sharp and her lips thin and disapproving, painted a deep burgundy, almost brown. She wore torn jeans and a very short tee shirt. Hunter tried not to stare at the ring in her navel.

"Yeah?" she said. Her voice was loud and raw.

"Is Theresa Jagpal at home?" Al pulled his badge out of his pocket, held it ready.

"Are you the cops?"

"RCMP," said Al, offering his badge.

She barely glanced at it. "Jag!" she yelled over her shoulder. "Jag! It's them!" Then she swung the door open, almost grudgingly, and motioned for them to enter. "Sit there," she said, pointing to a futon sofa. She was barefoot.

Al and Hunter exchanged glances. There were no other chairs in the room, just cushions on the carpet. Hunter walked across the room and stood there, staring out the window, which looked out on an overgrown lawn with a weathered picnic table under a moldering plum tree. A slender, almost anorexic, young woman entered the room. She was brown skinned and fine featured with huge dark eyes, and her black hair was swept up into a knot high on her head, ringed by a yellow cloth band. She looked uncertainly from Al to Hunter, and Al motioned her to the sofa. Al perched himself on the edge of the futon, at the opposite end so he could face her, his knees higher than his hips. Teresa Jagpal seemed to cower into her corner of the sofa, her limbs curled into her body, narrow bare feet swallowed by the cushion. Her thin fingers played with the folds of her tunic. The woman with the ring in her navel leaned against the wall, her arms crossed, one bare foot pressed flat against the wall. Hunter remained standing by the window.

Al glanced at the friend.

"You want me to leave? Is that it?" she said. When Al shrugged, she turned to Teresa Jagpal. "You want me to stay, Jag, I'll stay."

Teresa shot her a weak smile. "Yes, Hellen. Stay."

The name hit Hunter like a fist in the solar plexus. This coarse, abrasive young woman, she didn't look or sound or act like a Helen. He took a deep breath, quietly, and folded his arms, trying to keep the image of his dead friend's wife from occupying his attention.

"Your name?" asked Al. "For my notes."

"Hellen Brooker. Double el in Hellen, make sure you get it right."

Hunter nodded, although no one was watching him.

"Are you a relative?"

"No. I'm a good friend."

Teresa looked at her sharply. Al looked to Teresa for confirmation and after a moment's hesitation, she nodded, eyes downcast. "Yes," she said. "Hellen's a friend." Her voice was softly vibrato, like the low notes on a flute.

"First of all," said Al, "let me once again express my condolences on the loss of your husband. I know this isn't pleasant, having to answer police questions at a time like this, but under the circumstances, we need to know more about your husband and the days preceding his death."

"We weren't married." Teresa looked down at her hands. There was a filigreed silver band around the ring finger of her right hand.

Al pursed his lips. Hunter could tell he found this difficult. Almost anyone would.

"Can you tell me, when was the last time you saw your... you saw Greg?"

"Friday morning, just before I left for work. I came in - to the bedroom - and kissed him good-bye."

"Did he say anything about his plans for the day?"

"He didn't say anything. Just smiled. Or maybe he said, Bye. I'm not sure." Her eyes were so big and dark, they looked like an organ that shouldn't be exposed to air, like a heart, slippery and pulsing and vulnerable. "How did he die? Can you tell me how he died?"

Hunter looked at the floor, but only briefly. He wanted to see her reaction. He wanted to see the reactions of both of the women.

"Uh...," said Al. "The results of the autopsy should be available today. I don't know how much of the information will be released. It's quite possible, though, that your... that Greg froze to death..."

Hunter didn't believe the dark eyes could get any larger, but they did.

"... in a refrigerated trailer."

"Refrigerated trailer? What was he doing there?" she asked.

"The investigating officer believes that somehow he was locked inside a trailer full of frozen meat."

Teresa drew her breath in sharply, glanced quickly over at her friend. Hellen Brooker's mouth was a hard, thin line. Her head swiveled almost imperceptibly from side to side.

"Meat? A meat trailer? But why?" Teresa's voice had risen, lost its melodious quality. "The why is still under investigation, Ms. Jagpal. Perhaps you can help us out." Al's voice was patient, gentle. "Did Greg have any reason to be visiting a company called Hanratty Meats in Lake City?"

Again the dark eyes met those of Hellen Brooker, then shifted to her hands. She was twisting the filigreed ring around her finger. "I... I don't know. Greg wasn't part of..." Hunter followed her gaze to the wall behind Hellen. There were three identical posters that screamed, "End the slaughter!" above pictures of baby animals: a sad eyed calf, a yellow chick, a smiling piglet.

"That's our thing," volunteered Hellen. "Greg wasn't into it."

Al nodded. "Had Greg been acting different lately? Did he seem worried or excited about anything?"

Teresa shook her head. A muscle in her jaw pulsed raggedly.

"Do you know of any reason why anyone would wish to hurt him?"

She bit her lower lip, hesitated. Al had just opened his mouth to speak again when she said, "No. Of course not. Why would anyone want to hurt Greg? He lived for his music. He was totally non-violent, a very gentle man. Very gentle." The dark eyes began to overflow. She pulled a stuffed tiger from under her elbow and

82

hugged it against her chest, letting her chin fall between its tufted ears.

Hunter looked away, looked instead at Hellen Brooker. She was watching Teresa, but there was no compassion in her face. Al continued his questioning, covering the usual areas: did Greg have a car, who were his friends, where did he work, how did he spend his time The car, a 1986 Hyundai, was missing. Then came the awkward part.

"You said you last saw him on Friday morning, isn't that right?" said Al.

"Yes."

Al cleared his throat. "Your first contact with our office was yesterday morning, six full days after he disappeared. Can you tell me, Ms. Jagpal, why you waited so long to report him missing?" His voice was low, but had an edge that left no doubt about the implications of the question.

Teresa first dropped her eyes, as if she were ashamed. "I guess... I guess I was scared," she said.

"Scared of what?"

"Scared that maybe he didn't want me looking for him, that he didn't want the police looking for him."

"Why wouldn't he want the police looking for him?"

She glanced up at her friend, whose eyes were riveted on Teresa's face. She paused and her mouth moved in silence, as if she were rehearsing what to say. Finally she answered, "Hellen said he might be on a binge," her voice so soft Hunter had to strain to hear it.

"Why? Has he done that before?" asked Al, looking from one woman to the other.

Hellen shrugged. Teresa just shook her head, her chin stroking the tiger's ears.

"Then why did you think that might be the case?"

"I thought, maybe..." She looked at the corner of the ceiling, then closed her eyes. "I thought maybe Hellen knew something that I didn't."

Hellen frowned, shrugged her shoulders. "It was just an idea, Teresa. I didn't want you to worry so much." Still frowning, she addressed Al. "Can't you see she's getting upset? Why don't you respect her grief and leave her alone?"

Al ignored her. "Were there problems with your relationship, Ms. Jagpal?" he asked Teresa. "Was there any reason why your husband might have been despondent, might have considered running away?"

Teresa's mouth twisted into an agonized grimace. Her shoulders began to shake, and she covered her face with one slender hand as the other arm clutched the stuffed tiger. It was clear that she was crying, but her sobs were almost inaudible, as if she were afraid to make a sound.

"Ms. Jagpal?" prompted Al.

"Can't you leave her alone?" Hellen moved quickly to the sofa and put her arm around Teresa's shoulders. "Fuckin' pigs!" she snarled. "Leave her the fuck alone."

Al paused for a minute, and Hunter suspected he was debating whether to remove Hellen from the room. Instead he just repeated his question.

Teresa Jagpal shook her head.

On the way out, Hunter took a closer look at the posters on the wall. Below the cuddly pictures, there were some lines – poetry? Hunter couldn't tell – that read:

> *I have feelings.*
> *I love, I play, I hurt, just like you do.*
> *I am a creature of peace.*
> *I will not hurt you.*
> *Please respect my right to live, as I do yours.*
> *Please don't let me die in pain.*

Each poster had an insignia of some sort in the lower right had corner, something that looked like an anchor on its side.

Back in the car, Hunter suggested Al might want to interview the wife again, but alone next time.

"I think I'll just do that," said Al. "Or maybe you'd like to take a crack at it. You're single, free of professional... uh... constraints." He raised his eyebrows suggestively.

84

Hunter looked at him sharply. "What?"

"That young woman is damned attractive, maybe in need of a strong shoulder to cry on, you know what I mean?" He raised his eyebrows again, the corner of his lip curled. "Hey? Why not?"

Hunter decided he wasn't going to dignify the comment with a reply. "I don't know why you married guys think being single is some kind of party. It's not, by a long shot. It's you married guys who've got it made. By the way, how's Marta? Seems like years since I've seen her."

"If it's been years since you've seen her, then you don't know what you're talking about, saying us married guys have got it made." Al snorted softly.

"Why?"

"Two hundred and eighty pounds is why. Ever been to bed with a sumo wrestler?"

Hunter tried to think of something encouraging to say, but couldn't. "How does Marta feel about it?" he asked instead. He'd never been overweight himself, but knew a lot of heavy people who were comfortable with their size.

Al waved his hand in disgust. "She's always talking about diets, but that doesn't stop her from eating lunch at McDonalds and having ice cream before bed every night. And get this. She orders diet sodas. What's the good of a fuckin' diet soda when you're pigging out on a Big Mac with double fries? I say anything about it, and she looks at me like I've just murdered her pet cat. Christ!"

"Do you think Teresa Jagpal is hiding something?" Hunter said, sorry that he'd led the conversation off track.

"Maybe." Al sighed. "Look," he said. "I shouldn't have said anything about Marta. I feel like such an asshole. She's a good wife. She's just not the little pixie I married, you know what I mean?" He paused, sighed again. "I guess I feel cheated, you know what I mean?"

"Sure," said Hunter. He felt sorry for them both.

Teresa closed the door of the bedroom, pressing softly so the latch slid home with a click as soft as the tick of a clock. She didn't want Hellen to hear that she had left the bathroom. She didn't want Hellen's sympathy. Not that Hellen would come pounding on the door, insisting to be allowed inside. Teresa didn't think so anyway. She turned and leaned her back against the door, her hands pinned behind her buttocks. This had been their room, and now it was hers.

Greg's waterbed, his only contribution to the household furniture. She'd hated it at first, but he'd been so proud of it. She pictured the room with her old bed, its sheets neatly tucked under the mattress. She could have all five drawers now, if she cleared away Greg's underwear and socks from the chest of drawers. Its top was cluttered with guitar picks and bits of notepaper he emptied from his pockets, each making small dark islands in the sea of dust. It would take less than a minute to sweep them into a Safeway bag and tuck them in the back of the closet, wouldn't it? Why would she want to save them? In case Greg came back?

Teresa took a deep breath. Greg was dead. Dead. She mouthed the word, trying to understand it. Get your head around it, was what Greg would have said. Greg was dead and his death felt as foreign to her as much of his life had been, just another secret he kept from her. Instead of missing him, she was already itching to clear away his things. She knew she should be ashamed of how she felt. She pulled her hands from behind her back and covered her eyes, willing herself to cry, but no tears came.

She felt a tug at the carpet beneath her heels, and heard a soft sound, like the popping of tiny bubbles. She opened the door, and Grey Tiger slipped around the corner like liquid mercury, rubbed up against her bare shin. "Tiger," she said. "You can sleep with me again tonight." And she picked him up and nuzzled his neck, soft as a breeze and smelling of rain. "I love you, Tiger," she said, and started to cry.

Sitting next to Al and discussing the next step in the investigation felt good to Hunter, like sliding his feet into an old pair of slippers. It had always felt right, being a homicide detective.

In addition to a calendar Greg had kept that showed the clubs he was scheduled to play at, Teresa Jagpal had given Al a few names. Three of them were friends, fellow members of a sometime band called Carrot Rampant, and one was Greg Williams' brother, a Vancouver city cop. Al was on the phone to the VPD before they'd reached Kingsway, and by four o'clock the three of them were sitting in a quiet booth inside the Knight and Day restaurant at Lougheed and Boundary. Chad Williams had sandy hair buzzed at the temples, and his biceps strained against the short blue sleeves of his uniform.

"That little bitch." Chad Williams' voice barely rose above a whisper, but it erupted with the thrust of a greased piston.

"I'm sorry," said Al. "I should've..."

"No. No, it's not your fault. How could you know she hates my guts?" He looked away, covered his mouth with his hand as he took a deep breath through his nose. He wore a heavy ring with an oval jade stone. "Fuck!" he said, and shook his head. "He was fucked up, sure, but he was still my brother."

Al and Hunter exchanged glances.

"Fucked up?"

Chad Williams sighed again. "Useless. His idea of working was planting his ass on a stool and playing the fucking guitar. That whole scene stinks. Bars, late nights, booze, drugs... hanging out with drunks and losers. It's no way to live, man." He took another deep breath, squared his shoulders. "So how did it happen?" Then he shook his head and repeated, "That bitch! She could've left me some kind of message. That fucking little bitch."

Al told him what they knew. "Do you have any idea what your brother would have been doing inside a meat trailer?"

"Hah! That's some kind of irony for you! My dear brother, since he met his little Paki princess, had become a holier than thou vegetarian. Made me sick. He hangs out in skuzzy bars, smokes enough dope to curdle his brains, and then he has the nerve to tell me it's barbaric to eat steak."

"Was he some kind of activist?"

"Activist? Like, did he parade around with signs and throw paint on fur coats?" Chad Williams rolled his eyes. "Wouldn't put it past the Paki and her friends, but not Greg. All Greg was passionate about was his music. Damn that bitch! She got him started on the vegetable kick. My wife invited them over for dinner when he first shacked up with her, and the bitch turned up her nose at the whole meal. Had my poor wife in tears. Wasn't much point in even talking to him after he got hooked up with her."

"When did you see your brother last?"

Chad shrugged. "Couple, three weeks ago. I gave him three hundred bucks."

"Why?"

"Cause he needed it, that's why. I told you he was a fuck up, couldn't make enough money to even pay his rent. I told him it would be the last time." Chad rubbed the back of his neck. "I'll have to call Mom. Shit. I'd better go pick up his stuff, fast. I hope that bitch keeps her hands off of it. Mom would probably like some of Greg's things, keepsakes, you know?"

"Have you ever heard of Hanratty Wholesale Meats? Know anyone who works there?" asked Al.

"Not that I can remember. Jesus! Between her and those night crawler buddies of his, his stuff's going to disappear in no time."

"Have you ever seen either of these people?" Al pushed the coffee cups aside and placed mug shots of Ray and Sharon on the table.

Chad studied the photos, then shook his head. "Not that I can remember," he repeated.

"Do you know of anyone who might want to hurt your brother?"

"Besides me, you mean?"

Al raised his eyebrows.

"I would've liked to beat some sense into him," said Chad. He clenched his jaw and shook his head, slowly, his eyes closed. "... but I sure didn't want him dead."

"What next?" asked Hunter as they got back into Al's car. "Hanratty's?"

"I was showing the morgue picture around there yesterday morning at about the same time Jagpal came in to the detachment to report Williams missing, before we made the I.D."

"And?"

"Nobody had ever seen Greg Williams, fresh or frozen." Al backed the car out of the parking spot, nosed it out of the lot.

"Anything about activists?"

Al shook his head. "Didn't come up, and I didn't ask." He paused. "Funny, isn't it? how she doesn't want anybody calling him her husband. Tom Fong says she told him the same thing. Living with a guy for two and a half years makes him more than a boyfriend or a live- in lover, if you ask me."

"Maybe it's a culture thing," suggested Hunter. "What was your read on the interviews at Hanratty?"

Al accelerated across Boundary Road on an orange light and headed east on Lougheed. He shrugged. "One or more of them could have been lying, but there was nothing solid. I guess we'll just have to keep on shaking the tree, see if anything falls out. I'll put an APB out on Williams' car. When and if it turns up, that could point us in a new direction. With any luck, right outside of our jurisdiction."

Hunter nodded, watched the new buildings along Broadway slide by until they'd turned right and headed up Gilmore, past the Home Depot. "I'll let you know if I see anything suspicious."

"Huh? Where?"

"At Hanratty's," said Hunter, "when I'm picking up their next load."

"I knew you'd come in handy somewhere along the line. When's that going to happen?"

"Monday afternoon. And then I'll be on my way back to California."

"Well, I'd better make use of you over the weekend, then. I'll give you a choice between checking out the victim's previous employers and tracking down his band buddies. What's your pleasure? Skuzzy bars or weirdo musicians?"

Hunter tilted his head back, looked quizzically at Al. "Are you asking me to do some actual investigating?"

Al sighed. "Have you any idea how many open files I've got sitting on my desk? The only reason I freed myself up to do this right away is because it's fresh and maybe we can get lucky and turn up a hot lead. You think I'd be letting a civilian in on this if I could pull manpower from the detachment?"

"Thanks." Hunter snorted softly.

"Hey, no offense. You're not just any civilian. You were always a better detective than I was, and I'll be the first to admit it. But it's not kosher..."

Hunter nodded. "I know. I appreciate you letting me in on it. I'll take the skuzzy bars."

"Now, when I asked you to check them out, I figured... Like I said, it's not exactly kosher." Al pulled into the detachment parking lot. "If you start asking questions, you can't exactly say you're on police business."

"Impersonate a police officer?" Hunter smiled. "Never."

"Well, how... ?"

"I'll just see if I can scare up some witnesses that are worth your time to interview. How's that?"

"Yeah." Al grinned as he reached for the ignition. "It's probably better if I don't know how."

CHAPTER
NINE

After he left the detachment, Hunter fought his way through Friday night traffic across the Second Narrows bridge to the place he called home. It was a one-bedroom basement suite in a forty-year-old house owned by two elderly brothers. Because it was on a hillside, like most of the homes on the North Shore, the basement was only underground on one side. Hunter's suite had a sliding glass door that opened into the back yard, a shady moss-infested lawn that sloped down toward a stand of tall cedars. Between the cedars you could glimpse the changing face of Burrard Inlet, blue with glistening wrinkles on this sunny summer day, but gray and motionless as slate on countless others.

His rooms were filled with heavy air, so he left the door open as he dumped his bag of clothes onto the floor. The laundry room, on the other side of a door off his living room cum kitchen, he shared with his landlords, a doctor and a scientist, both retired. He changed into shorts and a tee-shirt, found a can of Kokanee in the fridge, and carried it outside. The cool grass felt good to his bare feet, and he had already settled his bum into a lawn chair before he remembered that he hadn't checked his answering machine. "It can wait," he decided, taking a long cold slug of beer.

"You're back. I'll bring your mail." Hunter looked up and over his shoulder to see his landlord, Gord Young, standing on the main floor sundeck. The old doctor saluted, then disappeared. A minute later, he lowered himself into a lawn chair next to Hunter, dropped a stack of mail at Hunter's feet, and popped open a beer for himself. Gord was in his seventies, but still had plenty of hair that wasn't gray. He wore baggy shorts, and a threadbare tee-shirt with faded bicycles across the chest above the words BICYCLE STANLEY PARK. "How was your trip?" he asked. "Short one this time, wasn't it?"

Hunter thought about it. He'd only been gone a week, but it seemed like two. "Long enough," he said. "Ever seen a frozen corpse?"

"A few," answered the doctor. "Back on the prairies."

Hunter's phone started to ring. He shrugged apologetically, snugged his beer into a nest of grass at his feet, and scooped up his mail before he went inside. It was Sharon's lawyer, Alora Magee.

"Ms. Watson gave me your number," she said. "She said you might be able to help." Alora had that same professional but friendly manner of speaking as Chris did when she talked to someone on business. Cheery, but just slightly aloof. Hunter's ex-wife worked for a big real estate firm, in the legal department.

"Help in what way?"

"Sharon Nillson isn't talking. I like to try to be a step ahead of the prosecutor, find out what we're up against in time to go on the offensive, as it were. Ideally, I'd like to know what they're going to find out before they do. So far Sharon's given me exactly nothing to work with. Ms. Watson said you'd been talking to the police in Burnaby."

"Ms. Watson? Did she let you call her Ms. Watson?"

Alora laughed. It was a genuine laugh, not just a polite one. "I guess you know the answer to that already," she said. "El, then. From the sound of her, I suspect she'd have your head if you ever tried to call her Ellie. Did you find out what they have against Ray and Sharon, other than the evidence from the trailer?"

"They're still trying to get a fix on the victim. He was a musician just barely making enough to live on. No record. No history of trouble. I might know more over the weekend." Hunter had answered the phone at his desk in the small cubbyhole that served as his office. He sorted through his mail as he spoke. A couple of bills,
92

ad mail and an auto club magazine. "Do you want me to call you if I find something out?"

There was a hesitation. "I'll be away," she said, "in the mountains. How about if I call you on Monday?"

"I'll be on the road," he told her. "On my way back to L.A."

"Really?" she said, sounding pleasantly surprised. "Well, it's early days yet. It won't hurt to wait a day or two for information. Maybe we could get together... ?" She let it hang like an unfinished sentence. "Oh. El said she was sending something down for Sharon next week. With you?"

This was the first Hunter had heard of it, but it sounded like something El would do. "Probably."

"So we'll have to get together anyway. How about dinner? Will you be here Tuesday?"

"Wednesday," he said, which was fine with her, so she named the place and time.

He thought she was about to hang up, but instead she said, "I've been thinking about what you said."

"What did I say?"

"About the fact that you wouldn't be able to defend a client who was guilty." She paused. "It's fundamental to the legal profession, I guess. Somewhere along the line, we have to ask ourselves, are we in it for money or for justice? And if we're in it for justice, why aren't we just as interested in getting justice for the victim as for the accused?"

"It's the system. You do the best you can within the framework of the justice system."

"I guess you know the system pretty well yourself. El said you used to be a detective."

Hunter stiffened, tossed a piece of ad mail into the waste basket beside his desk. "Yes," he said.

"I guess what I'm trying to say is, I wish I could believe - truly believe - that Sharon is innocent. Right now, I just don't know."

After he hung up, Hunter debated going straight back outside to join his landlord and finish his beer, but there were messages on his answering machine, so he pushed the button. All three messages were from his daughters, Janice and Lesley, one from each of them just saying Hi! Catch you later! but in the last message Lesley invited him to the Sunday barbecue. "It'll be just cazh, nothing fancy. In case you're worried about it being Mom's birthday, you don't have to bring a present or anything. Maybe just wine. But it's been eons since we've seen you so it would be nice if you could come." She rang off on a cheery, "See you Sunday, Dad!"

"You know, Gord," Hunter said to his landlord as he sat back down and picked up his beer, "as comfortable as I am living at your place, I miss the responsibility of being - I don't know - part of a team." He wasn't being totally honest. He missed his family, and sometimes, like now, it hurt like hell, but he couldn't say that, even to Gord. He took a sip of beer. It was warmer and flatter than before the phone call, but still good. "You know something I really miss?"

"What?" said Gord, pushing his glasses further up on his nose. His cat, a Siamese, trotted across the grass from under the laurel hedge, the skin under its belly swinging like an empty fur sack, and rubbed up against his bare legs, then Hunter's.

"Cooking on the barbecue," said Hunter, reaching to pet the cat's head. "My wife would make the potato salad and whatever, my daughters would set the table, and I'd cook the steaks. And I was damn good at it, if I do say so myself." The cat tried to bite him but he pulled his hand away in time. He had no illusions about Sunday. At best, he would still be only a guest. He smiled wistfully, then finished off his beer.

"You're hired," said Gord. "I've got two rib eyes in the freezer."

"Great," said Hunter. "I need to keep in practice."

They grinned at each other, but Hunter could read it in the old man's eyes. They both knew that it just wouldn't be the same.

Friday nights used to be fun.

Russell was still at his desk when the night crew came in, the Iceman file open on the desk in front of him. If it weren't for the filming of that damned TV pilot in Vancouver, he and Jennifer would probably be sitting over martinis somewhere in Santa Monica right now, getting ready for a two hour meal with a good cabernet, followed by good sex at Jennifer's apartment. But she was out of town, and he'd been out of circulation for so long now, he didn't know who else to call. He stroked his tie thoughtfully. It was interesting that he was even considering that option. Until recently, he'd assumed that he and Jennifer were on the verge of making the big leap: a house, a minivan, and babies. The whole enchilada. Something had changed. Maybe they just weren't spending enough time together.

He reviewed the coroner's report for the umpteenth time. Bruising on the neck. Someone had used force on the victim, and that somebody had to be both skilled and strong, especially if he'd had to hoist an unconscious Greg Williams into the back of the trailer from the ground. The husband could have done it alone, but if the wife did it, she had her husband's help. Either way, it didn't look good for Ray Nillson. Russell smiled as he thought about the little surprise he had in store for Nillson on Monday. Another visitor. A very persuasive one.

He closed the file and scooped up his keys. It was frustrating being here in L.A. county when so much of the investigating had to be done in Vancouver. He didn't trust the Mounties. Not that he thought they were dishonest, or even incompetent, just that he knew he could do a better job. This case was clicking for him. Maybe, with Merv away on vacation for the next two weeks, he could talk the boss into letting him spend some time up in Canada, following up leads generated by the RCMP. No question about it, the Iceman was his case. Merv's vacation had been timed perfectly, now if only he could get closer to where the answers were bound to lie.

Russell headed out to his car, not sure where he would go from there. The sun was already low in the sky. He was hungry, and could use a drink. As he pulled out of the parking lot, he flipped open his cell phone. He'd call a couple of buddies, see if anything was shaking. Maybe he'd even call his Mom and Dad. If worse came to worst, he could pick up a video and a six pack, and order in a pizza, home alone.

The first bar Hunter hit on Saturday afternoon was the farthest away from home, Fraser's Dock, the place where Greg Williams played the last gig of his life. Hunter had been warned about the manager, the sensitive guy who'd been sorely pissed off at Williams for dying and missing his Friday night gig. The Fraser River sparkled with the July sunlight, and two dirty gray river gulls fought over what was left of a hamburger bun in the parking lot. Hunter pulled his Pontiac in beside an old Cougar with oversized rear tires.

It was dim inside, quiet at this early hour, except for the sporadic clack of billiards coming from the far corner. A burly young man with a thick neck whose dark beard was only slightly longer than his close-cropped hair was fiddling with the connections under the levers that delivered draft beer.

"What'll you have?" he asked, a smile in his voice if not on his face.

Hunter hesitated, decided to order a beer. "Pale Ale would be good," he said, nodding toward the acrylic head of one of the levers. "You the manager?"

The young man nodded, filled a pint glass and clunked it on the counter.

Hunter took a sip. It was good, cold and good. He slipped a photo of Greg Williams out of his shirt pocket and laid it on the bar. "You remember this guy?"

The manager glanced at the photograph, snorted. "Picker. He wasn't all that good, but the chicks liked him. Who are you?"

"An investigator."

The manager's eyebrows rose.

"Helping the police with their inquiries," he added.

"They told me the guy's dead. He was whacked?"

"That's what we're trying to find out. You see him talking to anybody here?"

"Just the chicks."

"Any in particular?"

96

The man scowled, hesitated briefly before he said, "Just the locals, come in here to flirt, dance a little. He didn't stick around after his gig, though. Left alone."

"No fights, no arguments?"

Another hesitation. "Nope."

"Ever see either of these two?" He showed separate photos of Sharon and Ray.

The manager shrugged. "I don't recognize 'em, if that's what you want to know. In this business, I might've seen 'em half a dozen times, but with all the customers in and out of here, who can remember?"

Hunter handed the man one of Al Kowalski's cards. "If you think of anything that might help the police, please give Corporal Kowalski a call."

The manager barely looked at the card, slipped it in his shirt pocket. "What about all his shit? I've got all his fuckin' amps and speakers takin' up space in my office."

"Hang tough for a couple of days, chief. I'll have someone pick it up."

Hunter managed to visit five drinking establishments on Saturday night, left five pints of beer - minus a few good swallows - sitting on polished bars, and learned that Greg Williams was a competent musician but no star, although he managed to attract a regular crowd of female fans. Nobody seemed to remember Sharon or Ray. That night Hunter left his clothes lying on the bathroom floor. They reeked of smoke, and so did he.

Hunter would have forgotten his ex-wife's birthday if the girls hadn't reminded him. It had been five years since Chris had asked him for a divorce, and he had long since stopped thinking of her as his wife. She was the mother of his daughters, and nothing more. But as he dressed for the barbecue on Sunday, choosing his least-old shirt and a pair of chinos that he never wore on the road, he couldn't help wondering why he'd been invited specifically on her birthday, and it surprised him to feel a flutter of nervousness about seeing her. He wondered again if the girls were trying to get them back together again. At the beer and wine store at Greystone Mall, he chose a bottle of Pouilly Fuissé. It was stupidly expensive, but it had been her favorite wine. And on impulse, he bought flowers at the IGA, a mixed bouquet with freesias.

Hunter's ex-wife and daughters lived in a three-bedroom townhouse across the street from Burnaby Mountain Golf Course. He found a parking spot on the street, and sat for a moment in the car, collecting his thoughts, then started up the sidewalk carrying the flowers and wine. He realized that the chinos were uncomfortably tight at the waist, and it made him angry with himself. He should make the effort to get more exercise. Sitting in a truck for days on end could be deadly for a man who didn't keep active during his hours off. He climbed the stairs to their second floor entrance and rang the doorbell.

"Dad! I knew you'd be on time!" Lesley stood on her tiptoes to kiss his cheek. He inhaled the scent of her hair, like green apples. She was wearing shorts and what looked like a sleeveless man's undershirt over a bathing suit top. She had tiny gold chains around her wrist and ankle, and he thought she was the most beautiful girl he'd ever seen. "Are these for Mom?" she said in a whisper, examining the flowers, and she smiled.

Hunter followed Lesley into the living room, and Janice came in from the sundeck, crossing the carpet to give him a hug. "Hi, Dad," she said. "I'm sure glad you came." She was wearing a simple lime green shift, her long hair in a lopsided ponytail above one ear. Hunter thought she could be a model. "Can I talk to you, like, in private?"

"Wait until your father's had time to sit down and have a beer." Chris appeared over Janice's shoulder. "Hello, Hunter. Nice to see you," she said with a smile.

"Happy birthday," said Hunter, holding out the bouquet. He wondered briefly if he should kiss her cheek, but it seemed too awkward, with Janice right there. "Twenty nine, isn't it?" he said, deadpan.

"Yeah, right, Dad," said Lesley. "You knocked her up when she was nine."

Chris laughed, and Hunter looked at the floor, uncomfortable but not wanting to show it. Perhaps he wasn't around the girls enough. He wasn't used to hearing them speak like that.

"Would you put these in water, hon'." Chris handed the flowers to Lesley. "And get your father a beer." She turned to Hunter, and he held out the wine, still inside its brown paper bag. "Wine! Thanks," she said, and "Here, Janice, put this in the fridge." She didn't even look inside the bag. "Come outside, Hunter. There's someone I want you to meet."

A man stood up at their approach. He had a tumbler with what looked like scotch and soda in his left hand, and he offered Hunter his right. "Lance Macauley," he said. "I've heard a lot about you."

"Lance the lawyer," said Lesley from behind Hunter's back. Chris shot her a wicked look, then turned to Hunter with a smile.

"Lance is in real estate law, of course. I met him through work, as you probably guessed." Chris used her friendly, professional voice, making an effort to sound relaxed but Hunter knew her too well to be fooled. "Our firm is selling suites in a big Brantford Group development, and Lance is their lawyer."

"I fell in love with her voice on the phone," said Lance with a grin. "Sit down, make yourself comfortable. What'll you have? Oh, here's Janice with a beer. Is that okay?"

"Yes," said Hunter, deliberately taking the furthest chair from this unexpected host. Why hadn't the girls warned him? he asked himself, but he already knew why. If they'd told him about Lance the lawyer, he wouldn't have come. He made himself engage in polite small talk, which was not his forte. Lance carried the lion's share of the conversation.

Chris sat on the edge of her chair, sipping on a glass of white wine a little more frequently than she used to. Hunter felt sorry for her. "Janice, you wanted to talk to me?" he said at the first reasonable opportunity, and Janice led him into the kitchen.

She pulled something out from underneath the telephone and handed it to him with a big grin on her face. It was a glossy brochure advertising the Isuzu Trooper. "What do you think?" she said, pointing to a photograph of a white vehicle with zigzags of color on its side. "Isn't it just perfect for me?"

He smiled. "Perfect," he said. "You're going to buy it?"

"Well," she said, looking at the ceiling and rocking her shoulders back and forth, "The dealer has a used one, just thirty thousand kilometers on it, and I'd like to buy it, but..."

"But?"

"I don't have enough money for the down payment." She looked at him expectantly, batting her eyelashes, her lips in a tight little smile.

He nodded. "I see." What he saw was that his oldest daughter was asking him for money, and he wasn't even sure he could make the payment on his truck this month. "I guess your mom can't make you a loan?"

She shook her head. "Lance said he'd lend it to me, but I'd rather get it from you."

Hunter hesitated. How could he come up with the kind of money she'd need?

"Mom said I should take Lance up on his offer. She said, For God's sake, your father won't have that kind of money. He's just a truck driver. She's turning into such a snob." Janice shook her head in disgust. "But I don't want Lance's money, Dad. It just doesn't feel right to me."

"Good," he said. "How much do you need?"

Hunter excused himself even before the girls brought out the birthday cake. He told them there was something he had to do, which was true. He still had three bars to visit, looking for information on the dead musician. Lance the lawyer had barbecued the ribs and chicken, never missing a chance to pat Chris on the buttocks or grab her round the waist as she passed. Chris was delighted with the Pouilly Fuissé and drank two glasses within half an hour, while Lance polished off the rest of the bottle. To Hunter's disgust, Lance decided to show him to the door.

100

"Great meeting you, Hunter," said Lance. "You've got great taste in women, judging by your ex. Chris is a great gal, a real pleasure to do business with, and vice versa, if you know what I mean." And he slapped Hunter on the back.

Hunter stopped dead, then slowly turned around to face the man, aware of the look of horror on Chris' face, but too angry to care. "Look here, chief," he said in a tight, low voice, raising a hand in front of his chest, like a cobra. "If Christine lets you swat her with your clumsy paws, that's her business. But don't you ever - EVER - touch me again."

Lance took a step backwards. "Hey, buddy. Take it easy, pal. I was just being friendly." He bumped into Chris, who was glaring at Hunter from behind his shoulder, and looked from side to side as if he were trapped.

"Christ, Hunter! Don't be such a tightass!" said Chris. "Why don't you consider someone else's feelings, for a change."

"Leave him alone, Mom."

"Yeah, leave him alone," said Lesley.

"Happy birthday, Chris," said Hunter, turned on his heel, and walked out the door.

Of the bars Greg Williams had worked in the past few months, the closest to home was the Blackburn Pub in east Burnaby, and Hunter arrived there just after ten o'clock on Sunday night. Through the smoke, Hunter could see a girl in a leopard skin leotard singing into the gray ball of a microphone, and behind her a long-haired youth playing electric guitar. He made his way up to the bar and asked to see the manager.

"Not here," said the bartender.

"When will he be back?"

The young man shrugged, fingering a small gold hoop in his ear. "What do you need him for? Maybe Pat can help."

"Pat?"

"Yeah." A waitress signalled him from farther down the bar. "Hang on," he said, and left Hunter standing there while he beered up four pint glasses and squirted bar cola into a shot of whiskey. "Hey,

Pat!" he hollered across the room, grabbing two wine glasses from a rack over his head. "Pat! Some guy here wants to talk to Clifford."

Pat had lots of wavy, almost kinky, hair, auburn with hints of gold, tied loosely in a scarf that seemed to be slipping down her back. She had earrings that looked like long black raindrops, and was wearing a tight black skirt and a slinky purple blouse. "Can I help you?" she said, looking him up and down. "You're obviously not here for the open mike," she added, jerking her head in the direction of the leopard skin leotard.

Hunter smiled. There was an openness about her that he liked. "You can help me if you know this man," he said, producing Williams' picture. He had to raise his voice to be heard over the music.

"Sure. That's Greg Williams. He was playing here..." She looked up at the ceiling with a frown. "Shit! My life's a blur. I guess it was the week before last. What about him?" A big man heading for the bar jostled her arm, and she stuck an elbow in his ribs. "Watch it, Bub! C'mon," she said to Hunter. "Let's go talk in the office."

Hunter followed her through a door into a dark hallway, then into a small office. Pat sank into the big armchair behind the desk, kicked off her shoes. There was nowhere for Hunter to sit. "So, what's this all about?"

"Greg Williams' body was found in California a few days ago. We're trying to find out how he got there..."

"Body? Greg's dead?" Her eyes widened, and she left her mouth open.

Hunter nodded. "He might have been murdered."

"So Greg's dead." She shook her head. "Poor bastard. What happened?"

"When did you see him last?"

"After his last gig. Saturday night." She consulted a calendar on her desk. "I guess it was the eighth."

"Did you notice him talking to anybody in particular, arguing maybe?"

102

Pat ran a thumb up and down her chin. "God! Do you know what you're asking!?" She laughed. "I can't even remember what happened twenty minutes ago, let alone two weeks!"

"Take your time," said Hunter.

"Let's see." She reached behind her head, frowning, and pulled the scarf out of her hair. It spread out across her shoulders like a waterfall. "I remember he spent a while talking to some guy in a booth over by the stage. That was unusual. It's usually the girls who want to talk to... uh, wanted to talk to Greg. He was one of those sensitive looking guys all the girls want to take care of, you know? Puppy dog eyes? So I remember the guy, sort of. He looked pretty clean cut, almost like a cop. No offense. I like cops." She smiled, then stopped, narrowed her eyes. "You are a cop, aren't you?"

Hunter shook his head.

"Then why am I talking to you? Why are you asking these questions? You made me think you were a cop."

Hunter pulled one of Al's cards out of his chest pocket, and she stood up, met him halfway to take it. "I'm assisting the RCMP in their investigation," he said, "sort of like a freelance investigator."

She nodded. "Okay then. I can phone this guy and check you out if I want, right?"

"Yes."

"Okay." She ran the corner of Al's card back and forth across her lower lip. "So this guy I saw talking to Greg looked almost like a cop."

"Can you describe him?"

"Uh... pretty big, I think. I mean, tall and muscular. Not like you." She smiled. "No offense, but you're more... uh... compact. He was more of a jock. Not quite so... uh... tidy looking."

He smiled, just a half smile. "Hair color?"

She reached up and touched his hair, the scarf dangling from her fingers. The scent reminded Hunter of the freesias in his ex-wife's bouquet. "Light brown, verging on blond, sort of like yours."

Hunter ran his hand across his hair, nudging hers away. "Would you recognize him again?"

She smiled and tamed her hair with the scarf again before answering, watching Hunter watching her, almost daring him to look at the slinky blouse tightening across her breasts. He kept his eyes on her face. "Would I recognize him? I don't know if I would. He looked like a lot of guys."

"Were they arguing?"

"Not while I was watching." She shook her head. Her raindrop earrings brushed her jaw. Then she suddenly frowned, stabbed the air with a finger. "Wait!" she said. "I do remember something about that night. There was a fight in the parking lot. The bouncers said a guy got beat up."

"Was Greg involved?"

"No. He was on at the time. He'd been talking to that guy I told you about on his break, then he went back on stage, and half way through his set my bouncers disappeared. I went out to see what they were up to, and they said there'd been a fight. Couldn't have lasted very long, though. They'd all driven away by the time I got there."

"Any of those bouncers here tonight?"

She shook her head. "No. It's just part timers on Sunday. But, you know, I remember something else happened. A woman who used to work here, waited tables for the last few years, went up to the stage just as Greg announced his break. She and Greg were standing there talking, then all of a sudden she stormed out of here, practically ran somebody down at the door. He followed her out."

"You know her name and how I can get in touch with her?" asked Hunter.

"Might be hard to get hold of her," said Pat. "And I don't know her name now, but it used to be MacNeil."

"She changed her name?"

"Yeah," said Pat. "Sharon married a trucker."

CHAPTER
TEN

Hunter turned down his landlord's suggestion for a quick nine holes at Gleneagles Golf Course with a sincere "Next time, I promise," and was sitting in Al Kowalski's office by ten o'clock on Monday morning.

"Did she ID the photo?"

Hunter sighed, grim faced. "Yes," he said. "Ray's, too. Seems the Blackburn Pub is where he and Sharon met."

Al Kowalski shrugged. There was something a little different about him today, but Hunter couldn't quite put his finger on it. Hunter tried to remember if Al had worn a mustache, or maybe he'd just had a haircut. "You knew when you started this that the answers might not be what you wanted to hear," said Al, handing him a mug with the RCMP crest embossed on one side.

Hunter took a swallow of coffee. He didn't consider what he'd found out at the Blackburn to be proof of Sharon's guilt, but he had to admit it didn't look good. It meant that she and Ray were lying about more than just finding the body. "How did you make out with the band?"

Al snorted. "You know," he said, "if anybody had told me twenty five years ago when I was grooving to the Doors and the Rolling Stones that one day I'd be an old fogey like my father..." He shook his head, tapped his coffee mug with the end of a pencil. "I found the three surviving Carrots all together, practicing in their studio."

"Studio?"

"Yeah. I went to the first guy's house, and was redirected to that industrial area along Still Creek. It appears that Greg Williams and his buds had some pretty serious aspirations. They've got a rented space above a warehouse, make their own recordings. Experimental stuff. I listened outside the door for a couple minutes, which was a couple minutes too long. A little too much feedback and not enough melody for my tastes." He rolled his eyes. "I never thought I'd hear myself say stuff like that."

"Greg's brother said he had to lend him rent money. Who's financing this studio?"

"My guess is that one of the band has a rich daddy. None of the Raging Carrots has a solid day job." He looked down at his notebook. "One of them does part-time warehouse work, one of them works at a gas station, the other one is... uh... between jobs right now. They opened the windows as soon as I got there, but there was a delicate stink lingering in the air. My guess is, given their technological bent, at least one of them is also into hydroponics."

"If their grow operation was big enough, they wouldn't need a rich daddy."

"Crossed my mind." Al drained his coffee mug.

"What did they say about Greg's death?"

"They'd already heard. The drummer - a guy named Max - said Williams was clean. No enemies, no trouble. The others pretty much agreed."

"You going to run them all on Cee-PIC?"

Al frowned. "Jesus, Hunter! Do I look like I need busy work? You just finished telling me that one of the prime suspects was seen arguing with the victim a week before his death, and lied about knowing him. Why would I waste my time on investigating a bunch of Carrots?"

Hunter searched for a suitable rejoinder but all he could come up with was, "Beets me," which Al didn't seem to appreciate. "The fact

106

that Sharon knew the victim could be coincidental. That could be why they're afraid to admit finding him in their trailer."

"Yeah, right. And I could be the next King of England. Give me a break."

Hunter set his empty mug on Al's desk. "What next?"

"Like it or not, I'm going to follow up on your lead, check out Sharon Nillson's background, explore the connection between her and the deceased." Al shrugged an apology. "That's the most productive use of my time."

"Where is this studio? Mind if I check it out?"

Al leaned back in his chair and looked at Hunter, his eyes narrowed in thought. Hunter realized that Al had dyed his hair. Friday it had been pale brown streaked with gray, and now it was so dark it almost looked wet. Hunter wondered if Al had dyed it before or after becoming an old fogey. Al shrugged uncomfortably in response to Hunter's question.

"I won't mention your name," said Hunter. "It won't be for days, maybe not until next week. This afternoon I'll be on my way to California."

Al sat up, interested. "Right. I want to ask you something. You've pulled one of these reefer trailers before, right? If someone climbed inside, unbeknownst to you, and then banged and hollered to be let out, would you hear him?"

Hunter shook his head. "I doubt it. If he's banging on the trailer doors, he'd be forty eight feet of trailer away, and separated from your cab by seventeen tons of frozen beef, an insulated trailer wall, the refrigeration unit, moving air, and an insulated sleeper wall." He checked them off with his fingers. "In addition to the hum of the reefer, there's engine noises and traffic noises. My guess is no, but we could test it this afternoon before I leave, if you want."

"You're hauling the same stuff?"

"As far as I know. I'm picking up a load of frozen meat at Hanratty, and heading for the same warehouse in Orange County."

"You ever been inside a trailer with frozen meat?" asked Al.

"Just to check the loading. Never with the door closed."

"How cold is it?"

"Damn cold."

"How cold is that?"

"It'll probably be specified on the bill of lading, but my guess is about zero degrees Fahrenheit."

Al shuddered. "I wonder how long a man would last."

"Three to five hours."

"How do you know that?"

"I asked my landlord about it last night."

"Your landlord?"

"He's a retired doctor."

"You've been busy on this case." Al ran his hand through his hair, perhaps a little self consciously. "That means, technically, that he could've been locked in that trailer anywhere more than three or four hours north of where his body was found."

"No..."

"Oh, right. Of course. He was frozen solid. How long would that take?"

"My landlord didn't know, for sure. An educated guess might be ten or twelve hours. That would mean the victim would have had to enter their trailer at the latest just south of the California - Oregon border, if they drove straight through. If they stopped somewhere for the night, it could just as easily have been south of Sacramento."

Al rolled his eyes.

"I know," said Hunter. "Technically it's possible, but if the victim lived here it doesn't make any sense."

"Right," agreed Al, then winked. "Unless the victim's car turns up in San Francisco."

The traffic to Annacis Island was slow enough that it gave Hunter time to think. He could ask El to have Greg Williams' amps and speakers picked up at Fraser's Dock, and to store them at her warehouse. Then when he got back from California, it would give him the excuse he needed to visit the studio on Still Creek. He winced. Getting caught up in this investigation was going to cost him money in lost working time, income that he could ill afford to lose.

108

He wasn't looking forward to asking El for a loan, but there was no way he was going to let his daughter borrow money from Lance the lawyer. No way.

He parked his Pontiac against the chain link fence in Watson Transportation's yard, and did a walk-around inspection of the Blue Knight before starting the engine, then left it idling as he went in to talk to El. She was on the phone, as usual. He paced the floor in front of the counter, once stooping to pick up a perforated strip of paper that was nesting in a dusty corner, depositing it in El's wastebasket. He hated asking for money.

"Good thing this isn't a union outfit," said El as she put down the phone. "The Teamsters would have a fit, you doing janitorial work like that. So, what's the news? What did your RCMP buddy have to say?"

Hunter brought her up to date. The phone rang, so she dealt with it quickly, then put all of her lines on hold to keep it from ringing again. When she heard about Sharon knowing the victim, she buried her face in her hands. "Shit."

"There's still hope," he told her. "Maybe someone else with a motive will turn up."

"I'm glad you said that," she said.

"There's a possibility the victim and his cohorts were involved in drugs, maybe doing a little smuggling." He looked at her pointedly, and she understood his meaning.

"Not a chance. Ray wouldn't have had anything to do with stuff like that. Ray hates drugs. He's very outspoken about that."

"How about Sharon?"

"Ray married her. That's got to tell you something." She shook her head glumly. "Shit," she said again. "Is there anything I can do to help?"

"As a matter of fact, there is. A couple of things." He told her about Greg Williams' equipment at Fraser's Dock, then said, "The police don't have the time or money to pursue every lead, which means most of their focus will be gathering evidence that supports their case against Ray and Sharon. I'd like to spend more time on investigating this myself, because it may be their only hope, but I'm

109

pretty tight already, financially. Any chance you could give me an advance?"

"No problem," she said, unlocking a drawer beneath her desk. "How much?"

When he told her, she went totally still for fifteen seconds, her eyes wide. Then she took a deep breath and wrote the check. "You realize, Hunter, that if it had been anybody else but you, he wouldn't have had a snowball's chance in hell."

Before he left, she handed him a Wal-Mart bag with the top folded over. "What's this?" he asked.

"A care package for Sharon," she said. "The lawyer said she'd make sure Sharon gets it. Can you deliver it to her, that Magee woman?"

Before he tucked the bag under the bunk of his sleeper, he opened it and looked inside. There was a sealed manila envelope addressed to Sharon, plus about a dozen small paperback books, their spines wrinkled from use. Harlequins. Hunter smiled and shook his head.

For a woman the other drivers called Big Mother Trucker, El Watson was turning out to be an incredibly soft touch.

"For the record, Russell, I don't like this," said Jeff Feldman. The two of them were standing in front of the men's room door, waiting.

"What you like doesn't matter a whole hell of a lot, does it?" said Russell. He smiled smugly, jingled the change in his pocket as he rocked on the balls of his feet. "The man phoned me and begged me to let him talk to Ray. He flew all the way from goddamn Minneapolis at haying time for this, so how could I say no?"

"If you were doing this for compassionate reasons, you wouldn't insist on monitoring the visit," said Feldman, drily.

Russell laughed aloud. "Compassionate reasons? Look who's talking about compassionate reasons. What exactly motivated you to represent Nillson? He doesn't have much in common with your usual clients. He drives a fuckin' truck, not a Maserati."

110

Feldman looked at his watch, his jaw rigid. Russell was pleased. He must be right on target. Being able to rub Feldman's nose in it would make solving this case just that much sweeter.

"So when are you planning to call the first press conference, Jeff? The public is dying for news about the Iceman's killer. Oh, I see. You want to be front page, top of the hour. You're waiting for a slow news day."

A man in an ill-fitting polyester sports jacket came out of the men's room and nodded to Russell, and together the three of them headed for the elevator.

"I'd like to caution you not to say anything that might be used against your brother," said Feldman in a low voice.

"This man's not your client, Jeff. He can say whatever he damn well wants." Russell took the man by the elbow. "I know you're a law-abiding citizen, Mr. Nillson, a man who was raised in a God-fearing home and who believes in the American justice system. That's why I trust you to speak with your brother. Mr. Feldman, here, as your brother's lawyer, wants to win this case at any cost." He turned to Feldman. "Think of what it'll do for your reputation. Next time O.J. gets in trouble, you'll probably be the first one he'll call." Then back to Nillson. "I'm sure you'll use your own good judgement, Mr. Nillson." As they stepped onto the elevator, Russell happily returned Feldman's scowl.

"What happened, Ray? You can tell me."

"Yeah, tell him, Ray," Russell urged under his breath from the other side of the one way glass. Feldman cautioned them both for the tenth time. Russell snorted. "Don't listen to that prick of a lawyer, Ray. Tell your brother how it happened."

Dan Nillson was leaner and more weathered looking than his brother Ray, but he had that same ruddy face, the same earnest blue eyes. He'd stood up when Ray was led into the room, took a few tentative steps forward as Ray's handcuffs were removed, seemed to want to reach out and touch him. But Ray had just nodded, barely looked at his brother before he sat down behind the table, so Dan had stood, looking helpless and bewildered for several long seconds, before he, too, sat down.

"Nothing to tell," said Ray. He looked toward the glass, as if searching Russell out. "Nothing to tell," he repeated.

Dan Nillson's shoulders drooped. "I know you couldn't kill a man, Ray. You got to tell them everything you know. You can't throw your life away for a... a..."

Ray slammed the table with an open palm. "Don't you say it, Dan! Don't you say nothing against her! You never met her, and you don't know nothing about her!"

"You met her in a bar, I know that. You told me yourself."

"She was working there. I was the one that was drinking."

"You were her ticket out of there. You were her opportunity, and she took it. She took you."

"You don't know nothing about her!"

"But I know you, Ray." Dan leaned forward, his face intense. "You're a pushover when it comes to a pretty face. You let Beth Watkins walk all over you."

"Sharon isn't Beth Watkins, not by a long shot. Sharon's no spoiled brat. She appreciates me. She's had a hard life, doesn't take nothing for granted." He started tracing circles on the table with one sturdy finger. "Sharon's given me more than she's taken. You don't know nothing about her, Dan."

Feldman looked tense. He rubbed his neck under the collar of his button-down Calvin Klein shirt.

Dan was silent for a moment, his head bowed. Then in a quiet voice he said, "Think of Momma, Ray."

"Momma's dead."

"She'd be heartbroken to see you in jail."

"Momma's dead," Ray repeated tonelessly.

"I've come all this way," pleaded Dan. "Let me help you, Ray."

"You shouldn't have come. There's nothing you can do. Go back to the farm. They got more use for you there."

"But I did come." He put one hand over his eyes, then ran it down his face with a sigh, turned to Feldman. "You must be a good lawyer," he said. "Do you think he'll get out of here?"

112

Before Feldman could answer, in a flat voice Ray said, "He says if I plead guilty to manslaughter, I could be out of jail in eight years."

Dan Nillson jumped to his feet, knocking the chair over behind him. "Guilty! Sweet Jesus, Ray. I can't believe... I can't imagine... Sweet Jesus! Did you kill the man, Ray?"

Ray looked up at his brother, then back down at his finger, still making loops on the surface of the table. "I'd never kill anybody, Dan, if I could help it."

Dan stood there, open mouthed, watching his brother make loops.

"I couldn't just kill a man," repeated Ray. "You know that."

Hunter arrived at Hanratty Wholesale Meats at about two thirty. The frozen meat was in an insulated freezer, but the entire warehouse felt like the inside of a refrigerator. In spite of the warm July day, Hunter had brought a jacket with him and put it on. Al Kowalski had questioned the employees already, but Hunter watched them closely as his trailer was being loaded with packaged beef. The two men manning the forklifts were clean cut, wearing white uniforms like butchers, and looked to be in their early twenties. They worked without speaking. The shipper was barrel chested and had rosy cheeks. He strolled over and stood beside Hunter, rocking back and forth from heel to toe and jingling keys or change in his pockets.

"Cold for you?" he asked with a grin, nodding at Hunter's jacket. He had a hearty voice with what Hunter took for a German accent, making his pronunciation halfway to "kalt". He wore a short-sleeved shirt, yellow, with a blue tie.

Hunter grinned back, hugging himself and feigning a shiver. He didn't know the man, but judged him to be friendly and maybe talkative. He decided to play the role of a guileless, garrulous driver. "Well, chief, I heard a guy froze to death in your last meat shipment. Me, I don't intend to take any chances." He laughed, encouraging the shipper to join him, which he did.

"First time a thing like that happens!" The shipper shook his head, and let air rush through his teeth, making a whishing sound.

"Cops were here. Christ! Like they checking to see if we ship human meat as well as beef!" He guffawed.

"You know the guy?" Hunter asked.

The shipper pushed his lips out, shook his head again. "Never see him before. Poor bastard."

"How'd he get in the trailer?"

"I'd sure as hell like to know that answer myself. I almost fired your goddamn company because of it, you know? Big hassle. Sure doesn't make our American customer very happy, he's got cops looking over all his shipment." He jingled his coins some more, shook his head again with a little laugh. "That El, she won't let me go. You got a tough boss, man."

Hunter grinned, steered the conversation back. "Here I thought the frozen guy was one of those animal rights fanatics, like the ones who go around setting laboratory rats free, and he was trying to liberate your cows."

The shipper grinned back. "He wasn't such a smart guy then. Our cows arrive here already cut in half and skinned, hanging from big hooks. Pigs, too."

"You ever get animal rights protestors bugging you?"

"Not much."

"Not much?"

"We have once a little gravity."

Hunter frowned. "Gravity?"

"You know, on the walls. Sprayed on paint."

"Really? You've had graffiti here? What'd it say?"

"Graffiti. Graffiti," he repeated, practicing the word. "Oh, something stupid. Stop the slaughter. Save the Earth. Something stupid." The red of his cheeks began to spread to his forehead and neck. "You and me, we're human beings, for God's sake. We're not cows. We're not rabbits. What? So they want all the cats and dogs to eat nothing but grass, too? They want lions and bears to eat nothing but goddamn carrots? To hell with them. If my wife wants to wear fur, Goddamn, they can't stop her wearing fur."

"Does she?"

"Does she what?"

114

"Does your wife wear furs?"

"Damn right she wears furs. She's got money. She's got style. Why wouldn't she wear furs?" The more worked up he got, the redder his face became. He looked like a good candidate for a stroke.

"Did you ever find out who did it?" asked Hunter.

The shipper shrugged, made a face. "How?" he asked. "You have to catch them when they do it."

"Any signature? You know, these groups usually like you to know who they are."

"Oh, sure. Some funny thing that looks like, oh, maybe like an anchor lying down. I look for it sometimes other places, you know, other graffiti, but I never see it."

"An anchor lying down?"

"Ya. Come. I show you." He led Hunter over to the corner of the warehouse that served as the shipper's office. Behind a counter there was a desk, some filing cabinets and shelves, and a computer workstation. Hunter noticed there was a small electric heater blowing hot air toward the desk.

The shipper took a Polaroid photograph from under his blotter and held it out for Hunter to see. The signature seemed to be two initials in stylized block letters. It looked most like the initials EB, or perhaps EC, but the first letter could have been a T lying on its left side, which is why it looked like a sideways anchor, and the second letter could have been an E. The effect was like a twisted ribbon, almost creating an optical illusion. Hunter had seen it before.

"You see this somewhere," said the shipper, "you come back and tell me. I'd like to catch these guys, make them pay."

"Make them pay? How?"

"You know, pay for the painting. We must paint over the whole damn side of the building before it looks right again." He shook his head disgustedly. "Eight hunnert bucks."

CHAPTER
ELEVEN

Hunter called Al Kowalski from the warehouse phone at Hanratty Wholesale Meats and arranged to meet him on a quiet street in Lake City. When Al pulled up behind the trailer in an unmarked car, Hunter left the Blue Knight's engine running and walked back to meet him.

"Well, Al. You want to do the yelling or the listening?" he asked with a smile.

Al smiled sardonically. "I'll do the listening. You got a jacket or something?"

"Yes, but I hope I don't need it." Hunter unlocked the padlock and threw open one of the trailer doors. "How long do you need to listen for, anyway?"

Al shrugged, peering into the back of the trailer. "Not very full, is it?" he said. There were two rows of skids, each skid roughly four feet cubed. That left about three and half feet of clearance between the top of the skids and the ceiling of the trailer.

"Right," said Hunter. "But the load's already maxed out on weight. There's almost thirty four thousand pounds of frozen meat in there."

"And there'll soon be thirty four thousand and... what?... a hundred and eighty?"

116

"Whoa. How long do you intend to leave me in there?" asked Hunter.

Al grinned. "Start pounding and hollering as soon as I close the doors. I'll listen from here, then I'll go climb in the cab for a bit, see what I can hear from there. Can you get up to the front of this box?"

Hunter nodded, then hoisted himself up into the trailer, boosting himself onto the top of a skid chest first, scrambling to his knees, then tucking his feet under him in a squat. "I'll pound on the back doors for a full minute, so you'd better do up the latch. Then I'll go up and pound at the front."

"And yell."

"And yell," agreed Hunter.

"Need a flashlight?" Al said, easing the door shut.

"That would be cheating," Hunter said through the crack. Then the door closed and he was in darkness. It wasn't that cold. At first.

He pounded on the back door, his fist landing with dull thumps. The sound didn't seem to go anywhere, as if it were being sucked up and swallowed by the insulated door. The experience reminded him of those dreams where you run and run and run for your life, but never seem to move. "Hey!" he yelled. "Let me out of here!" His voice hit the walls and crashed back into his eardrums. "Hey!" He pounded again on the door, then heard Al's muffled voice telling him to move up front. Hunter gave the door a hard shove, then a kick, and sucked in his breath. It wouldn't budge. He tried to imagine how he would feel if he didn't know Al was there to let him out, and a shiver coursed up and down his back. Goddamn. He was helpless.

There were narrow gaps between the pallets, so he made his way carefully, moving in a crouch, and feeling his way along the cold, plastic wrapped surface with his hand. His fingers were already beginning to feel numb from their contact with the cold door, and now the frozen cartons. His left foot slipped off a frosty edge and into a crevice between two skids, and he cursed as he almost lost his balance. He was thankful his ankle hadn't lodged in tight, and, having learned his lesson, moved over to the right hand side of the load so he could keep one hand on the trailer wall. The noise of the refrigeration unit grew louder, and the air blew colder. Once or twice his head brushed the billowing plastic sleeve that hung from the ceiling. Finally he was at the front wall of the trailer, where he banged and hollered for what he judged to be a full minute before stopping to listen, his hands tucked into his armpits. He heard nothing but the loud hum of the reefer and his own breathing. His thigh muscles ached from the cramped position and the cold.

Hunter was only half way back when the door swung open and let in a flood of daylight. He heaved an involuntary sigh of relief, and said nothing until he was out of the trailer and able to step into the sun. It felt good to stretch his legs. "Well?" he asked Al.

"They never would've heard anything up front. The back, yeah, at least in a situation like this where there wasn't much other noise."

"That's about what I figured."

"Not that it would have made any difference."

"What do you mean?" Hunter rubbed his palms together, trying to warm his hands.

"I mean, if they wanted the guy dead, what difference would it make whether they could hear him screaming his head off?"

Hunter waited, imagining how the victim would have felt, and knowing from Al's expression that he had more to say.

"I followed up with a couple more witnesses this morning," Al continued. "That argument the victim had with your friend's wife, they raised their voices enough for one of the waitresses to hear the end of it."

"And?"

Al referred to his notebook, recited emotionlessly, "God damn you. You used me, and I never got a damn thing out of it. You owe me." He shot Hunter a meaningful glance. "Then Williams replies, You're alive aren't you? Isn't that worth something? And she says, You're going to pay for screwing me around, you bastard, and he says, If I hand 'em over, I'd be the one getting screwed, Share. Then she starts to leave and Williams says, Wait, Share. I'll make you a deal, or something like that, and he follows her outside."

"What's all that supposed to mean?"

Al scratched his chin. "It means that she threatened him."

118

Or maybe he threatened her, thought Hunter, but that was almost as bad in terms of a motive for murder. "But what was it all about?"

"Drugs, maybe. I'm thinking maybe she was a courier. They made some kind of deal and she was trying to welsh on it, sounds like. The important line is, You're going to pay for screwing me around, you little bastard. The other witness heard the same thing."

"They say anything else?"

"Sharon Nillson and the victim had a friendly relationship over the last couple of years, according to the witnesses, and often spoke together privately when Williams was playing there. Nobody knew any intimate details, but one of the waitresses speculated - and took pains to assure me she had no first hand knowledge - that Williams might have been selling Sharon cocaine. She had a drug problem, ended up in rehab."

Hunter didn't like the way this was shaping up, another lead pointing to Sharon. He shook his head and was about to head toward his cab when he remembered the graffiti at Hanratty meats and told Al about the signature. "I had someone look into that," said Al. "Every meat warehouse in the Lower Mainland has been hit in the last few months. I can't see animal rights graffiti as a motive for murder. By the way," said Al, "how did it feel?"

"What?"

Al jerked his head toward the trailer.

Hunter took a deep breath and looked down at his hands, which he was clenching and unclenching to get the blood circulating. He stared into Al's face for several seconds before replying.

"It was a horrible way to die."

Alora Magee wasn't ready to give up on her new client. So far, she'd learned nothing useful from Sharon Nillson, because Sharon refused to talk about the circumstances surrounding the frozen body. Alora knew they needed something to open up the lines of communication between them, something to break the ice. Break the ice. When that analogy occurred to her, her mind wandering as she sat at her desk polishing the final draft of a brief, Alora groaned aloud, and decided

119

that "building a bridge" would be a better label for it. With a free hour at the end of the day on Monday, she decided to give it a go.

Sharon Nillson shuffled into the visiting room and Alora had to look to see if she was in leg chains. She wasn't. The guard removed her cuffs and left.

"Are you okay?" Alora asked. "You don't look well." Sharon's skin was pallid, her hair hung in lusterless strings, and there were dark circles under her eyes.

"There's a crazy woman in my cell," she said. "If I don't get out of there, there'll be two crazy women."

"She keeps you awake?"

"No. She keeps me asleep. That's the only way I can escape from her." Sharon closed her eyes and worked her jaw. "If I have to listen to her and look at her, that woman will drive me stark raving mad." She shuddered and opened her mouth as if she were about to scream. "A troll. She's an ugly troll."

"I'll see what I can do," said Alora, knowing that all she could do was complain to the Sheriff's Department "I'd like to help." When her client didn't respond, she said, "We need to help each other, you and I. We have to communicate better if I'm going to build a good case for you."

Sharon just took a deep breath and lowered her eyes.

"I can tell that you're uncomfortable with me," Alora started with a sentence she'd partially rehearsed, "so I thought that perhaps if I told you a little bit about myself, it might help to break... to break the barrier between us." Gawd. She'd almost fallen into the ice analogy again. "Yuck. I almost sound like a social worker, but trust me, I'm not the touchy feely type. I just want us to find some common ground so we can work together. We don't need to be friends, you don't even need to like me, we just have to come to an understanding that we're both working toward the same goal. Am I making sense?"

Sharon barely nodded. Alora noticed that Sharon was fiddling with her hands underneath the table again, so she clicked open her briefcase, which she'd left on the floor beside her chair, and extracted the emergency pack of cigarettes. "Would you like a smoke?"

120

Sharon reached for the pack and tapped it against a knuckle. Three cigarettes flipped out onto the table. "Sorry," she said.

"Okay," said Alora, wondering where to start. With the basics, she decided. "I'm thirty seven years old and I've never had kids. How's that for a start?"

Sharon was busy lighting a cigarette. She nodded as she inhaled, then said, "Me neither. Go on," and settled back in her chair. Smoke curled out her nostrils.

"I've been a lawyer for five years, and before that I tried teaching school, but I hated it." Alora realized that her education could turn out to be more of a barrier than a bridge, so she quickly continued. "On weekends, I ride my bike, mostly in the mountains." She watched Sharon suck deeply on her cigarette and decided that sports probably wasn't going to be much of a bridge either. "I have a sister and a brother, both younger, and my sister is married with two kids, so I'm an aunt. How about you?"

"My kid sister - my only sister - OD'd on heroin," said Sharon, her voice emotionless.

If she'd intended it as a slap in the face, it worked. "I'm sorry," said Alora, putting her fingers to her lips. They were both silent for a moment, and Alora scrambled for something neutral to say. Hobbies? Pets? "I used to like to ride my bike alone, when I had a dog. Then I lost my dog, so now I only go on organized rides, or ride with friends."

There was a spark of interest in Sharon's eyes. "How did you lose your dog?" she asked.

Alora squirmed in her chair. The death of a dog couldn't compare with the death of a sister. Was this another mistake? "I had to put him down," she said. "He wasn't even ten yet, but his hips were really bad. Dysplasia. It's very painful. Have you heard of it?" Sharon shook her head. "He was a German Shepherd," added Alora. "It's very common in Shepherds."

"I have a Pomeranian," said Sharon, her eyes averted. "Ray gave her to me."

"You must miss her," said Alora. Another faux pas? She hastened to add, "And Ray, too. You must miss them both."

Sharon nodded, kept her eyes lowered. "Life's a bitch."

"What did you say her name was? This bitch," she added with a smile.

"Peaches," said Sharon, acknowledging the joke with a soft snort.

Alora didn't like small dogs. They weren't strong enough to give her any sense of comfort, not powerful enough to frighten a man, to ward off a stalker. "My dog's name was Brutus. I... uh... got him for protection."

"A guard dog?"

"You could say that."

"I've never had much worth stealing," said Sharon.

"Oh, no," said Alora. "It wasn't that I was worried about burglars. It was..." She didn't really want to have to talk about this, but Sharon was looking at her with interest now. Maybe this would be the bridge. "...it was my ex-husband. He threatened me." She felt compelled to add, "I was very naive when I married him. I didn't know. He wasn't violent before the wedding, so I had no idea." She shook her head. "It was a mistake."

Sharon looked thoughtful, sat tapping her front teeth with a thumbnail, her cigarette hovering inches from her nose. "Did he beat you?" she asked.

Alora closed her eyes, involuntarily recalling the nightmare of that day. "Only once," she said. "It scared me so much I ran away from him, filed for divorce." She shivered, feeling suddenly exposed and cold. "That made him angry. Very angry."

"Scared? You're lucky you had the guts to run away. Once you let it happen the first time, it just keeps getting worse," Sharon said. "They want to own you, like you're a car or a truck, or a dog. If you walk away, that's an insult to them, so they won't let you go." She held the flimsy aluminum ashtray with one hand, tapped the cigarette against its edge. "Once they got their teeth in you, they're like a pit bull. You ever seen a pit bull lock its jaws on someone?"

Alora shook her head.

"I have. A friend of mine. We'd been partying, and the guys were getting pretty pissed. Just beer, but they'd been drinking all day. My friend, Verna, she'd had enough of her old man mouthing off at
122

her, so she said she was leaving, and she got up to go." Sharon squinted across the table, a bitter smile twisting her lips. "The bastard sicced his pit bull on her. It got its teeth into her here, right at the back of her thigh." She stood up and grabbed her leg just below the buttock. "And its jaws locked shut. Verna screamed and tried to run but it just stayed there, hanging off her, like it was attached. First her husband laughed. The bastard laughed! Then he tried to call it off. He called and whistled and when it wouldn't let go, he started to kick at it. Verna was crawling along the ground screaming like crazy, and the dog still wouldn't let go. So finally Gary beat it over the head with a crowbar." She shuddered. "It was awful. The dog went into convulsions and died, its mouth all bloody, and Verna was still screaming and crying, her eyes almost bugging out of her head. Then Gary booted the dead dog halfway across the yard, and came back at Verna, yelling at her and threatening her with the crowbar, like the whole thing was all her fault."

"Jesus."

"I wish I'd never seen it."

"It must have been horrible."

"I wish my boyfriend had never seen it either," Sharon continued. "He held it over me, brought it up every time he got drunk. He said he was like that pitbull, that he'd never let me go unless I killed him."

Alora nodded. This was familiar territory for her. Too familiar.

Her client smiled bitterly. "But the bastard forgot to add, until he found a younger, more attractive woman who was willing to put up with his shit."

"Lucky for you," Alora said, shaking her head. "So you've been there, too."

"I've been there." Sharon took a last deep drag on her cigarette and stubbed it out. "I've been there so many times that I thought that it was my fault. I thought I'd never know anything different. But I was wrong."

"Ray?"

Sharon nodded, her lips pursed tight.

"He must be a very special man. I'd like to meet him one day," said Alora. It occurred to her how absurd that was. As if they would meet socially one day, go out for dinner or a walk on the beach. Even if Ray and Sharon were both acquitted, if their marriage held together after the strain of a trial, there was little chance of any kind of social evening together. Except for abusive men in their pasts, she and Sharon had so little in common. And Alora was trying to forget about her abusive man.

"You're still afraid of him, aren't you?"

Sharon's question took her by surprise and Alora caught her breath, realized she didn't have to answer because Sharon already knew it was true.

"Does he know where you are?"

"I don't know," Alora said, shaking her head. "It's been a few years. I don't know."

"Maybe," said her client in a grim voice, "you should get another dog."

Hunter eased The Blue Knight and its trailer load of beef into one of the parking slots north of the border, then tucked his clipboard under his arm and walked up to the U.S. Customs office. It would be nice to be able to discuss Ray and Sharon's border crossing with one of the customs inspectors, but he didn't hold out much hope for getting cooperation. In fact, even bringing it up could jeopardize his chances of getting across the border smoothly tonight. The U.S. Customs inspectors weren't particularly friendly toward drivers, and were quick to wield their bureaucratic power against anyone with a bad attitude. Asking questions would probably fall into that category. Hunter decided to leave that part of the investigation entirely to the RCMP

As luck would have it, however, he was given an opening. He'd placed his paperwork in one of the stacked boxes and stood over in the waiting area to watch. One of the inspectors, short with a dark complexion, pulled out Hunter's paperwork and called out, "Hey! Tom. This one's for you," and flung the bundle of papers across another inspector's desk. "How about this time you make sure there's no human carcasses in with the beef," he said with a gruff laugh.

124

The man behind the desk grinned at his colleague, then straightened out the papers and studied them before getting up from his desk. He was wearing dark glasses and had fresh pink scar tissue on one cheek. Hunter strolled over to the counter and identified himself before he could be called. "Trust me," he said. "There's no body in there this time. An RCMP detective and myself both looked."

"Let's hope not," said the inspector, looking up. Hunter couldn't see his eyes behind the dark glasses, and hoped he hadn't said the wrong thing. Even polite small talk could backfire on a driver trying to stay on a customs man's good side. "But we still need to take a look inside. Bring 'er around to the dock." Just routine for a meat shipment. The man's voice wasn't particularly friendly, but it didn't sound menacing either.

"You betcham," said Hunter, and left to comply.

When Hunter swung open the back doors, the customs inspector was standing at his shoulder, along with an inspector from the Department of Agriculture. "What have we here?" asked the Food Safety man, stepping toward the nearest skid. Winking at the customs inspector, he added, "Any frozen corpses on board?"

"Were you two the ones who inspected that load?" asked Hunter.

The Food inspector deferred to the other man, who answered with a question of his own. "Did the RCMP really inspect this trailer before you left?"

"We conducted a little experiment," said Hunter, reasoning that if he shared some information with them, they might reciprocate. "The detective wanted to know if you could hear a man yelling and pounding from inside the trailer." He smiled. "That was my job."

"And could you?"

"Hear? He said he could hear some from back here, but nothing from inside the cab."

"You undercover?" asked the Food inspector. He'd checked the labels on the rearmost skids, made some marks on the paperwork on to his clipboard.

"Not anymore." Hunter left it deliberately vague. "So you two saw nothing unusual about the load or the drivers?"

125

The Food inspector shook his head, then looked sheepishly at the customs inspector. "I'm afraid I was a little... uh... under the weather that day, so it wasn't exactly a close inspection. And Tom there wasn't much help. He'd done a face plant from his mountain bike the weekend before - right, Tom? - and was suffering from a painful road rash."

The customs agent lifted his dark glasses to reveal faint yellow circles under his eyes.

"Shit, Tom. You don't need those anymore." The Food man turned to Hunter. "He thinks he's Tommy Lee Jones."

"I didn't know mountain biking was a contact sport," said Hunter.

"Great sport," the customs man said, deadpan. "As long as you keep your face off the gravel."

"Thanks, chief," said Hunter. "I'll keep that in mind." They gave him the all-clear sign, and he swung the doors of the trailer closed, fastening a heavy padlock on the latch.

To Hunter's relief, without any further delays he was back behind the wheel, heading down the I-5 toward Seattle. If the customs and Agriculture inspectors had been as lax with their inspection when Ray and Sharon had come through, there was no doubt that a man could have hidden deep in the darkness of the trailer and not been discovered at the border. If that were the case, why would Greg Williams have wanted to be in that trailer? He had no arrest record, so presumably, if he wished to enter the country, he could have done so openly. It seemed unlikely that Williams had resorted to smuggling himself across the border in a refrigerated trailer.

If the two U.S. agents both remembered the load, there was little doubt that the trailer had been opened and at least a cursory inspection performed. So a man in the trailer against his will, unless he were unconscious, could have used that opportunity to escape. Russell Kupka had said there was evidence indicating that the victim could have been unconscious, that perhaps he woke up somewhere past the border and found himself lying on a bed of frozen meat, padlocked inside a moving trailer. Woke up to the cold. Woke up to the dark.

126

In spite of the heat, Hunter shivered. He reached for his radio, and cranked up the dial.

When El was finished at the office, she left her pickup parked behind the warehouse and fired up the old Hino that Wally did local pickups and deliveries with when there was less than a trailer load involved. She'd bought an extra sandwich from the lunch truck, so she munched on it as she drove. She had the foresight to buy the cheese and lettuce, so although the lettuce was limp, the bread wasn't soggy. The worst of rush hour was over, but it was still bumper-to-bumper from Brunette Avenue to the Port Mann Bridge. Once she was past 200th Street, it was clear sailing all the way out to Chillwack and Fraser's Dock pub.

The bar manager was so happy to get rid of Greg Williams' equipment that he helped her carry it out to the truck. El scribbled out a waybill for him and signed it off, then, tempted by the smell of freshly cooked french fries, decided to have dinner in the pub before heading back down the highway. It was pretty quiet in the pub, being Monday night, so the waitress took her order right away, then returned with a glass of Coke. She set it down, but remained beside the table, resting one hand on the back of a chair.

"So you picked up Greg's stuff, huh?" the waitress said.

"Yeah," said El, paying close attention to the young woman for the first time. She was blond and curly, with round red cheeks that looked out of keeping with the heavy eye makeup she wore. Corn fed, and bored with life in the country. "You knew him?"

The girl nodded, her mouth drooping mournfully.

"You like him?" El asked.

"I guess," the girl said with a little shrug. "Did you take the tapes and stuff?"

"What tapes?"

"His tapes. You know, with his songs on them."

"Yeah, I'd better take them, too. Where are they?"

The girl came back a couple of minutes later with a large manila envelope. She handed it to El, then said, "He said I could have one."

El was already busy looking inside the envelope. She pulled out a stack of photographs, eight by twelve glossies of Greg Williams in three different poses: one a close up of his head and shoulders, one of him seated with a guitar and looking past the camera, one of him with the guitar and his eyes looking down. You could call him handsome, she supposed, but he was a little too close to pretty for El's tastes.

"Greg said I could have one," the girl repeated.

"Huh? Oh, here." El handed her a few of the glossies. She noticed the bartender heading toward them with a frown on his face. "Take your pick."

"And a tape, too. He said I could have a tape."

"Melissa..." said the bartender, a note of warning in his voice. He grabbed the glossies from the girl. "What do you want with these? You'd better not be mooning over that little prick. I told you, the only way I'd let you work in the bar was if you didn't get friendly with anybody."

"You want your waitresses to be unfriendly with the customers? What the hell kind of stupid idea is that?" El couldn't help herself.

He scowled at her. "I don't mean that kind of friendly." He turned back to the girl, grabbed her by the arm. "And that goes double for scumbag musicians like him. You hear me?"

"Hold on there," said El. "No boss has a right..."

"Stay out of this." He must have realized he was talking to a paying customer, because he added, "I'm not talkin' as her boss, I'm talkin' as her big brother."

El's mouth made an O. So maybe that gave him a right to get personal with the girl, but he was still an asshole.

"Especially this scumbag," the bartender said to his sister, slapping the glossies hard against the back of the chair.

"Ow. Let go. You're hurting me." The girl glared at him. "And don't talk about him like that. Greg wasn't a scumbag."

"He was a fuckin' scumbag," he said, ripping the glossies in half, then in half again, and throwing the pieces to the floor. "Now, you leave this lady alone and get back to work. Go."

It was almost enough to make El lose her appetite. Almost. When the girl showed up with her burger and fries, El slid one of the cassette tapes across the table under a napkin. "Here," she said. "Just don't let your brother see it." They both looked toward the bar, and were relieved to see him busy with a couple of customers.

"He can be such a jerk sometimes," said the girl.

"Why didn't your brother like Greg?" El asked, picking up the biggest french fry on her plate. She blew on it, then nibbled off the end. It was still hot enough to burn her mouth.

"He's just jealous. He's jealous of anybody that girls like better 'n him."

"The girls liked Greg, huh?"

"Well, yeah. Who wouldn't?" She looked over her shoulder and saw that her brother was watching again. When he turned his attention back to the beer glass he was filling, she scooped the tape up off the table and slipped it into her pocket. "Thanks, eh?"

El shook vinegar and salt on her fries, then dug into the meal. She wished she could've asked the waitress a few more questions, but whenever the girl got close to El's table, the bartender watched her like a hawk. When she finished eating, El left the girl a two-buck tip and went to settle her bill at the bar.

"How come you didn't like Williams?" she asked him as he opened the till for her change. "Was it something about him in particular, or you just don't like musicians?"

"The guy was a scumbag," he said, slapping her change down on the counter. He turned his back to her, which El took as a sign that he didn't intend to continue the conversation.

"Thanks," she said, lowering her voice to add, "... asshole."

There was no tape player in the Hino, and by the time she got home, got the dogs walked and fed, she wasn't in any shape to listen to a tape of a dead guy, scumbag or not, singing. Hell, she wasn't in any shape to listen to anybody sing, not even Phil Collins.

She threw the manila envelope on the kitchen counter and went to bed.

CHAPTER
TWELVE

Before leaving the house on Tuesday morning, El slipped one of Greg Williams' tapes into her shirt pocket, planning to listen to it at some point during the day. She wished she could listen to it on her way in to work, but she'd driven the Hino straight home from Fraser's Dock, and it had no tape player. The old truck did have a radio, so she flipped it on to catch the six o'clock news.

After two or three hot political items, the newscaster turned to crime. "The RCMP revealed that they've located the car belonging to a Burnaby man found dead in Southern California last week," he said. "The car, found yesterday in a restaurant parking lot in Mount Vernon, Washington, is being towed to Vancouver for forensic examination."

"Jesus!" said El. "I wonder if Hunter knows about that yet." She knew he would check in with her sometime during the day, and she was already looking forward to the call so she could tell him about her visit to Fraser's Dock. She wondered what the victim's car being abandoned in the U.S. meant to the case against Ray and Sharon. How could he have gotten into their trailer in Mount Vernon? And why?

When she arrived at the office, she backed the Hino up against the chain-link fence. It wasn't going to be used today, and she decided she'd pick a time to unload Greg Williams' equipment when she could be sure no one would walk in on her. She took the tape out of her pocket and examined it in the daylight as she walked to the office. There was a telephone number on the insert, presumably where the singer could be reached for a booking or to inquire about purchasing another tape. Would it be the studio? She put on a pot of coffee, unlocked the warehouse door, and looked through the night's curled up faxes before she tried the number. As she suspected, there was no answer, but she reached a voice mail box.

The male voice on the recorded message was smooth and could pass for sexy. "Thanks for calling Whistlestop Studios. This is Greg Williams. I'm not able to take your call right now, but if you'll leave a message, I'll get back to you as soon as possible."

"Yeah. Sure you will," she said, and hung up.

Sharon woke to a humming. It was rhythmic but tuneless, growing in intensity. It took her a few seconds to remember where she was, just until she opened her eyes. Across the cell, her cellmate's naked foot, long knobby toes with yellowed pads, hung over the side of her bed, twitching in time to the buzz from her throat. The woman caught Sharon's eye, and with a leer threw back the sheet. Her hand worked between her legs as her pasty buttocks slacked and stiffened. "Oooooh. Watch me, Princess. Watch me. I'm coming."

Sharon gagged and hid her head under her pillow. "Please, God. Get me out of here. Please, God. Show me the way. Please. Please. Please. Please. Please."

"Alora Magee. A-lor-a Ma-gee." Russell reread the message slip, frowning. According to the note, she'd called just five minutes before he walked in the door. The name was familiar, but... Of course. Alora Magee was Sharon Nillson's lawyer. As soon as he reached his desk, he picked up the telephone and punched in her number.

The woman got right to the point. "What can I do to get Sharon moved into a different cell? It appears that her cellmate is a thoroughly unpleasant individual and is making prison life very

131

difficult for her. Sharon's under a great deal of stress and I'm worried about her mental health." The voice was competent and assertive.

"Not my department," Russell told her. "I'm a detective, not the warden." He'd always suspected that women who made an effort to sound competent and assertive were doing so to mask their incompetence and insecurity. "If your client wanted to bunk with a member of the PTA, she shouldn't have murdered her dope dealer."

There were a few seconds of silence, then the lawyer said, "What? What do you mean?"

"Prison inmates aren't known for their pleasant personalities and social skills..."

"No. What do you mean, she shouldn't have murdered her dope dealer?"

Russell smiled. Gotcha, he thought. Suddenly Ms. Clever Lawyer's not nearly so sure of herself. "Just what I said. Appears that the Iceman, before he became an Iceman, was Sharon Nillson's snow man, or at least, the two of them evidently had a long lasting, secretive relationship of some kind, which led her coworkers to assume he was selling her cocaine."

"Sharon knew the victim?"

"She didn't tell you? I thought you and Feldman were hotshot lawyers. How come I know more about your clients than you do?" There was another period of silence which Russell liked to imagine expressed the female lawyer's stunned disbelief. He leaned back in his chair, stroked his tie. "Ray's hick brother from Minnesota has a better fix on your client than you do, and he's never even met her. But then, I guess you defense lawyer types can't afford to be good judges of character. You probably sleep better when you delude yourself into believing your clients are innocent."

"I just do my job. Guilt or innocence is for the jury to decide." The voice was back to being competent and assertive. "Getting a guilty client off - not that I'm aware of ever having done so - would affect my conscience a lot less than putting an innocent man in jail."

"Don't get huffy, Ms. Magee. Or have you forgotten that you called to ask me for a favor?"

"That was a mistake, obviously a result of me being a poor judge of character. Or should I say, a bad judge of poor character?" The phone clicked in Russell's ear.

"Ha!" he said, getting up from his desk. "Sanctimonious bitch. Thank God I got out of law before it was too late." He tossed his empty coffee mug in the air and caught it behind his back, headed for the coffee machine.

"Is there anything you want to tell me?" Alora had dropped everything and told her secretary to reschedule her morning appointments, pleaded an emergency and managed to get in to see Sharon on short notice. If anyone had asked her why it was so important that she talk to her client this morning, she wouldn't have been able to give a rational reason. She didn't know herself.

"Have you got those cigarettes?" Sharon looked even worse than yesterday, but Alora had no sympathy for her today.

"No," she said, staring stonily across the table at her client.

Sharon seemed to realize that something had changed. Her mouth dropped open as she studied Alora's face, then opened and closed several times before she said. "What? What is it that I'm supposed to tell you?"

"The truth."

"You won't believe the truth." Sharon dropped her eyes. The fingers of one hand plucked repeatedly at the limp strings of her hair.

"Try me."

"Ray and me had nothing to do with that man's death."

"With whose death?"

"Who... ?" Sharon glanced up, then dropped her eyes again. "You know who. That man the police say was in our trailer."

"Who was he?"

"I don't know who..."

"That's bullshit!" Alora exploded, slamming the table with an open hand.

Sharon's head jerked upright, as if she'd been hit.

"You did know him, and the police know that you knew him. I've been honest with you, it's time you did the same for me." That was exactly it, Alora knew, the reason she felt hurt and angry enough to march straight down here this morning. She had dropped her guard, confided in this woman, this stranger from somewhere a thousand miles and million life experiences away, and this stranger had mocked her, not by betraying her confidence, but by refusing to entrust Alora with her own. Looking steadily into her client's eyes, Alora continued, her words cold and clipped. "Say it. You knew the dead man. You knew Greg Williams. The people you used to work with have told the police that you and he knew each other, knew each other very well. It's time you told me, Sharon..."

Alora leaned forward, sliding her hand, palm down, until it rested in the middle of the table. "Tell me, Sharon. How did that same Greg Williams end up dead in your trailer?"

Sharon felt as if her stomach had just dropped to the floor. She closed her eyes and struggled against a wave of nausea and heat that worked its way up through her chest to her throat. She clutched at the table, afraid that she would slide off her chair. How could this be happening? How could her life with Ray have gone so suddenly and so horribly wrong?

"Talk to me, Sharon."

The lawyer's voice held no trace of compassion. Ray was right. Lawyers, cops, they were all the same. Sharon said nothing.

"The more you lie, the weaker your case becomes. There's no reason for an innocent person to lie. Doesn't that make sense to you?"

"You already think I'm guilty."

The lawyer took a deep breath. Her mouth twitched a little before she spoke, as if she were trying to keep a strong emotion under control. Sharon realized with a start that it was anger. Why was the lawyer so angry? "You're innocent until proven guilty. I'm your lawyer. It's my job to present evidence of your innocence to the court, evidence that I'll have a hard time finding without your cooperation." She paused. Her stare made Sharon uncomfortable. "If you want someone else to be your lawyer, just say so. I'm no pit bull. I'll let you go."

Sharon shook her head. Yesterday she had begun to believe Alora Magee could be her friend, and now the woman had turned against her. If only she could talk to Ray, just for a minute. He said not to say anything to anybody. Would he be angry with her if she trusted this woman? She was so confused and frightened and tired of being under siege, right this minute all she wanted was to put her head down on the table and cry like a child. Her eyes began to sting.

"I have half a mind to walk out on you," said the lawyer, her voice now weary. "Why won't you tell me what really happened? Why won't you help me to help you?"

"I need to talk to Ray," said Sharon, and lay her head on her arms. She felt the tears start, felt their heat on the skin of her arm. "Please," she said into the table. "Please."

"If you, or Ray, locked Greg Williams in your trailer, you must have had a good reason. Did he threaten you? Or was it an accident? You just wanted to scare him. You didn't know he would freeze to death. Is that it?"

Sharon raised her tear stained faced from the table. "Ray and me never knew there was anybody in our trailer. We never hurt anybody."

When she didn't say anything else, the lawyer spoke again. "Is that all you have to say?"

Sharon nodded.

The lawyer looked disgusted, took a deep breath and shook her head.

"Help me," said Sharon. "Please."

After spending his obligatory eight hours off the road at the truck stop in Yoncalla, Oregon, Hunter stopped for a late breakfast near Grants Pass. He called El's 800 number from the restaurant. "Just checkin' in," he said.

"They found Greg Williams' car," El told him, "in Mount Vernon."

Hunter frowned, puzzled. "Any idea how long it had been there?"

"They don't tell you stuff like that on the news," she said.

"You got some kind of log on Ray and Sharon?"

`"You mean, when they might've passed through there?"

She put the phone down while she looked, and he could hear her thump something heavy on the desk and riffle through pages. Then he heard her phone buzz, and found himself on hold, listening to Garth Brooks singing about friends in low places. A couple of drivers walked past on their way out of the restaurant, arguing.

"He's got every right," one of them said, settling a baseball cap on his head.

"The hell he does. He got a responsibility. He expects her to be there when he gets home, then he got a responsibility..."

El came back on the line. "That's about half way to Seattle, so it looks to me like they would've been passing through Mount Vernon at about six o'clock on Friday night."

"Sounds about right," said Hunter. He had passed by at roughly the same time the day before.

"That's a reasonable place to stop for supper, I guess."

He couldn't argue with that. "I wonder what Williams was doing there?"

"Shopping?" she ventured. "Something he couldn't buy on our side. Maybe drugs? You said he might've been into drugs."

"More likely he was selling something, if he and his buddies had a hydroponic garden somewhere. But what would that have to do with Ray and Sharon? They'd just crossed the border themselves." Hunter scratched his jaw. He hadn't shaved, only taking enough time to wash his face and grab a cup of coffee when he left Yoncalla. "Unless they met by accident." He sighed. "I wish those two would talk."

"You find out anything yesterday when you made the pick up?"

"Just that somebody painted graffiti on Hanratty's walls that had something to do with animal rights."

136

"And the victim was into animal rights?"

Hunter shrugged lightly as he spoke into the phone. "Either him or his roommates. We don't know enough about him yet."

"I found out last night that he was a scumbag."

"A scumbag? What kind of a scumbag?"

"I don't know. Is there more than one kind?" When Hunter didn't say anything, El continued. "That's the opinion of the bar manager at Fraser's Dock. I got the dead guy's equipment, like you said."

"Thanks, El. Hang on to it. I'd like to deliver it to his studio myself when I get back."

El told him she'd managed to line up a return shipment from L.A., and that it would be ready on Thursday morning. "You should have your load off in Anaheim before noon tomorrow, so that gives you the rest of the day to fart around. Think you can get in to see Ray again?"

"I'll see what I can do."

Back on the highway, Hunter was impatient. Usually he enjoyed daylight driving, relaxing deep in the driver's seat and enjoying the strong pull of the big diesel and the steady hum of tires against the asphalt. He enjoyed the feeling of getting somewhere, noting with pleasure the mileage signs that signaled his progress. He liked to peer at the farms and the small towns he passed, imagining a life there far different from the life he himself had led, a life with an old-fashioned family, a simple life built on physical labor and lifelong relationships. No suicides. No divorces. No ex-wife's new boyfriends. But today, he found Ray's problem more compelling than daydreaming about happy imaginary lives. Hunter had been a bulldog as a detective, and he hadn't shed the habit along with the job. He wanted to solve this case. He wanted to know who was guilty. Even if it was Ray, he wanted to have that sense that he'd unraveled the knot, uncovered the truth, in some way closed a loop that needed closing.

"Talk to me, Ray," he muttered, passing the exit for Yreka, California. "Talk to me."

CHAPTER

THIRTEEN

Hunter arrived at the warehouse in Anaheim at nine thirty on Wednesday morning, and was lucky enough to find a warehouseman ready to start unloading his trailer. The man was dressed in white, like a chef, and had an infectious smile, teeth yellow compared to his uniform, but brilliant in contrast to his black skin. "James" was embroidered in red above a buttoned pocket.

"A burn baby load again, huh?" James said, taking a look at the bill of lading Hunter handed him. "Han-RAT-y in BURN-baby, Canada." He put the waybill on a clipboard and hung it on a hook beside the door. "Here's the beef, man," he called to a younger, thinner warehouseman who rounded the corner of the cold storage locker.

"You get these shipments every week?" Hunter asked.

James shrugged. "Mebbe once or twice a month."

"Were you here for the load that arrived last Monday?"

"'Deed I was. That one created some excitement, let me tell you. Next thing you know, the police was here crawlin' all over it."

"They find anything?"

The black man shrugged. "Who knows? Held us up all Tuesday morning, goin' over everything with their little magnifying glasses and vacuum cleaners. Half the stuff woulda already been shipped outa here if they hadn't made us hold onto it. The boss was some mad about the hold up, I'll say that." He tossed the last sentence over his shoulder as he headed for the forklift.

Hunter watched him unload, nudging the big tines of the forklift under a skid, lifting it just enough to pull it out a foot or two, away from the other skids, then running the forks in deep and lifting the skid well off the floor. One by one, he transferred the skids from the truck to the warehouse floor. The other warehouseman slit the shrink wrap with a single deft pull of his knife, then peeled it off and away before moving the skid into the cold storage locker with a second, smaller forklift. James turned off his motor while he waited for the other man to catch up, and Hunter leaned against the frame of the forklift to talk to him.

"Say, chief..." Hunter glanced at the warehouseman's chest and corrected himself, "James, did you talk to the drivers who made the delivery last week?"

"Sho' did. I like those two, the big guy and his woman. They's nice easy goin' folks compared to some of the tight-ass drivers come in here." James grinned and jabbed Hunter lightly on the shoulder with his fist. "They's quiet and polite, just like you."

Hunter smiled. "They're friends of mine."

James nodded his head thoughtfully and added, "I could tell they was grievin', but they still had a smile for me, still had a good word, you know what I mean?"

"So they were upset about something?"

James frowned, nodding slowly. "Grievin'. I figure they was grievin'."

"How's that?"

"Well, they was standin' just over there. The young lady, she kept watchin' him close like, like she was real worried about him. The big guy wasn't sayin' nothin'. When I stopped my motor, just like now, I heard her say, Ray, honey, we's got to talk, kinda pitiful like, like maybe he was mad at her for something. That's what I figured at first, anyways. But he didn't look mad. She started to ax him something, or tell him, I wasn't sure. What happened... she started sayin'. What happened..., but that's all what come outa her mouth before he shushed her, gentle like, then when he didn't know I was lookin', he gave her a long hug." James sighed.

"Just kind of put his arms 'round her like he was comforting a little kid. She pressed her face into him like she was cryin' on his chest, and he kissed her on the top of her head. It weren't none of my bidness, so I never said nothin', I just pretended I never saw it. Looked to me like somethin' bad had happened, and they was grievin' over it, both of 'em. Then, a'course, next day the police was all over the shipment here, made a pile a trouble for us, let me tell you."

"Did you tell the police about the drivers?" Hunter asked.

"Nope. The police never axed, and I never woulda said nothin' if they had. Them two was grievin', ain't no bidness of the police."

El was preoccupied. Twice during the morning she forgot to get back to a holding phone line, resulting in a late pick up and one very pissed off shipper. Things slacked off a bit around eleven o'clock, so she pulled the envelope containing Greg Williams' tapes and photos out from under her desk and called a friend at United Terminals.

"Hey, Paddy, could you do me a favor? Could you check a couple of phone numbers in the Criss-Cross and see if you can come up with an address for me?" She read off the two numbers under Greg Williams' name on the outside of the envelope.

Her buddy came up with two addresses, one in a residential area in southeast Burnaby, the other on Still Creek, in an industrial area. It wouldn't hurt, she figured, to drive by and take a look at these places, see if anything clicked into place. Hunter would be pleased, she thought, if she had some of the legwork done before he got back from California. When the lunch truck arrived, she bought a sandwich and a bottle of juice, asked Wally to man the Watson office while she was gone, then headed out the door, with no specific plan in mind.

The residence, presumably Williams' home, was an older three-story house, not far from Kingsway's commercial hubbub and traffic. The house could have used a handyman's touch and a few thousand dollars worth of exterior renovations. It seemed to be divided into

140

suites, since there were two doorbells and mailboxes at the main door, which was on the front porch, and what looked like a separate, ground level entrance at the side of the house. The address she had been given applied to the ground level door. El drove past once, then circled the block and drove past again. From the road, she couldn't see anything at the back of the house, nor were there any large windows at the front of the house, so she couldn't even tell if there was anyone home.

She parked a couple of houses away and was just about to get out of the truck when she glanced in the rearview mirror and saw an athletic figure in navy blue pants and shirt, possibly a uniform, stride down the sidewalk from the direction of the door. Briskly, he crossed the street, got into a nondescript Ford, and drove away.

El swung the pickup's door shut again and sat there a moment, considering. The man could have been a cop, but he wasn't wearing the tan uniform of the RCMP. Maybe he was a fireman, or just a security guard on his way to work. She hadn't seen him standing at the door as she drove past, so he must have been around the back or even inside. Could he have been a gas or hydro-electric employee? Not likely. A visitor to the home, friend or relative of Greg Williams or his wife? Maybe. Which would mean someone was home.

Curiosity got the better of her, and, taking a clipboard with her as a small measure of disguise, she walked purposefully up to the door and knocked. There was no answer, so she knocked again, banging with her fist. "Hello! Anybody home?" she called in her best foghorn voice. Still no answer, so she rattled the knob and was surprised to find the door unlocked. She stuck her head in the door and hollered again, "Hello there! Anybody home?" There was silence.

She wondered if Hunter had been mistaken, or if she had heard him right. He'd said that Williams had a common-law wife, but this apartment was a mess, not typical of a woman at all, in her experience. Books and papers were spread all over the living room floor beside a plank and brick bookcase, and the bare wooden frame of a futon couch was pulled out from the wall, the futon itself propped crookedly behind it. CD's and CD holders were scattered like a deck of cards in front of a black metal stereo stand. She heard water running through the pipes, as though a toilet had flushed. "Hello?" she called again. When there was no answer, she walked across the living room, picking her way through books and sheet music to a small kitchen.

The kitchen, too, was a mess. At her elbow, a ceramic cookie jar in the shape of a teddy bear was lying on its side, threatening to roll off the counter, so she righted it before it occurred to her that this was no ordinary lived-in mess. Cupboard doors were open and drawers pulled out, their contents dumped on the counters and the table. The apartment had been tossed. Either the place had been burgled, or someone had been looking for something. She thought back to the figure she'd seen leaving the property, and began to wonder if it had been a cop. Maybe he'd been called in by a neighbor reporting the break in. In any case, she didn't feel comfortable being here.

"What the hell am I doing?" she said aloud. Carefully, she lay the cookie jar back on its side the way she'd found it and took one last brief look around at the mess, then headed for the door. She was half the way down the sidewalk when a small Honda pulled up against the curb and a young woman with spiky red hair got out. Standing at the driver's door and leaning across the roof of the car, she looked El up and down through narrowed eyes and asked, "You looking for somebody?"

El lifted up her clipboard, glanced at the blank waybill on top, and said, "Yeah. I'm supposed to pick up a box of personal effects to ship to Winnipeg. You know anything about it?"

"From who?" the woman asked, not hiding her suspicion.

"Uh... ." El glanced at the clipboard again. "It just says 7135 Elwell."

"You're on the wrong street." From her tone of voice, the woman might as well have added, "Stupid".

"Oh. No wonder there's nobody home." El saluted, smiled innocently, and continued walking. "Thanks, eh?"

The woman continued to stare at her until she'd turned onto the sidewalk. "Elwell's that way." The voice scraped like a rasp against the back of El's neck.

El stopped, looked over her shoulder. She'd had enough of this woman, whoever she was. "No shit?" she said, not expecting an answer, and not getting one. Checking her rearview mirror as she turned the key in the ignition, El could see the woman still watching until she drove away.

"I'm hoping to see Ray again while I'm here."

"I'm the detective collecting evidence against your buddy, not his social director," said Russell into the telephone receiver. "Talk to his lawyer." Hunter Rayne's call had come just as Russell had finished going over the notes he had taken during his last phone conversation with the RCMP.

"I'll be seeing Mr. Feldman later," said Rayne, "but if you've got a few minutes, I'd like to talk to you first."

"I'll give you three." Russell checked his watch, then leaned back in his chair, stretching his back. "So. Talk."

"I'm in your building. I thought maybe we could sit down together. Maybe I could buy you a coffee or something."

"Why?" Russell said before he realized that he could answer his own question. He had a niggling feeling about this guy, a feeling that Rayne's interest in the results of this investigation went beyond concern for a friend. He might have more of a stake in it than he was willing to let on. Why not give him a chance to say or do something that would tip his hand?

"I was working on the investigation with Al Kowalski of the Burnaby RCMP on the weekend. I'm might have some information you can use."

"Whose side are you on, anyway?"

"I'm on the side of the truth."

Russell doubted that, but agreed to meet him in the parking lot, and as he shrugged into his suit jacket, he shook his head at the irony of it. This guy figured that he could help his buddy Nillson by

143

helping Russell and the RCMP? There was something wrong with that picture. The man was either absurdly naive, or consummately devious. According to Russell's earlier conversation with Al Kowalski, Rayne had been a first rate detective, a dedicated one, and highly thought of in his department. Then why the hell did he quit? Why would anybody quit being a detective to become a fuckin' truck driver?

"You won't tell me why you wanted to become a trucker, so tell me why the hell you wanted to quit being a cop?" Russell asked when the two of them sat down across from each other at a table in Starbucks.

Rayne's jaw stiffened and he nodded slightly. "It was just time," he said, their eyes locking.

Russell waited for him to go on, but he didn't. "And now," he suggested, "you're tired of being a truck driver and want to be a cop again, right?"

The trucker ignored the comment, asking instead, "Have you talked to Al Kowalski in the last couple of days?"

"Yeah. I've talked to Kowalski."

"He told you about our experiment with the trailer?"

"Yeah. What does it prove?" Russell stirred the whipped cream and powdered chocolate into his cappucino.

"It proves that the drivers wouldn't have heard the man calling for help if he'd been locked in there accidentally, or by someone else."

"We've been over this, Rayne. That story would be a hell of a lot more credible if it had come from your buddy himself... at the same time he reported finding the body."

The trucker nodded his head in reluctant agreement. He poured sugar into his coffee. "I saw them in Oregon the day before and they were relaxed and happy. According to a man in the Anaheim warehouse, when they arrived to deliver the freight they were visibly upset. I still believe they didn't know he was in the trailer until it was too late." When Russell responded with a shrug, Rayne asked, "Anything on the padlock?"

"No damage, no sign of tampering, if that's what you're asking, which is another reason why it's hard to swallow your version of
144

events." Russell wanted to let Rayne do most of the talking. Without being too obvious about it, he wanted to goad him into saying something Russell could use against him or his friends. "Yeah, somebody could have picked the lock or Nillson could have forgotten to secure it at the border or something. If that's the case, why don't your innocent friends say so? It's not up to me to come up with their defense."

"No, but like any good cop, you're anticipating their defense so you can plug the holes in your investigation before the case comes to trial."

That was almost a compliment, and Russell was pleased in spite of himself. "So if you've thought this all out, how do you explain the fact that Sharon Nillson knew the victim and didn't admit it?"

Rayne sipped at his coffee, put down the cup. "Scared to admit it, is my guess."

"Hah. Weak."

"What about the car?"

"What about the car?"

"The car was found some fifty miles inside the United States border. The Nillson's trailer was loaded in Burnaby. I don't see how the location of the car supports a case against Ray."

Russell laughed, licking whipped cream off his upper lip. "You got your nerve, you know that? Why the hell should I share the prosecution's theories with you? You're about to toddle over to visit Feldman, and help him shore up his case with information you expect to pick up from me?"

Rayne wore a little smile, as if he had a secret, but Russell could see his jaw working. He could tell that his jab hit home, that he was pushing Rayne's buttons.

"I can understand your frustration," said Rayne. "It can't be easy for you, with your witnesses a thousand miles away. You have to rely on what the RCMP tells you."

Russell was surprised that there was no sign of anger in the trucker's voice. "I hope to remedy that soon," he said.

"That's good. That'll give you a better feel for the victim, interviewing the witnesses directly. If you're like me, your gut instincts work better when you're face to face."

"You got that right. And I've been face to face with Ray Nillson and his wife a couple of times now," said Russell. "My gut's pretty sure they did it."

"I admire your confidence, especially since you know how carefully you've got to dot your i's and cross your t's if the prosecutor expects to make a case that'll stand up to a lawyer the caliber of Jeff Feldman."

At the mention of Feldman's name, Russell put down his cappuccino, said nothing. The trucker had said nothing overtly offensive, but Russell felt his anger rising.

"I've never met Sharon's lawyer, Alora Magee. What's she like?" asked Rayne.

"Low profile, unlike your friend, Feldman, a lawyer of such high caliber that his main objective in taking on this case was the publicity."

"Didn't he tell me that you and he were old school friends?"

Russell snorted. "Going to school together didn't make us friends. You know, sometimes I have trouble picturing you as a cop. Are you always this naive?"

"Yes." Rayne half smiled. "I guess I am."

Russell snorted. "Yes. Yes. What are you? A fuckin' army private?" he said irritably. "Can't you ever say 'yeah' like everybody else?"

"Sure. If I wanted to."

"Once a Mountie, always a Mountie." Russell wasn't getting any satisfaction from this conversation, and decided it was time to terminate it. He drained the last of his cappuccino, then said, "I guess you haven't spoken to Feldman recently."

"Why do you say that?" asked Rayne, getting to his feet.

"Because," said Russell, with a smug smile. "He's so worried about losing the case, he's threatening to drop your friend as a client."

146

CHAPTER
FOURTEEN

When Hunter entered his office, Jeff Feldman was sitting behind a pile of books with his jacket off and his sleeves rolled up, could have passed for a college student except for the huge oak desk. He tossed his pen lightly onto a yellow legal pad and stood up to shake Hunter's hand. "Thanks for coming in," he said. "I hope you've got some information for me, because I can use all the help I can get on your friend's case."

Hunter pulled up a leather-upholstered chair and sat down. "I hear you're not too happy with your client," he said.

"I guess you could say that. I'm not getting anything from him, except for continual requests to speak with his wife. And with you."

"With me?"

"He's pinning a lot of hope on you. And none on me. I'm just his lawyer. I'm just the shmuck who has to present his case in court. You, you're the white knight crusading against the dragon." He laughed. "I can't get through to him. I'd hate to admit I've come up against a case I can't even manufacture, let alone win, but I've got better things to do than to butt heads with a reluctant client. If I wanted that kind of client, I would've gone to work for the public defender's office."

"I wish I could help."

"Maybe you can. I don't have time to take you there this afternoon, but I'm due for a phone call to see if Ray's decided to tell me anything. You game to try talking to him again?"

"Sure. Thanks." It was what Hunter had been hoping for.

"Maybe if you can get him to talk to you about what happened - if you can get him to say anything at all - it'll put a hole in the dike and he'll start talking to me." Jeff picked up the phone and dialed.

It took a while for him to get Ray on the line, so Hunter gave Jeff a rundown of what he'd found out in Burnaby, the speculation that the victim and his friends had been involved with drugs, and the fact that Williams' car had been found in Washington state. Jeff jotted a few things down as they talked. Once Ray was on the phone, Jeff handed the receiver across the desk to Hunter.

"Have you found out who did it yet?" Ray asked.

"No, I haven't, Ray, and you're not helping matters by withholding information. Why didn't you tell us that you and Sharon knew the victim?"

There was silence on the other end of the line.

"Did you think the police wouldn't find out?"

"I just hoped, I guess," he said.

"And now the police have found the victim's car near the I-5 in Mount Vernon, Washington. You have anything to say about that?" Hunter paused, but again, silence. "I hope we don't find out tomorrow that the police found your fingerprints all over it. If you know anything about it, speak up now. If you're innocent, you've got everything to gain and nothing to lose by telling me the truth. This time no one from the sheriff's department or the prosecutor's office, not even your lawyer is listening in. It's just you and me this time, Ray."

Ray cleared his throat. "I'm sorry, Hunter. If I knew for sure that talking to you or to anyone would help us... help Sharon... but I don't know who I can trust. I know I can't talk to the police, and from what I know of lawyers... Well, I just can't take the chance. People like that twist things around. I can't play those games, Hunter. I can't think fast enough. I just can't take the chance."

148

"You do realize that it looks worse when you lie, or conceal facts? Have you thought of that?"

"Of course I've thought of it. It's eating away at me, not knowing what to do."

"How do you expect Jeff to prepare your case? How do you expect him to be able to prove your innocence?"

"I thought the police, or you, would find evidence that somebody else might have done it. I really hoped..."

Hunter sighed. "Will you work with me now? We'll take it one step at a time. Where did Williams get in your trailer? Mount Vernon?"

"I don't know."

"Assuming you didn't put him there, when did you find out he was there?"

Silence.

"Ray? Did you hear me? When did you find out Williams was in your trailer?"

"I'm afraid..."

"Afraid of what, Ray?"

"I'm sorry, Hunter. I'm afraid I just can't tell you right now."

"Are you saying that he wasn't in your trailer? The evidence is pretty clear-cut, Ray. You're making it harder on yourself by denying it."

"I said, I can't tell you." His voice was monotone, almost dead.

"What *can* you tell me?" Hunter was beginning to feel frustrated.

"If you can't find out who did it," said Ray, "I'll say whatever they want me to say if they'll just let Sharon go."

"We've been over this ground before. If you're thinking about confessing just to get Sharon out of jail, you're throwing away your future, yours and Sharon's both. She won't thank you for that, Ray, letting yourself get jailed for something you didn't do."

"I've got to go now, Hunter."

"Do you understand me, Ray?" said Hunter, but the line was already dead. "I don't get it," he said to Jeff as he handed back the telephone receiver. "He's not a stupid man. Why is he being so stubborn about this?" He exhaled, shaking his head in disbelief, then held up his hand. "No, you don't have to tell me. He's protecting his wife. What does she have to say?"

Jeff shrugged. "For that," he said, "you'll have to ask Alora Magee."

"What's missing?" the police officer had asked. When Hellen had arrived home to evidence of a break-in, she had immediately called both Teresa and the RCMP. Teresa was home before the police arrived. When neither she nor Hellen could answer the constable's question, he said, "Go through your belongings and see if anything's been taken."

Teresa stood at the door of the bedroom, felt the energy drain from her shoulders through her hips and disappear through her heels. Splotches of white fingerprinting powder mottled the varnished surface of the chest of drawers; its round brass knobs were dusted with soot. She fought an urge to walk away, close the door behind her, and never come back. What were they looking for? How would she ever know what was stolen?

What if what was stolen was another of Greg's secrets? She didn't know what he did at night when she was asleep. Sometimes she would hear him come in from his gig, hear him rustle in the kitchen, hear the sounds of voices on the TV in the living room, then hear the click of the back door. What was he doing outside in the dark? What if he owned something that was worth lots of money and never told her about it? His old record albums? His CD's? His sheet music? He had tons of sheet music, things he'd written himself. She would never know if some of it was missing. She would never know if it was worth anything. Could some of it be valuable? Was some of it stolen? How would she ever know?

She started with the closet. Boots and shoes littered the floor outside it, so she knelt and began to sort through them, at first placing Greg's in one neat row, hers in another. Then, picking up one of Greg's old ragged sneakers by the laces, she got to her feet and searched the room, looking for a place to put it. His shoes didn't belong in her closet any longer. Her eyes kept coming back to the
150

waterbed. Greg's waterbed. She tossed the sneakers, one after another, watching the fat ripples of their landing lift the edges of the quilt, remembering how, in the early hours of morning, Greg would get into bed and she would rise and fall, her eyes closed tight, rise and fall, pretending not to have wakened, rise and fall, until he'd become still. She thought of the times, just hours before she had to get up for work, when he had crawled into bed and wrapped his arms around her from behind, his naked skin cold against her own, his breath over her shoulder smelling of marijuana and beer. She would pretend to be asleep when he moved his hips against her, and the feel of his erection would stir a desire in her that she struggled to ignore. The bed would go, she decided. The waterbed would definitely go.

Her clothing, picked up from the floor of the closet and shaken out, went back on hangers, which she spaced evenly from one end of the chrome bar to the other. Greg's shirts and pants, his two jeans jackets, one frayed at the cuffs and one still inky with blue dye, landed on top of the shoes on the bed. Was any of Greg's clothing missing? She couldn't tell. She remembered what he'd been wearing in the photograph the police had shown her, the photo with his eyes closed and his skin the color of yogurt. The blue and green striped polo shirt he'd bought at Value Village. It angered her that he had died in a second hand shirt.

Teresa slid the closet door shut, then faced the chest of drawers and squared her shoulders. Some of the clothing had been strewn on the floor, and some trailed out of the half open drawers like weeds between cracks in the sidewalk. The top drawer was where she kept her panties and nighties and brassieres. The intruder, whoever he was, had pawed through them. Even if it meant staying up half the night at the laundromat and being sleepy at her keyboard tomorrow, she'd have to wash them all before she put them away again. She dragged over the hamper and opened the lid. Inside were Greg's black jeans and his green shirt and a pair of his socks. She stared at them for a full minute, then picked up the hamper and shook it over the waterbed.

"What are you doing?" Hellen stood in the doorway, a hairbrush in her hand.

"There's no point in putting Greg's clothes away." Teresa pulled out the drawer still half full of Greg's underwear and socks and dumped it out onto the growing pile on the waterbed. "I'm cleaning out his things."

"What are you going to do with them?"

Teresa struggled to pull the little drawer out of Greg's night table. It contained nothing but junk, as far as she could tell: guitar picks, an extra steel tube for playing slide guitar, business cards and snatches of song written on napkins and scraps of paper. Once worth nothing to anyone but Greg, and now, worth nothing even to him. When she'd first moved in with Hellen, her brothers had helped her move the few pieces of furniture she had bought. She couldn't ask them for help moving the waterbed out. She couldn't let them guess that she had been living with Greg as man and wife. She dumped the contents of the night table drawer onto the waterbed, and said, "I'll put it in bags for the Salvation Army, and call them to pick up the bed."

Hellen just stood there, watching Teresa work, and languidly running the hair brush through her short hair. Teresa wondered if she would ask for the bed. If she does, Teresa thought, I will chop it into small pieces and burn it. "Did you find anything missing in your room?" she asked.

"No," said Hellen. She stepped inside the room and nudged a sweatshirt, one of Greg's, with her toe. "Whoever it was sure made a mess but I can't think of anything that's missing, can you?" She picked up the sweatshirt and held it out to inspect it.

Teresa shook her head.

"It gives me the creeps, thinking that Greg's murderer might have been here, going through our stuff," said Hellen. "I wonder who that fat woman was. I can't picture her as the murderer, but you never know."

Teresa didn't want to think about it. She took a deep breath and covered her face with her hands, trying to keep from telling Hellen to shut up and go away.

"Poor Jag. All this has been so awful for you." Hellen said, putting a hand on Teresa's shoulder. "Where will you sleep tonight?" She pulled Teresa close in a hug. "You can sleep with me if you like."

152

Teresa pulled away. "No, Hellen. I'll be fine."

Hellen shrugged. "This is a nice sweatshirt," she said, holding it up against her chest.

"Yes," said Teresa, taking it from her. She stood there stiffly, waiting for Hellen to leave.

Hellen smiled, then raised the hair brush and resumed brushing her hair. "I think I'll put on the kettle," she said, "for tea."

When she had gone, Teresa looked around the room. "What's missing?" the police officer had asked her. What would he say if she told him the truth? What would he say if she told him, "It was me. I was missing from this room. I'd moved over so far to make room for Greg that there was hardly anything of me left." She hadn't recognized how little was left of her in here until after Greg was gone. She smiled to herself as she used Greg's sweatshirt to wipe the fingerprint powder off the brass knobs of the chest of drawers, then dropped the sweatshirt on top of the pile on the bed.

She'd moved over for Greg, and that was a mistake. She wasn't going to move over again now for Hellen.

Hunter took the Overland exit off the Santa Monica freeway and had no trouble finding the Italian restaurant Alora Magee had picked for their meeting. As he drove slowly into the lot beside it, looking for a suitable place to park the Freightliner, a dark haired woman wearing khaki walking shorts and a white shirt got out of a small black Audi and flagged him to a large parking spot behind the building. By the time he had turned off the engine and opened the door, she was standing beside the truck with her hand stuck out.

"Hi," she said, smiling. "You must be Hunter. I'm Alora Magee." Her handshake was firm, her hand neither cool nor warm. He liked her instantly. "Where's the rest of your truck?" she asked.

"I left the trailer at the truck stop. Parking this thing is enough of a challenge." He prepared to close the door, but she stopped him with a hand on his arm.

"I've always wondered what it felt like to drive one of these mothers," she said. "You mind if I look inside?"

153

"Be my guest."

She climbed into the driver's seat and sat there, her hands on the wheel and a grin on her face. "Cool," she said, laughing. "Do I look like a trucker?"

"About as much as you look like a lawyer."

"I'm not what you expected?"

"To tell you the truth, I didn't give it much thought." And he hadn't, but for some reason it surprised him that she was so informal and friendly. She seemed self-assured and uncomplicated, as straight-ahead and cloudless as a spring wind.

"I did," she said. "You look a lot like I expected, based on what Sharon said about you."

He raised his eyebrows. "She told you what I look like?"

She frowned, wrinkling her nose. "Not exactly. She said you were a really nice man but that most people didn't want to mess with you. I figured that put you somewhere between Roy Rogers and Charles Bronson."

"Old guys. You got that part right."

"Old? You? Well, maybe mature." She clambered down out of the truck, and he climbed back inside, pulled the Wal-Mart bag El had given him out from under the passenger seat.

"Before I forget," he said, handing it to her, "here's a care package for Sharon."

Alora reached in and pulled out one of the books. She held it up so they could both see the cover and looked at him sideways, a smile dimpling one cheek. "Forbidden Desire?"

Hunter coughed and looked away. "They're not from me."

"That's what they all say," she said with a laugh. She opened to a random page and cleared her throat. "Jasmine could feel the muscles of his back through the wet fabric of her nightgown. She felt her nipples tingle and harden, and she buried her face in his neck, hoping desperately that he couldn't feel the heat of her unbidden desire," she read. "Whew!" She fanned her face with the book. "Hot stuff."

Hunter could feel himself begin to blush, made himself think of something else. "Did Sharon tell you she knew the victim?"

154

Alora looked sideways at him again, her eyebrows rising lightly, as if she recognized his discomfort and found it amusing. "No. It appears she's taken a vow of silence when it comes to the case. She won't say much of anything." She paused, frowning. "Do you have any idea why?"

"Yes," he said. "That's exactly what Ray's doing. It seems to me that he's refusing to say anything at all rather than take the risk of saying something that might incriminate his wife, and my guess is she's doing the same to protect her husband."

Alora slapped the book lightly against her thigh. "You sure these aren't yours?" she asked slyly. "That's a pretty romantic notion you've come up with, for this day and age."

"I guess I'm old fashioned," he said.

"I guess you are." She dropped the book back into the bag, pulled out a manila envelope. "What's this?"

"I don't know. It's from El."

"El?"

"My dispatcher, Elspeth Watson. You spoke to her, I believe."

She nodded. "Of course," she said, sliding an enlarged photograph out of the envelope. "Peaches!" she said with delight, looking up at him for confirmation. "Sharon will be happy to have this. She told me about Peaches."

"El's got a soft spot for yappy little dogs. She has one of her own."

"These books are El's, too?"

"I guess so."

"From her voice, I'd pictured her more as a woman who'd own a Rottweiler and read Stephen King. Someone tried to interrupt while she was on the phone to me, and she swore like a longshoreman."

Hunter laughed softly. "El's one of a kind."

Alora Magee looked at him sideways again. "You really like her, don't you?" she said, slipping the photo back into the envelope.

He crossed his arms, leaned back against the Blue Knight's fender. "You don't waste any time getting personal, do you?"

She looked embarrassed, and it surprised him.

"Just kidding," he said. "Yes, I like her. We're good friends." He had on occasion admitted to himself that over the last few years El had become his closest friend. He felt the familiar shadow pass over his heart as the image of Ken Marsh came to mind, a friend whose death had never ceased to haunt him with guilt and regrets. Ken had been the closest friend he'd ever had, and he didn't expect to have another friend like that again. He pushed Ken's image away. "I make it a rule to stay on the good side of any woman who weighs more than I do," he added, and immediately regretted it. He felt as if he were betraying El.

Alora laughed. "Swears like a longshoreman and is built like one too, huh?"

He was grateful to her for seeing it that way. "And proud of it," he added with a grin.

"You know, many people would have said swears like a trucker, rather than a longshoreman. I would have..." She openly looked him up and down. "... until today." Before he had time to speak, she said, "Let's go eat," turned on her heel, and walked away.

Russell had been just about to put on his jacket and head home. Not home, exactly. He figured he had time for a quick workout and a shower, then he was planning to pick up a bottle of red wine, maybe even a Stonestreet cabernet, change into something sexy, and go to Jennifer's for pasta. She was only in town for the night, and had invited him over for linguini putanesca with capers and anchovies. He was looking forward to a fine spicy evening for the first time in two weeks. He didn't know when Jennifer would be back again, so he was prepared to make the most of it.

Then the phone rang. A shooting in a high school parking lot during a junior league baseball game on the school diamond. "The DOA's a sixteen year old kid," said the officer on the scene.

"Fuck!" said Russell, slamming down the receiver. "Fuck! Fuck!" He shrugged on his jacket and headed for the car.

He drove to an upscale neighborhood in Glendale, a high school that Russell had quarterbacked a football game at almost half a

156

lifetime ago. The coroner's investigator was already there. "Glad you could make it," he said, glancing up from where he squatted next to the victim. The boy's body was slumped against the rear wheel of a car, one arm clutched to his stomach. His shirt was a collage of colors, under laid with dark circles of blood that stretched from underneath his chin to the crotch of his jeans. "No mystery where this homicide occurred," said the investigator, bracing his hand on one knee to get to his feet. "C'mon guys. Let's finish with the pictures so I can look under his shirt."

The photographer moved in, and Russell and the investigator stood aside.

"You're the detective handling the Iceman homicide, right? I heard you've got someone in custody. How come the body's still in our cooler?"

"The deceased is from out of state. There's a hold up getting the official I.D."

"What kind of hold up?"

"The RCMP says the position of next of kin is in question. The wife reported him missing, but the brother says she's got no right. Common law relationship," explained Russell. "Gross, huh? Fighting over possession of a corpse." He made a disgusted face, then noticed a beckoning gesture from one of the first officers on the scene, who had been canvassing the crowd for witnesses. As Russell walked toward the police cruiser, he noticed a TV news truck pull into the parking lot and swore under his breath.

"Couple of kids witnessed the shooting," said the officer, meeting him half way and pointing to the back seat of the cruiser. The cop glanced over toward the body, then snorted and shook his head, as if he still couldn't believe what he was seeing.

The two girls in the back seat of the police car, slender and pale and wearing tight-ribbed sweaters and blue jeans, held each other and whispered back and forth as Russell approached. He sat sideways on the front passenger seat with the door open, listened to what they had to say. Evidently the victim, who they referred to as Pellegrino, had been a bully, and earlier that week had stolen a Bulls cap from a younger student named Ashton.

"So, like, Marnie has this big crush on Ashton..." Here Marnie covered her face and slouched further into the seat. "... so we were, like, following him to see where he was going when he left the game, but, like, we didn't want him to see us or anything, and he was acting real nervous, like, looking over his shoulder and stuff, and he went over there behind that truck, and didn't come out again." She pointed to a truck parked next to the car where the body was. "I guess because it was parked beside Pelligrino's car."

So they'd hung back, waiting to see where Ashton was going, and finally Pellegrino had come out to his car, stuck the keys in the front door. Pelligrino had turned around, as though Ashton had said something, but the girls couldn't hear what, and then they heard the shots and saw Pellegrino grab his stomach as if he'd been kicked. "He had, like, this real surprised look on his face, and then he walked a couple of steps, then fell back against the car. We just screamed." They hugged each other tighter. Marnie started to cry.

"So you didn't actually see this Ashton do the shooting."

"No, but we knew he was there."

"Did you see him after the shooting?"

"No. We just started to run, you know?" She glanced out the open door, did a double take, her eyes widening. "Look! There's Ashton with his dad."

Russell looked through the windshield of the police cruiser at a small group of people who had approached a uniformed officer. A boy of about fourteen, tall and slender with a square jaw and a blond shock of hair falling across his forehead, stood downcast beside an older man wearing the pants of an expensive suit with a light windbreaker, as if he'd come home from work and not had time to change his clothes. With one hand, the man gripped the boy by the elbow.

"Here's Detective Kupka now," the uniformed officer said to them as Russell approached, then turned to Russell and spoke in a low voice. "This is Mr. Everett Slocum and the boy is his son, Ashton. Mr. Slocum caught his son trying to sneak a .38 back into its hiding place in the closet. When confronted, the boy confessed to shooting the victim. He said the victim had stolen his ball cap."

158

Russell saw that Slocum was holding a Bulls cap in his free hand. The boy stood meekly at his side, his shoulders drooping in a posture of complete resignation.

The kid reminded Russell of himself at fourteen. He remembered how his gut had twisted when a Neanderthal senior had taunted him after a fumble his first time on the field. Cupcake, he called him. That Cupcake is a loser. Cupcake is a bum. Cupcake has butter on his fingers, get that pansy off the field. If he'd been unlucky enough to have had a gun, he would've shot the bastard. He couldn't help feeling sorry for the boy. Why had his father brought him here? He should have contacted a lawyer.

Before he had time to ask any questions, Russell heard a man's voice from behind his shoulder. "Don't say anything, Everett. Don't let Ashton say anything."

Russell set his jaw and spun around. It was Feldman.

"What the fuck are you doing here?" Russell asked.

"My client," said Feldman to Russell, nodding toward the boy, then addressed the boy's father. "I called as soon as I got your page, and Lisa told me where you were. I wish you'd waited to talk to me before you brought him down here." To the boy, he said, "Ashton. How's it goin', buddy? I'll be your attorney. I'll try to make things as easy as possible for you, but you're going to have to go through some very unpleasant moments until we can get you remanded to your father's custody. Stay cool, and don't talk to anybody about what happened. Nothin' but your name, rank, and serial number. Got that?" He punched the boy lightly in the shoulder. "That's my man."

"There are witnesses. I already know what happened," said Russell. "Did you bring the gun?" he asked Slocum.

Slocum looked to Feldman.

"Wait here a moment, Everett," he said, laying a hand on the man's shoulder. "I'd like to talk to the detective first."

He guided Russell about twenty feet away. "Everett Slocum is my neighbor," he said. "In his distress, he followed his first impulse to bring his son here and make a clean breast of it. The boy needs help, not punishment. You'll get the gun. You don't need to bully them to get their cooperation. Above all, we don't want this to turn into a media circus, so I'd appreciate it if you could escort the boy out of here immediately, with as much compassion as you can muster. He's not a criminal. He's just a kid who was bullied to the breaking point."

"Shit, Feldman," said Russell. "You out of your mind? You're screaming police brutality and all I did was look at the kid." He saw Feldman's glance take in the TV van. "Say, you really lucked out. Two media cases in the space of a month. You must be on cloud nine."

Feldman shook his head, a crooked smile on his face. "Believe what you want, Russell. These people are my friends, and not a damn thing about this incident is lucky, not for me, not for him, and not for the victim." He turned to walk away, then swung back with a frown, and added, "I don't know what kind of sophomoric grudge you've got against me or why, but have the decency not to let it affect how you behave toward that poor kid."

Fifteen minutes later, the crime scene unit in place and doing their job, Russell escorted the boy, Ashton Slocum, to a waiting police cruiser. Another TV news van had arrived, so there were now two cameras following their progress, microphones thrust toward Russell's face. Keeping his head down, he hurried the boy past them and ignored questions from the reporters. When the boy was safely secured in the back seat, Russell waved the cruiser away and headed toward his own vehicle. The cameras and microphones had disappeared, and as he stepped into his car, he saw why. Jeff Feldman, looking impeccable in his Armani suit, was giving them a sound byte.

"Asshole," muttered Russell. Who was Feldman calling sophomoric? Russell's evening was ruined. He'd be tied up for hours. Jennifer was leaving for Vancouver again tomorrow and God knows when he'd see her again. He was genuinely sorry about the kid. It wasn't his fault that he had a publicity seeking legal weasel for a neighbor.

Russell burned rubber leaving the scene.

CHAPTER
FIFTEEN

Alora secured both deadbolts, then the chain latch. She looked at her watch. It was only eight fifteen. Good. An early night. She could go to bed with the new Connelly novel she'd been looking forward to. Right. Good thing the evening had ended early. Sure. That's what she tried to tell herself.

She had been prepared to like Hunter Rayne. Right off, she'd liked his voice over the telephone. Then when she heard from Elspeth Watson that he was a retired RCMP detective and was investigating Sharon's case on his own time, purely out of friendship, she'd wondered at first whether he was just a busybody flake, but from the way El and Sharon talked about him, she'd soon begun to picture him as some kind of Lone Ranger, a crusader for justice and the rights of the downtrodden. Yes, she'd set herself up. She'd let her imagination turn him into a hero, a possible savior, not only for her client, but for herself.

When he said the Nillsons were each saying nothing in their own defense in order to protect the other, she'd kidded him about being a romantic. Hah. Who was she kidding? As it turned out, *she* was the romantic one.

She kicked her sandals off into the closet, nudged them straight with a bare toe, then stripped off her tailored shirt and shorts, replacing them with sloppy cotton sweats. She had honestly believed that Hunter Rayne liked her, too. He was friendly and warm. They'd talked about the Nillsons, about California, and about the mountains in British Columbia. They'd compared notes on their respective professions: lawyering versus driving up and down the interstate. He told her he was divorced and had two grown daughters, and she told him she was single and disillusioned with dating so she was trusting her future love life to fate. Had she sounded desperate? She meant to sound nonchalant, and thought she'd succeeded. They'd laughed about it, anyway.

Alora padded barefoot to the kitchen, pulled a club soda from the fridge and mixed it with orange juice and ice. The drink in her hand, she slid open the door to the balcony, stepped outside and leaned against the railing. This was all the tiny balcony was good for, leaning against the railing and sipping a drink. Although the sky was still pale, with a broad streak on the horizon the color of cantaloupe, the lights of the city had begun to stand out, shivering in the dusk. She'd moved to the high-rise after the dog died. She felt safe from her ex-husband here, but captive, like Rapunzel in the tower, waiting for someone to rescue her from her prison of fear. Maybe she would let go of her fear if there was a man she could trust to protect her. Maybe she *was* desperate.

She went back inside and picked up her book, then settled into the corner of the sofa, her feet tucked underneath her, but she didn't turn on the light. They had been finishing their wine, snug in the candle glow, leaning on their elbows into the flow of talk that washed back and forth across the table. She felt comfortable with him, sure of his good will.

"That's a beautiful ring," she said. "Can I see it?"

"I can't take it off without soap," he said, tugging on it gently to make his point.

She reached her hand across the table with a come hither wiggle to her fingers. "I just want a closer look," she said. "What is that stone? I've never seen one reflect the light like that. It's magical."

"It's a star sapphire," he said, laying his hand flat on the table.

She picked up his hand, feeling a small thrill at the warmth of his skin. She turned his hand this way and that in front of the candle,

162

admiring the play of light inside the round stone. "Nice," she said, looking up at him, but not letting go of his hand.

"Thanks," he said, gently pulling away. Pulling his hand away, and pulling himself away.

"You really are old fashioned, aren't you?" she said.

He cleared his throat to reply, but only shrugged. Pulling away, further away. Sitting up straight, and looking around for the waiter, and signaling for the check.

Alora put her drink on the side table and clicked on the light. She opened the book and stared at the first page. He thought she was coming on to him. He must have. And maybe she was, but why did he pull away? Was it something about her? She chided herself for being so sensitive. It's about him, obviously. He could be involved with someone else. Maybe he has some kind of rule, a code of ethics that doesn't allow him to get involved with women outside of his hometown. They talk about sailors having a girl in every port. What about truck drivers? He wouldn't be like that.

Alora sighed. Yeah. What about truck drivers? In the past five years she'd dated two medical doctors, two marketing executives, one college professor and even a judge. Why on earth had she even entertained the notion of getting romantically involved with a man who drives a truck for a living?

"A moment of insanity on my part," she said aloud. "Thank God the man had the good sense to pull away."

It was not yet nine o'clock in Burnaby, and sunset was still half an hour away. El Watson had parked her Ford pickup, twelve years old and robin's egg blue, on Still Creek Avenue about a block away from what Greg Williams had called Whistlestop Studios. She'd already driven past the address, and discovered that the building which housed the studio was set back from the street behind another warehouse, and that her pick up would be conspicuous parked in that lot at this time of day, now that most of the businesses were closed. She clicked a thumbnail against a front tooth, considering her course of action.

She had gone home after work, fed and walked the dogs, then fed herself and tried to watch TV. She couldn't sit still, her mind doing loops around the implications of what she'd seen at Williams' house earlier in the day. The fact that the place had been turned upside down was a critical development. With Ray and Sharon both in jail in California, how were the police going to explain away the fact that someone else was more than a little interested in the dead man's possessions? Even if evidence proved that the man had died in the Nillsons' trailer, it didn't necessarily follow that they were the ones who put him there.

She had sat on the couch, the dogs fighting over her lap, and stared at the phone, willing Hunter to call. She wished he would keep his cell phone activated on the road so that she could call him, but he said he didn't make enough money to allow his dispatcher that convenience. Well, shit, she'd decided, shooing the dogs off her lap. If she couldn't talk to someone about it, if she couldn't do something about it, she was going to bust just sitting around home. At least she could stake out Williams' studio and try to find out more about the guy. So here she was.

El turned the key and the Ford shuddered back to life. Musicians probably wouldn't pay much attention to a dirty pickup truck parked in an industrial section. Hunter had made it clear that he wanted to be the one to deliver the equipment she'd picked up from Fraser's Dock, so she wasn't going to screw things up by going inside, but what if she just parked close enough to have a view of the door? She decided to go for it.

She drove into the yard in front of the building and backed the Ford up to one of the doors in the adjacent warehouse, a spot that was already in shadow. There was an old Chevy Blazer, a metallic brown, parked outside the ground level door of the studio, and the lights were on upstairs. She turned off the ignition and slumped down in her seat. Through the open window of the truck, she could hear the thrum of a base guitar and the rhythmic thud of drums, broken now and then by a frantic tattoo, but she could see nothing except what might have been the top of someone's head moving around, then dropping from sight and reappearing. The drummer? It told her nothing.

The first hour went by excruciatingly slow. The daylight disappeared, and she felt more secure in the darkness. She tried to think of what Hunter might do, but had to admit that she didn't have a clue. Maybe it came from years of experience, but Hunter always seemed to know what to do, and made it sound like common sense. Uncommon sense was more like it. Some of the drivers gravitated to him for advice, others found him downright spooky. She looked at her watch. If the musicians were to leave, should she follow them? Should she sneak around the back onto the railroad tracks to see if she could get a better view? She rummaged under the seat for a flashlight, turned it on but it was dead. Scratch that idea. Instead, she popped the top on a can of Coke and placed it on the console beside her, then tore open a bag of ripple chips. Between crunches the sound of thunder, she could hear the fizzing of the cola, and the soft ebb and flow of the music from the warehouse, and the distant swish of traffic on Highway 1, and her own slow breathing, and she fell asleep.

She woke with a start to the sound of a slamming door. Her neck was stiff and her feet were cold and her bladder was uncomfortably full. Then she heard the whine of the Blazer's engine coming to life, and ducked down behind the dashboard just as its lights came on. She pushed the button on her watch to illuminate the dial and saw that it was almost two o'clock. "Shit!" she swore, knowing that she couldn't start up and follow the Blazer at this time of night without them knowing where she'd come from. When she looked up, she saw a taillight disappear around the end of the second warehouse, heading for Still Creek. "Shit!" she said again, then looked up at the studio windows. They were dark.

She started her pickup, then thought better of it and turned off the ignition. She had to pee. While she was at it, she thought, since her eyes were accustomed to the dark, why not poke around a little? She stepped out of the truck and slammed the door, loud as a rifle shot. The silence as she walked across the parking lot - or was it the anticipation of a pee? - made her shiver. A few security lights from the offices at the other end of the warehouse illuminated the area in front of the doors, but what was out there in the dark, in the tangle of grass and skinny green alders beyond the back of the building? She tried the door to the studio, but it was locked. The small window in the door showed nothing but blackness behind a brief veil of condensation from her breath. Was there a fire escape? Some means of getting to the second floor from the outside?

Her footsteps crunching on gravel, she walked around the corner into deep shadow, running her hand along the building's corrugated siding until she was half way down its rear length. Leaning against the wall for support, she yanked her sweatpants down to her knees and squatted to pee. The exquisite relief was spoiled by the annoying fact that droplets splashed back on her thighs and buttocks. She tugged her sweatpants back up and stepped away from the building to look up at it. Slashes of reflected light indicated the location of windows on the upper floor, but she couldn't make out any means of access at the rear. She saw no point in continuing, and had already turned back when she thought she heard a car and stopped, holding her breath to listen. She could identify no sounds beyond the white noise of an industrial yard: the faint hum of lights, the distant swish of traffic. She walked on, the crunch of her footfalls all she could hear, rounded the corner, heading toward her pickup, and found herself caught in a sudden blaze of headlights. She ducked back around the corner, and heard a man's voice yell, "Hey, you! Stop right there!"

"Shit!" she said to herself, started to run with the sinking feeling that she couldn't run as fast or as far as the body behind that voice. Her mind raced to the consequences. A trip, a fall, a physical tussle on the gravel? Who was it? One of the musicians coming back? A security guard?

"Police!" the voice continued.

"Shit!" she said aloud, and stopped dead.

Russell left the captain's office with the first smile he'd had on his face in the past eighteen hours. So, maybe Feldman had upstaged

166

him last night, and maybe he hadn't been able to see Jennifer, but at least now he could move forward with the Iceman investigation. Russell grabbed the empty coffee mug off his desk and looked inside. Whew! It could use a rinse. He headed for the men's room, whistling. The captain had just okayed a trip to Vancouver. The D.A. wanted more to tie the Nillsons to the victim. Since they were short a man with Merv on vacation, Russell had to volunteer to go on his own time on the weekend, but that didn't bother him at all. Because in Vancouver, he could not only spend his days interviewing witnesses first hand and visiting sites relevant to the Iceman case, he could also spend some time with Jennifer. And it was about time.

She'd been less than understanding last night when he'd called to let her know he was going to be indefinitely delayed. "Don't come after midnight," she'd said. "I have an early breakfast meeting and then have to rush straight to the airport."

"What's that got to do with me spending the night?"

"I've had a rough week, Russell. I'm bagged. I need my sleep."

"I've got my key. You won't even have to get up."

"Getting up isn't the point. It's waking up."

"Don't forget, Jen, it's been a while. It'll be over so fast, you won't know what hit you."

"I can hardly wait," she said, without enthusiasm. "No, Russell. Let's save it for next time."

"And when is next time?" Russell didn't try to hide the frustration in his voice. "I'd like to see you once in a while, Jen. Is that too much to ask?"

There were a few seconds of silence, then Jennifer said, "This isn't working for us anymore, is it?"

At that point, Russell had been entering the parking lot at the crime scene. "I gotta go," he said. "So can I come by?"

"No," she said. "I'll call you on the weekend."

Russell examined his face in the mirror above the sink as he ran hot water into the dirty mug. By the time he'd finished dealing with Ashton and his father last night, Feldman hovering in the background like a bad smell, then taken a run back to the crime scene, it had been close to two a.m. When he got home, feeling bad about the kid and imagining Jennifer lying in her bed alone, hot and juicy under the covers and smelling of sweat and Chanel, he'd been too wired to get much sleep. It showed. There were puffy pouches under his eyes, and tiny red webs in the whites. He wiped the crud out of the bottom of the mug with a paper towel, then rinsed his face with cold water, patted it dry with paper towels, and slapped his cheeks a few times. What the hell. By the time he got to Vancouver on Saturday, he'd be irresistible. He'd look like a million bucks.

The foxy chick was at the coffee machine again. She was wearing a purple leather skirt and matching shoes with three-inch heels. Man! Those legs.

"Hey," she said. "I was hoping I'd bump into you again." She sidled up next to him and bumped him with her hip, then eyed him from beneath heavy lashes. "How ya been?"

"Cute trick," he said, jerking his hip in her direction. "But I can't do it back to you, 'cause that would be harassment." He filled up his coffee mug, adding, "... and that's against department policy, know what I mean?"

"I like a little sex-u-al harassment now and then," she drawled, taking his coffee mug and setting it down beside the machine. She grabbed his hand, clicked her ballpoint pen, and wrote a telephone number across his palm. "Call me, okay?" she said, smiling over her shoulder at him as she walked away, swinging that purple skirtful of young hips.

"Not on your life, baby," Russell said under his breath. "It ain't gonna happen." Even if things were falling apart with Jennifer, he wasn't desperate enough to have casual sex with a woman who worked in the same building, let alone the same office. When you say goodbye, you've got to be able to cut the cord. Not that he wasn't tempted, maybe a little too tempted after last night. He licked his palm, stood on one foot, and rubbed his palm against his other sock.

By the time he reached his desk, the foxy chick's phone number was too smudged to read.

Sharon had no desire to talk to Alora Magee, but she was happy to get out of her cell and away from that disgusting troll and her irritating voice. Outside of the cell and away from Angie, she felt the relief of moving from a nightmare to a plain old bad dream. When the guards ushered her into the interview room, Alora was already there with her briefcase open on the table. The lawyer sat square to the table, leaning on her elbows with her chin propped up in one hand, as if she were tired. She looked up and smiled, perhaps with a hint of apology, as if she felt bad about the unpleasantness of their last meeting. She indicated a chair with a wave of her hand, but Sharon didn't feel like sitting down.

"I'd like to walk around a bit, if you don't mind," she said, trying not to sound hostile. The lawyer wasn't so bad, after all, and the longer she could stay here, away from Angie, the better.

"You like these?" the lawyer asked, throwing a small paperback onto the table.

Sharon picked it up, turned it over. A romance novel. "I've never read one," she said with a shrug and set it back down.

"Your friend sent a bunch of them."

"What friend?"

"Shit. I don't know what's the matter with my brain. I've forgotten her name. Oh, here," she said, pulling an envelope out of her briefcase and sliding something out of it. "El. Her name's El."

She passed a sheet of paper across the table, and Sharon saw there was a note scrawled on it. The note said:

> *Sharon -*
> *Thought this might keep you company.*
> *She's being well taken care of, and*
> *expecting to be home with her Mom soon.*
> *Good luck.*
> *El.*

Sharon turned it over, and her heart did a sudden lurch. There was Peaches, smiling up at the camera with her aren't-I-a-clever-girl

169

look. Sharon felt as if the wind had been knocked out of her, and groped for a chair.

It hit home, hard. It hit home that her reality had become this ugly building full of unhappy people, full of resentment and bitterness and perversion. Her sole pleasures had become the blessed oblivion of sleep, and getting out of sight and hearing of that horrid and nauseating cellmate of hers. Ray and their life together had become a dream, an internal movie of memories that she could sometimes escape to when it was quiet enough for her to shut out her surroundings, but it wasn't her reality any more. Imprisonment was her reality, and something as simple and precious as this little dog was beyond her reach. If she'd ever in her life thought that jail wouldn't be such a bad deal, now she knew how sadly she was mistaken. She was suddenly overwhelmed with a feeling of self-pity, a surge as strong as floodwaters knocking her off her feet. She lay her arms and head on the table and began to sob, loose racking sobs, till she was bawling, tasting salty tears like a heartbroken child, letting herself really cry for the first time since this whole thing had started.

She didn't know how long she'd been crying, but she gradually became aware of a hand stroking hers. She drew her hand away, took several deep breaths and sat up, keeping her eyes down. She didn't need sympathy from anybody, least of all some skinny California lawyer with nice skin who had it made. She hurriedly wiped her cheeks with the back of her hand, took more deep breaths until she felt in control. When she finally looked across the table at Alora Magee, the lawyer had her hands clasped on the table in front of her, as if in prayer. She had a wan smile on her face.

"You're the second person in twelve hours to pull away from me as if I had the plague," she said, then shook her head. "I'm sorry. My problems are pretty inconsequential compared to yours." The lawyer pulled a pack of tissues out of her briefcase and slid it across the table.

Sharon nodded her thanks as she pulled one out, then turned away to blow her nose. She felt a surprising sense of relief. The crying helped. There was a faint scent of leather on the tissue. "You don't have to apologize," she said. "It would be nice to think about somebody else's problems for a change."

Alora shrugged. "Just the usual baby boomer's angst, I guess. One day I woke up and discovered that I was in my late thirties and had no man in my life. Look at me." She stretched her arms out from her sides, palms up. "I'm not so bad looking. Nice hair. Good teeth." She bared her teeth and Sharon couldn't help but laugh, although it sounded more like a hiccup. "Yet sometimes it feels as if I'm as far away from finding a man to grow old with as I am from walking to the moon." She let out a sigh, began to stroke the top of her briefcase with an index finger.

A man to grow old with. "God! I'd give anything right now not to love that man! That's what hurts so goddamn much." Sharon covered her eyes with one hand and took a few deep breaths through her mouth. Her nose was plugged and her eyes stung from the crying. "You know? Last year at this time, being in jail like this would have been a piece of cake compared to what I'm feeling now. I could've just waltzed through this like it was summer camp. But you know what? With Ray I had a taste of heaven out there..." She raised her arm, gesturing toward the high windows. "... and now it hurts like hell to lose it."

"You can't lose what you ain't never had. That's what the song says." Alora smiled sadly, but this time Sharon didn't find her sympathy offensive.

Sharon leaned back in her chair, put her palms to her cheeks, and thought about it. Would she have given up the pleasure she'd found with Ray in order to avoid this pain? It was a tough question, coming at her in the middle of the pain. Suddenly she was dying for a cigarette. "Have you got a smoke?"

"Sure. Special for you." Alora slid a pack of cigarettes and matches across the table, and watched while Sharon took one out and lit up. It had been so long, the first drag made her dizzy, but she sucked in another lungful and held it for the hit.

"Ray changed my life." She took another deep drag and blew it out slowly. "God! He changed me. I never knew I could feel so good about myself. Self respect. He gave me my self respect." She

171

smiled wistfully and added, "I guess sometimes it's better to have somebody like that and lose them than to never have them at all."

The lawyer looked so sorrowful, Sharon almost started to cry again. Instead, she picked up the photograph of Peaches and found herself laughing and crying at the same time. "This little punkin' head... this picture... it's kind of like a picture of what me and Ray had together. See? See how she's got that light in her eyes? A little mischief, a little fun, a lot of love, like she knows she's absolutely adorable. A symbol." She held the photo up, shook it a little. "This is a symbol of how much love we had and how good it was." She took a last drag on her cigarette and stubbed it out. "God! It hurts like hell, but I wouldn't have missed it for the world."

"Sharon," said Alora, leaning forward with a bemused expression on her face, "why are you speaking in the past tense?"

Sharon bit her lower lip. "It's over, isn't it?"

"Is it?"

"They think we're guilty. We've got no way to prove that we're not."

"And are you?"

"Shit," Sharon said, getting to her feet. "I almost forgot that you're one of 'them'."

The big Freightliner swallowed the gray tape of highway at sixty miles an hour, hour after solitary hour. Hunter's thoughts kept drifting back to his evening with Alora Magee. She was attractive, pleasant to be with, but when she'd shown her interest in him, he'd backed off. What's wrong with me? he thought. What kind of magic was he waiting for? He thought about Chris settling for Lance the Lawyer. Settling? Who was he to judge? Maybe the companionship of Lance the Lawyer was better than none at all. No. There was a good reason for his own behavior.

In spite of the yearning he felt for intimacy in his life, he was on the road at least twenty days a month, never spending enough time in one place, including home, to get to know anyone well. In spite of the undeniable attraction he felt for Alora, there couldn't be a future
172

with her, and he wasn't interested in a relationship without a future. Old fashioned was right. Old fashioned, and too old to change.

A J.B. Hunt rig passed him, the driver giving him a comradely salute. Hunter smiled and nodded, took a few seconds to pick up the thread of his thought. Why couldn't there be a future with someone like Alora Magee? He hated analyzing things to death like this, but he had been wrestling with his solitude for too long to ignore it anymore. Was it just because she lived in California, in one place, and his home was in Vancouver, although he spent precious little time there, as his daughters would attest. No. It was more than that. He hadn't let himself explore his feelings, nor acknowledge them even to himself, but he felt a strong connection with Ken's widow, uncomfortably strong. He had tried to interpret it as something less than it was. He felt responsible for Helen, he was prepared to admit that. He could tell himself over and over again that he wasn't responsible for Ken's death, but the guilt remained like an indelible stain. Shouldn't he have known that Ken was close to the edge? Shouldn't he have been there for him?

Hunter felt the familiar churning in his brain, the restlessness that made him want to bust out and run, run until his lungs burst and his legs collapsed like rubber hose. He had often wondered, reluctantly and with distaste, if that was what had attracted him to life on the road. Running and running and always getting ready to run again. If he just kept moving, maybe he could leave the guilt behind. He couldn't argue it away, because it wasn't a rational thing. It bedeviled him and tormented him and wouldn't let him rest. After Ken's death, because of Ken's death, Hunter had sullied everything he held sacred. He destroyed evidence, he betrayed Ken's last wishes, he failed to show the integrity he'd always prided himself on, the courage to be honest and open. Was it compassion, or was it cowardice and shame? Or was it, plainly and simply, for her? For Helen.

Hunter felt a need to talk to someone, take his mind off the subject, so when he stopped for fuel in Santa Nella, he called El from an outdoor payphone.

"It's about time," she said.

"I called when I left L.A., and you weren't there." Wally said he'd pass the message on, but Hunter didn't want El to give Wally a bad time, so he didn't elaborate. Wally was a good, steady worker, with the patience and good nature to put up with El's occasional bellowing.

"Yeah, yeah. I know. Listen, though. Something interesting happened at Greg Williams' house yesterday." He could hear the familiar squeak of her captain's chair as she rocked back and forth.

"What happened at Greg Williams' house?"

"I was there just pokin' around, seeing what I could see, and what I saw was that somebody tossed the place."

"You were there? What were you doing there?"

"Like I said, just pokin' around. There was nobody home, but the door was open..."

"For God's sake, El. Don't go taking risks like that. Besides walking a fine line with the police, you don't know what kind of trouble you could get yourself into. Don't forget, there's already been one murder, and if Ray and Sharon didn't do it, whoever did is still out there. Don't put yourself in danger."

"Aw, come on, Hunter. What danger? Nobody knows who I am and I'm not about to pick a fight with anybody, but did you hear what I said?" She didn't stop for breath, let alone to give Hunter time to respond. "Somebody trashed the place before I got there. Somebody had been looking for something, I guess. What do you think it was? Doesn't that pretty much let Ray and Sharon off the hook?"

Hunter took the receiver from his ear and shook his head before saying, "You shouldn't have gone there."

"It's significant, isn't it? that the place was tossed?"

Hunter rubbed his jaw. "Could be."

"What do you think it means? What do you think they were looking for?"

"Supposing, first of all, that it wasn't just a break in. A coincidental occurrence."

"Yeah. Supposing."

174

"Who knows?" Hunter watched a driver hoist a flat of Anderson's pea soup into his truck before following it inside. It was a new Freightliner, probably equipped with a microwave.

"Drugs maybe?"

"That's a possibility." Hunter pictured Teresa Jagpal, her slender body curled in the corner of the couch, shivering like a frightened rabbit, although she hadn't been shivering, or had she? In any case, he could imagine what effect a break-in would have on her, timid as she was. "Another possibility," he announced, "is there could very well be a dispute over the man's estate. There's no love lost between the victim's wife and his brother, and although the relationship was common law, if she and Williams lived together long enough she's still entitled to inherit. If the victim's brother felt strongly enough about it, and from what I've seen of him, he did, then he might have tried to get his hands on anything of value that belonged to the victim before the wife had a chance to dispose of it."

"Ugh! What an ugly thought. The poor guy's not even buried yet and they're squabbling over his pitiful possessions."

Hunter heard another phone ringing in the background and knew what was coming. Before she had a chance to put him on hold, he said, "I'll let you go now, El. Talk to you tomorrow."

"Wait!" she said. "That's important information, don't you think?"

The last thing Hunter wanted to do was to encourage her, but he didn't have the heart to bring her down. "Sure, El," he said.

"Run with it, Hunter," she said, just before the line went dead. "Run with it, okay?"

CHAPTER

SIXTEEN

After supper, Sharon curled up on her bunk, facing the wall, and tried to read. Her cellmate was lying on her back with her legs bent, one knee crossed over the other, bouncing one foot up and down and humming to herself. The witch was looking for any excuse, Sharon knew, to speak. The best thing Sharon could do was pretend to be asleep, so she lay there silently, holding the book low and turning the pages, when necessary, with as little movement as possible. After about an hour, the humming stopped, and was soon replaced by an open-mouthed snore. The witch was asleep. Sharon had read no more than three pages.

Very quietly, and with one eye on her cellmate, Sharon pulled back her mattress and pulled a ragged copy of Time magazine out from beneath it. She opened it to just inside the back cover, and a soft, sad smile crossed her face. Peaches was so sweet and innocent. Her heart melted at the sight of that eager little face. She felt overwhelmed with love and sorrow. Peaches was inseparably mixed up in her heart with everything else: Ray and the truck and their favorite CD's and the meals they shared on the road, the takeout coffees and the rented videos and snuggling into the bunk together at some quiet spot just off the highway. God! The heat of his skin, the smell of him. How she missed it all!

The witch choked on a snore and coughed herself awake, and Sharon let the magazine fall closed. She didn't want the witch to touch Peaches, not even with her eyes. She didn't want Peaches tainted by so much as a thought from that perverted mind.

"You awake, Princess?"

Sharon could hear the soft scrape of dry skin against skin, and tried not to imagine what part of the witch's disgusting body was being rubbed and scratched. She clenched her jaw, willing the witch to leave her alone.

"Yoo hoo! Prin-cess!" the witch called softly in a lascivious singsong voice. "Wake up, honey cup. Have I got a sweet deal for you!"

Sharon gritted her teeth, remained silent and still. She could hear the soft smacking sound of wet lips and tongue, imagined she could smell the fetid breath.

"How about you scratch my back, and I'll scratch yours. How does that sound, pussycat? Huh?" She chortled, then raised her voice. "Let me suck your tits." Smack. Smack. "C'mon. You'll like it. How about it, honey cup?"

The woman from the next stall piped up, "Shut up, you old hag! Ain't nobody wants to touch you wif' a ten foot pole!"

The witch's voice became manic. "Shut your face, cunt! I ain't talkin' to you!" Then soft, sulky. "Come on out, Princess. Play with me."

Sharon hugged the magazine to her chest and began, soundlessly, to weep.

At four o'clock on Friday afternoon, a uniformed RCMP officer walked into the office of Watson Transportation on Annacis Island and stood politely behind the counter.

"Are you Elspeth Watson?" he asked.

"That'd be me," said El. "What can I do for you?"

"Do you own the blue Ford pickup parked outside?"

"Yeah, the old clunker's mine."

"Staff Sergeant Al Kowalski wants me to bring you down to the Burnaby detachment. He has a few questions for you."

"Now?!"

"Yes. Now." The young Mountie was still being polite, but his voice took on an edge.

El tsk'd and threw down her pen, picked up the phone. This Al was a friend of Hunter's after all. She'd just explain how busy she was on Friday afternoons. "What's his number?" she said, then "Never mind. Here's his card. I'll just give him..."

"I'm sorry, you'll have to come with us." The Mountie motioned to someone through the window, then stepped around and took the telephone receiver out of her hand. El punched in the last number anyway. "Now," he said.

El stiffened. "What the hell...?! Let go of my phone! Let go of my arm. Wally!" she bellowed. "Wally, get in here! At least let me talk to my warehouseman, so he can take care of the office for me." A second officer came through the door.

"Wally!"

El was escorted to an interview room, and made to wait. She tried taking deep breaths to calm herself, but her face was burning and she couldn't stop doing things with her hands, flexing them repeatedly, or running them up and down her thighs. The officers who had transported her in the RCMP cruiser - she'd felt like a prisoner locked inside the back seat, and like a fish out of water without a vehicle of her own - had been polite and would only tell her that she was wanted for questioning. In her usual forceful manner, she'd demanded to know why she couldn't drive her own pickup, but they said that they were only doing their job, and added that if she didn't quiet down, she'd make things worse for herself. Worse? Worse how? she'd asked, a little more quietly. They hadn't answered, and she then had to admit that she was not only angry, she was scared. What the hell did all this mean?

When Kowalski arrived, he was accompanied by another uniformed officer. "Ms. Watson," he said to El with a grim nod, then turned and spoke to the other officer as if she weren't there. "Is this the woman?"

The officer nodded. "Yes, that's her." For the first time, El paid attention to his face, her forehead creasing with a bewildered frown.

"You," she said, then sighed. He was the officer who had caught her sneaking around the back of the building on Still Creek Avenue. She opened her mouth to remind him of her explanation, which had been something vague about scouting out a new site for her business, but realized that with Al here, any kind of a lie would only make her look worse. She shut her mouth and waited to hear what this was all about. The uniformed officer left, and Al sat down across the table from her.

"I'm going to give you a chance to explain this," he said, "but let me tell you that it doesn't look good. You could be facing two counts of breaking and entering, and quite possibly a charge of obstruction of justice. I'd sure like to know what you thought you were going to accomplish."

"Breaking and entering?!" She looked at him in disbelief. "What the hell are you talking about? All I did was try the knob. It was locked, so I left. Ask the officer, there. I wasn't inside the building, and never have been." She thought about the sound equipment she'd picked up from Fraser's Dock, still locked in the back of the Hino in Watson Transportation's yard, and her stomach did a loop-di-loop.

"Which building?" he asked.

"What do you mean, which building? You know very well which building."

"Where were you at one fifteen Wednesday afternoon?"

"One fif..." The penny dropped. Two counts of breaking and entering, he'd said. They knew she'd been at Greg Williams house. That spiky-haired bitch had taken down her license plate number and reported it. "Listen, Al," she said. "You know I'm straight. I'm a friend of Hunter Rayne's, for God's sake. He'll tell you. I'm just trying to help out, but I'd never do anything illegal. Christ! B and E's. Obstruction of justice! What's all this about, for cryin' out loud?"

He sighed like a man losing patience. "Where were you at one fifteen Wednesday afternoon?"

She let out a big breath and rolled her eyes. "Balmoral Street," she said resignedly.

"What were you doing on Balmoral Street?"

"I went to see if there was anybody home at Greg Williams' house." Her mind was going ninety miles a minute, trying to decide what kind of reasons to give. "The door was open and I could see that the place had been trashed, but I didn't do it." Nobody had seen her inside, had they? No. There's no way that spiky haired woman could've seen her before she walked out onto the sidewalk. "There was nobody home, so I never went inside. Like I said, I'm straight. Hey. I'm on your side. Law and order. I just wanted to find out more about the guy, so I could help Hunter figure out why he'd gotten himself killed." She leaned forward and stabbed at the table with her index finger. "Ray and Sharon Nillson didn't do it. The fact that someone tossed his place proves it."

"That may be," he said, motioning her to stand. "We'll need your fingerprints."

After watching the sprawl of the L.A. basin in its nest of yellow haze disappear beneath the burnished aluminum curl of the 757's wing, Russell settled back in his seat and decided it wasn't too early for a drink. He was nervous, but it had nothing to do with flying. When he stepped off this plane, he was going to be out of his jurisdiction, out of his comfort zone. He was going to have to depend on the cooperation of a foreign law enforcement agency, and foreign witnesses. Sure, Canadians looked just like Americans and almost talked just like Americans, but Russell wasn't confident that they thought like Americans. After all, they were so damn polite, they had to be hiding something. It was spooky, discomfiting. And that wasn't all that was eating at him. Now he was also entering Jennifer's world, a world in which she'd been spending most of her time over the past three months, a world she was becoming more and more acclimatized to as she became more and more alienated from him.

180

Their relationship had been changing, and it had something to do with Vancouver, and he was afraid to find out why.

She didn't know he was coming. They hadn't been spending enough time together, nor even talking enough on the telephone, for him to have mentioned the case to her. So today he would be showing up in her new world unannounced, and - what frightened him the most - quite possibly unwelcome.

The passenger beside him was a middle-aged woman wearing jeans and Reeboks and tapping away on a laptop computer. The flight attendants came by with the service cart, and his neighbor leaned way back in her seat so he could see the attendant better, and stayed that way, looking uncomfortable but maintaining a polite smile, until he had received his can of beer.

"Why are Canadians so damn polite?" he muttered out the window.

"Pardon me?" she said.

Russell looked at her sideways. She, too, had ordered a can of beer, and had closed up the laptop but left it sitting on the meal table. She was trying to open a bag of beer nuts.

"You're a Canadian, aren't you?" The way he said it bordered on an accusation..

She smiled. "You can tell?"

"You're polite. Canadians are so damn polite."

"If you say so," she said. "I guess we're trying not to disturb the elephant." She was trying to pull the seam on the package apart.

"Huh?"

"Canada has been compared to a mouse sharing its bed with an elephant."

"You think that's why?"

"No. Probably not. But we were never the rebels that you Americans were. We still have the Queen of England on our money. Look." She dug into her jeans pocket and pulled out a handful of coins. The Queen was on every one of them. "Colonial mentality, I guess," she said, putting them back. "We started off being respectful to Britain, now we're respectful to the United States. We should have a war and conquer somebody. That might help us snap out of it."

She held a corner of the package in her teeth and pulled. The bag ripped from top to bottom, spilling nuts on her computer and into her lap. "Shit!" she said. She picked up one of the spilled nuts and threw it in her mouth. "There. I said shit. Is that better?"

"It's a start," said Russell.

They both drank some beer. Russell looked out the window, then turned back to his neighbor. "Tell me something," he said. "Is it contagious?"

"What?"

"The Canadian thing. The politeness."

"No," she said firmly. "My guess is if you hang around Canadians long enough, you'll experience a sort of uncontrollable backlash. You'll get meaner and ruder, just to compensate for all the stifling politeness around you." She emptied her beer glass. "Feel better now?"

"Yes," he said, thinking of Jennifer, wondering why she was becoming more distant, more reserved. For some reason, he also thought of Feldman. Feldman, the picture of an up-and-coming young criminal lawyer, delivering his sound byte for the TV news. Feldman was married, and Russell wondered if there was a baby on the way. Fuck Feldman. "Yes, I do feel better. Thanks." But he didn't.

She nodded, then went back to her computer. Russell didn't speak to her again for the rest of the flight.

Hunter crossed the border at noon. He pulled the Blue Knight into the yard at Watson Transportation well before one o'clock and left it running while he went inside. El's pickup was parked outside, so he knew she'd be there. She was always there on Saturdays, and occasionally even on Sundays. He'd never known her to take a vacation. "When I need a vacation, I'll be the first one to know, okay?" was what she said to anyone who suggested it might be a good idea.

The door was unlocked, but there was no one in the office. Papers were scattered across El's work surface, and a pen lay on top,
182

as if she'd just thrown it down. A half empty coffee cup sat beside one of the telephones. He proceeded into the warehouse and called out to her, but there was no answering holler, no sound at all. He stuck his head into the coffee room. The light on the coffee maker was on and the pot on the burner was half full, but there was no sign of El. Then he heard the back door of the warehouse slam, and the scritching and scrabbling of nails on the concrete floor. Seconds later, those same nails were scratching on his jeans, just above his knees.

"Hey, Hunter! Am I glad to see you!" El bellowed from the back of the warehouse as soon as she came into view from behind a wooden crate. "Peaches! Pete! Behave yourselves! Down! Get down! Don't let them jump on you, Hunter. It's not polite."

Once he'd parked his rig where she indicated, Hunter came back inside and poured himself a cup of coffee. El looked uncomfortable, her jaw set stiffly, as if she were facing an unpleasant task. "What is it?" he asked. "What have you done now?"

"I fucked up," she said, turning her coffee cup around in circles. "I fucked things up for Ray and Sharon."

Hunter took a sip of coffee, leaned back in the chair with his legs stretched long in front of him, trying to work out the kinks after hours on the road. "How?"

"Remember I said I'd been to Greg Williams' house, and his house had been tossed? Well, seems that the woman I saw outside took down my license number or something and gave it to the police."

"And?" Hunter raised his brows.

"And your buddy Al considers me a suspect."

Hunter took a swallow of his coffee. "He knows you went inside?"

El nodded.

"How does he know? You told him?"

El cleared her throat and looked away. "Fingerprints," she muttered.

Hunter sighed.

"I only touched one goddamn thing! It was a cookie jar, and I was afraid it would roll off the counter, so I put it upright, and when I realized I shouldn't touch anything, I put it back the way it was."

"So did you explain that before he found it out for himself?"

"No," she said.

"Damn," he said quietly. "Still, if that's all they've got, they probably won't charge you."

"There's more," she said, with a weak smile. "They think I tossed the studio as well."

Hunter sat bolt upright, almost spilling his coffee. "They found the equipment I asked you to pick up and think you stole it?" He couldn't blame anyone but himself for that.

El shook her head. "It's still in the Hino. I guess we should get rid of it, huh?"

Hunter gave a sigh of relief. "See if you can set it up for tomorrow afternoon. But then... why would they connect you with the studio? You've never even been there."

She cleared her throat again, and her smile got weaker. "The police caught me there late Wednesday night."

"What?!"

"I was just being nosy, parked outside watching to see who was there. I wasn't gonna do anything or talk to anybody, just watch. But then I fell asleep, and when I woke up I had to... uh... go around the back of the building for a minute, if you know what I mean." She ran a hand back over her forehead, leaving a lock of hair standing straight up. "I never went inside. Honest. But I'm not worried about me. It makes me sick that maybe I've made it look worse for Ray and Sharon. If they didn't think it was me, they'd think it was somebody else, and that would take the heat off of Ray and Sharon, right?"

Hunter took some slow breaths. He hoped Al Kowalski didn't think that El had done these things with Hunter's knowledge. "What did Al say? Did he say anything about your motive for doing these break-ins?"

El looked aghast. "I didn't do the break-ins!"

"I know that." He held up his hands to calm her down. "But if Al thinks you did, why does he think you did it?"

184

She looked at the floor, swung her chair to and fro a couple of times before she answered, "I told him I was doing a little legwork for you."

"Shit!" said Hunter.

El's eyebrows rose, as they did every time she heard him use a four-letter word, a rare and meaningful occurrence. "But I don't know if he believes me. Seems the cops went to see Wally last night, asking him about suspicious shipments, and there were a couple of cops in here this morning going through my waybills." She stabbed the air in the direction of the filing cabinets with an indignant finger.

Hunter stood up. "I'm going to have to talk to Al." He took a last swallow of coffee and put his mug down on El's desk. "Shit," he said again, and rubbed his jaw. "So they went through your waybills. Maybe they're more interested in who your customers are than in you. Did they search the premises? Or your house?"

She shook her head. "That's one good thing, anyway."

"If they didn't take the trouble to search the premises, it would mean that nothing was reported missing from Williams' house or studio. Whoever broke in must have been looking for something neither Williams' wife nor the other band members knew about, or wanted to admit knowing about."

"I never thought of that. It must've been pretty small, if they pulled out CD's and books off the bookshelf looking for it, don't you think?"

Hunter shrugged. "Small could be anything from a safety deposit box key to an incriminating photograph. Obviously, if they tossed both places, it wasn't easy to find, and quite possibly wasn't found in either place. I wonder if forensics turned up anything in Greg Williams' car."

"You could ask Al."

Hunter snorted softly. "If he'll even talk to me."

She looked at the floor again. "Sorry," she said.

Hunter had tried to call Al Kowalski from the Watson office, and although he hadn't succeeded in getting through to him, he did find

185

out that Al was on his way back from the airport and expected at his office within the half hour. Instead of going home to shower and change as he usually did after a week on the road, Hunter drove straight to the Burnaby RCMP detachment. He wanted to find out right away how he stood with Al after El's little escapades.

Al came out to the reception area to meet him. His face was grim as he signaled Hunter to step outside. They walked across the parking lot, and Al half sat on the hood of a police cruiser, his arms folded across his chest.

"Jesus, Hunter. What the hell do you think you're doing?"

Hunter met Al's question with a calm voice and a steady gaze. "I assume you've already concluded that El Watson didn't commit the break-ins, or you would have charged her. Do you consider her guilty of anything other than showing poor judgement by letting her curiosity put her in the wrong place at the wrong time?"

Al snorted. "How about obstructing a police investigation, possibly tampering with a crime scene? Did you suggest to her that she poke around?"

"You know me better than that, Al." Hunter's first inclination was not to dignify the question with an answer, but he thought better of it and decided that, as weak as a verbal denial might sound, he wanted it on the record. "Absolutely not. I never asked her to get involved. In fact, I strongly suggested that she not do so."

"Then why did she?"

"Because she's El Watson, and she makes up her own mind about things. She's soft-hearted and bull-headed, and she's my boss, so why should she listen to me?"

"Does she realize what her behavior has done?" Hunter nodded, but before he could speak, Al continued. "She may not have hurt herself much, but she did hurt her friends. I don't know your boss, and I don't know what she's capable of. If she'd taken something - anything - I would've charged her, but it's not worthwhile to prosecute her for breaking and entering because, as far as the complainants can tell, nothing was taken. It would be a waste of our time, and of taxpayer's money. However, we have a witness and fingerprints that place her at the scene, which is enough evidence to make it hard to justify looking for anyone else. You follow?"

Hunter nodded again. El had been right. "Meaning that the B & E's haven't thrown the case against Ray and Sharon into question, that you're not looking for an unknown person with a motive relating to Williams' murder."

"Right. Because we've already got your busybody boss, whose motive was to create a diversion to take the heat off her friends." Al shifted his position, still leaning against the fender of the car. "Well, your boss's little scheme didn't work."

"For what it's worth, I believe her." Hunter smiled wryly. "Somebody else committed the break-ins. She was just in the wrong place at the right time."

Al stared Hunter in the eyes for a moment, then straightened up, indicated the door. "Let's go inside. You'll find this interesting."

Hunter looked at him curiously, then followed him inside.

Standing with his back to the door, hands in his pockets, and gazing at what he could see of the sky out of the window in Al's office was Russell Kupka. He whirled around on a heel as he heard them enter, and his eyebrows shot up when he saw Hunter. "Well, look who's here," he said in a flat voice. "The eighteen-wheeled crusader."

Hunter looked over at Al, saw him frown as he slid in behind his desk.

"Okay, where were we?" said Al.

"What's he doing here?" said Russell. "I don't think it's a good idea to discuss the case in front of civilians, especially civilians with a stake in the outcome."

Hunter had just pulled over a chair, but he remained standing. He was prepared to leave without argument, for Al's sake.

Al waved at them both to sit down. "I told you before. Hunter is on the case as a consultant, at my request."

Russell turned his back to Hunter, and spoke as if he weren't there. "You just finished telling me about the complications he's caused, him and his friends. Until we know just to what extent they're involved, I don't think the guy should be here."

"I said the suspect was someone Hunter works with. Hunter had nothing to do with it."

"How do you know?"

"I know."

"It's okay, Al," said Hunter. "I'll call you." He started to put his chair back.

"No, Hunter. I want you here. I'm counting on your help." Then Al turned to Russell. "Now, do you want me to fill you in on what we've found out, or not."

Russell glared, first at Al and then at Hunter, but yanked his chair aside to make room for Hunter's and sat down. Hunter quietly followed suit.

Al leaned forward, positioned some notes in front of him on the desk. "Okay, first about the break-ins we mentioned. Our prime suspect for the break-ins is Elspeth Watson, proprietor of Watson Transportation, who was responsible for dispatching Ray and Sharon Nillson to handle the load of frozen beef from Hanratty's Wholesale Meats. As far as the remaining occupants of both the house and the studio can tell, nothing was taken at the time of the break-ins, so the motive does not appear to be burglary. We don't know if the motive was strictly mischief, to disrupt our investigation, or if someone, either Watson or someone else, was looking for something. We consider it a strong possibility that Watson committed the break-ins in an attempt to divert suspicion from her friends, the Nillsons."

"Why?" said Russell. "What's her stake in this? Isn't it possible that, whatever is behind this murder, the Nillsons weren't working alone?" He glanced pointedly at Hunter. "Don't bother comparing this Watson broad to Mother Teresa. I've told you before, character testimony doesn't cut it with me."

Al nodded. "We've been following that line of investigation as well. She's clean. So far, we've come up with nothing that points to illegal activity at Watson Transportation, but we're now running the names of Watson's customers past Narcotics, as well as Customs and Immigration, to see if any of them set off alarm bells."

Hunter didn't like the direction this was taking, but felt it wasn't his place to object. He did, however, want to make a point about the

188

fingerprints, so he leaned forward and addressed Al. "You have fingerprints from the house, you said. Have you identified any fingerprints besides Elspeth Watson's?"

"There are half a dozen unidentified prints here and there, plus prints from Williams and his wife, and their friend, Hellen Brooker."

"Elspeth's were on one item only?"

"Yes. A cookie jar."

"She had an explanation for that, I believe."

"Yes."

Russell snorted. "What the fuck does it matter?"

"But her fingerprints weren't anywhere else?"

"No."

"And at the studio?"

"A few partials on the glass of the door, as if she'd been peering inside with her hands against the window, but nowhere else."

Russell was looking at the floor and rubbing his nose. Hunter nodded for Al to continue. He could tell that both Russell and Al had drawn the same conclusion that he had, whether or not they were prepared to admit it. El had left prints, so she hadn't been wearing gloves. If she'd touched anything else, her prints would be in more than one place. The logical conclusion was that she had not been the one to commit the break-ins. Even if she had, with that scant evidence it would be impossible to get a conviction.

"The next item of interest," Al continued, "is the victim's car. As you both know, it was found in a restaurant parking lot just off the highway in Mount Vernon, Washington. We had it towed back to Burnaby, and it was gone over by our forensics team. We haven't found any specific forensic evidence linking it to your suspects..." He nodded at Russell. "... but we do have the usual assortment of fibers from the upholstery, dirt and bits of gravel from the carpet, both inside the vehicle and from the trunk. There's also some paint, a metallic green paint, that the lab says was recently rubbed off against the rim of the trunk, as if an oversized article was riding in the open trunk, possibly a lawnmower or child's swing set or bicycle. And they did find something interesting under the seat." He bent down and lifted a paper bag onto his desk. "This," he said, and placed a tape

189

recorder not much bigger than a deck of cards on the desk in front of him. "Listen," he said, and pushed a button.

The recording started with a confident and pleasant male voice singing snatches of song. "I want to be at home with you, baby, home alone with you" was one of the lines, sung over and over again with variations in melody and cadence.

"He's writing a song," explained Al.

Then there was what sounded like the last half of an expletive, followed by "Learn to drive, you dick head!"

Al interrupted the tape again to say, "Voice activated."

There was the sound of a cell phone ringing, and the same male voice saying, "Whistlestop Studios." A pause, and then "It's about time. Where?... Yeah, if I don't get hung up in the border line up." A longer pause. "In the parking lot? Is there a coffee shop or something? Okay." The voice became impatient. "Of course I've got it." After that, they heard the beep of a cell phone button, then a low and disgusted "Stupid bitch."

"The telephone company checked Williams' cell phone record, and it looks like he had a call from a pay phone in a Cloverdale mall, just off the Pacific Highway leading to the U.S. border, at about four p.m. on Friday. We can surmise that he was on his way to meet someone on the Washington side of the border, most likely in Mount Vernon, where his car was found," said Al. "Would you agree?"

Russell leaned forward. "Is that all that's on the tape?"

"Yes, but that's not all we have," said Al. "The phone company was able to access Williams' cell phone voicemail. They sent me this recording. The call was a reroute from a cell phone tower in northwest Washington." He punched some numbers into his telephone, and a woman's voice could be heard above a cloud of background noises.

"I don't know what went wrong, but we've waited as long as we can for you. We have to go. Don't do anything, okay? Please. I'll call you when I'm back, probably early next week."

Al punched another button on his phone and paused. "The message came in at 6:30 p.m. on Friday the 14th. I'm betting it's Sharon Nillson." He looked pointedly at Hunter. "Is it?"

190

"I wouldn't swear to it, but it sounds like her," said Hunter.

"You know it is," said Russell, leaning back and crossing his legs. He snorted. "Of course it is. You can verify it with their cell phone records, can't you?" Al nodded.

"Did you find his phone in the car?" asked Hunter. Al shook his head, and Hunter turned to Russell. "Was the phone found on the body? Or a wallet?"

"Nada," said Russell.

"So we can assume that whoever locked Greg Williams in the trailer cleaned out his pockets first."

"Or later," suggested Al. "When the body was dumped."

"No," said Russell. "Only pockets you could have access to with him curled up like a frozen pretzel would've been the back ones, and I know from experience you could barely get a finger in them. And if he'd had a jacket with him, he would've been wearing it, and you couldn't have taken it off him without breaking his arms."

"What else was in the car, Al?"

Al looked down at the notes on his desk. "In the trunk, there was a six string guitar in a case. Other than that, just some music paraphernalia: guitar picks, sheet music, some kind of microphone. And a pair of boots."

"Boots?"

"Yeah. Ordinary looking, like short cowboy boots, brown, no tooling or anything on them."

"Probably looked better on stage than sneakers," volunteered Russell.

"Did his wife have anything to add?" asked Hunter. "Anything else missing, maybe?"

Al shook his head. "She says there might be a jacket missing, but for all she knows he could've left it at a gig somewhere."

Hunter looked over at Russell, who was nodding silently and frowning.

"What are your plans now, chief?" he asked.

CHAPTER
SEVENTEEN

To Russell's way of thinking, the right people were in jail. All that was left was to tie up enough loose ends to satisfy the district attorney. Over the weekend he expected to obtain a recap of the investigation from the RCMP, conduct follow-up interviews with some of the witnesses, and have an evening free to spend with Jennifer, or at least to find her. He'd pictured dinner together somewhere nice, with good wine - he was ready to run up his Visa bill - and a steamy evening in the hotel room. Something fluttered at the top of his stomach every time he thought about calling her. What if she wasn't happy to find out he was here?

So with that on his mind, Russell wasn't too pleased with the way things worked out. Al Kowalski had suggested that Russell, as the primary investigator, retrace the route the suspects and quite possibly the victim had taken on their last day in Vancouver, from Hanratty's warehouse to the border and then beyond that to the restaurant parking lot in Mount Vernon, Washington. Russell had to agree that the idea had merit, the best way to familiarize himself with the layout and what the RCMP had discovered so far. "Sure," Russell had said. "Let's go."

Al shrugged apologetically. "I can't, I'm afraid."

"You got somebody can take me?" Surely they'd be able to spare a constable and a car.

192

"Sorry. This is a weekend. We haven't got enough manpower to go around as it is." Al nodded toward Hunter. "Maybe if you ask him nicely..."

Russell clenched his jaw. He didn't like the idea one bit, but he needed to keep Kowalski on his side, so he twisted his mouth into a smile. "Well?"

The trucker sighed and rubbed his neck.

"If you're sincere about wanting to know the truth, Hunter, I'd suggest you take this opportunity to get inside the investigation," said Al. It sounded like a challenge, or perhaps a warning.

The trucker sighed again, then nodded. "Okay, chief," he said. "I guess I don't have time to go home for a shower..." Russell looked at his watch and made a face. "I didn't think so," said the trucker. "Let's go."

Now the two of them were on their way to the border, driving down a two-lane road that seemed ludicrously small to connect with a major U.S. Interstate. They passed through residential areas with a semi-rural look to them - large properties, some with fences and barns - and a few clumps of light industrial, and now there were farms to either side of the road, some with neat rows of vegetables. Hunter Rayne's car was an anonymous-looking white Pontiac, and he had the radio tuned to a station identifying itself between songs as JR-FM. Country and western. Russell faced the window and rolled his eyes. It figured.

They'd hardly said two words to each other since leaving Hanratty Wholesale Meats, but something had been niggling the edge of Russell's mind. Rayne had been noticeably alert in the wholesaler's warehouse, following the warehouse manager's every move through narrowed eyes with the concentration of a cougar watching a fawn. The RCMP had virtually ruled out any involvement on the part of Hanratty's employees, so what had made the trucker that keen about covering old ground?

"What's your take on Hanratty?" Russell finally asked. "You think there might be something there?" He couldn't help wondering if Rayne's attention had been directed, not toward picking up new information, but rather toward preventing the warehouse manager from saying something incriminating about his pals, the Nillsons. Or something incriminating about himself?

The trucker shrugged slightly, made a face. "I don't know." He tapped the steering wheel lightly with his fingers, frowning in thought. "I don't like coincidences," he continued. "I've known them to go either way, and that makes them hard to read."

"What coincidences?" Russell reached forward and turned down the radio. It wasn't loud, but it was interfering with his concentration.

"The victim and his girlfriend and roommate were strongly against eating meat, and into animal rights, according to the victim's brother. There had been animal rights graffiti at Hanratty, with a tag that matched the signature on some posters at the victim's home. It might mean nothing, or..." The trucker shrugged again.

"Pretty weak. Kowalski told me that's already been discounted. That tagger's been all over town. Doesn't even rate being called a coincidence, in my book," said Russell. "Now, if, for example, the shipper had been seen arguing with the victim the week before..."

Rayne shot him a wry glance. "I get your point," he said, and they lapsed into silence again.

As they approached the border, Rayne explained the normal procedure a trucker would go through at the border. He pointed out two parking areas where the Nillsons' rig may have been left unattended while the drivers visited the customs brokers to get the paperwork in order, one the lot behind a duty free store, and the other designed specifically for big rigs, but with limited capacity. As they waited in the line-up inching toward the booths where passenger vehicles were required to report, he also pointed out the raised booth where a simple freight clearance could be accomplished without the drivers having to get out of their cabs. "Because they were hauling meat, Ray and Sharon would have had no choice but to stop for inspection, so they would've parked and gone inside. Given the circumstances, it's unlikely they would have knowingly arrived at the border with Williams in their trailer."

"With the car being found in Mount Vernon, it makes more sense that he would have been put into the trailer there," agreed Russell.

After a few questions, the customs inspector waved them through, and Rayne pulled the Pontiac into a parking spot to the left of the booths. Russell had called ahead, and he knew the customs inspector he wanted to talk to was on duty and expecting him. He got out of the car before Rayne had even turned off the ignition, and strode toward the building on the commercial vehicle side. He wanted to make it clear to Rayne and anyone else that this was the U.S.A., and it was his turf, not Rayne's. He stepped inside the door and looked around. There were long line-ups of people and luggage in front of the only two customs inspectors behind the counter.

He heard a voice say, "Russell. This way." Russell turned and saw the trucker holding open the door and motioning him back outside. Russell swore under his breath.

The trucker matched strides with him and was there to open the door for him on the other side of the building. Russell approached the counter and cleared his throat, waiting for attention from one of the inspectors. One of them looked up from the paperwork on his desk, then back down again. The others didn't even look up.

"Hey, chief! How's the shiner?" he heard Rayne say from beside him, and one of the customs inspectors looked up.

"Hello again," he said to the trucker, and glanced over at Russell. "You brought the LAPD back with you. Not in the reefer, I trust."

Russell wasn't amused. "Russell Kupka. L.A. County Sheriff's Department, Homicide Division," he said coldly. He couldn't tell for sure if it was the same voice he'd heard over the phone, so he said, "You're Inspector Donohue?"

Donohue nodded, stood up behind his desk. "Let's go outside," he suggested. "I'll show you the layout."

Russell followed Donohue as the customs inspector explained where the Nillsons' rig had been parked, and how the inspection was carried out. "We had him back it up here and open the doors. Stu isn't on duty right now - he was the agricultural inspector that day - but as I told you on the phone, I know for a fact he didn't look at any more than the rearmost skids of that load. There's really no justification for inspecting every skid in every trailer. As a consequence, full inspections are generally made at random, or if we

195

have a reason to be suspicious. In this case, we had no reason to offload the goods."

"What would have made you suspicious?" asked Russell.

"If the shipper had been red flagged because of non-compliance in the past, or if we'd received a tip about irregularities with the load, or in some cases, we decide to take a closer look if the driver seems nervous or in some way makes us suspect he's got something to hide. There's a lot of drugs, marijuana in particular, moving into the U.S. from B.C. Some big hydroponic grow operations north of the border, high-tech stuff."

Russell stole a glance at Rayne. The trucker was standing at a slight distance from the two of them, his posture relaxed, arms folded across his chest. It occurred to Russell that a trucker could boost his income significantly by ferrying drugs in so-called routine loads. "So if these drivers had done anything to arouse suspicion, you'd have examined the load more closely?"

"If we thought it was drugs, we would've brought in the dogs." Donohue motioned Russell to move away from the loading dock, and the three of them stood silently for a moment, watching a fifty-three foot trailer being backed into position for inspection. "Amazing how accurate some of these drivers can be. I have trouble backing up my kid's toy wagon."

"How about your bike?" asked the trucker with a sly smile.

"No problem. At least I've never gone over the handlebars backing up," the customs inspector answered with a grin.

Russell ignored the exchange. He pulled a small notebook out of his jacket pocket and referred to it. "You told me over the phone that you remembered the drivers. You know: the wife's a Canadian and has applied for her green card?"

"Right," said Donohue. "The blond and the big guy. Seemed friendly enough."

"You remember anything else about them since we last spoke?"

The customs inspector shook his head regretfully. "Sorry."

"So there were four of you standing around back here, is that right?"

"Right. We only needed the one of them to open the door, but she came with him. That's when we talked about the green card business, while Stu was poking around the back of the load. The big guy was pretty quiet. The wife did most of the talking."

"And when the inspection was finished?"

"The driver closed the doors and we left."

"And they drove away?"

"Not immediately, no. There was some paperwork to clear up, so they had to wait a couple of minutes before they could leave."

"They waited here?"

Donohue shook his head, jerked his thumb in the direction of the office. "At the counter out front."

"And you don't think anyone could have gotten into the trailer during that time?" asked Russell, gesturing at the open loading dock.

"Not with the back doors padlocked shut."

Hunter dropped the California detective off at the Villa Hotel in Burnaby. He was hungry. He'd suggested stopping for a meal at the restaurant in Mount Vernon, but in reply, Russell had wrinkled his nose as if he'd encountered a bad smell and then informed Hunter that he had to rush back for a dinner engagement in Vancouver. They didn't do much in Mount Vernon except examine the site. The local police had canvassed the restaurant and surrounding shops, and hadn't been able to turn up a single person who remembered seeing the car arrive, and only a couple who'd even noticed the police making a fuss over it before it was towed away. On the drive back, the detective seemed distant and preoccupied, and they had exchanged very few words.

Leaving the hotel, Hunter couldn't decide whether to turn left or right. Should he head straight for home, pick up something to eat along the way, or should he drop in at his daughters' place to see if one or both them might be free for a late dinner? He thought of Lance the Lawyer, and decided to pull over and phone instead. He couldn't stomach the thought of seeing his ex-wife's lover again, and hoped that at least the man would never answer the phone.

"Hello?" It was Christine. "Hello?"

Hunter wasn't sure what to say. He hadn't spoken to his ex-wife since the night of the barbecue, and she'd been none too happy with him then. "Hi, Chris. It's me," he said.

For a moment he was afraid she was going to hang up. Then, in a tight little voice, she said, "The girls aren't home."

"I'm sorry about the other night," he said. "I shouldn't even have come."

"It wasn't your fault," she said with a sigh. "The girls." She paused, sighed again. "We were both kind of set up, if you know what I mean."

"They're too young to know better."

"You don't have to like him." There was a hostile edge to her voice.

"I know that, Chris. I'm sorry." He knew he should drop the subject right there, but he didn't. "I guess I've lost my patience with drunks."

There were a few seconds of taught silence, then, "Fuck you." Hunter winced. She never used to swear. "It was different when the drunk was your buddy Ken, wasn't it? I couldn't say a bad word about him without you calling me uptight. You never once admitted what a lush he was."

"And you pitied Helen for putting up with it."

"That was an entirely different situation."

Hunter gritted his teeth. He wanted to continue to argue with her, he wanted to stand up for Ken the way he'd done a thousand times before, but he knew it would only make things worse. "Tell the girls I called," he said instead.

"Fuck you," she said again, and his phone went dead.

Hunter turned the phone off and tucked it back in its case. He didn't want to think about it. His face expressionless, he put the car in gear and turned its nose toward the highway to the North Shore. On a day like this one, he figured, the best thing was to cut your losses and head for home, drink a few beers and eat take-out food sitting in front of the television with your brain turned off until you fell asleep.

198

The worst of it was, Hunter knew that she'd been right.

When Russell walked into his room at the Villa Hotel, there was a flashing light on his telephone. He knew it couldn't be Jennifer, because she still didn't know he was in Vancouver. He wanted to talk to her directly, not exchange voice mails, so he hadn't left one. He picked up the receiver and punched the button to retrieve the message.

"Detective Kupka, this is Chad Williams, Greg Williams' brother. I understand from speaking to the RCMP that you're the primary investigator into my brother's murder, and I'd like to discuss it with you. Please call me as soon as possible so we can set up a meeting. You can reach me through the Vancouver Police Department..." He'd left a number for the VPD Vice unit, and another number for his cellular phone.

A second message followed: "Detective Kupka, this is Chad Williams again. I'm off duty now, and you can reach me directly at my cellular number. Please call me immediately when you receive this message."

And a third: "This is Chad Williams. I'm waiting for you in the cocktail lounge of your hotel. Either page me, or join me here as soon as possible. I'm in the booth at the northwest corner, farthest from the bar."

"Shit!" said Russell. He dialed the number of Jennifer's hotel, which he'd already tried twice since his arrival that morning. Again, there was no answer in her room, and he declined to leave a message. "What the hell," he thought, "It saves me tracking him down. I'll go have a drink with Williams and by then it'll be time to try again."

The lounge was dark and quiet, with comfortable armchairs in earth tones and rose, and low round tables with varnished cherrywood surfaces. Chad Williams stood up as Russell approached, and the two men shook hands across the table. "What'll you have?" asked Williams as the waitress approached.

Russell looked at Williams' half empty glass. It looked like ginger ale. "What are you having?"

Williams pushed the glass away. "Now that you're here, I'll switch to beer. I'll have a Kokanee Gold," he said to the waitress.

"Make that two," said Russell, and sat down.

"And a shot of Johnnie Walker Black," added Williams.

Russell shrugged. "Why not?" he said, taking off his jacket and loosening his tie. "It's been a long day." He leaned back, relaxing into the chair, and studied Williams. He was squarely built and only slightly gone to flab, quasi-military haircut, unmistakably a street cop. "What can I do for you?" Russell asked him.

Williams' eyes widened, and his nostrils flared. "My brother is dead and you ask me what you can do for me? You can tell me what the fuck is going on with your investigation, for starters."

Russell held his hands up. "Sorry, pal. Bad choice of words on my part. Like I said, it's been a long day." He leaned forward, his elbows on his knees. "How about I start over? First off, my sincere condolences on the loss of your brother. I know you're a fellow cop, and I guess that made me lose sight of the fact that you're a victim here, too. I'm sorry if I sounded insensitive."

"Okay, just don't jerk me around. Tell me where you're at now. I want to know what happened to Greg."

"How much have the RCMP told you so far?"

It turned out that Chad Williams knew the basics about the crime scene, the cause of death, and the suspects. Russell filled in some of the details, and while they discussed it, the waitress arrived with their drinks.

"That's where we're at so far," said Russell. "I'm here looking for more evidence to support what we've already got, which is pretty strong, even though circumstantial. I know we're on the right track, but I'd really like to uncover the motive." He pulled photos of Ray and Sharon Nillson out of his coat pocket. "You ever seen either of these two people?"

Williams studied the photos, then shook his head. "They the drivers?"

Russell nodded. "We know for a fact your brother's body was in their trailer. Now I want to find out how and why he got there."

200

"Sorry. I don't know many of my brother's friends." He paused to watch the waitress set down their drinks. "What about Greg's car? I heard they found the car. Was there anything in it?"

"Nothing to link him to the suspects, as far as we can tell. Fingerprints belonged mostly to your brother, his wife..."

Williams grunted. "Don't call her that," he said.

"Hey! Whether or not I call her that, legally..."

"Legally shit!" said Williams, and slammed back his shot of scotch whiskey. "If Greg had wanted her to be his wife, he would've married the bitch!"

Russell shrugged. "Outa my hands, pal." He found Williams' volatility irritating. He didn't owe this asshole anything.

"I'm sorry," said Williams. "It's a sore point with me. I warned Greg about her, about getting mixed up with a broad he wouldn't want to bring home to mother. You stick with her for too long, I said, and she'll own half of you. Not worth it for a piece of tail, I told him. Get out before it's too late. But he wouldn't fuckin' listen. She'd turn those big cow eyes in his direction and his brains turned to mush."

Russell downed his own shot of Johnnie Walker. He felt its trail of fire from the back of his throat right down to his belly, and the relaxing warmth spread down to his fingertips and toes within seconds. He sighed. "You want to hear about the car or not?" he said.

Williams nodded.

"There was a guitar. An acoustic guitar in a case..."

"Don't let her have any of that stuff. Anybody gets his stuff, it should be me, not her."

Russell glared at him.

"Sorry I interrupted. Go on." Williams raised his beer to his lips, as if to prevent himself from speaking.

"And a tape recorder with a tape in it."

Williams' beer glass hit the table with a thud. "A tape? What kind of a tape? What was on it?"

Russell frowned, and put his head back to take a few long swallows of his own beer. He was extending a courtesy here. He wasn't obligated to tell this man anything, and he certainly didn't intend to jeopardize the investigation by revealing things that could become important evidence. He put his beer down, then shrugged. "A song your brother was working on, I guess. Nothing of great importance, as far as I could tell."

"A song? No conversations? Were there any other tapes?"

Russell's mouth twitched in irritation. "I said, a tape - a single tape - and I think the RCMP homicide detectives and myself are pretty good judges of whether or not it contained anything relevant to the case." Williams looked chastened, and in a moment of uncomfortable silence, they both turned their attention to their drinks.

The waitress arrived with a second round. Russell began to protest, but Williams said, "It's on me, Detective. I appreciate you being so forthcoming with me." He pushed the second shot of Johnnie Walker toward Russell's right hand, and raised his own glass. "To my little brother," he said.

Russell had no choice but to drink.

Eighty minutes and two more rounds later, Russell was sick of hearing Chad Williams rant about his brother's choice of women and careers. He had to agree that being a bar musician wasn't the most practical choice of vocations, but he would have to meet this poor woman for himself, and after tonight, he was feeling inclined to give her the benefit of the doubt. It was the American way, wasn't it? to root for the underdog.

Chad Williams' confided what he called "valuable tips", including some general information about Greg's band, their rumored drug involvement, a suggestion that there was valuable recording equipment in the band's studio. "All the stuff that belonged to Greg should come to me. Don't let that little bitch get her hands on it, or those slack-ass musicians he hung out with."

Here we go again, thought Russell, then looked at his watch and groaned. "Look," he said, getting abruptly to his feet. "I gotta go. If you think of anything else, call Al Kowalski, will you? He'll make sure I get the message." Then he hustled himself out of there before Williams had a chance to protest.

Waiting for lights out, Sharon tried to sit still but she couldn't. She had already paced up and down the cell for nearly two hours, until she literally felt like climbing the walls. She was so wired, she felt like her head was ready to explode. But what she wanted was to calm down so she'd be able to slip into the sweet oblivion of sleep as soon as the lights went out, so she forced herself to sit down on her bunk and try to read.

Almost against her will, she looked up. The witch was sitting cross legged on her bunk, and when she caught Sharon looking, she licked her lips and patted her crotch. "Taste of honey, Princess. I'm savin' it for you."

Sharon's jaw stiffened and her breath started coming fast and shallow.

"It's you and me, Princess," she sang in a lascivious voice, then cackled like the witch she was. "Forget about your old man. I'll be your honey pot and you be my hungry little bear. It's you and..."

Sharon lunged across the cell. She didn't want to touch the disgusting creature with her bare hands, so she swatted her across the face with her paperback, once, twice. It took her surprised cellmate a few seconds to raise her hands to her face, and when she did, Sharon tossed the book away. It hit the cell bars and dropped to the floor, but Sharon had already picked up the woman's pillow and begun whacking her about the head and shoulders. The woman was still cackling, screaming in delight as if this had been part of her plan, and Sharon realized the pillow wouldn't hurt her enough to shut her up.

Sharon began screaming back at her. "Shut up! Shut up, witch! Shut the fuck up!" She was only dimly aware of clanging and cheering coming from the other cells. "Shut up!" she screamed, her voice beyond her control, and grabbing the pillow firmly at each end, she lunged again at her cellmate, driving the woman's head back against the wall. It hit with a dull thud and Sharon pinned her there, her knees across the woman's bony thighs. The woman squirmed and Sharon felt the bony hands first flailing at her chest, then grabbing at her arms. Suddenly and without warning, a thick arm circled Sharon's neck and she felt herself being dragged backwards, and the pillow being yanked out of her hands.

"Cool it!" a deep female voice bellowed into her ear as she was hauled back to her bed and made to sit down. "Cool it!" She didn't struggle, and the guard's grip on her gradually relaxed.

Sharon started to sob.

"It's okay, honey," the guard said, her voice almost gentle. "I won't hurt you. You just take a deep breath. Calm down and it'll be okay."

"That... that... woman... she's..." Sharon had to stop to take three or four deep breaths. "I just..."

"I know, honey. I know. She's pretty disgustin', I know that. But she ain't gonna hurt you if you don't let her."

Another guard was standing over Sharon's cellmate, talking to her in a low voice. "Keep your hands to yourself, Prentice, and don't provoke her, hear? You want to get out of here in one piece, you don't mess with your neighbor, hear?"

"Can't you move me?" pleaded Sharon. "Can't you get me away from her?"

"Prentice is a little crazy, but she ain't gonna hurt you. You got to grin and bear it, honey. This ain't a long term thing here. It's just temporary. So just grin and bear it, and don't make more trouble for y'self by causing a stink over it, understand?"

The guard handed her the paperback, and cautioned her one more time before she closed the cell door. "Just take it easy, don't make trouble for y'self."

The door clanged shut, and they listened in silence as the guards' footsteps receded down the corridor.

"Hee, hee," said her cellmate.

"Oh, for God's sake! Will you SHUT THE FUCK UP!"

204

CHAPTER

EIGHTEEN

Russell's head felt like it was stuffed with steel wool. He blinked against the sunlight flooding his hotel room, wishing he'd had the foresight to close the drapes the night before. He lifted his arm to shield his eyes, noticed that he still wore his shirt. He lifted the bedspread, realized that he hadn't even had the foresight, or whatever it took, to undress, or to even take off his shoes. "Fu-uck," he groaned, and closed his eyes. His tongue worked sluggishly against his coated teeth.

A vague memory surfaced. Chad Williams in the hotel bar. He had come back to his room to call Jennifer, and finally left a message for her to call back. While he was waiting to hear from her, he opened the mini-bar and ate a jar of roasted nuts. Then he'd made himself a drink, and ate a chocolate bar, and phoned her again. And again. By the time he got hold of Jennifer it was two a.m. and his mini-bar was half empty and he was drunk. "Fuck," he said again, as the memory sharpened. He'd made an ass of himself, big time, and he didn't know if he'd be able to fix it with her. She'd been working long hours, she said, then made it clear that she didn't want to see him this weekend at all.

He stripped off his shirt and balled it up to stuff in his suitcase, then folded his slacks carefully and hung them on a towel rack in the bathroom. He stood under the shower for fifteen minutes, as hot as he could stand it, in an attempt to steam the wrinkles out of his slacks, then followed up with five minutes of cold, trying to clear his head. When he emerged to dress, he heard the fading beep of his dying cell phone. He'd left it on and forgotten to put his other spent battery on the charger. "Fuck," he said one more time. Downstairs, he forced himself to eat a fruit plate for breakfast and inhaled three cups of black coffee before ordering a rental car. He walked outside into the sunlit parking lot and set about studying the map they supplied. He had no intention of depending on anyone else for transportation today, not the RCMP, and especially not that trucker.

His first stop was Greg Williams' home. It didn't look very far on the map, but the lights and traffic along Kingsway, plus the minor detours he had to make in order to locate the right street, stretched the drive into more than half an hour. Teresa Jagpal had been expecting him, having been contacted the day before by Al Kowalski by way of introduction. She met him at the front door, a pliant brown-skinned girl with big dark eyes, and although she suggested sitting in the living room, he asked if they could sit at the kitchen table. He felt more in control at a table, somehow. The chairs were moveable, and the situation simulated the interview rooms he was used to.

There was another woman standing at the stove, waiting for a kettle to boil. She ignored them both until Teresa asked Russell if he would like some tea. He asked for coffee.

"Do we still have that coffee, Hellen?" Teresa said to the woman with the kettle. The woman turned around. She had short spiky hair - hennaed, he thought - and lipstick of a similar shade, stark as a raw wound against her pallid skin.

"There's a jar of cheap instant - cheap and old - if you want," the woman said directly to Russell. Her voice was as garish as her lips. "We don't do caffeine."

"You live here, too?" asked Russell.

While the woman seemed to be searching for an answer - a disdainful one, judging by her smirk - Teresa spoke. "Yes. The house belongs to Hellen's aunt."

206

Russell introduced himself and offered his hand. The woman let him take her fingers, then let them fall away. "Good old L.A.," she said, and turned back to the stove.

Russell snorted softly. Affected boredom bored him. He motioned Teresa to take a chair, then pulled out one for himself, moving it close to her with only a corner of the table between them, and with his back to the other woman. He leaned forward and spoke softly. "As I believe Corporal Kowalski told you, Teresa," he began, "we think we have the persons in custody who are responsible for the death of your husband, Greg. I'd just like to go over some things with you, see if there's anything you can tell me about your husband that will reinforce or refute the theory we've developed." Russell resisted the urge to attribute the theory to himself alone. A 'we' would carry more authority, he reasoned.

Teresa Jagpal squirmed in her chair, seemed about to say something when the woman behind him slammed a cupboard door. Russell frowned, trying to look troubled rather than irritated, and it seemed to work, because Teresa said, "Perhaps we can wait until Hellen is finished. Are you nearly done?"

The woman named Hellen banged two mugs on the counter and replied, "Do it yourself, then," before breezing into the other room. Russell heard the small rustling noises of her sitting down and turning pages, and although he knew she could still hear them, he was glad that she was gone.

He guided Teresa Jagpal through a description of her husband's last days, his habits, and his friends. Everything she said pretty much tallied with what he'd already heard from the RCMP, but he felt more comfortable getting it right from the horse's mouth. The guy lived for his music. His wife was a fan, but was not a musician herself, nor a drinker, so she seldom went to his studio or went to his bar gigs, unless they were close by. He'd left her no money, no insurance, and no will.

"We weren't married, Greg and I," she said. "We never thought of ourselves as husband and wife, so it's hardly surprising he would ... um... that he wouldn't leave me anything." She seemed embarrassed by this statement, and wouldn't meet Russell's eyes. She was hardly the bitch that Chad Williams had described. He wondered why the burly cop had felt so threatened by her, especially in relation to his dead brother's estate. "Well, he didn't have much anyway. Greg was very talented, but it takes time to build a reputation in the music business, you know? He needed to meet the right people, make the right connections before the money got better. It was just a matter of time, he always said." She raised her eyes briefly, looked away again. "Greg didn't have much," she repeated.

Thinking of what Williams had said about the recording studio, he asked "What about the equipment in the recording studio? Isn't that pretty valuable stuff?"

Teresa shrugged, looking confused. "I don't know anything about equipment. I know he went to the studio a lot to practice. I don't think it was his own equipment." More quietly, almost to herself, she added, "Was it?"

Russell frowned. "Did he keep any papers here? Receipts, bills of sale, that type of thing?"

She offered him a strained smile. "His desk is outside in the carport. I don't really know what's in it." She led Russell out the door, across a weedy lawn and into a cluttered carport, explaining that she'd had the neighbor help carry Greg's things outside, and was waiting for the Salvation Army to pick them up. Lumpy black garbage bags surrounded a small wooden desk, painted rusty brown. A waterbed frame leaned up against the carport's weathered posts.

"After the break-in, all the drawers were empty and there were books and papers scattered all over the floor. I just scooped them up and put them back in the desk, but I didn't really look at them." She said the police had given them a cursory examination, but hadn't shared any conclusions with her.

"That's because they didn't have any," said Russell, opening a drawer and riffling through a sheaf of mismatched papers, mostly handwritten notes with what were presumably song lyrics, mixed in with photocopied pages of performance contracts with the name of the booking agent at the top. Russell noted the amounts, shook his head. According to these, the guy was working for peanuts, never grossing more than a couple of hundred dollars a week. Flat on the

208

bottom of one drawer was a manila envelope, which he pried out with a fingernail. He shook it and a stack of papers slid out, the first a bill of sale from an electronics store with Greg Williams' name on the top line, for a piece of recording equipment worth over $3000. Scrawled at the bottom was 'Paid in Cash'. There were at least half a dozen such invoices, for varying amounts, some considerably higher in value. Russell whistled softly. "Your husband have an inheritance last year? Savings from a previous job? Where'd all this cash come from?"

Teresa leaned closer to read the receipts. She shook her head, looking bewildered. "He mostly got paid in cash at the gigs, but he never had that much." She looked away, obviously uncomfortable. "He didn't... I don't understand... why didn't he tell me? Why didn't I know about this?"

"You were supporting him?" Russell asked gently.

"Well, temporarily," she said, but her breath quickened. "He... he was waiting for a break, like I said. I knew he'd pay me back one day." She looked in his eyes briefly, then away again. "Greg contributed what he could," she added, but they both knew that she could no longer believe that.

Russell shook his head, examining the bills of sale.

"Maybe the whole band chipped in," Teresa suggested.

Russell smiled. As if a group of musicians would trust one of their number to register a purchase this size in his own name. Maybe, being "artists", they didn't know any better, but Russell doubted it. "Did Greg have a bicycle?" he asked.

She hesitated, a pained looked on her face. "He never told me about that, either. Did he buy a bicycle, too?"

Teresa followed him back to the house. The woman with spiky hair still sat in the living room, ignored them as they returned to the kitchen. Teresa sat back down at the kitchen table, her back stiff, her mouth closed but lips working silently while he wrote a few things in his notebook, then he referred back to his previous notes.

"What can you tell me about Hanratty Meats?" he asked.

She raised her wide eyes to his face. "Hanratty Meats? I don't understand," she said, looking briefly toward the door to the living room. "I don't understand what Hanratty Meats would have to do with Greg." He opened his mouth to speak, but she didn't wait for a response. "I know he was found in a trailer full of meat, but I don't understand why he would be, or why he would have gone there. Greg wasn't like that."

"Wasn't like what?"

"Wasn't an activist. He was a musician. That's all he really cared about. He'd never get involved in protests or meetings or anything."

"Meetings?"

"You know. Animals rights groups or save the whales or... things like that." She spoke the last words at the end of a breath. Minutes seemed to pass before she inhaled again.

"You're familiar with Hanratty Meats then?"

"As far as I know, Greg never had anything to do with Hanratty Meats." She frowned and sighed. "Not that he ever told me," she added then, emphasizing the word me.

Russell studied her curiously for a moment, debating whether to pursue this line of questioning further. She was being evasive, in her quiet way, but she'd still told him what he expected, and wanted, to hear. He, too, didn't believe Hanratty Meats had anything to do with the reason why Greg Williams died. He pulled Ray and Sharon Nillson's mug shots out of his jacket pocket and laid one of them on the table for her to see.

She leaned over the picture for a few seconds, then looked up at him. "I don't know this man," she said. "Is he...?"

"Look again," he said. "Have you ever seen him before?" When she shook her head, he put Sharon's photograph on top of Ray's. "How about this woman? Have you ever heard of Watson Transportation?"

Again she shook her head. "No. No, I don't remember seeing either one of these people. Are they the ones who...?" She didn't finish the question, and Russell ignored it, instead arranging the photographs side-by-side and motioning for her to look again.

"I... I don't know these people," she said. "If they did it... I don't know why. I don't know why anyone would want to hurt Greg." She

210

buried her face in her hands. "I don't know. Why is there so much about him I don't know?"

After the detective from California left, Teresa excused herself with a headache, told Hellen she was going to lie down. She stayed in her room until she heard Hellen leave the house, then peered through a crack in the blinds to make sure Hellen was really gone, watched her get in her car and drive away. When Hellen's car had turned the corner out of sight, Teresa went to the back door, parted the curtains in its little window to look out at the yard. It had rained during the night, and the grass was still wet, as if with heavy dew.

What other secrets had Greg kept from her? If he had thousands of dollars to spend on equipment for his studio, why had he always looked so embarrassed and ashamed when he told her he was broke, thanked her with tender kisses when she picked up his share of the rent, seemed so truly grateful for her financial support? Could he lie to her so easily? What else had he hidden from her? She thought again of his nighttime excursions into the back yard, and the burglar who had torn the house apart but taken nothing. Could Greg have stashed something outside?

Teresa walked barefoot across the unmowed lawn, taking simple pleasure from the feel of the soft wet grass beneath her soles and around her toes. She touched the rough bark of the plum tree, let her hand slide down its length as she bent to examine the roots, and around its circumference as she circled the tree. No hiding places there. She stood on tiptoe and thrust her fingers into the V between the branches, again worked her way around the tree to look and feel from all sides. There was nothing there, either.

She cast a glance around the yard and then focused on the old doghouse where the little gray cat liked to play. The carpet, she thought. She put one hand on the mossy roof as she knelt to peer inside. The front of the carpet was still wet from the rain and she was loathe to touch its mildew blackened edge. She reached inside and felt the surface for any lumps or bumps. It was smooth and even to the touch. She leaned her shoulder inside the dog sized door and

211

began to feel along the underside of the roof, jerking her hand away as it came across the sticky threads of a spider web inside. Perhaps if she tipped the doghouse on its end, she could examine the inside from without. She did so – it wasn't as heavy as she thought it might be – but didn't have to look inside. Duct taped to the plywood underside of the doghouse was a square of green plastic.

Teresa let the doghouse fall and spun around to see if anyone was watching. When she saw no one, she tipped up the doghouse, ripped the duct tape off the plywood, then settled the doghouse back down into exactly the same spot, taking care not to trap the long grass that surrounded it underneath its base. She looked around her again before running back to the house, the plastic square tucked close against her chest.

Greg had kept too many secrets from her. Now it was time for him to share.

Russell's next destination was Whistlestop Studios. It was even harder to find than the victim's home, so he stopped at a gas station and bought a coffee, casually asked for directions as he sorted through his American coins looking for Canadian quarters. It wasn't all that far, but en route he had to wait for a freight train, a seemingly endless string of grain cars peppered with rust and graffiti. Russell sipped at his coffee and tried to revive some sense of optimism about his relationship with Jennifer. Was it really as bad as he thought when he woke up this morning with his brain leached out by alcohol? By the time the train passed and he put the car into gear, he'd decided that yes, it was as bad as he thought. Maybe worse.

The studio was on the second floor of a boxy warehouse with light blue aluminum siding. He took the stairs two at a time in an attempt to punish himself for last night's drinking. The upstairs door was open, and he looked in to see two unkempt young men watching another one work the buttons and dials of a piece of electronic equipment, black and brushed aluminum with blue and green LED displays. A thundering riff from a base guitar started and immediately

212

stopped as the operator became aware of Russell's presence. All three stared at him without smiling.

"Are you the Carrots?" he asked, stepping inside. The room was sparsely furnished: a couple of scarred trestle tables and several stacking chairs of the types that populate church basements and school gymnasiums. There were some garish rock music posters and a few pen and ink drawings taped to the wall that ran between the door and the window.

"No," said the one manning the hardware. He was, Russell thought, surprisingly healthy looking for a musician. He seemed exceptionally fit, and his cut off blue jeans and muscle shirt exposed shining planes of tanned skin. "We're part of a single carrot," he added, turning back to the machine. He wore a purple bandana on his head, pirate like. Russell looked for a gold hoop earring but couldn't see one.

"Three quarters of a carrot," added one of the others.

"The fourth quarter is here in spirit," said the third. The first musician spun around, eyes wide in mock alarm. Baring his teeth, he raised two fingers in the sign of a cross toward two or three spots on the ceiling.

"And that would be Greg Williams," said Russell, producing his ID and holding it out to each of them in turn. "Is there somewhere I can talk to each of you about him, one at a time?"

"Why?" said the first musician, dropping his exorcism and turning to Russell with a grin too much like the Joker's for Russell's comfort. Either the man had never grown out of the role of class clown, or he was half crazy. "We keep no secrets from each other! We're like the Three Musketeers, all for one and one for all. Right, guys?" His grin faded. "Ayeee! Agree with me, you slime dogs, or I'll make cat food out of you! En guard!" he growled, snatching up a drum stick and wielding it, with sound effects, as if it were a rapier.

The second musician frowned, shifted uncomfortably from foot to foot. "Get serious, Max."

The other one shrugged and spoke to Russell. "I got no problem with it. Can't tell you much, but I got no problem." He turned to Max. "We could use the mad room, eh?"

213

Max, who turned out to be the drummer and to all appearances the lead Carrot, led the way to a tiny back room, probably intended as a supply closet, but now furnished with a mattress on the floor and a child's bedside lamp, shaped like a clown. One of the clown's arms had broken off. A mountain bike leaned up against one wall. Max rolled back the mattress with his foot and rearranged two mismatched chairs, then ushered Russell and the second musician in with a sweeping bow. "Entrez," he said, rolling the r like a Frenchman.

"Why is it the mad room?" asked Russell, after the door was closed.

"Oh, it's just that Max kind of took it over, and we call him Mad Max because... well, you see how he is, never serious for a minute and kind of off the wall, you know?"

Russell had a line of questioning that was meant to elicit information about Greg Williams, his final weeks, and the band itself. He was also fishing for information about the equipment in the studio. Who paid for it? How was it paid for? His thinking was that if there was dirty money involved in the purchase of the equipment, that same dirty money, or the means by which it was obtained, could have supplied the motive behind Greg's murder. The more he thought about it, the more convinced he became that smuggling was involved. Drugs across the border by truck. God knows there were enough truckers showing excessive interest in the case to make him wonder. The first Carrot, who was the bass guitarist, didn't have much new to say or was effectively playing dumb. He had long blond hair and a goatee, and wore a navy blue tee shirt and faded jeans. There was a silver ring in his left nostril.

"The stuff belongs to Greg and Max. I don't ask questions, man. You know, don't look a gift horse in the mouth, that's what they say, right? I appreciate having the stuff, but I'm no techie. I'm just the bass player, man. Half the stuff was already set up here when I started last fall. Could be rented... hell, could be stolen for all I know." He shook his head and pressed his lips together. "I got nothin' I can tell you. Greg and Max made things work here. I'm just along for the ride. They write the songs. I just play my licks and go home, man."

214

The keyboard player wasn't much better. The only thing he added to Russell's fund of knowledge about Williams was that Williams took his music a lot more seriously than he should have. "Like, not to speak ill of the dead and that, but he wasn't that good. Me? I know I'll never be more than a second rate musician, and that's okay by me. I got no pretensions. I love to play. I'm gonna play anyway, and if somebody wants to pay me a few bucks to do it, even better." He grinned, exposing a broken front tooth, then he shrugged his shoulders and tweaked the ends of his droopy mustache. "But Williams figured he could make big bucks if he sent a decent demo to L.A. or Nashville or something. Him and Max had ambitions. Shit. I liked the guy, but he was no Bryan Adams. He wrote a couple of songs that weren't too bad, but, shit. He was no Springsteen, that's for sure."

When Max came in, he turned the chair around, straddled it and hunched himself around its back. His knee bobbed with some arcane rhythm, the heel of his black boot stopping just short of the floor with every beat. "So, who iced the poor bastard? You guys figure it out yet?" he asked, then grinned like the Joker.

"You and him get along?" The guy just shrugged. The RCMP had told Russell that Max Curry and the other band members had solid alibis for the afternoon of Greg Williams' last trip to the border, but the drummer's extreme nonchalance about his friend's death raised Russell's suspicion. "How long did you and him play here together?"

The drummer made a show of counting to thirty on his fingers, then said, "About four years. We've only had this space since last fall, though. Before that we practiced in my Dad's garage." He frowned then soberly said, "No, five. It was the same year I started working at Toilets R Us. "

Russell consulted his notes. The RCMP had said Max Curry worked part-time at a wholesale plumbing supply warehouse. He was doing a shift there up until five o'clock of the day Greg disappeared. Stronger alibis than that had been broken. Russell clenched his jaw. He ached to tell this smart ass to can the humor, but knew that was

215

exactly what he wanted and he'd be damned if he'd give the guy the satisfaction of reacting. "That your bike?" he said instead.

Max nodded, surprised at the question. "My mean green wheelin' machine," he said.

"Nice," said Russell. Then, "You got receipts for all that equipment out there?"

"I don't see how that's any business of the L.A. Po-leece," Max replied with the Joker's grin. "Care to enlighten me?"

"If you're referring to the possibility I might prosecute you for possession of stolen property, you're absolutely right. I won't, and I couldn't if I wanted to. I'm trying to find out more about your buddy Williams. If that's his equipment, I want to know. If it is, I want to know where he got his money from." He grinned back at the drummer. "If you're scared of being suspected of his murder, relax. Don't get your gaunchies in a knot. But if you want to confess to it and take the fall, just for fun, be my guest." Russell pulled his dead cell phone out of his pocket. "Just say the word and I'll call in the Mounties."

Max snorted. "Everybody's got to be a comedian. Why don't you leave it to the real funny guys, like me and Saddam Hussein, huh?" He stood up, sliding the chair out from between his legs, stretched his arms and back, then sat back down. "Yeah, Greg brought the stuff here. You never heard the expression, don't look a gift horse in the mouth? Why take the chance that his stinkin' breath'll make you puke."

"Horses don't eat meat. It's carnivores whose breath stinks," said Russell. "So where'd Williams get the bucks?"

Max held up his hands, pleading ignorance. "I asked him the same question. He answered me with a question of his own."

"What's that?"

"'What the hell difference does it make to you?'" He said it as if the question were addressed to Russell.

Russell stiffened, waited in silence for him to continue.

The drummer sniffed, kicked the chair leg lightly with the heel of his boot, then said, "That's what he said, and I said, 'I guess it doesn't, man' and we left it at that."

216

"I hear you had a break-in here. Looks like they weren't after your equipment."

"Yep, that's what it looks like," said Max. "Whoever it was, they dumped the contents of a couple of Greg's cardboard boxes all over the floor. Most of it was his sheet music and shit. I don't know if they found what they were looking for, because I don't know what all was in them in the first place."

Max stood up, turned his chair around and sat down again, then tipped the back against the wall, balancing on the back legs. The right knee started to bob again, marking complicated time to some unheard tune. Russell tried not to watch it.

"What kind of a relationship did you have with Greg Williams?"

Max gestured with a limp wrist. "I swear, Officer, we were just good friends," he said in a falsetto. Then, "Only thing we really had in common was our music. Except for the women, of course. But that was before."

"The women?"

"Well, we did some stuff together as two couples. You know. We went out for pizza, had parties at home, that kind of shit. I was living with Double Hell..." He shuddered visibly. "And Greg was shacked up with her little friend, Jag. You must've seen Jag, right? Greg's old lady?'

"Teresa Jagpal? Yeah."

"Then you probably met Double Hell, the Wonder Bitch."

Russell assumed he meant the woman with the spiky hair, and nodded.

"Hell hath no fury, like the Wonder Bitch. You know what she did? We decided right up front when she moved in with me that we'd hang loose, you know? No strings. An open relationship. It was even her idea. Well, then she decided I wasn't staying home enough and she started getting on my case. Finally I told her I was fed up, she was hangin' all over me and bitchin' every time I stayed out all night. I was sorely tempted to beat the shit out of her, but I didn't. So I told her I was moving in with my sister and setting her free. That's how I put it, setting her free. I thought she'd like that. So I come back to pick up my drum kit, and she'd fuckin' cut the skins to ribbons with the biggest knife she could find. She's one scary chick, man. Don't think Fatal Attraction didn't flash through my mind. I've steered clear of her ever since."

Russell looked at the drummer appraisingly. He had no reason not to believe him. "How did Hellen and Greg get along?"

Max snorted. "Double Hell was nice as pie to Greggie after I split with her. She had him convinced that I had it coming - the knife bit - and me and Greg weren't exactly bosom buddies at the time so it didn't take much convincing on his part. He could be such a supercilious little prick sometimes..." He rolled his eyes, his lips twisted in a disgusted sneer. "I think he was poking her, after she moved back in to her aunt's place there. I know she was trying to get him more involved in her animal rights shit. I swear she'd shoot a man dead for kicking a dog. Like I said, she's a crazy bitch. Anyway, Greg didn't exactly confide in me, but I think they started fucking."

"So you and Greg didn't get along?"

Max scrunched up one side of his face, drew a sibilant breath through closed teeth. "Let's just say we didn't always agree on the direction to take the band or our music. Sometimes he behaved as if the music was just there to showcase his voice, and I wasn't all that crazy about his voice. Aspartame. No edge to it. The chicks seemed to like it, though. I gotta give him that. Let's just say that he liked to sip champagne and I like a good slug of Jack Daniels. Nothin' personal, but we had our disagreements from time to time."

Russell steered the conversation back to money. Max remained adamant that he didn't know where Greg's money came from. He'd never seen Sharon or Ray Nillson, nor heard of Watson Transportation. Either he was involved and hid it very well, or the drummer from Carrot Rampant was telling the truth.

Joker or not, as he headed back out to his car, Russell decided that Mad Max had been telling the truth.

Sunday morning, Hunter and his landlord had made the trek up Highway 99 to Squamish, to the closest golf course where they were able to book an early tee off at short notice. Standing on the first tee,

218

Hunter took a deep breath and swung his fat-headed driver once or twice, easy and relaxed. It felt good. He was suddenly thankful that he had kept his promise to Gord, and taken the time to golf. Sometimes he forgot how good it felt to let himself play - not golf specifically, just "play". To do something for the sheer joy of it.

Gord was holding his five wood above his head, twisting his body left and right to loosen up his spine. In his seventies, it often took some time to get the stiffness out of his joints. They hardly said a word as they waited for the threesome ahead of them to hit to the green and move out of range. There was a light breeze to take the hot edge off the sun, and it carried the liquid melodies of a robin, as well as the chirps and warbles of a few birds Hunter didn't recognize. He inhaled deeply of the scent of fresh cut grass. Gord's drive went straight down the middle about a hundred and forty yards. He nodded with satisfaction. "I'll take that," he said.

Hunter's first drive sliced wildly out of bounds, so he took a mulligan and used another ball. It still went right but stayed on the fairway, about twenty yards or so beyond Gord's. They grinned at each other and walked off the tee box. "I should do this more often," said Hunter.

"You should," agreed the old doctor, grabbing the handle of his pull cart and walking on.

When they finished the round, Hunter managing to break a hundred in spite of being out of practice, thanks to a couple of strategic mulligans, while Gord ended up with about a dozen strokes more, they headed back down the highway to Horseshoe Bay, looking for a quiet table in the Troller Pub to relax over pints of ale and a late lunch. "I met my ex-wife's new boyfriend last week," announced Hunter halfway into his first pint.

The old man nodded. "And?"

"Nothing," said Hunter with a shrug, playing with the corner of his napkin. "She likes him, and I guess that's all that counts."

Gord raised his beer mug. "Good thing you don't have to like him," he said with a twinkle in his eye.

Hunter smiled. "Okay," he said, leaning back. "You're right. I'm having a hard time liking him. He's a real jerk, and I think she deserves better. No, I think the girls deserve to see their mother with somebody better." He shook his head. "I never understood it, in all the years attending domestic disputes while I was a member. Why do so many women settle for abusive men?"

"He's abusive?"

"Maybe not physically. He's obnoxious. It's not that he's overtly mean to her, but he doesn't show her enough respect. Or am I being old fashioned again?"

"You're allowed to hate him, if it makes you feel better."

The waitress set down a basket of onion rings and they each took one, then another.

"It's not that I'm harboring a secret desire to get back together with my ex-wife." Hunter picked up the thread of the conversation again, gesturing with an onion ring. "It's... well... ." Hunter sighed. "He did the barbecuing. He's now part of what used to be my family, and I'm part of..." He shrugged. "... nothing."

"You can't hold him responsible for your choices."

"Hey! You're the one who said I could hate him."

Gord shrugged apologetically. "Sure, go ahead. I just didn't want you to forget that being on your own is ultimately your choice. It's something you can change, if you really want."

"I guess I haven't wanted then." Hunter smiled wistfully. He thought of Alora Magee in California, and he thought of Helen Marsh, widow of his friend Ken. He hadn't spoken to her more than a couple of times since Ken's death. "Or wanted enough."

They were halfway back to the house, Hunter driving his landlord's Mazda through a surge of ferry traffic along the Upper Levels Highway, when Hunter said, "I wish at least that he'd burned the chicken."

Gord grunted in agreement, and Hunter was glad he'd been able to talk to somebody who understood.

CHAPTER
NINETEEN

After leaving the Carrots' studio, Russell pointed the nose of his rental car north and then west, which, according to the map, was downtown. Jennifer was staying at the Holiday Inn Harborside, which he understood was right in the heart of Vancouver. He didn't expect to find her there, but he wanted to get familiar with this place she didn't share with him, he wanted it to lose its mystery and mystique. He wanted to uncover its warts.

The highway turned into a street named Broadway, which gradually became more and more commercial until block after block was an endless line of retail stores and restaurants, with an occasional office tower or hotel. Here and there, through a gap between buildings, he could see mountains rising up north of the city, higher and greener than the hills around L.A. The signs told him to turn, and he did, heading across a six lane bridge toward the mountains. Water, a deep blue and littered with small boats, stretched in both directions beneath the bridge. Soon he was in downtown canyons, surrounded by concrete and glass. The usual big city mixture of tourists with cameras and derelicts with green garbage bags, students with backpacks and tailored men and women in expensive suits. He turned again, heading west, and soon found the hotel: a deep brown building on a street near the waterfront, quiet because it was Sunday.

He watched a group of elderly Asians clamber into a mini-van, and took the parking place when it pulled away.

He turned off the ignition and sat there, staring at the building. The glass of the front entrance was dark, so he couldn't see inside. The doors opened, and a middle aged couple walked out, the woman in a lemon yellow dress with white shoes and purse, the man in a suit. Dressed for a wedding. They were followed by a young family, the kid with a red and blue knapsack, the mother in Birkenstocks and khaki shorts. She stopped, studying a book of some sort, then pointed in the direction Russell had just come. They set off that way, the kid skipping and the father grabbing the knapsack to hold him back at the curb.

Just a hotel, like any other. Nothing secret. Nothing scary. He wondered whether he should go inside, call her room. Maybe he could send up flowers, something from the gift shop, as an apology. Or would she resent him coming here to her hotel, intruding on her world uninvited, especially after last night? Would she give him the chance to apologize, now that he was sober? He knew he couldn't leave it like it was. Before he left Vancouver, he had to talk to her again, or at least try. He locked the car, and, smoothing his hair, crossed the street to the hotel.

When Hunter and his landlord arrived back home, there were two messages on his answering machine. One was from Jeff Feldman. Ray Nillson had just fired him, he said, and he thought Hunter would like to know. Hunter shook his head. Maybe Ray could relate better to an older lawyer, someone a little more homespun than Feldman. In any case, there was nothing Hunter could do about it today. The next message was from El, confirming that he could deliver Greg Williams' amps and synthesizer to the studio on Still Creek that afternoon. "Wife doesn't seem to be home, but there's somebody at the studio, and like you said, we'd better get them out of my Hino today."

Hunter stowed his golf clubs, washed the smell of onion rings off his hands, grabbed his car keys and headed out the door. When he rounded the corner of the house, he saw Gord standing beside a cherry red vehicle talking to the driver. Before he could make out who it was, Gord turned around and pointed at him, and the driver's hand began waving excitedly.

"Want to go for a ride, Dad?" It was his daughter, Janice. Her younger sister Lesley sat beside her.

"Pretty jazzy lookin' wheels you got there, doll," said Hunter. They grinned at each other.

"Yeah. C'mon for a ride, Dad. I'll sit in the back," said Lesley. The girls both opened their doors and stepped out of the car while Hunter continued his inspection of the little Tracker, nodding appraisingly.

"Want to drive it, Dad?'

Hunter looked at her, trying to decide whether she wanted him to say yes or no. "Yes, if it's okay with you."

They took a spin around the block, Hunter making all the appropriate noises - lot of pep, just the right size for you, must get good gas mileage - then apologized for having to cut it short. "I'm afraid I've got a delivery scheduled for this afternoon." He was going to suggest he drop by their place on his way home, but remembered last time.

As if she were reading his mind, Lesley said, "Mom hasn't invited Lance over again since her birthday."

"Oh? She's stopped seeing him?"

"No. But I think it embarrasses her for us to see them together."

"Yeah, Dad. He makes her feel embarrassed. I guess you made her take a hard look at him. He's obnoxious. I don't think he'll last."

Hunter just smiled.

When Hunter backed the Hino up to the building that housed Whistlestop Studios, it was already close to five o'clock. The lower door was unlocked, so he let himself in. Before he was halfway up the stairs, a young man wearing cut-off jeans and a mesh muscle shirt came out on the upper landing and called down to him, "You the delivery guy?" He had a purple bandana on his head.

"You betcham," said Hunter. "You with..." He pretended to look at the waybill. "... Whistlestop Studios?"

"You got it," said the young man, starting down the stairs. "Yo! Piano-man. Get your fat ass out here," he called over his shoulder to someone still inside.

"You want to carry some of these things up those stairs, you're welcome to," said Hunter, rolling up the door of the Hino and climbing into the back. He handed a rectangular case to the man, who close up turned out to be not quite as young as Hunter had first thought, maybe late twenties or early thirties. The guy pretended to drop the case as Hunter handed it to him, then groaned with the effort of picking up a mike stand. "Better your back than mine," said Hunter, as he pushed the remaining equipment and speakers to the edge of the truck's floor. Another musician, this one taller and sporting a bushy brown mustache, grabbed a synthesizer keyboard and headed upstairs as Hunter jumped down from the truck. As he maneuvered one of the heavy black speakers to get a good grip on it, Hunter noticed that half the back of it was covered by thick black tape. He poked at it, felt around it some, and then shoved the speaker as far as he could back along the floor of the truck. He hoisted himself up behind it just as the two men emerged from the doorway for a second load.

When they had disappeared inside again, Hunter gently peeled back the edge of the tape. A sealed padded envelope, securely bonded to the sticky side of the tape, came away with it. Once he'd ascertained that there were no wires involved, he ripped the tape with its envelope free of the speaker and tossed it into the dark recesses of the truck box. Then he jumped down and unloaded the remaining equipment onto the concrete pad that fronted the building before pulling the truck's door shut. Starting up the stairs with the bulky speaker, he met the musicians on the stairway. "The last two pieces are just outside the door," he told them, and pushed past them toward the top of the stairs.

Inside the studio door, Hunter stopped and looked around. Al was right. There appeared to be a lot of money tied up in this studio, judging by the amount of recording equipment, most of which looked

224

relatively new. The two musicians came in, each carrying a black amp, and were followed by another young man carrying two McDonald's bags. The three of them were joking about his timing, missing out on the grunt work.

"Give us your hamburger, you goddamn shirker," said the man with the bandana. "All you bass players do is move one lousy finger, anyway. What do you even need to eat for? Say, you! Truck driver! You play lead guitar by any chance? We need a new fretboard virtuoso."

Hunter deposited the speaker he was carrying in the corner with the others, nudged it up next to its mate. "Somebody quit on you?"

"Somebody died on us, man. Hitched a ride to California in a refrigerated trailer and arrived a popsicle."

Hunter laughed as if it were a joke. "Can't help you unless you need a second violin," he said. "You serious about your friend?"

"Ah. A fretless man. What do you think, guys? Replace old Greggie with a fiddler?" When they snorted, he persisted. "I'm not kidding, you turds. Seriously, man. How well do you play?"

Hunter smiled. "Purely second fiddle, chief." He pulled the waybill out of his back pocket and looked for a place to lay it out.

"Shut up and eat, Max," said the tall one with the bushy mustache, then turned to Hunter. "Don't mind Max, but he wasn't kidding about our lead guitarist. Froze to death in a reefer."

"You know, I think I heard about that on the news," said Hunter. "How'd it happen?"

The one called Max stopped unwrapping his Quarter Pounder and gazed at Hunter with widened eyes. "It's a mystery," he said, in a deep Boris Karloff voice. "Nobody knows who put him there, but everybody in this room wanted him dead. M-m-m-wah, ha, ha, ha-a-a-a."

"Shut up and eat, Max," said the thin blond one.

Hunter spread out the waybill on a trestle table by the door. "X marks the spot," he said, pulling a pen out of his shirt pocket and indicating where to sign. Max stepped forward. "Why did you all want him dead, just so I don't repeat the mistake."

Max held his hamburger in his right hand, signed with his left. "We couldn't stand listening to his sucky voice one more minute. Right, guys?" He gestured at a drawing on the wall. "Sang like a fuckin' fairy."

Hunter looked at the drawing. It was pen and ink, done as a caricature, tiny bodies and big heads. The band was all recognizable: Max on the drums, grinning like the Cheshire cat, the bass player looking half asleep, the keyboard player with circles around his eyes as if he were wired, and Greg Williams with the biggest head of all, out front caressing his electric guitar, looking effeminate and sporting tiny wings. One of grinning Max's drumsticks was raised above Greg's head.

"He thought that picture meant he sang like an angel," said Max, took a massive bite of his hamburger. "Fuckin' idiot," he mumbled.

"Talented artist. One of you do this?"

"Max's girlfriend," said the thin blond man, the bass player.

Max swallowed. "Ex girlfriend. Psychotic ex girlfriend." He took another bite. "Scary psychotic ex girlfriend."

"Does she do these on commission?" asked Hunter. "What's her name?"

"You don't want to know," said Max.

"Hellen Brooker, double L," said the bass player, dipping a french fry in ketchup.

"Thanks, chief," said Hunter, folding the waybill up and tucking it into his pocket. "Good luck with your talent search."

"Auditions are next Saturday," mumbled Max, his mouth full of french fries and hamburger. "Bring your reefer for the losers."

Hunter climbed into the Hino and slammed the door, sat there for a moment, lips pursed, drumming his fingers on the steering wheel. He wasn't sure what to make of what he'd just learned. According to the signature on the caricature he'd just seen, Hellen Brooker had designed the posters on the wall at Greg's home, and was also responsible for the graffitti on the wall at Hanratty Meats.

El's truck was still parked in front of the office when Hunter parked the Hino in the Watson Transportation yard on Annacis Island.

El was at her desk, scowling over a large book with pictures. "According to this book of Wally's, Peterbilt isn't a Pomeranian," she said, as he walked behind the counter.

"Was he supposed to be?"

"That's what I paid for. The guy in the pet shop said he was a purebred, but didn't have papers. He said I could register him if I wanted to show him."

"Do you?"

"No. That's not the point. What's that?" she asked..

"Cassette tapes," said Hunter, tilting the envelope toward her so she could see inside. "Have you got any gloves?" She rummaged under her desk and pulled out a pair of heavy leather work gloves, marked with grease. Hunter looked them over, frowned. "How about a handkerchief or something? We don't want to ruin evidence by putting fingerprints or anything else on these." She handed him a Kleenex from the box on her filing cabinet. He carefully pulled one of the tapes out and examined it. It wasn't a miniature tape like the one Al Kowalski's men had found in Greg Williams' car, just a regular cassette tape that would fit in any tape player. He held it in the light from the window, far enough away for him to focus on the writing without using his reading glasses. "Sieg Heil, it says." He pulled out a couple more and read, "Toupee + S. This one's Yo, Bro! and this one's Snakeskin Boots + R."

"What are they? Song titles?"

"Could be. You'd recognize Williams' voice, wouldn't you?"

"Yeah, I think so. I've heard his other tape. Where'd you get 'em?"

"In the truck. Must've fallen off a speaker or something." He arched one eyebrow.

"Yeah, right."

"You got a tape recorder we can play these on?"

El shook her head. "Not in here."

"Your truck or mine?" They chose hers.

The first tape they played was Snakeskin Boots + R. The quality was poor. There were a few muffled words, and some thumping sounds, as if someone had jostled the recorder, then a female voice said, "How's it hangin', Big Dog?" The voice was breezy and cheerful, sounded slightly familiar.

A deep male voice, "Aren't you a naughty little thing tonight. You're wearin' that slippery shirt I like. You look so sexy in purple satin, Ruby, honey. Let me feel..."

"Talk about naughty! Not here, sugar. People can see."

A low laugh. "You're damn right people can see. They can see your little nipples, hard as jelly beans. Gawd, I'd love to suck on one right now."

"Hang on there, sugar. I need a drink first."

Another female voice, "Something to drink, sir?"

"Glass of your best chardonnay for the lady, another scotch for me."

El stopped the tape. "Sure doesn't sound like the Blackburn, does it?"

Hunter shrugged, motioned her to restart the tape.

A little more banter, then the woman called Ruby's voice, "Hey, sugar, I bet I can guess how old you are."

"Why'd you want to do that?"

"I'm good at it. And I'm a gambler. How 'bout you? How 'bout if I don't guess right, you can feel me up right here at the table?"

"Now you're talkin', sweet stuff. How old do you think I am?"

"We-e-e-ll, let's see. You got some laugh lines here... and here... and I can see a little gray here... and here..." Her voice was slow and seductive. "You got stamina in bed like a sixteen year old, but I know you gotta be older than that, 'cause I know that you're married and your kid's even married, 'cause you told me so... I'll guess that you're... you're forty two."

A big male laugh. "You're so far wrong, sweet stuff! You come over here and let me slip my hand..."

"Chardonnay for the lady, and a scotch for the gentleman." The sound of drinks being set on the table. "Have you had a chance to look at the menu? No hurry. I'll come back in a while." A few seconds passed.

"How do I know you're not forty two?"

"Well, I'm tellin' you I ain't forty two."

"Prove it. Let me see your driver's license or something." A hesitation. A light moan and the woman's voice again, "Yep. You're right. Hard as a jelly bean."

"Okay, okay. Here's my driver's license. Look."

"Chester Culligan, 1385 Fulton Avenue, Fort Worth. Chester. That's a very dignified name, Cowboy. Uh, where's the date? Oh, here. You were born February 7th, 1942. Wow! I can't believe it. You don't look nearly that old."

"Heh, heh, heh... pay up. You lost the bet, you little hussy. You bring your little jelly beans over here where I can reach 'em without everybody seein' it."

"Just for a minute, okay? We don't want them throwin' us outa here before we eat, right?"

Rustling sounds and a giggle, followed by a low laugh. "M-m-m-m. What I wouldn't give to put that little jelly bean in my mouth right now." More giggling and rustling.

"Speaking of candy, did you buy the stuff? You got a little nose candy to make us randy, Cowboy?"

"I don't need nothin' but you to make me randy, sweetheart."

"Did you?"

"Yeah, I got it. I always get it."

The tape continued for several minutes longer, then ended abruptly in mid-sentence, as if the tape had run out, but after a few seconds of silence, a male voice announced the date, and gave the location as a hotel restaurant in downtown Vancouver.

"Sounds like Williams' voice. What do you make of that?" asked El.

"Blackmail," said Hunter. "The woman named Ruby was setting the man up, and I'll bet Williams was doing the dirty work."

They let it run until they were sure there was nothing else on the tape, then rewound it and put on another tape. This one was labeled,

Sieg Heil + S. It started much the same, with a few unintelligible words and background noise, rustling and thumping.

A man's voice with a thick European accent said, "Give me a hug, Blondie. How's my girl tonight?" That was followed by the sound of a lip smacking kiss.

"Do I ever love your sweater, Mike. You always have such nice things." It was a woman's voice, not Ruby's. "Ooooh. Is it cashmere? It's so soft, I could just crawl right inside it with you."

The man laughed. "Not right here, Blondie. I let you wear it later, right next to your skin, eh?"

"M-m-m-m. That'll be so nice. It's a beautiful sweater. Did your wife buy it for you? She has such good taste. In clothes and in husbands, right?"

A laugh. "She picked a good husband to provide for her, so she can buy nice things. I think sometimes she likes the things better than the husband."

"That's hard to believe, Mike. She must be crazy. Or maybe you just wore her out, you're such a stallion!"

"Men don't get old so fast as women. It's a fact. I'm fifty eight, and I'm still as strong as a young man. Feel this! Blondie, feel this!"

The woman made appropriate remarks, then said, "I don't believe you're really fifty eight. I think you're just saying that to impress me. You're probably... oh... I'd guess you're really only forty five. Am I right?"

"No, I'm telling you. I'm fifty eight."

"No, you can't be. I know, let me see your driver's license. You're being carded. Show me your driver's license so I know you're old enough to drive."

"To drive?"

"Yeah, to drive me." A giggle. "Vroom, vroom. Uh-oh. Maybe you should check my oil." Another giggle. "C'mon let's see your driver's license."

"I don't know..."

A sudden change in tone. "You don't trust me? I thought we were truly friends, Mike. I really thought you liked me."

"Don't look so sad, Blondie. We are truly friends. Here, look. Here's my driver's license. See?"

"My goodness! How do you pronounce your last name? Van der... Van der Vieler..."

"Just Mike," he said. "You see the date?"

"Yes, you're right. August 5th, 1937. You really are 58. I can't believe what good shape you're in for someone your age. You're like a young man, a young stud." Her voice lowered. "Did you bring me a present, Mike? Like usual?"

"Of course, Blondie. I think you shouldn't do it so much, but I buy it from your friend like usual. Your white powder is safe in my pocket. Here, next to my little soldier."

The woman laughed. "You're such a tiger!"

When the tape finished, El's head was down, rolling from side to side on her forearms on the desk. "Goddamn it. Goddamn it all to hell. Goddamn it," she said over and over again. She raised her head to look at Hunter. "Sharon. Sharon was in on it, too. That goddamn whore. He did it, didn't he? That poor lovestruck schmuck. Ray did it for her." When Hunter didn't respond, she raised her head, frowning. "Aren't I right? Please tell me I'm wrong."

Hunter shook his head sadly, wishing he could answer her question. "The only thing I can tell you for sure after listening to these two tapes is that Greg Williams was playing with fire. We've listened to one out of ten tapes, and been introduced to two men who might have wanted him dead. This second man could easily have wanted revenge on them both. What better way than to frame one for the murder of the other?"

El frowned again. "You're right. Do you think we can find this Mike guy?"

He smiled, shook the envelope full of tapes. "I think I'd like to find out just how many Mikes and Chesters there are in here before I turn these tapes over to the RCMP"

El pushed the rewind button. "The dogs' dinner will just have to be late," she said, looking at her watch. "I'll go make us some coffee."

Russell's last scheduled stop that day was the Blackburn Hotel, where he planned to interview one of the witnesses who had seen Sharon Nillson arguing with the victim. The witness's name was Pat Stevens and she was the assistant manager. When he introduced himself, the woman rolled her eyes, clicked her tongue against her teeth in an exasperated tsk. It wrenched his gut. She reminded him so much of Jennifer.

"Not again," she said. "I've already been over it - thoroughly - with the RCMP. I must've said the same thing to at least three people - no, four. I signed a statement and everything. Didn't you read it?"

Russell wanted to reach out and touch her hair. It was streaked with gold, lighter than Jennifer's, but just as long, its fullness caught up behind in a careless band of cloth. She wore lipstick that made her full lips look freshly licked. He found himself licking his own. "I'm sorry, but it's very important I talk to you myself. I have questions that weren't answered in the statement. Is there somewhere we can be alone?"

At that, she smirked mischievously, raised and lowered dark lashes as she looked him up and down. "Why, Detective!" she said. "That's the best offer I've had all day." Abruptly serious again, she sighed and called out to the bartender. "Send a free round over to table four. If that doesn't make them happy, I'll be back as soon as I can." Then she motioned for Russell to follow her, shaking her head. "Some scumbag's claiming he found a slug in his salad." Her earrings clinked softly. "Well, he probably did, but so what? A little extra protein never hurt anybody. Besides, it's only this big. Just a cute little baby one." She held her thumb and index finger at eye level, a quarter of an inch apart. Her fingernails were the same color as her lips. Then she giggled. "Oh, yeah. You're from southern California and you probably think I'm talking about a bullet or something. You ever seen a slug? Like, a snail without a shell?"

She let them into a little office, where she sat in a chair behind the desk and motioned Russell to sit on a stack of liquor boxes piled in front of it. "A little pilferage problem," she explained. "When the bartenders need a new bottle, they've got to get it from me or the

232

manager." She shook the key ring she'd used to open the door. "You sometimes wonder if there's an honest person left in this world."

"Does that include Sharon Nillson?"

"You mean Sharon MacNeil? That was her name when she worked here, anyway." Pat pouted thoughtfully. "Sharon was as honest as anybody. I liked Sharon a lot. She reminded me of that Shirley MacLaine movie, Sweet Charity. You ever see that? Poor woman gets kicked in the teeth a hundred times but still won't stop chasing rainbows." She smiled up from underneath her lashes. "Sorta like me."

Russell remembered the movie. He remembered wanting to see the guy that jilted her get his head kicked in. He thought about the suspect, Sharon Nillson, the hard set of her jaw when she refused to speak, the defiance in her eyes. Could he believe she was vulnerable and scared underneath that hard veneer? "Tell me more about Sharon. It doesn't have to be anything you'd swear to in court. Just tell me what you knew of her, so I can get a better picture of her as a person." He leaned forward, elbows on his knees. "She doesn't talk much, you see."

"Sharon? Not talk much? Hah!" She grinned. "You're pulling my leg, right? Sharon's one of the friendliest, most talkative people I know. That's why she and that trucker she married hit it off so well. A shy guy. I hardly ever heard him say a word." She opened a drawer and pulled out an ashtray and a package of cigarettes, then lit one up and inhaled deeply before she spoke again.

Russell found himself remembering how it tasted, kissing a woman who had just smoked a cigarette. Without thinking, he licked his lips again. She caught him doing it and half smiled.

"Sharon had the balls - if you know what I mean - to do what she had to do to survive, but she was a kind person, more sensitive than she let on, I think. You know the old movie stereotype of the good hearted hooker? Well, that's Sharon." She tapped the cigarette on the rim of the ashtray. "Is this the kind of stuff you want to hear?"

Russell had been so distracted, it took him a couple of seconds to react. "Sharon Nillson was a hooker?"

Pat made a seesaw motion with the hand that held the cigarette. "She worked here as a server. But using a little... uh... deductive reasoning, something you as a detective are probably familiar with..." She winked, and he smiled. "Some guys used to always sit in her section, you know? And go outside with her on her breaks, and she'd come back all lit up, so I gathered she was exchanging favors for a hit of coke, if you know what I mean? Remember, this is nothing I'd swear to in court."

"An addict?"

She nodded, setting her earrings swinging. One of them caught briefly in her hair. "Booze, too, sometimes. Occupational hazard. She got suspended here after a couple of bad incidents, then she cleaned up real well, went through a program, and the boss let her come back to work. As far as I know, she was clean from then on."

"What was her relationship with Greg Williams?"

"Nothing special, far as I know. They talked, like everybody does. Hell, I talked to him sometimes, too."

"Do you think he was selling her drugs?"

She shrugged. "Maybe they went outside together a couple of times, I wouldn't have paid that much attention. Sharon took a lot of her breaks outside. Musicians..." She shrugged. "... they're in and out all the time. I'd never seen them arguing before, if that means anything. They got along fine. Like I said, nothing special." She crushed out her cigarette, looking up at him from under lowered lashes as she did so. "How long are you in town for, Detective?"

It was almost eleven o'clock when Hunter pulled into the driveway of his landlord's house. His landlord was on his knees at the edge of the driveway, a flashlight in one hand and an old sneaker in the other. There was an earnest look on his face, no sign of distress. Hunter turned off the ignition and set his parking brake before strolling over to ask what was going on.

"The cat," explained Gord, directing the flashlight under a rhododenron bush. "Puss, puss, puss, puss. I don't like her to stay

234

out at night because of the raccoons and coyotes. Puss, puss, puss, puss." He shook the sneaker.

"What's with the sneaker?"

Gord thrust the sneaker under the bush, then pulled it out slowly. "It's the shoelace. I'm trying to lure her out with the shoelace." There was a rustling in the rhododendron, then a pale skinny Siamese leg shot out toward the sneaker and just as quickly disappeared. "Puss, puss, puss, puss."

"Can I help?" asked Hunter, squatting down beside his landlord.

"Could you stand back over there..." He motioned toward the dark side of the rhododendron. "... and grab her next time she comes out?"

Five minutes and two tries later, Hunter had his two hands circling the cat's wriggling body, holding it far out in front of him so her claws wouldn't catch on his shirt. Gord got to his feet as fast as his age would allow him and led the way to the front door, letting them all inside just in the nick of time. The cat seemed to turn in its skin, snagging Hunter's sleeve with its teeth, and he threw it to the carpet as if it were made of molten metal.

"Holy Mackerel!" said Hunter, examining his sleeve for holes. "She's doesn't much like being picked up, does she?" The cat was glaring at him from under a chair.

"That's why I let you do it," said Gord.

"Thanks," muttered Hunter. "You wouldn't happen to have a tape recorder, would you? One with a good microphone?"

Before carrying his own portable radio-cassette player up to Gord's living room where the tape recorder was, Hunter phoned Al Kowalski's home from his downstairs suite. Al's wife, Marta, answered.

"Sorry, Hunter. Al's not home," Marta said. "Either he's still working or unwinding somewhere with a couple of other cops. Weekdays, weekends, it doesn't matter. Seems like I never see him anymore." Her voice was cheerful, but Hunter sensed the hurt behind her words. He imagined Christine saying the exact same words about him five or six years ago. It made him sad. He asked her to have Al call him as early in the morning as he could.

There were only three of the twenty tapes that Hunter wanted to make copies of. He wasn't sure what he'd need them for, but he didn't want to chance the originals being somehow misplaced. The first tape was one of several with Ruby's voice on it. He couldn't help but think she might hold the answers to Greg Williams' murder, and a copy of the tape might be necessary to help track her down, and ultimately to persuade her to cooperate once he'd managed to find her.

There were three male voices on the second tape, one of them Greg Williams. There was the sound of two car doors slamming, then Williams introduced one of the men to the other, sneaking in a name for the sake of the tape. "Mr. Brantford, this is the gentleman who can give you what you're looking for."

"We don't need last names," said one of the other voices irritably.

"Sorry. Colin, then. This is..."

"Shut up. No names at all." The voice of the third man sounded familiar to Hunter, but he couldn't place it. "You know this guy? How do I know he's not a cop?"

"Trust me. He's not a cop." It was Williams' voice. "He's having a party, invited a friend of mine, who suggested he come here to buy... uh... refreshments."

"What friend?"

"A girl. You wouldn't know her, but she's okay. Trust me. She's okay, he's okay, you're okay, I'm okay." A weak laugh.

"You've got cash?" A brief silence. "Did he tell you how much?"

Williams again. "He's good for it."

"Listen, bud. My cash isn't the problem. With this big an investment, I want to be sure of what I'm buying, you know what I mean?"

"Peruvian. Pure. Very clean."

"You think I'm an idiot? You let me do a line first, before I commit to buy."

"It's good coke," said Greg Williams.

The other male voice said, "Show me the cash. I don't give you a free sample until I know you came prepared to do more than just kick tires."

236

"You think I'm not good for it?" said Brantford, sounding disgusted.

"He doesn't know who you are," said Williams.

Brantford swore, there were a few seconds of silence, then, "See? Yankee dollars. You happy now?"

A sigh. "Yeah. Sure. Here, do a line."

Williams' voice sang softly, "Cocaine, cocaine, goin' 'round my brain."

Hunter's landlord wandered in from his kitchen carrying a glass of milk and a peanut butter sandwich. "Thought you might need a midnight snack," whispered Gord, putting the milk and the sandwich on the coffee table in front of Hunter. "I'm heading off to bed. Just turn out the lights when you're done." He paused as if he recognized something, listening intently for a few seconds with a quizzical frown on his face.

The buyer was saying, "Seems pretty good. Where'd you get this stuff?"

"Peruvian. That's all you need to know. You want it or not?"

"Yeah. I'll take it. And it had better be good right to the bottom of the bag. You don't ever want to make me mad, dude. Trust me."

"Turn on the light." The sound of a car door opening. "I want to read the numbers on these bills."

Hunter stopped the recording tape. "You recognize that voice? It's driving me crazy. I've heard that voice before. I'd swear I've met this man, but I can't for the life of me place the voice." He scratched the back of his neck. El had found one of the male voices familiar, too, but not the same one. Put in their own context, they'd probably be easier to identify.

"That's Colin Brantford, isn't it?"

"You know Brantford?"

"Doesn't everybody in Vancouver? At least, everybody who watches the TV news."

"I guess you'd have to watch it more than once every couple of weeks," Hunter said. "I must miss at least eighty percent of the news in this town. My dispatcher does, too, evidently. Who's this Brantford?"

237

"Department store scion, invests in all kinds of high profile things. Lately, though, he's been denying - rather lamely, I might add - rumors that he'll be running for mayor of Vancouver this fall."

Hunter nodded his head thoughtfully. "I see. Is he the buyer or the seller?"

"He's the one that said, You don't ever want to make me mad."

"How about the other voice? That's the one that sounds familiar to me."

Gord shrugged. "Haven't a clue," he said. "Good night."

Hunter was tired when he was finished recording the third tape, thanks in part to the milk and sandwich, which he found unexpectedly pleasing, making him think for the hundredth time how lucky he was to have Gord Young for his landlord. After turning out the lights upstairs, he returned to his own suite and stowed the duplicate tapes in his desk, put the originals on his kitchen counter. As he stripped off his clothes, he wondered how Al and Russell would react to the tapes. He visualized picking up a rock on the beach and watching a dozen tiny crabs scurry to find new cover. Instead of making their job easier, the tapes had suddenly turned up a collection of men with motives at least as compelling as Ray and Sharon Nillson's might have been, some with the money or connections to arrange a frame up.

At least as good a suspect as the high profile man with family money, running for political office, was the man on the third tape Hunter had just made a recording of, a man who not only risked losing his reputation and livelihood, but also his freedom, and with that, possibly his life. A man who, in Hunter's estimation, was the lowest of the low, a man who not only broke the law, but who was a betrayer of everything Hunter had held sacred for the best part of his life.

The man on the third tape was a dirty cop.

CHAPTER
TWENTY

"I could call room service."

"No, don't bother. That'll be just fine. It's the company that's important." She said it with a delicious little grin.

Russell studied her face for a few seconds, smiled slowly back at her. Pat's resemblance to Jennifer was only superficial. Jennifer would have bitched unless he'd had a decent bottle of Chardonnay sent up, with an iced wine bucket and stem glasses. Generic mini bar wine would never do. Russell unscrewed the cap off the miniature bottle of white wine, poured half the bottle into the tumbler and handed it to her. Then he unscrewed the top off the bottle of red, and poured some for himself.

"Here's to the hospitality industry," Pat said with a wink. She took a sip, then put down the glass and began to remove her earrings. "I like hotel rooms. There's no beating around the bush. You invite a girl in and, voila!, she's not only in your bedroom, she's sitting on your bed and putting her jewellery on your nightstand." She paused before adding, "And stuff." Beside the earrings was a condom.

Russell laughed. "There's something to be said for not beating around the bush. You're pretty good at it yourself." He was leaning against the TV cabinet, in no hurry to get close to her, and he wondered why. He wanted her. There was no doubt about that. But he found watching and listening to her refreshing and delightful, a soothing balm to the cuts that had stung him since his last conversation with Jennifer. His eyes strayed to the room's phone. No flashing light. No call to even acknowledge the gift basket he'd asked the hotel to send to her room that afternoon. No reason not to spend the night with Pat.

Pat picked up her glass and began to play her tongue along the rim, glancing up at him with a sly smile.

In the past three years, since he and Jennifer had started seeing each other, Russell had had sex with only one other woman, and that was near the very beginning of their relationship. He had never again even been tempted. Jennifer, by dint of her strong personality and high self-esteem, demanded and was willingly accorded sole rights to his emotional and physical allegiance. Until today. Last night she'd kicked him away like a flea-bitten mutt. She'd called him disgusting. "Dismissed," he mouthed into his wine glass, as if it were a revelation.

He put down his glass and started to take off his jacket, but before he could shrug his way out of it, Pat was in front of him with her hands gripping his lapels and her warm belly pressing against his. He felt the wet heat of her breath against his neck as she whispered, "Let me do that, Detective," then began to explore his chest and shoulders with her hands under his jacket. He felt the heat and rush of his blood in his ears, and as her tongue began to caress the corners of his lips, he shuddered and pulled her into an urgent kiss, overwhelmed by a sudden hunger.

She slipped his jacket off, pulled him gently by his tie toward the bed. Then she dropped her hands and, shoulders back, seemed to offer herself to him. "Undress me first," she said, her voice already husky with arousal. As soon as he'd dropped her blouse to the floor, she turned her back to him and lifted her arms to encircle his neck, arching her back. His hands felt weightless as he began to stroke her naked breasts, tentatively at first, gently tweaking her nipples until they grew and hardened. She sighed and pressed against him, moving her buttocks rhythmically against his groin until he thought he would go mad with his hunger for her and had to pull away to undo his belt. They both removed their remaining clothes, frantic to be naked and touching. "Hurry, hurry," she whispered, with a pained intake of breath as she waited for him to fumble with the condom. Arms

240

snaking around her, Russell boosted her hips up against his and was inside her before he lowered their locked bodies to the bed.

The second time was slower and tastier, and the third time playful and less urgent. It was almost midnight when they shared a can of Budweiser from the mini bar, sitting cross-legged and naked on the bed. Russell studied her face. She was stroking his hairy calf as if it were a kitten, and smiling, like they'd just shared a good joke.

He tucked his fingers in the fold of her leg, feeling the hard bulge of her calf as she flexed it. "Strong legs," he said. "You a runner?" He wondered if he'd made a mistake in asking. Thus far she'd made no move to get to know him, except physically.

"Mountain biking. It's like pumping iron with your legs." She said nothing more, just plucked the beer from his hand and took a long pull. Russell supposed her silence meant she didn't care if he shared her interests, outside of sex.

"Why did you come on to me?" he asked her.

"You're a stud. What can I say?"

"I mean..." Russell frowned, trying to figure out how to word it so he wouldn't sound too serious. Or too glib. "I get the impression you wanted to sleep with me because I was only going to be around for one day. Was that part of it?"

"Maybe. Or maybe it's just that you're a stud." She ran her knuckle gently along his jaw line, then pulled his head closer for a tender kiss. She sighed. "You cain't lose was you ain't never had. Isn't that how the song goes?"

He nodded, and it suddenly made sense. No long term relationship, no breakup, no heartache.

"Why? You planning on coming back?" she asked.

Her voice was hard to read. Russell wasn't sure what she wanted to hear. He'd gladly see her again, but he was afraid that wasn't why she was asking. He shrugged. "I don't know," he said, honestly. The phone began to ring. "This was sort of a one time thing. I mean, me coming to Vancouver."

"Aren't you going to get that?" she asked. "Or would that be your wife?" She made a wry face, and Russell couldn't tell if her expression was self deprecatory, or mocking him.

"I don't have a wife," he said as he reached over and grabbed the receiver. "Kupka," he barked, as if he were in the office.

"Sorry, baby. Did I wake you?" It was Jennifer.

"No, you didn't wake me." He uncrossed his legs and tucked them under the sheet, thinking as he did so how stupid it was to worry about his nakedness. It was just a phone call. Pat looked as if she was about to giggle, so he put a finger to his lips to caution her. She grabbed it playfully in her teeth.

"I'm sorry about last night," said Jennifer. "You know how I hate drunks, though, Russ. But it's been eating at me all day, talking to you like I did. I was tired. I'm sorry."

"That's okay," he said.

"I left the shoot early tonight, because I want to make it up to you," she said.

"That's not necessary."

"I brought your goodie basket with me. It's lovely, Russ. Thank you. Champagne, caviar, grapes and brie, and... um... looks like melba toast. But they won't give me your room number."

Russell's stomach dropped. "You're here?" He tried not to look at Pat, who had been fondling his fingers and was now staring at him curiously and intently. He had to turn away, putting his feet to the floor.

"I'm in the lobby," Jennifer said. "Give me your room number and I'll be upstairs in thirty seconds."

"Uh... just give me a couple of minutes, would you? I'll... I'll come down." He was afraid to look at Pat, but he felt the bed start to quake, heard muffled laughter.

"I think we'll be more comfortable..." Jennifer fell silent as the penny dropped. "Is someone in the room with you?"

Pat's laughter erupted out loud, and Russell slapped his palm over the mouthpiece of the phone. "Sorry," she gasped between giggles, brushing his arm with her bare breast as she slid off the bed and padded toward the bathroom. "It's just such a classic. It's like an old movie."

Russell heard a click.

"Jennifer?"

242

Sharon couldn't sleep. Angie was snoring softly, and as hard as Sharon tried to shut out the sound, she couldn't. Her cellmate's presence was a nightmare in itself, and Sharon had grown to dread every second of contact between them: every word, every glance, every ugly gesture. Now even the sound of the woman's breathing was abhorrent to Sharon. Her only chance for oblivion, her only reprieve from Angie's intrusion into her consciousness, was sleep. Sleeping so much during the day made it harder to sleep well at night.

During the dark hours of turning and tossing, acutely aware of every cough in the cell block and the occasional sounds of pee and running water, Sharon tried repeatedly to lose herself in fantasies of being back on the road with Ray and Peaches. She hugged her pillow to her chest, trying to imagine she was cuddling Peaches, trying to call up the hum of Ray's eighteen wheeler and the sound of his voice as he told stories of growing up on the farm, trying to drown out the soft snoring from across the cell.

Finally, less than two hours from wake up, Sharon fell asleep.

El arrived at her warehouse at five, as she usually did on Monday so she could have everything under control by the time the phones started to ring. After turning on the lights, she went directly to the lunchroom and started the coffee, threw her lunch bag into the fridge. Ever since she and Hunter had listened to Greg Williams' tapes yesterday, she'd been trying to get her head around what she'd heard. Ray Nillson's bride was some kind of prostitute, and had been part of a blackmailing scheme. Ray didn't deserve that. Ray was a straight-up guy with a heart as big as the Rocky Mountains. Surely he hadn't known about Sharon before he married her, had he?

El collected the few faxes that had come in overnight and carried them over to her desk, threw them onto the pile that served as her in-basket. Beside her phone was the book on dogs Wally had loaned her, open to the page on Pomeranians. El paused, hovering over the picture, reading the description one more time. Peterbilt was much too big to be a Pomeranian, and besides, he was black, which was very rare for the breed. She'd been duped into paying for a purebred dog who turned out to be nothing of the sort. She felt cheated and it made her mad. If she could get away from the office, she'd pay a visit to that damn pet shop this afternoon. "If I don't get some satisfaction, I'll rip his face off," she muttered, slamming the book with her fist.

Is that how Ray felt? If that scumbucket blackmailer Williams had told Ray that his wife was a whore and a junkie, wouldn't it have made Ray mad? It must have, she reasoned. If being sold a... a... whatever misrepresented as a purebred Pomeranian made her mad enough to want to stomp the pet shop owner, finding out the truth about his wife must have been ten times worse for Ray.

As much as it troubled her, El had to admit it was just possible it could have made easy-going Ray Nillson angry enough to kill.

For a moment Sharon didn't know where she was. She'd been in a deep, deep sleep, and waking was like fighting her way up from under water. Until she opened her eyes, all she knew was that she was lying on her stomach, her head on a thin pillow. First she saw the blue lines of the cotton twill mattress through the thin sheet, then the gray prison blanket, and she remembered.

"Wakey, wakey, Princess. Rise and shine!" The voice of her cellmate grated against her senses like fingernails on a blackboard.

"Shut up," she mouthed into her pillow, knowing that to say it aloud would have the opposite effect of what she wanted.

"Prin-cess," Angie continued in an irritating sing-song voice that reminded Sharon of schoolyard taunts. "Oh, Prin-cess! See what I've got?"

Sharon turned her head to the wall, trying to ignore her cellmate, but the edge of the Time magazine lying on the blanket caught her eye. Suddenly wide awake, she grabbed at the magazine, turned over and jerked herself to a sitting position. Angie was prancing in the middle of the cell in an undershirt and panties, holding up the photograph of Peaches.

244

"See what I got?" she repeated, then lapsed into a distorted baby talk. "Cute widdle puppy dog, fuzzy wuzzy widdle puppy dog, does my widdle Princess miss her widdle fuzzy widdle muttsy?"

"Give me that," said Sharon. It took all the willpower she could muster to speak quietly, her voice quivering with the effort. Her head seemed on fire with rage. "Give me that picture."

Angie held it out toward her, but when Sharon reached for it, she snatched it back and twirled clumsily away. Holding it out again, but further away this time, she started her demented cackling, like a cartoon witch. "Looky, looky! Princess is angry." Angie's voice changed again, became charged with hostility. "You fuckin' little bitch. You think you're so special. Well, fuck you. And fuck your precious little mutt." With that, she tore a strip off the photograph and tossed it toward the toilet.

Sharon lunged. She came at Angie and straight-armed both hands against the woman's bony clavicles. Shock on her face, Angie staggered backwards, lost her balance. Her shoulder blades slammed against the wall as she fell, her head following with a thunk. Grinning viciously at Sharon from the floor, she began to crumple the remainder of the photograph in her fist, then threw back her head and began to cackle again. "Poor little princess."

Sharon grabbed the woman's shirt and pulled her off the floor. "You had no right," she said, her voice low and shaking. "You had no right." She bunched the thin cloth in her fists, exposing her cellmate's tiny wobbling breasts.

Angie's skeletal hands came up toward Sharon's face, her fingers heading for Sharon's eyes. Sharon shoved her away, and again Angie hit the wall. "Eyow!" she snarled, like a cat, and scrambled to her feet. Sharon brought her knee up toward the scrawny throat, caught her under the chin. Angie's mouth snapped shut with a click of her teeth, and she fell back again, hard, her head hitting the wall first this time.

By this time, the prisoners up and down the cell block were whooping and hollering, cheering them on, although Sharon hadn't been even dimly aware of them until her cellmate fell silent. With a groan, Angie's skinny body curled itself into a foetal position on the floor, her hands tucked in against her flaccid breasts.

Sharon snatched up the remains of Peaches' photograph and retreated to her bunk, where she sat, her chest heaving with each gulp of air, wiping the two halves of the picture against her nightgown, trying to clean them, trying to straighten them. Two guards appeared at the barred door, began to unlock it.

"What's all the ruckus? What's goin' on here?"

One of them walked over to where Angie lay, the other planted herself in front of Sharon, her hands on her hips. "I know Angie's a pain in the ass, but you just makin' more trouble for yo'self if you get physical 'bout it."

The other guard spoke into her walkie talkie. "Get a medic down here, on the double. We got one out cold, and she's started breathin' funny."

Sharon held the torn picture against her chest and closed her eyes.

"You got these where?"

"That envelope was left behind on the floor of my truck after I transported some equipment for Whistlestop Studios." Hunter repeated what he had told Al the first time, word for word.

"And how did you happen to be transporting something for Whistlestop Studios?"

Hunter smiled.

"Right," said Al. "I guess, for the moment, nobody has to know that."

"I suggest you play this one first," said Hunter, pointing to one labeled Yo, Bro!

Like most of the others, the tape started with a confusion of noise, snatches of different voices, thunks and a rustling sound, possibly of clothing rubbing against the microphone. Fading in and out and in again behind it all was a country and western song. This went on for approximately thirty seconds, then a voice spoke clearly.

"Yo, bro! What's happening, man?"

246

"That's Greg Williams," said Hunter. Al Kowalski nodded, put down his coffee and leaned toward the tape recorder, both elbows on his desk.

The tape continued. "Little brother," said a voice in greeting. "You having a beer?"

"The cop?" Al raised his eyebrows at Hunter's nod.

The tape went on with small talk, a few minutes about Greg's bar gigs, some mutual friends, and professional sports, then Greg Williams asked, "Those your new wheels in the parking lot? That awesome Cherokee Limited?"

"Fine machine, eh? I took it off road last weekend. Beauty. Sheer beauty."

"Must be taking a helluva chunk out of your paycheck. Donna give you a hard time about it?"

"Bought and paid for, little brother. Free and clear." You could hear the grin in his voice.

"On a cop's salary? What's your secret, bro? You win the lottery or something?"

"Let's just say I came across a windfall, a nice little windfall."

Greg's voice, more quietly. "C'mon, bro. I'm flesh and blood. You can tell me. How'd you ever come up with the scratch to buy that baby outright?"

Chad's voice dropped, almost to a whisper, and Hunter could visualize the two of them leaning in across the table. "It's not strictly legal - kind of a gray area - but nobody gets hurt, you know what I mean? Me and my partner do a bust, right? Catch this guy cold with a nice stash of white stuff. He says, forget this ever happened, and you can have my stash. The stuff's got a street value of more'n a hundred grand. Me and my partner look at each other, then look back at the asshole dealer, and say, Forget what ever happened? He hands over his stuff, we sell it to another guy owes us a few favors, and voila! A new truck for me and a swimming pool for my partner."

"Jesus, Chad! Aren't you afraid they'll figure it out, you having all that money all of a sudden?"

"They don't know I don't have a rich uncle just died, or that my wife's aunt didn't just win a jackpot in Vegas, do they? They don't even know that maybe Donna doesn't have a bigger income than she does, do they? It's none of their business."

"But you're a cop. Didn't you swear to uphold the law or something? You know, I, Chad Williams, do solemnly swear..."

Chad snorted audibly. "After a couple of years of busting your ass to get the goods on these assholes, then seeing the fuckin' judges turn them back out on the streets with a fuckin' slap on the wrist, you're nothing more than a sucker if you don't try to get a piece of the action. We're no knights in shining armor; we're just mindless pawns in a game where nobody else plays by the rules. I'd have to be stupid not to take advantage of the situation."

There was a pause, a clinking of glasses. "Here's to you, bro. You're a true entrepreneur." Then, "What would happen if they did find out?"

"Let's not go there."

"I'm curious, though. What would happen?"

"I'd lose my job, spend a few years in jail, and probably end up losing my wife and kid to boot." A pause. "Like I said, let's not go there."

The tape went on, back to small talk and jock talk and eventually Chad said, "Gotta go, little brother. My partner and his wife are coming for dinner, and Donna's waiting for me to bring home the steaks and beer." Soon after that, there was an abrupt end to the noise as the tape recorder was switched off.

"Jesus!" said Al, clicking off the recorder. "Greg Williams was blackmailing his own brother."

Hunter nodded. "Might be worthwhile showing his photo to some of the witnesses, see if he might have been the man seen arguing with the victim the night Sharon was there."

"Sure. I could get the VPD to fax it over." He shook his head. "His own brother."

"And there's more," said Hunter, glancing at the stack of tapes. "More tapes, and more people who wouldn't be sorry to see Greg Williams dead."

"Who are they?" asked Al, reaching for another tape.

248

Hunter beat him to it, handed him one marked Silver Spoon, one of the tapes he'd made a copy of the night before. He wanted to make sure Al had a few new suspects firmly in mind before he heard the tapes with Sharon's voice on them. "You'll recognize at least one of the men on this tape. Silver Spoon. And I'd sure like to know if you recognize the other voice. It seems familiar to me, but I can't quite place it."

Al whistled softly as the tape played. "Brantford, huh? Involved in a drug buy. If this was made public, it would sure as hell screw up his chances of becoming mayor, wouldn't it? Our little guitar player was playing with fire." They listened silently as the tape continued, then came to an end, Williams reciting the date and location a couple of seconds after the first click. "Sorry. The second voice doesn't ring a bell with me, but Brantford's is hard to mistake."

"Maybe I'm wrong," said Hunter. "You got time to hear the rest of them?"

"What else have we got?"

"The rest of the tapes involve men spending the evening with... well, with prostitutes from the sound of it. During the conversation the woman manages to get some kind of ID on the man, usually off his driver's licence, then gets him to admit to making a cocaine buy. By the end, Williams has a tape he can threaten the man with. From the sound of it, all the marks were married and well to do. They all had something to lose."

"These women would definitely be worth talking to. Do we know who they are?"

"There are two of them. One of them we don't know, but once again, the voice sounds familiar to me. With your permission, I'd like to try to track her down."

"And the other one?" Al's phone started to ring, and he held up his hand to get Hunter to wait. "Kowalski," he said into the receiver.

Hunter got up to pour himself more coffee. When he came back, Al was off the phone, and had begun tucking the tapes back into the envelope.

Hunter sat down and sighed heavily. "The other woman was Sharon. Sharon Nillson," he said.

Al stopped what he was doing, looked up at Hunter with a crooked smile. "So these tapes wouldn't have gotten your friends off the hook after all."

"Reasonable doubt."

"Might have worked."

Hunter frowned. "What do you mean, might have worked?"

"That phone call," said Al. "It was your friend, Russell Kupka. It appears that Ray Nillson has confessed."

On his drive back from LAX, Russell hadn't been sure how he felt. Unsettled might have been the best word. Unsettled and uncertain. He knew now it was over with Jennifer - she would never forgive him for that humiliation - but, as yet, he felt no sense of loss. Pat had jollied him out of his funk, and she ended up staying the night. A sense of her floated like a mist around him: a taste, a touch, a tightening in the groin, and kept drawing his attention away from the here and now. Uppermost on today's agenda was a meeting with the chief, wherein Russell would be expected to produce evidence of enough progress on the Iceman case to justify his trip to Vancouver.

He went over it again in his mind. He'd found out that Sharon Nillson had been an addict and quite possibly a prostitute, a woman on the fringes of criminality in spite of not having a police record. He had seen proof that Greg Williams had been living beyond his visible income, which pointed to some illicit means of financing his studio. He'd seen for himself where Greg Williams' car had been found, a spot easily accessible by an eighteen-wheeler. There were additional details that helped flesh out the case, that supported his theory, and others that made him just a little less certain... Chad Williams had been a little too intense about his brother's belongings, for one thing, while Teresa Jagpal had maybe been a little too quick to clear them out of her house. And Pat had liked Sharon, sympathized with her, painted Ray Nillson as a guy in a white hat, Sharon's knight in shining armor.

Russell shook his head. He couldn't afford to get sentimental about suspects. The scent of Pat's body tickled his memory, became

250

so vivid he could taste it on the back of his tongue. Maybe he could swing another trip to Vancouver after all.

"Well done," said the chief with a mystifying smirk on his face. "I should send you out of town more often."

Russell was just sitting down, hadn't said more than hello. "I don't understand," he said. "I don't know what you've heard..."

"One of your suspects nearly killed her cellmate with her bare hands." The chief leaned back, put his feet up on the desk as if the news were a signal to relax. "She probably has killed her, in fact. The woman just hasn't had the good grace to die yet."

"What? When?" Russell was still on the edge of his chair.

"Just this morning, while you were 25,000 feet above Oregon."

"What happened?"

"Who knows? Something about the cellmate tearing up a picture of her dog. Just goes to show what she's capable of, though." He smiled. "Her and that brute of a husband."

Without thinking, Russell found himself saying, "I don't have any firm proof yet that he was involved. I have some leads to follow up, but..."

"If he wasn't involved," said the chief, smugly tossing what looked like a handwritten statement across the desk, "then why the hell did he confess?"

I should be happy, Russell told himself. I am happy. He re-read the statement as he waited for Ray Nillson to arrive. I was right and the case will be closed. He had phoned the Burnaby RCMP to let them know, then arranged to meet with Ray. He didn't have to. It was all here, in the suspect's own handwriting. But Russell couldn't accept it. He didn't believe it. He wanted to hear it for himself.

Ray was shown into the room, his cuffs removed. He sat down across from Russell without once looking up from the floor.

Russell cleared his throat. "Thanks for talking to me," he said. "You know you don't have to, don't you?"

Ray nodded.

"You got yourself a new lawyer yet?"

Ray shook his head, frowning. It was clear he had no intention of getting a new lawyer, if he could help it.

"You said in your statement that, while your wife was asleep inside your truck, you stopped to talk to Greg Williams. Where was that?" Ray hadn't been told where the victim's car was found. If he could name the spot, it would be strong confirmation that his statement was accurate.

"I don't exactly remember." Ray Nillson sat with his back straight, eyes straight ahead and unfocussed, yet he seemed at ease. He seemed to be a man at peace with himself. His voice was a steady monotone.

"Which side of the border was it on?"

"I don't exactly remember."

"Surely you can..."

"The American side. Yes, it was on the American side." He chewed on his lower lip, seemed to come to a decision. "Ferndale. I had stopped to go to the bank in Ferndale but I saw Greg Williams there and I changed my mind."

Russell nodded. So far, so good. "Why was Greg Williams there?"

"Coincidence, I guess." Ray shrugged. "I don't know," he said.

"Did you recognize him?"

"Yes."

"Where did you recognize him from?"

Ray frowned slightly. "I seen him play at the Blackburn a few times."

"In your statement, it says he made you mad. How did he make you mad?"

"He said something bad about... he insulted my wife."

"What did he say?"

"I don't remember."

"Approximately, what did he say?"

For the first time, Ray's eyes narrowed and his voice lost its robotic monotony. "If it was something that made me mad, I wouldn't repeat it. Ask me all you want and I'll never repeat it."

"Then what happened?"

"Just like I wrote..." Ray gestured at the statement which lay on the table in front of Russell, his voice again became expressionless. "I got him in a choke hold and he passed out, so I put him in the back of the trailer. I didn't want to leave him there in the street."

"You knew it would kill him?"

Ray hesitated, then answered, "I didn't know."

"You didn't intend to kill him?"

"No."

"Well, if you didn't intend to kill him, why didn't you let him out before he froze to death?"

Ray shrugged. "I forgot he was in there, I guess."

Russell stroked his tie. There was no question in his mind that Ray Nillson was lying, but just how much was a lie and how much was the truth? He had to get Ray to drop the script. He had to make him speak from his gut. He trained his eyes on Ray's face, seeking the still averted eyes. "When you and your wife opened the trailer to dump the body..."

"Sharon didn't know. My wife didn't know anything. She was asleep in the truck."

"She was asleep when you put him in, and she was asleep when you took the body out?"

Again Ray gestured toward the statement. "That's what I wrote, and that's exactly how it happened. Sharon didn't know a thing about it. She's completely innocent."

"Innocent women don't assault their cell mates. An innocent woman wouldn't kill a fellow inmate."

Ray's eyes met Russell's. Russell saw a flicker of fear. "What the hell are you talking about?"

"Your wife. She beat up the other woman in her cell this morning. The woman is on life support and will probably die."

"No!" Ray leaped to his feet, his big hands gripped the edges of the table as if he were about to heave it over. Russell tensed, ready to move. "No! Sharon's gotta get out of here. You've got to let her go!" The trucker looked around him, wide eyed as if the walls were on fire, then seemed to recollect himself. He took a few deep breaths and sat down.

"You're lying." The eyes were straight again, and calm. The automaton had returned. "You're trying to shake me up, but I know you're lying."

"If you don't believe me," said Russell, getting to his feet, "watch the evening news."

CHAPTER

TWENTY-ONE

When her pager went off, Alora was in court defending a woman who had shot her abusive husband in the knees. The bastard was playing it to the hilt, wheelchair and meek demeanor, and according to the judge, Alora wasn't allowed to introduce a recent videotape of him riding his motorcycle, nor bring up the threatening notes he'd been sending to his wife almost daily since the attack. It was another hour and a half before court recessed for the day and she was finally able to call her secretary to find out what the message was. When she heard about Sharon's new problem, she rearranged her schedule as best she could and headed straight for the county lock-up, hoping she'd have time to stop somewhere and pick up a sandwich before her afternoon appointments.

Hurrying to the jail from her car, she recognized Detective Russell Kupka standing just outside the front door, a microphone thrust toward his face like a metal detector searching for gold fillings. They were still trying to make news out of the Iceman. There was just one female reporter and one cameraman, but it was one too many of each as far as Alora was concerned. She turned her head away as she got closer. They weren't likely to know who she was, but there was no sense in tempting fate. The last thing she needed was for her ex-husband to see her on the news and be told her new name and where to find her.

Then she heard Russell's voice say, "There she is now. That's her lawyer right there. Alora Magee." Alora's heart did a flip flop as she made a dash for the door.

"Ms. Magee," called the reporter. "Ms. Magee, please wait." Alora had no intention of waiting, but three heavy set African American men approached the door from the opposite side and she was forced to step back as the doors swung outward. "Why did Sharon Nillson attack her cell mate?" asked the reporter, barely pausing to breathe. "Does your client have a history of violence? Will you be having her evaluated by a psychiatric expert?"

Alora wished she hadn't brought her heavy briefcase. At least with a file folder or a small portfolio she could have held something up to obscure her face. Maybe if she said nothing, they wouldn't use the footage on the news. Make it dull. "Please," she said, pushing the microphone away. "I have nothing to tell you. I haven't even talked to my client about this yet."

She should have known that the reporter would interpret her reluctance to talk to mean that she had something to hide. The questions began again, "Ms. Magee, how does your client feel about her husband's confession in the Iceman murder case? Will your client be pleading guilty as well?"

Confession? Alora let down her guard, turned to seek out Russell Kupka and was caught full face by the TV camera. "I have nothing to tell you at this time," she repeated to the reporter. Kupka was still standing on the walkway, smirking as if he found her discomfort amusing. "Detective Kupka," she said coldly, striding over to him. "Can I speak to you for a moment." The camera and microphone were still in her face. "Inside," she said, and motioned for the detective to precede her.

Before stepping toward the door, Kupka turned to the reporter and made a throat slashing gesture. "Cut," he said. "Now go away."

"What is this?" Alora dropped her briefcase and stood with her hands on her hips, like an angry mother. "What did she mean, Ray Nillson has confessed? Why wasn't I told?"

Kupka put his hands up in front of him in mock surrender. "Hey. I just found out about it this morning myself. You'll get the documents through channels eventually."

"Come on, Detective. I have to know what he said. Did he implicate my client?" She frowned. "I guess I should call Jeff Feldman."

"Won't do you any good."

"What?"

"Nillson fired Feldman yesterday. My guess is Feldman wouldn't let him confess - wouldn't have made very good press for our rising young attorney now, would it? - so Nillson fired him. As far as implicating your client goes, according to her husband she slept through everything."

"Did he say why he did it?"

"Nothing that makes sense. In fact, I think he made the whole thing up."

"You mean you don't think he killed Williams?"

"I didn't say that. It just seems to me that he's lying about what happened, and how it happened." Kupka ran two fingers along his tie, pulling it out in front of him. Alora found the gesture oddly sensuous, as if he were stroking a cat. "The body was in their trailer. That's irrefutable."

"You're beginning to sound as if you're not so sure about the rest of it," said Alora, cocking her head to one side. "You having doubts?"

"Don't ask me to help you do your job, Magee. I think I answered that question once and for all when I arrested the two of them."

El parked her truck in the loading zone in front of Fur 'N Feathers Pet Shop. She tucked Wally's dog book in her armpit, then scooped up Peterbilt with one hand and Peaches with the other. She yanked the door open and Peterbilt yelped as the glass bumped his nose. The rumpled pet shop owner looked up from sprinkling dried bugs, dropped the bug box into the turtles' pool, and snatched it back out with a gasp.

"Can I help you?" he asked, holding the bug box up in front of his chest, like some protective talisman.

El grunted. "Remember him?" she asked, thrusting Peterbilt toward him. Peterbilt wriggled, and she had to swing her arm to keep him balanced. "Stop it, Pete!" she snarled.

"Uh... did you purchase him here?" the pet shop owner asked, bumping into the turtle tank behind him.

"You're goddamn right I purchased him here. For three hundred and fifty bucks, remember?"

"I... uh... I... is there a problem?" He had backed clear of the turtle tank, and was inching gradually toward the counter. When he was within five feet of it, he turned and bumbled hurriedly in behind it.

"You're goddamn right there's a problem. You told me he was a Pomeranian, remember?"

The pet shop owner looked from Peterbilt to Peaches and back again, then looked wide-eyed at El. "He's not?"

"This..." El thrust Peaches under his nose and shook her. The book dropped from El's armpit, bounced off the edge of the counter to the floor, and Peaches squirmed off of her forearm with a little squeal. Peaches and Peterbilt skittered across the countertop, knocking over cat toy displays and flyers. "That..." continued El, pointing at Peaches, "is a Pomeranian. This..." She grabbed Peterbilt, who was sniffing at the Visa machine, by the scruff on his back, "is a... a... who knows what?"

"A what?"

"You're the goddamn expert. You tell me!" She scowled at him.

His mouth worked, but no sound came out. Peaches tried to climb his chest.

"Look. Look at this." El retrieved the book from the floor, opened it to a page about Pomeranians, and jabbed at it with her finger. "Up to ten pounds. Ten pounds! What is he? The Shaquille O'Neal of Poms? Rarely black, it says. Look at him! You told me he was a Pomeranian. I should sue you for false advertising. You

258

charged me three hundred and fifty bucks for a Pomeranian, and you didn't deliver. That's downright fraud."

The man held Peaches away from his face as her paws scrambled against the arborite, nails ticking like a tiny tap dancer. "You want to return the dog?"

"No!" El looked at Peterbilt's twinkling eyes and her jaw dropped. "No," she said, her voice dropping. "I don't want to return the dog."

"I can't give your money back unless you return the dog."

"I don't want to return the dog."

"What then?"

"I want you to explain yourself. I want you to stop cheating people like that!" Her voice rose to a shout again, and a customer just coming through the front door changed her mind and backed out again, setting a bell tinkling near the ceiling. "I want you to fuckin' apologize." Peaches cringed, and Peterbilt eased his nose past the edge of the counter, priming his haunches, poising to dive. El scooped him up against her chest. "Apologize!" She lunged across the counter, grabbing at the man's collar, but he drew back in time, drew his hands up toward his chin.

"I'm sorry," he stammered. "I didn't know. The breeder sends them, and they're just little puppies, and you can't always tell. There are no real papers for most of these dogs, you know. Not official ones. I must have told you that. There never were."

El snorted, gathered up Peaches and the book.

"It wasn't my fault," he said, bolder now that El's hands were full. "I have to go by what the breeder tells me, you know."

"Fuck off," said El. It was all she could think of to say.

Three blocks away from the store, she pulled the truck over to the side of the road and jerked on the parking brake. Then she scooped Pete into her arms and buried her face in his ruff. "Oh, Petie, I'm sorry," she mumbled. "I don't care if you're a Pomeranian or a Heinz 57 or a goddamn turtle. You're my little guy, aren't you?" She kissed the top of his head and rocked him a little, scratching behind his ears. "You were worth every penny," she said, then spat air, once, twice, three times, to blow a hair from between her lips.

259

"Every fuckin' penny."

Alora had to wait ten minutes before her client was shown into the room. Sharon Nillson looked worse than ever, her hair dangling in dull, twisted strings, skin pallid, and her eyes circled by grim shadows. She managed a tight smile. A resigned smile. She picked up one of the cigarettes that Alora had placed on the table for her, lit it, and took a deep drag.

"Tell me what happened, Sharon."

"I lost it," she said. "Why the hell didn't they move me, like I asked? She wouldn't leave me alone, and I finally lost it. I didn't want to hurt her, I just had to make her shut up."

Alora nodded. "I documented your requests to be moved. If you're charged, we'll throw the blame back where it belongs. Don't worry." She hoped it would be as easy as she was trying to make it sound, but knew it wouldn't.

Sharon sighed. She scratched at her scalp with the fingers that held the cigarette. "I hope Ray doesn't have to know. That's the worst thing. I don't want him to feel bad about me, you know?" She smiled wanly. "I'm not saying that I don't want him to think badly of me, because he won't. He's always so understanding. It's just that he'll feel bad for my sake, you know what I mean? He'll worry. I don't want him to know."

They sat silent for a few minutes. Alora hesitated to tell Sharon about Ray's confession because she didn't have enough information yet, but she was afraid not to. She was afraid of what hiding it from her would do to the fragile trust they seemed to be building between each other. "I've just been informed that Ray confessed."

"No." Sharon closed her eyes, then lowered her head. Her body went so still she seemed to have stopped breathing, but after half a minute her chest heaved with two shuddering breaths. "He's lying for me," she said. She paused to light a second cigarette off the stump of the first. "You know that, don't you, Alora? Ray's lying for me."

"I don't know that, Sharon," she said softly. "You tell me."

260

"Okay. I will. Write this down or tape record it or whatever you do. I'm going to tell you what really happened." She sighed two or three times, chewing on her lips in concentration, then took a deep drag on her cigarette, letting the smoke out as she talked. "I thought Greg Williams was my friend. He played the bar where I worked a couple times a month, and we used to talk. This was up in Canada, eh? So, there was this guy used to come in to the bar. He was married and had a pretty fancy job so he had money, but he liked a different kind of good time, something he couldn't do with his wife. We got to talking, and he said he liked me. He said he'd treat me to some good blow if I'd party with him, you know? Cocaine. I was really hooked on it at the time, couldn't afford as much as I needed to keep happy. After the first couple of times with this guy, I knew I was in for trouble. Turned out he was a real asshole who liked to hurt women. He'd pull my hair, twist my arm, anything to make me scream and cry. It turned him on. He did worse stuff. One night he came to the bar, said he'd be back for me after I got off work. When I went outside on my break to have a smoke, I was so scared and ashamed I started to cry. I wanted the coke so bad, but I hated what that creep did to me. Greg was on his break, too, and he saw me crying, asked me what was the matter. He seemed to care so I told him all about it."

Sharon closed her eyes, remembering. "Greg said he could help. He said he'd loan me this little tape recorder he used to write songs, and I could tape Jake saying stuff that he wouldn't want his wife to know, or his boss. Stuff that might even get him in trouble with the law. I was to get him to say that he'd bought cocaine, and the kind of things he liked to do in bed, whatever I could get him to talk about. And I had to find out where he lived and stuff. It was easy. I just looked at his driver's license while he was in the shower. I made the tape and gave it back to Greg, like he said. A couple of days later, Greg talked to Jake, played him the tape, said if he ever hurt me bad, he'd be in big trouble. So Jake was pissed off. We saw each other a few more times, but he wasn't having fun anymore. I could tell he really wanted to hurt me, but he didn't. Then he just stopped coming

around. But by then I had two or three other guys buying me coke."
She looked up at Alora. "I know what you're thinking."

Alora didn't respond, other than to smile sympathetically. She'd been jotting down notes as Sharon talked, intending to fill in the blanks later, before she forgot.

"You're thinking I'm nothing but a whore." She sighed. "Well, you're right. I was selling my body for drugs. I used to tell myself I was just partying, that I never did it for money. Hah! If I'd had the money, I would've bought the drugs with it, so it was really just a shortcut, wasn't it? I was still just a whore."

She looked at the short stub of her cigarette, and Alora passed the package across the table. Sharon lit a third cigarette before she continued. "Greg said I should tape some stuff on all the guys I went with, just for insurance. He'd hold onto them for me, and if anything happened to me, he could take the tapes to the police. Or if the guys started getting nasty, he could do what he did with Jake. I said, okay. Of course, I still thought Greg was doing this for my sake, just to help me out, keep me safe."

Alora looked up from her writing and nodded, encouraging Sharon to continue.

"I found out a few months later he was doing it for Greg. He was hitting them up for money, but I didn't know, eh? One of the guys told me about it, said he couldn't see me anymore because of it, that he had to pay Greg a thousand bucks to get the tape back and he sure as hell wasn't going to let it happen again, and was I happy now. He was pissed off with me because he thought I was in on it. When I talked to Greg about it, he offered me a cut." Sharon paused, took a deep breath and rubbed her forehead with her palm. "You know, I actually thought about it, started working out what kind of money I would make if I slept with two new guys a week. Christ! What a wake up call! While I was just sleeping with these guys for coke, I could pretend I was still a half decent girl. A bar waitress who happened to be a party girl. But when I found myself actually thinking about blackmailing these guys ... What did that make me? It was about that time that I got drunk at work a couple of times, and they told me I had to get treatment or I'd lose my job. That and the
262

blackmail thing scared the piss out of me, so I went to treatment. I'd been sober for four months when I met Ray." She leaned back, her eyes wandered to the corner of the ceiling and she was lost in her thoughts for a while. Alora scribbled furiously, taking down as much as she could remember.

"Being sober, being with Ray, I almost forgot about Greg's tapes. We still talked some when he played the bar, and he seemed happy for me when I told him how well it was working out with Ray, but we never mentioned that other stuff. Well, after me and Ray got married, and we needed to get a green card for me so I could work with him on U.S. runs, I started to think about those tapes. There must've been at least half a dozen, probably more. I couldn't take a risk of somebody getting hold of those tapes and going to the police, because if I had a criminal record, it would make it an awful lot harder to get my green card. In fact, I might not even be able to cross the border into the United States. I'd quit my job by then, but I went back to the Blackburn to talk to Greg." She looked up at Alora, snorted softly and shook her head. "Guess what happened?"

Alora shrugged. "He wouldn't give them back?"

"Worse than that. He said I could have them all - all the ones he had left, because I think he just hit some of the guys up for a hundred bucks every month or so, and others he handed over the tape for a bigger amount, so some of the tapes were gone. So he said I could have them all back if I wanted to buy them out. Five thousand dollars, he said. I said, You know me, Greg. I don't have that kind of money. And he said, but that's a pretty nice looking truck your husband has. He must make pretty good money. Why don't you ask him for it?" She grunted, looked like she wanted to spit. "He knew I wouldn't want Ray to hear those tapes. It wasn't like Ray didn't know I'd had some problems. I told him I was an addict and did some things I was ashamed of. Hell, he's even been to a couple of AA meetings with me, just to keep me company. But that's not the same as hearing your wife making out with some asshole on tape. It makes me shudder to even think about Ray hearing some of the things I said to those guys. And the blackmail part. It would've just killed Ray to think I was in on stuff like that."

Sharon was silent for so long, lighting up and smoking another cigarette, staring down at her hands on the table, that Alora prompted her gently. "That was the night the witnesses saw you arguing?"

Sharon nodded. "I guess. It was just a few days before our last trip out of Vancouver. I got mad and yelled at him. Asshole. I don't remember what I said. Next day, I figured I didn't have any choice, so I called him up and said I'd meet him, pay him off. I didn't know where else to get the money, so I had to ask Ray. I said it was money I'd borrowed from Greg when I was using, that he was threatening to make trouble for me unless I paid it back. I told Ray I'd work it off, like a loan, and he just laughed. He said it was his gift to me, and would just mean he couldn't get me diamond earrings for Christmas this year." She smiled sadly.

"He's a special man, Sharon."

"Yeah. And now because of me he's in jail and I'm in jail and I just about killed that crazy woman they stuck me in here with. No. Not because of me. Because of that bastard, Greg Williams. I'm glad he's dead."

"How did it happen?"

"Ray couldn't get the money from any of the banks in Canada, because he keeps his money in a U.S. bank. I told Greg to meet us on Friday at the Wells Fargo bank in Ferndale, so Ray could get the cash. I don't know what went wrong, but Greg never showed up." Sharon paused, twisting a strand of hair around her index finger and frowning.

"Did Ray lock him in the trailer outside the bank?"

"I told you, he never showed up."

"Then how did Greg get into your trailer?"

"I don't know."

"What did Ray do with the money?"

"He never got the money. We were waiting for Greg and he didn't show."

Alora leaned back thoughtfully. She hadn't heard anything about money being found on the victim, but she didn't know. "Well, I guess Ray has explained it all in his confession," she said.

"No," said Sharon. "Ray couldn't have confessed to anything. He was lying."

"How would you know if he was lying? He said you didn't know anything about how Greg got into your trailer."

Sharon swallowed hard. "I'm really thirsty. Can I have a Coke?"

Alora went to the door, asked the guard if it would be possible to get Sharon a Coke. The guard motioned to a pop machine at the end of the hall, said she'd stay with Sharon but Alora had to get the Coke herself. When Alora returned, Sharon popped the top on the Coke can and took a long swallow, then asked for another cigarette.

"Go ahead," said Alora. "Why did you say Ray was lying?"

"Because Ray doesn't know what happened. Okay?" She took a deep breath. "He wasn't even there when Greg showed up. When I saw Greg's car stop at the red light at the intersection closest to the bank, I sent Ray to the gas station across the street to get me a Coke and some cigarettes, and told him to meet me back at the bank. I ran to the intersection and waved Greg over to our truck, on the other side of the bank. Ray didn't even see."

"So how did you get Greg into the trailer?"

"I told him that was where I'd hidden the money."

"And he just climbed in?"

"I unlocked it and climbed in first, then I helped him in. I pointed back into the trailer and said, look over there, and while he was looking around, I jumped out and locked the door."

"Didn't Ray hear him screaming and pounding on the door?"

"He didn't make any noise. I must have knocked him out first."

"How did you do that?"

"Shoved him and he fell and hit his head." She made a shoving motion with her two hands, tilted her head defiantly. "Just like that poor crazy woman did this morning."

"What happened to the money?"

"I told you, we never got the money. I just told Ray that we should go, that Greg hadn't shown up."

"Kind of hard to believe Greg would just jump into the trailer to look for the money."

"Well, he did." Sharon looked away.

"Where was his car parked? On the street? In the lot?"

"I don't remember. I was upset. I wasn't paying attention. I just can't remember."

Alora snorted softly. Sharon had to be lying to protect Ray. Alora didn't think this was the time to confront her about it, however. The wrong word now could destroy the relationship that had been so difficult to forge. "Sharon," she said softly. "This is a lot of information for me for one day. You've had a rough day yourself. Let's both sleep on this tonight, and get together tomorrow again. Okay?"

"What about Ray?"

"What about him?"

"You said he's confessed. I want everyone to know that he's innocent, that he was just trying to protect me."

"Nothing will happen overnight," said Alora, checking her watch. "I'll find out more about what Ray said before we get together again." She reached across the table and took her client's hand. "Look. I've got to rush back to my office for some appointments. If we weren't both so tired, I'd suggest coming back tonight, but I think it would be better if we both got a good night's sleep before we continued. Nothing will happen to Ray. Trust me."

Alora suspected that her client's willingness to quit for the day was due to the fact that she needed more time to think out her story. As she packed up her briefcase and Sharon was escorted from the room, Alora mused that her client would probably remember the story much better, or a much better story, twenty four hours from now.

Hunter was at the Watson Transportation office, pacing up and down in front of the reception counter. Because of the holiday weekend, the phone calls were few and far between and mostly from the United States, so every time El answered the phone with a sharp "Watson", Hunter glanced at her to see if it was the call he was waiting for. If the call didn't come in soon, he'd have to leave. He was scheduled to

266

pick up a load for Portland, Oregon, before five o'clock and the longer he waited, the worse the traffic would be.

"Christ, Hunter! You're driving me nuts. Sit down or go wash your truck or something." El pointed a thick finger at him. "What're you so nervous for? You'd think you were waiting for a call from a new girlfriend."

"I'm impatient to get out of here," he answered, sounding more irritated than he'd meant to.

"Is she pretty?"

"Huh?"

"Alora Magee. The one you're waiting for. Is she attractive?"

He shrugged. "I guess maybe." The phone started to ring.

"You guess maybe. Either she is or she isn't."

"Answer the phone."

"Tell me first if you find her attractive."

"Sheesh, El."

She smiled wickedly, let her hand hover eight inches above the receiver.

Hunter rolled his eyes. "Yes, she's attractive."

"Watson!" El started to write something, and Hunter had already turned away to resume his pacing when she said, "Hunter, it's for you."

"Now what?" said the voice on the other end of the line.

"I beg your pardon," said Hunter.

"First my client almost kills her cell mate, next I get caught by a TV news camera being surprised with the information that her husband has confessed to the murder, and then my client tells me her husband's lying, and that it was really her who locked Greg Williams in the trailer. I don't think I could take any more news on the Ice Man case today, thank you."

"Sharon confessed, too?" Hunter and El exchanged glances. "Do you believe her?"

"Why shouldn't I believe her?"

"I don't know. He won't admit it, but I believe that Ray confessed just to get Sharon out of jail. I want to know if he had reason to. Did she do it?"

"Either she's a rotten liar, or a brilliant strategist. I believe the story she tells me about knowing Williams, but then it turns sour. I don't think she killed him. I think she's lying to protect her husband."

"Does the story involve Williams blackmailing her... uh ... dates?"

"Her johns? Yes, it does. You've heard about the tapes."

"We found them. We've listened to them. As far as I'm concerned, the tapes have put at least a dozen more people on the suspect list, from Williams' own brother to a local politician. It didn't end with Sharon. There was another woman who took her place, a woman named Ruby, and she could be the key to solving this case."

"But the tapes also give the Nillsons a pretty strong motive." Alora's voice was somber. "Sharon talked about needing her green card."

Hunter couldn't disagree. "Detective Kupka let me talk to Ray on the phone this morning, and I believe he's lying, you've talked to Sharon and you believe she's lying, so the truth has to be somewhere between their two versions of events. Tell me what she's told you." He looked at his watch. "Just the nuts and bolts."

After Alora gave him a recap of Sharon's story, he said, "They're both lying about the location. That could mean they think there could be evidence or witnesses at the actual scene."

"What is the actual scene?"

"The victim's car was found in a restaurant parking lot near Mount Vernon, Washington. They're both talking about a bank in Ferndale. Why doesn't either one of them mention Mount Vernon?"

"Is there a Wells Fargo branch in Mount Vernon? Maybe they're mixed up."

"No bank where the car was found."

"Like you said, maybe they think there could be evidence there. Or could the car have been stolen and moved?"

"Possible. Or maybe neither of them knows where it happened."

"Well, that would be impossible. One of them has to know."

"Not if they were framed."

They were both silent for a moment, then Hunter said, "I thought I'd pay a visit to the Blackburn pub tonight. It's a good starting point to try to track down the other woman who made tapes for Williams. Could you ask Sharon if she knows someone named Ruby? Meanwhile, I've been trying to convince Ray to find a new lawyer. Do you know anyone maybe a little older and more homespun than Mr. Feldman?"

"I'll see what I can do."

Hunter hesitated. El was still sitting at his elbow, pretending to work. He felt he owed Alora an apology for the awkward way their dinner had ended the week before, but he didn't know what to say. "What time do you go to bed?" he asked. El glanced up at him, her eyebrows disappeared under her bangs. "Do you want me to call you tonight if I find out anything at the Blackburn?" he added.

El winked, signaled that she was going out to the warehouse, and rose from her chair.

Instead of answering his question, Alora said, "Do you remember saying that you'd make a poor lawyer because you could never defend a client you believed was guilty?"

"Yes," he said. He wondered if she was about to tell him she could no longer represent Ray's wife.

"Well, if you were me, you'd have no trouble defending Sharon Nillson."

Hunter smiled, but said nothing.

"Oh, and Hunter, call me anytime," she added softly.

Hunter said goodbye, put down the phone and was out the door before El could see him blush.

El insisted on coming with Hunter to the Blackburn, but she promised to stay in the background unless he asked for her help. She sat nursing a pint of pale ale and working her way through a basketful of timber-sized fried potatoes while he canvassed the staff. None of the servers knew anyone named Ruby. The bartender shrugged his shoulders. "Ask Pat," he said. "She's in her office."

Hunter tapped on the open door of the tiny office and a breezy voice said, "Hello again! How are you?" A familiar sounding breezy voice.

"Just tickety boo," he said. "And you?"

"Tickety boo? How delightfully corny. Come on in," she said, looking up from a stack of paperwork. "What can I do for you?"

"I'd like you to hear something." Hunter pulled the miniature tape recorder out of his pocket. "But before you do, I'd like you to tell me about Ruby."

Pat Stevens threw down her pencil and leaned back in her chair with an exaggerated sigh. "Shit," she said. "I should've known this would happen sooner or later. Close the door and pull up a case of CC and sit down."

Hunter found an unopened case solid enough to sit on and moved it to a spot where he could watch her as she spoke.

She sighed again, made a wry face. "A.k.a. Ruby. Yeah. I have champagne tastes, and at this stage of my career, a beer income. A friend I met at college listed herself with a high priced escort service, and told me what a gas it was. She went places with these rich guys, businessmen from out of town with fat expense accounts, mostly out for dinner at nice restaurants or to shows, and sometimes they ended up in bed, other times not. Sometimes she was just paid to attend parties of the rich and famous. Eye candy. Party favors. Not much different than going on blind dates or to pick-up bars, she said, and getting paid for it. Except you're expected to be easy. Well, we are, I told her." She laughed weakly. "Sounded like my kind of job, so I thought about it for a few weeks, then signed up. It was like a matchmaking service, and the girls are independent contractors, so you can call your own shots. As they say, the rest is history."

"And these?" Hunter held up the tape.

"Greg saw me once at one of the other clubs. I was with one of my least favorite clients of all time, some car dealership bigwig from Edmonton. Greg figured out what was going on and said he knew how we could both make a few bucks off jerks like him. Hey. Champagne tastes. I'm not about to turn down easy money. I put a clear twenty thousand in the bank in less than six months working maybe one day a week." She paused, lit up a cigarette and inhaled deeply.

270

"So I'd tape my clients, but only the ones I knew had a lot to lose, plus they were jerks or weren't regular enough or rich enough to keep. A few of them got pissed off and dropped me as soon as Greg made one of his friendly little phone calls, and a couple of them didn't give a shit. They just told him to fuck off, didn't give a shit whether or not he told anybody." She shrugged. "But about half of them were scared enough to pay him off. Of course, when it got back to the agency they dropped me. Thanks, Greg." She shrugged again, "Easy come…".

"Sharon Nillson got paid in drugs."

"Not me. I only do drugs socially."

"But on the tapes…"

"Yeah, I know. Greg's idea. He'd get a finder's fee for sending guys to do business with this biker named Toad, plus it added to the… uh… blackmail-ability of the client. If I could get the suckers to buy cocaine, they'd be in deeper, you know? Greg gave me half his finder's fee."

"Toad?"

"Yeah. A biker. He does his business from a sharp-looking RV, sort of a mobile operation. I see him in here once and a while. Greg told me who he was, but we don't officially know each other. He knows I work here, but I doubt that he knows my name."

"He and Greg knew each other?"

"Well, yeah," she said, taking a drag on her cigarette, then tapping it against the ashtray to knock off the ash.

"And this Toad would have known Sharon?"

Pat shrugged. "Maybe. Look, if I thought there was any chance Toad had killed Greg, I wouldn't even have mentioned his name. I have no intention of being found dead in an alley from an overdose. Toad was pissed off at Greg about a fast one he pulled, but they sorted that out and Greg learned his lesson, never tried it again."

"What kind of fast one?"

In spite of the fact that the door was closed, she lowered her voice. "This guy comes in here sometimes. Toad buys stuff off of this guy, like, he's a wholesaler you might say. Well, one night I phoned up Greg and told him I had this client who wanted to make a

271

big buy for some fancy party he was throwing. He had wads of cash in his pockets, could I send him over? Greg was here at the Blackburn, and he saw this wholesaler sitting around waiting for Toad, but Toad was late. So Greg went to this wholesaler and sweet-talked him into selling direct to this rich dude, and when Toad got here, expecting to get a new supply from his wholesaler, the guy had already split with the money from my client. Greg said that Toad was really, really pissed off."

"Pissed off enough to kill someone?"

"If he was that pissed off, he would've done it. He's a biker. They don't fool around. Greg said he told him he'd break every fuckin' one of his fingers and flatten his pretty nose if he ever messed with Toad's operation again. Greg wouldn't have taken any chances after that. The wholesaler had already left, but I think Toad was madder at him than at Greg because he'd stiffed him. Toad was expecting that stuff, so it left him high and dry. He said he was going to have to teach the guy a lesson."

"Did he?"

"Probably. I only ever saw the guy one more time."

"When was that?"

Pat sighed, looked up at the ceiling. "I think I told you about him the first time you were here. He was the guy who Greg was talking to the night Sharon got into an argument with him. That was the last time I saw the guy. Any of them, in fact."

"Would you recognize his voice?"

"No. I don't think I ever heard him talk, but he's straight looking, sort of a jock. Greg joked once that the only reason he didn't figure him for a cop was that he looked too much like a cop to be one. No real cop would be stupid enough to do business looking that much like a cop." She looked Hunter up and down. "Sort of like you, but you don't look anything like him. You're not a jock."

"Would you recognize him to see him again?"

"Of course."

Hunter pulled a piece of paper out of his shirt pocket. It was a photocopy of a selection of six photographs, headshots from the RCMP mug files. One of the photos was the one Al had asked the
272

Vancouver Police Department to fax him. "Do you recognize any of these men?"

Pat took the paper from him, stubbed out her cigarette as she looked it over. "No," she said, shaking her head and handing it back. "He's not on there."

"You sure?" He held it out again.

She took another look and nodded. "Absolutely."

Hunter thanked her. "Your client, the one who made the big buy, he wouldn't be a potential candidate for mayor of Vancouver, would he?"

She smiled. "You didn't hear it from me, cowboy."

"You showed her a photo line up? Can I see?" asked El as they walked out to the parking lot. Hunter handed her the paper, and she carried it into the glow of a floodlight. "Hey! That's him! That's the guy!" she said excitedly.

"How do you know?" asked Hunter, wondering if Pat Stevens had a reason not to identify the wholesaler she'd talked about. Was she afraid of what he'd do to her? Or what Toad would do if he found out she knew more than she should?

"Not the guy on the tape," El said, turning the page toward Hunter and jabbing Chad Williams' photo with her finger. "This guy. He's the one I saw leaving Greg Williams' house that day I touched the cookie jar."

CHAPTER
TWENTY-TWO

Alora worked late, as usual, and by the time she got home she was too tired to make a proper meal. She sipped on a glass of chilled wine and appeased her hunger with a plate of cheese and wheat thins while she thought about what to have for dinner, decided to throw together a salad and heat up a frozen pasta entree in the microwave. She watched a rerun of Seinfeld on TV from the kitchen counter as she washed and sliced tomatoes and cucumbers for the salad. She'd seen the episode at least twice already, but it didn't matter. Seinfeld and NYPD Blue seemed to have become substitutes for a social life of her own. People talked and laughed and fought with each other, and she experienced a little vicarious camaraderie and vindication, love and anger, emotions that seemed sadly lacking in her own life.

She tried to put work out of her mind in the evenings, but she wasn't always successful. She was thinking now of how ironic it would be if Ray and Sharon Nillson each believed that the other had locked Greg Williams in their trailer, and had each confessed to save the other, when in fact, if they had both simply told the truth, it might make the real killer that much easier to find. Love could be stupid. Love could be cruel.

It was almost nine when the phone rang. She looked at her watch, surprised that Hunter Rayne would be calling this early. She let it ring three times, taking deep breaths. "Hello?"

274

"You're looking good, Monkey." It was not Hunter Rayne.

At the first word of her ex-husband's voice, Alora felt hot and cold at the same time. She wanted to put the phone down, but knew it wouldn't help. He knew where she worked now. He knew how to reach her at home, probably manipulated someone at the firm into giving him her home number. He could be slick. She prayed he wouldn't be able to find out where she lived.

"Magee, huh? You married again or is that just a corruption of McGuire?"

"What do you want, Mike," she said, her voice as flat as she could make it. "We're expecting an important call." Her heart was thudding against her ribcage, and she cursed herself for letting him get to her, for being frightened enough to lie.

"We? So you are married. Looks good on you, Monkey. Who's the lucky man?"

"You and I have nothing to talk about." Alora realized she was standing rigid, as if she were frozen in place. Still, she didn't move.

"That was a nice suit you had on. Looked expensive. You and your husband must be making big bucks. He a lawyer, too?" When she didn't answer, he continued. "You take that pretty suit off yet, Monkey? I still miss your tits. You got nice tits. Does Mr. Magee appreciate your tits, Alora? Let me talk to him, okay? I got a real good lawyer joke for him."

"Good bye, Mike." There was nothing else to say. Reasoning with him had never worked. Alora hung up the phone.

As she expected, it rang again within thirty seconds. She glanced at the Caller I.D. unit. Both calls simply read "PRIVATE CALL". He was probably using a cell phone, so there'd be no way to block his calls. She let it go to her voice mail, dreading what the messages might be. Knowing he would call again and again before he gave up. Tomorrow she'd change her number. Again. Tonight she would simply turn off her phones.

And lie awake listening to their silence.

Hunter tried to call Alora Magee when he arrived home at eleven o'clock. He reached her voice mail, but he didn't leave a message. He went right to bed and slept like a log until his internal alarm woke him at five thirty, giving him just enough time to make coffee, shower and pack his duffel bag before leaving home. By quarter to seven, he was firing up the big diesel engine in the Blue Knight at the Watson yard on Annacis Island. In order to be sure its trailer load of cargo would be delivered in Portland by four o'clock that afternoon, he was allowing extra time for morning rush-hour traffic through Seattle, and possible delays at the border crossing or construction hold ups along the I-5.

As the engine warmed up, he went inside to talk to El. She was on the phone to Chicago and paused only long enough to wish him a good trip - "Call me from Portland," she said - so he just filled up his coffee mug from the pot in the lunchroom, and hit the road.

The border wasn't busy, and there were no problems with his clearance. He didn't even have to get out of the truck. As he passed, he saw a tractor-trailer unit very similar to Ray Nillson's backed up to the customs dock, one of the drivers leaning against its concrete wall smoking a cigarette. He wondered when would be a good time to try calling Alora Magee again. Portland would be soon enough, he decided. After she'd had a chance to talk to Sharon and get a list of the stops the Nillsons had made that trip, maybe even locate a suitable lawyer for Ray.

Less than an hour later, Hunter pulled his rig into the parking lot outside the restaurant in Mount Vernon where Greg Williams' car had been found. He felt this was as good a place as any to stop for breakfast. He found a window table where he could keep an eye on his truck, and ordered bacon and scrambled eggs, with a side of hash browns. As he stirred cream and sugar into his coffee, he thought about Williams' car. It made sense that if the Nillsons were guilty and this was where Williams entered their trailer, Ray and Sharon would steer police away from this potential site for witnesses or evidence. If Williams didn't enter the trailer here, then his car had been moved. If someone had known enough about their itinerary to frame the

276

Nillsons by putting Williams in their trailer, it would've been a small matter to plant his car somewhere else along their route.

Hunter delivered his load in Portland well ahead of the deadline, then headed straight for the Jubitz Truck Stop where he could settle into a booth with a table phone. He waited while the waitress cleared the table and took his order, then he dialed the number of Alora Magee's law firm. The receptionist asked his name, said, "She's expecting your call," and put him through.

"Did you call last night?" she asked. "I'm sorry, I had my ringer turned off."

Hunter wondered briefly if perhaps she hadn't been alone, decided it should not be his concern. "I found Ruby," he said. "She gave me some more pieces of the puzzle, but I'm still trying to put them all together. There's a man on one of the tapes I haven't got an ID on yet, but I think he may be the key to all this. Have you talked to Sharon again? Did they fuel up or keep any receipts from their Ferndale stop?" The waitress arrived with his pie and coffee. He nodded his thanks.

"Yes, I talked to her. She's sticking with her story, but says there's nothing to verify their stop in Ferndale."

"I'll be checking out the logistics at the Wells Fargo bank there on my way home today. The police were able to determine that Ray didn't make any bank transactions on July 14th. I'll ask if anyone at the gas station remembers him."

"I may have found a new lawyer for Ray."

"I appreciate that. I hope El can talk him into accepting a new lawyer. With any luck, he's not going to need one," said Hunter. "I'll call you later to let you know what I find out. That is, if you're going to turn your phone back on."

"Wait," she said. "Have you got a pen? I'll give you my new phone number."

"Oh," he said. He suddenly understood. As a Mountie, he'd met a lot of women who'd stopped answering their phones before a sudden change of phone numbers. The first time he'd seen them, many of them had purple bruises and broken bones. The last time he'd seen some of them was in the morgue. Alora Magee was smart.

She was savvy. He hoped she could keep herself safe. He took down the number. "Take care of yourself," he said, and immediately felt uncomfortable. He was getting too personal. "I'll call you tonight."

His next call was to Russell Kupka of the L.A. County Sheriff's Department. "I was wondering if you would do me a couple of favors," he said.

The detective laughed out loud. "Yeah, right. Why the hell I should I?" was his reply.

"Because if you do, and if I'm right, you'll have won yourself another all expenses paid trip to the beautiful Pacific Northwest."

She was due for a vacation so it wasn't hard for Teresa to arrange a week off. As soon as she got home from work, she pulled out an overnight bag and packed hurriedly, throwing in underwear and a nightgown and two or three changes of clothing, and hanging her beige linen suit on the doorknob.

Grey Tiger jumped in and out of her bag and chewed on its nylon straps. She picked him up and kissed the top of his head, then set him down beside the stuffed tiger on her pillow. She would take him. It had been many weeks since she'd seen her parents, and over six months since she had stayed the night in her old room at the farm. She couldn't have taken Greg there, never had. Her parents wouldn't have understood, and she feared her brothers would have understood too well.

She went into the bathroom she shared with Hellen, that they had both shared with Greg. She scrubbed her face with a rough washcloth dripping with cold water, feeling the need to wake herself up out of this bizarre dream. Greg, who was always handing her just a ten or twenty dollar bill to help with expenses, always apologizing for not being able to afford more, and telling her how one day he would shower her with gold jewelry and take her on a world cruise. How could he have paid cash for expensive recording equipment, thousands and thousands of dollars of it in the past year? What did all those little tapes contain? She had listened to part of one, played it in her answering machine, but it was voices from a world she didn't
278

want to be a part of, nor even know about, so she'd stopped the tape and bundled them all into a padded envelope and mailed it to the address on the policeman's business card.

She never really knew Greg, then, after all. He had kept so many secrets from her. Did Hellen know?

Perhaps Teresa was just the way they paid their rent and bought their groceries. Teresa's hard work had made it possible for Greg to pursue his music, and had supported Hellen's causes, her caustic crusade to save animals from people. What kind of human being loved animals over people? Did Teresa mean less to Hellen than a pig or a cow? Was she nothing to them both but a meal ticket? How could she have been such a fool for so long?

After she'd washed her face and brushed her teeth, Teresa put her toothpaste and soap and lotion in a zippered cloth bag. She would help her mother and father tomorrow, help to pick radishes and carrots and wash and bundle them for the market. She would squat on the earth in the hot sun, a shawl shading her head and shoulders, listening to the hypnotic buzz of flies and the swish and growl of cars and trucks along the road beside the field, and she would try to stop thinking about the past two weeks. Instead, she would think about the moment, or maybe think about nothing at all.

She would feel the sun drape its heat across her back and the soft soil cling to her fingers, she would smell the perfume of earth and green onions, and she would put behind her what had happened with Greg and Hellen, stop trying to understand why, after she had been so strong and willful in her refusal to relinquish control of her future to her parents, she had given control of herself to such people. How was she able to stand up strong to her parents the way she had after high school graduation, when she insisted on moving to the city to attend college and get a job, but then go limp like an uprooted potato stalk when first Hellen, and then Greg had started molding her life? How could she have let herself be told how to think and how to behave in order to fit into their world? How had she allowed Greg to hide so many secrets from her? Why hadn't she seen what was happening long ago? How had they made her feel so unworthy?

Teresa pulled on her oldest pair of jeans and a faded cotton tunic, slipped her feet into the cool, cracked leather of her oldest sandals. Now she would be herself again. Today she would think about what her future could be, would be, without Greg, and without Hellen. She would make resolutions. She would make plans. She would talk to her parents and her brothers about her life in the city, and about how she sometimes regrets leaving the steady quiet pace of the farm, and about how maybe now she will be willing to meet the neighbor they have long wanted to introduce her to. Just meet him. No promises.

Teresa had no intention of escaping from one prison just to enter into another.

Before she drove away, Teresa backed her car up to the carport and loaded everything she could of Greg's into the trunk and backseat of her car. She would dump them somewhere on her way to the farm, in a restaurant dumpster in Langley, or in an empty parking lot in Aldergrove, or even in a ditch beside the road. Anywhere, that is, that Hellen would never go.

It was early evening and the tavern wasn't busy, just a couple of loners at the bar and a few tables of twos and threes, talking quietly and drinking beer. A Reba McIntyre song played on the jukebox. Hunter sat with Russell Kupka in the shadows. The detective's hands kept moving, scratching his unshaven cheek, adjusting the strap of his watch, pushing his sunglasses up on his nose. "What if your suspect doesn't show?"

Hunter shrugged. The man was only five minutes late, hardly long enough to be a concern. His biggest worry was that he and Russell might be recognized. He pulled the ball cap lower over his face.

Russell put his hand up to straighten his hair, probably remembered that he was supposed to look scruffy, and scratched his scalp instead. "The local cops can't wait around all day."

Hunter glanced at the two plain-clothes policemen from Ferndale, Washington. This was their jurisdiction. They had ordered

280

two beers as part of their cover, and were sharing a plate of nachos. It was a warm day, so they were wearing shorts and tee shirts. "They'll be fine," he said to Russell. "I don't think Ferndale is a high crime town."

Russell spent the next few minutes watching Pat Stevens, dressed as her "Ruby" alias in low slung white jeans, a crimson silk sleeveless blouse top tied short just below her breasts, floppy straw hat and designer shades. "She's nervous," he said, and sniffed. "That's her second cigarette already. You sure it was a good solid ID?"

Hunter had given the LA detective the best vantage point, so he himself could only see Pat's left elbow from where he sat, but he suspected she wasn't half as restless as Russell was. "She picked him out of the photo line up you put together, no hesitation. She knows what she's got to do. She's told him she has a tape Greg made of his transaction with Brantford. If he was scared enough to kill Greg, Pat knows he'll think about getting her out of the way, too. She'll make it work." He took a deep breath, let it out slowly. "She's doing us a big favor, putting herself at risk like this. We'd better not let her down, chief."

"Don't lay that on me, Rayne. This was all your idea. I still don't know why I went along with it, letting a civilian plan a sting." He scowled into his drink, then stretched his shoulders. "So when I've heard enough, I'll stand up, and they'll make the arrest. I hope they're on the ball." The detective glanced at the Ferndale officers as he adjusted the earpiece that would pick up the signals from the wire inside Pat's blouse. The conversation would also be recorded. "I hate this waiting."

"Haven't done many stakeouts, have you?" Hunter said drily.

Russell glowered briefly, then started playing with a coaster, spinning it like a top. "Don't look now, but here he is."

The man walked into the smoky gloom of the tavern, scanning the tables. He wore a cowboy hat and sunglasses, just as eager to hide his identity as the rest of them, but Hunter had no trouble recognizing Inspector Tom Donohue of U.S. Customs and Immigration. Hunter lowered his head, obscuring his own vision with the peak of his cap, and pretended to be digging in his jeans pocket for change. Russell turned his face toward Hunter and said, "So... how's the wife and kids, Norm? You going to be able to stay for another brewski? Your treat." He took a sip of beer, whispered, "He didn't make us. He's sitting down. Shhhh."

Hunter smiled. He had no intention of saying anything.

Russell listened intently to what was coming through his earpiece. He kept his head turned toward the trucker beside him, but trained his eyes on the couple across the room, trusting that his sunglasses would mask the direction of his gaze. "So," he heard Donohue say, slipping into a chair across the table from Pat, a.k.a. Ruby. Ruby the call girl. Ruby the high class hooker. Pat, the woman who'd been haunting the corners of Russell's mind since the night he'd made love to her. "You've got something for me, I believe."

"You must want it real bad," said Pat. She had tucked her waterfall of hair up under the wide brimmed hat, and wore the big sunglasses in an attempt to keep Donohue from recognizing her. She hadn't been sure whether or not he had ever seen her working at the Blackburn. They hoped he'd take her as the call girl he'd heard about at the time of the transaction with Colin Brantford, and nothing more. Russell found himself recalling the smell of her hair. The hair of a hooker.

"If you say so. I haven't heard the tape, so I don't know. Do I?"

"Cut the crap, cowboy. I was there the night Greg made the tape. I saw it all go down from inside of Colin's Mercedes. I saw Greg and Colin get into your car, the Washington plates. A Ford, isn't it? White. So, tape or no tape, I know exactly what went down, and the kind of damage it can do to your... uh... career." There was an audible intake of breath as she took a quick drag on her cigarette. "Tell me, how did Greg find out where you worked?"

"How did you?"

"Like I said, I was Greg's partner. How did he find out? He never told me."

"Greg didn't know. How did you?"

" How much did he want from you? Five thousand? Ten thousand?"

"You say you're his partner. You know so much, you tell me."

"I forget, Inspector Donohue."

Donohue scowled and looked around quickly. "No names, bitch."

"You can call me Ruby." She took a leisurely drag, blew the smoke toward the wall. "Since you don't want to name a figure, I will. Let's say Greg asked you for ten thousand. Okay with you?"

"What's your point?"

"Well, I figure now it's worth much more than that. About four times more."

"What?!"

"I know what else you did," she said.

"You know what's on the tape."

"No. Read my lips. I know what else you did," she repeated. "You lucked out, cowboy. You were in the right place at the right time. Or let's say, Sharon and her husband were in the wrong place at the wrong time. You almost got away with it, didn't you? If it wasn't for me, no one would ever put it together, would they?" It occurred to Russell how she might have been right. If it hadn't been for that damned trucker's persistence in poking around, trying to prove his buddy innocent, none of them, himself included, might ever have looked beyond Ray and Sharon Nillson. Even now, he had his doubts about Rayne's theory, and didn't care to think of the consequences if they were wrong.

"I don't know what you're talking about."

"You put Greg in that trailer because those poor dumb truckers were there to take the fall."

"You're crazy."

"You killed him. I know you killed him." Cool and self-assured. She was good. Russell felt an absurd surge of pride, as if she were his to be proud of. He had to remind himself she was just a hooker.

"Yeah, sure. I didn't kill anybody, but if you think I did, then prove it."

283

Watching Donohue's face, listening to the tension in his voice, for the first time Russell began to think Rayne could be right.

"I can't prove it, but I'm sure once the police know what to look for, they'll find enough evidence to put you away." Russell felt the bulge of the search warrant in the rear pocket of his jeans. Would the paint on Donohue's mountain bike match the paint on the rim of Williams' trunk? Would the brown hairs found on the driver's side headrest match Donohue's? Would they find something more?

"Fuck you."

"No, pay me. It's that easy, cowboy." Pat shifted her position, leaning back, and the mike picked up the rustle of fabric.

Donohue didn't answer. He just sat ramrod stiff and glared at her. Russell shook his head. "He's not giving us dick," he whispered to Hunter. "Sweet fuck all." He turned his head toward Donohue and caught Donohue staring at him. His heart lurched and he cursed silently, turned away again and started babbling to the trucker the first nonsense that came into his head. "You ever slept with a professional, buddy? Purely as a business transaction, of course. Like, barter, you know? I'll fix your toilet if you lay my carpet, you know what I mean?" What if Donohue wasn't guilty, but he figured out what was going on and made a complaint? Would there be official repercussions? Russell's stomach tightened with dread at the thought.

Hunter Rayne glanced sideways at him, concern showing on his face for the first time. "What's wrong?" the trucker asked.

"He might've made us," whispered Russell, unable to hide the resentment that was building in his gut toward Rayne. "He's clammed up. I told you it was too much of a risk to use an amateur in this sort of operation. At the very least we should've sprung for a two way." Not for the first time this afternoon, Russell cursed himself for letting this happen. It would turn out to be a waste of time and money, and he would look like a total fool.

"You think he wouldn't notice? A teleprompter would've been nice."

"Shhh..."

Pat a.k.a Ruby was still trying. "Look. You must make a good ten grand every time you bring some of that fluffy white stuff across
284

the border. Put it down to the cost of doing business. You give me a couple weeks worth of your profits, I go away. I'll move to Montreal, forget I ever saw you. You can wake up every morning without wondering if this is the day you're going to get busted, the day you're going to lose your job and your wife and your free..."

Donohue leaned across the table. "You want to know where that money goes?" Russell could tell from the way the trucker's eyes shifted that he could hear Donohue's raised voice himself, even without a wire. "It goes to doctors, it goes to hospitals, it goes to therapists, and I need every penny of it."

Russell sensed Pat's hesitation, but she continued. "You look pretty healthy to me, cowboy."

"It's not for me. It's for my son. He's only five, and he..."

"Whoa, there. Stop. I don't want to hear about your son. He's your problem, not mine." She sounded shaken. "Just do a couple extra deliveries, pay me off and I'll be out of your life."

"He needs..."

"Shut up! I said I don't want to hear about it."

Donohue's back stiffened and he clenched his jaw. "You heartless bitch. You're playing with fire."

She laughed. Russell could tell it was forced, that she had become uncomfortable with her role. "What're you going to do? Kill me right here?"

Donohue said nothing, but his breathing became faster, uneven. His lips were clenched so tight they turned white at the edges. Russell sucked in his breath. Guilty or not, Pat was starting to get to Donohue.

"Well?" Pat repeated.

"Give me the tape." Donohue's voice shook. What Russell could see of Donohue's right arm was moving, as if he were reaching for something in his pocket, or tucked in his waistband. Russell snuck his own hand inside his jacket, inching up toward his shoulder holster. He heard the trucker beside him whisper, "Shit."

"Forget it," Pat was saying, blowing smoke across the table.

At the same split second that Donohue stood up, knocking over his chair, Russell leapt from behind the table, his gun drawn.

"Freeze!" he yelled. The two Ferndale cops scrambled to their feet and went for their weapons.

Too late. Donohue had reached across the table and grabbed Pat's throat. As she opened her mouth to scream, he thrust the barrel of his .38 between her jaws. "Back off!" he shouted in Russell's direction. "Back off and let me out of here, or I'll blow the back of her head off." Russell stood there, frozen, his gun still aimed at Donohue's chest. "BACK OFF!" Donohue jerked Pat's head around and her hat fell to the table. He grabbed a handful of her hair.

"Russell. Put your gun down." It sounded like his father's voice, calm and soft as velvet, but it was the voice of Hunter Rayne. Russell could only think of what a sticky mess Pat's hair would be if Donohue pulled the trigger, matted with blood and bone. He lowered his gun.

"Don't anybody follow us," said Donohue. He wrapped Pat's hair around his fist and yanked her toward him. Her sunglasses fell and were crushed under her knee as she scrambled across the tabletop, gagging on the gun. Her eyes were wide with fear.

"I see anybody walk out this door in the next five minutes, and she's dead. You understand?" He was speaking directly to Russell. "DO YOU UNDERSTAND?" He had the gun at Pat's throat now, his left arm clamped around her ribcage as he dragged her backwards toward the door.

Pat's eyes were on Russell, a silent plea for help. They bored like a laser into his brain and he thought his head would explode if he didn't chase that bastard and grind him into the dirt. He opened his mouth, drawing a breath to shout, "NO!", ready to run, but...

"Say yes." That calm voice in Russell's ear again, like water on the flame of his panic. Someone thinking for him when his own mind had shut down.

Russell slowly let out his breath. "Yes," he said, nodding. "Yes. I understand." Inside his head he began to pray for the first time in a decade. Please, God, don't let him hurt her. Please, God, get us out of this mess. Please, God, show me the way.

286

"This way." Hunter moved off toward the rear exit, but the detective didn't follow. Instead, he started toward the front door. One of the Ferndale men blocked his way. "Russell," said Hunter, raising his voice. "You heard what he said. Come with me. Now."

Russell and the two plainclothes officers followed Hunter through the rear door, which opened up behind a dumpster in the rear of the parking lot. Hunter held up his hand for the others to halt while he peered around the dumpster. As he had hoped, Donohue had taken Pat to his own vehicle, a white Ford Taurus. The man wasn't about to hijack someone else's car. Donohue wasn't a professional criminal, a fact that made him less predictable and possibly more dangerous, because he was acting out of desperation.

Donohue paused awkwardly beside the driver's door. Hunter could almost see him thinking. How would he get Pat into the car without taking the gun off of her? How could he get out of here with his hostage? He was tentative and uncertain, tried to mask it by being rough. He maneuvered her around to the passenger side, made her stand with her hands on the roof of the car while he got out his keys and opened the door, then had her get in, sliding across to the driver's seat while he sat next to her with the gun pressed against her neck. His lips moved.

"What's he saying?" Hunter asked Russell, who was cupping his ear to keep the noise of traffic from drowning out the transmissions from Pat's wire.

"He's apologizing. The stupid fuck is apologizing."

Hunter nodded. Donohue's panic had already subsided a good deal, and it might be possible to reason with him. "Stay here," he said.

"What the fuck do you think you're doing?" Russell grabbed Hunter by the arm and spun him around.

"I got her into this, I'm going to do my damnedest to get her out of it. You're not responsible. Stay here," Hunter repeated and walked out from behind the dumpster, casual and slow, as if he were strolling on the beach. He threw off his cap and tucked his sunglasses in his shirt pocket, then put both hands, fingers locked together, on the top of his head. Just as Pat turned the Ford into the exit lane, Hunter came out from behind a minivan and stepped in front of it. The car lurched to a stop. He shot a reassuring smile at Pat, nodded to Donohue. "Hello, chief," he said. "Can I talk to you for a minute?"

"Get the fuck out of the way!" yelled Donohue.

Hunter kept his voice low. "Give me two minutes. Then I'll step out of your way and you're free to go. Just two minutes. I'm not armed." He lifted his hands clear of his head to show they were empty. "I'm not even a police officer. I have no intention of keeping you here against your will, nor the authority to do so."

"Are you crazy?"

"Maybe." He smiled, putting his hands back on top of his head.

Donohue's jaw worked, and he scowled. "One minute. If this is a trick, she's dead." His gun pressed into Pat's throat. "So talk."

Hunter spoke, slow and even. "If you run, Tom, they will find you. Think about it. Where are you going to go that they won't find you? If you're able to elude the police, as a fugitive you'll never be able to see your wife and child. They'll suffer for you. They'll go through hell not knowing where you are and when your ordeal will end. And it will end. Badly. You know it will. You know the law. The worst thing you can do now is run."

"I've got no choice."

"Yes. You have a choice. Just like you had a choice when you sold the drugs. Just like you had a choice when you put Greg Williams in that trailer. You're a smart man. You knew the risk, and you made the choice to take it. From what I understand, you had good reason to. Well, you've gambled and you've lost. The game is over. You can't avoid paying a penalty for what you've done, but you can minimize your losses."

Donohue swung his head from side to side. "Fuck," he said. "Goddamn it. Fuck."

"You don't want to hurt anyone, Tom. You're a good man who has made a tragic mistake. Don't make it worse for yourself and your family. Slow down and think about it. You'll know what to do."

Donohue made no move, gave no sign of preparing to resume his flight, just sat sullenly, massaging his temple with his free hand.

288

Hunter stepped slowly around to Pat's window. He crouched down so his head was in the window, his hands harmlessly on the roof. Donohue took the muzzle of the gun from the woman's neck, aimed it directly between Hunter's eyes. Pat sat with her head pressed hard against the headrest, so tense her body was rigid. She closed her eyes.

"If you want me to," Hunter said to Donohue, "I'll help you get out of this mess. I'll take the gun."

The next fifteen seconds were among the longest in Hunter's life. He kept his eyes trained on Donohue's, trying not to look into the neat black hole where death lurked just inches away from his face. The corner of Donohue's mouth lifted, and Hunter ventured a quizzical smile.

Donohue shook his head, snorting softly. "You're right," he said, his mouth contorted in bitterness. "Fuck. It will only get worse. I wish to God I'd never crossed that damned border." With that, he opened his hand and let the gun spin loosely on his index finger. As Hunter reached for it, Donohue flipped it back into position and aimed it again at Hunter's face.

Pat whimpered softly. Hunter let his breath out slowly. Ten seconds passed like hours.

"You know what, man?" said Donohue. "I could've killed you, just like that. You're nuts. You're fuckin' nuts." He let the gun drop again, let it hang from his index finger. "Here," he said, extending his arm. "Take it. Take the fuckin' gun."

CHAPTER
TWENTY-THREE

Russell leaned against the trunk of his rental car, watching the Ferndale police Mirandize Donohue and prepare to transport him to the local jail, where he would remain until the official transfer to Russell's custody. Pat Stevens had been guided to the back seat of Hunter Rayne's Chevy, where she had crumpled and cried for a few minutes while the trucker stood beside her looking helpless. Russell now felt the pull of her eyes on him, but kept his head half turned away. He hadn't spoken to her except for a brief test of the wire when he'd first arrived at the tavern. Was she his lover, or a hooker? He didn't know what to say.

The trucker appeared at Russell's elbow. "Say, chief. You're better with the ladies than I am. Maybe you could go over and debrief our volunteer." He nodded over toward Pat. "She's pretty shaken up."

Russell took a deep breath. He couldn't very well hand this off to a civilian, and he couldn't very well ignore someone who had just risked her life to help.

"She asked for you," added Hunter.

"Great," Russell muttered. He ran a hand through his hair, then across his jaw, remembering how scruffy he looked. What the hell. She's just a hooker.

She was watching him as he started over, but when he got to the car her eyes were trained on the broken sunglasses she held in her hand. "Hi," he said. "You were terrific."

She didn't look up, just ventured a wry smile. "That's what they all say."

"I mean it," he said, ignoring his inadvertent double entendre. "That took a lot of guts. I appreciate it." There was a moment of uncomfortable silence. He rubbed his jaw and looked away. "You look like you could use a drink. You want to go back inside while we talk?"

He stood back to let her out of the car, thought better of extending his hand to help her. She stood up, then stumbled. He took hold of her arm to steady her. Her skin was cool.

"Sorry. I'm feeling a little shaky."

He let go of her arm and she hugged herself, as if she were cold. "I can't stop shivering," she said.

Russell appraised her flimsy blouse and the amount of skin it left bare. "It's pretty cool inside with the air conditioning. Maybe we should stay here." He guided her back to the car, and she slid over to make room for him. He sat, but left one foot out on the pavement. Russell took a couple of deep breaths, yawned, then coughed. He wished he hadn't let her get under his skin. He wanted her to apologize for leading him to believe... but what had she led him to believe? Nothing more than that he was a good fuck. That as one night stands go, he was a good one. Instead, he decided to apologize to her, show her it didn't matter. "Look," he said. "I didn't realize you were... uh... this close to the case. It was very unprofessional of me... the other night, I mean. You should have said something."

She said nothing.

"You could have told me!" It burst from him before he knew what he was saying. "You could have told me," he repeated under his breath.

She opened and closed the arm of her sunglasses, making soft clicking sounds. "If I'd told you, you would have looked at me differently." She shivered visibly, and began rubbing her arms.

He snorted softly. "Why would you care, Ruby? I don't imagine you're so hard up for one nighters."

"You see?"

"Big deal, Pat. Big fuckin' deal."

"You're the one who's making a big deal out of it. Look, I liked you, you liked me. We had fun. Is that so wrong?"

"It screwed up a good relationship."

She laughed. "A good relationship? If you'd had a good relationship with your little prima donna, I wouldn't have been there in the first place, would I?" She seemed to be warming up. "Don't lay that on me, cowboy."

He grabbed the door rim with one hand, preparing to get out of the car.

"Men are such hypocrites. Sure, it's okay for you to cruise the bars to pick up a good-looking stranger. It's something you all boast about in the locker room. But let a woman look for a little fun, and she's a whore."

"You are a whore."

"Look, asshole! I'm an escort. I keep men company, go to parties, shows, out on their boats. I've even had guys fly me to Chicago and New Orleans to be their escorts at business conferences. They're rich men, they're busy men, they don't have time to meet women. The money a guy pays helps me dress nice so I can look good on his arm. Who gets hurt?"

"Sure, but you notice they never take you home to meet their mothers."

"I've got a perfectly good mother of my own, thank you."

"Does she know?"

"Go to hell."

After Russell was back in L.A., he thought about what Pat had said in the hotel room. You can't lose what you ain't never had. Maybe she was right, but it didn't make him feel any better. He'd had his guts tied in knots by a whore. Stupidly enough, he wanted to see her again, but he knew he never would.

The hydro towers visible from the I-5 looked like an endless parade of long-legged stick men, and the oblique shafts of evening sun blessed even the worn asphalt with amber light. It was mid-September when Hunter and the Blue Knight fell in behind that familiar rust colored Kenworth on the California interstate and followed it from the Lost Hills turn off to the truck stop in Buttonwillow. As he stepped down from his rig, Sharon Nillson was waiting by the fender, and wrapped her arms around him in a bear hug, almost pulling him off his feet.

"I know you don't like it," she said, tucking a strand of blond hair behind her ear, "but I've been wanting to do that for months. I don't know if we'll ever be able to thank you enough."

He waved her gratitude away. "If it hadn't been me, someone else would've sorted it out."

"I don't believe that for a minute." She raised her voice to be heard above the growling engine of a rig as it passed, gearing up and snorting smoke. "How did you figure out it was the customs guy?"

"I figured it had to have happened somewhere you and Ray had stopped, better yet where your trailer had been opened, and when I started to look at the border as a possible site, the pieces started to fit. I couldn't place it at the time, but I knew I'd heard the voice on one of Greg's tapes before. There'd been bicycle paint on the trunk of Greg's car, and I knew that Tom Donohue had a bicycle, and he matched the description of the man who'd argued with Greg in the Blackburn the same night you did. He'd also shown up to work with a shiner, which I found kind of suspicious since the witnesses had mentioned a fight in the parking lot that night. I thought it could have been Toad and his biker buddies teaching Tom a lesson. Turned out I was right. Before we set up that sting, I got the police to show his picture to Pat Stevens, and she identified him."

"You know, if I hadn't been so scared of saying something that would make Ray look guilty, I would've told the police how long we were away from our truck at the border. We opened it up for the Food Safety guy to do an inspection, then we'd both gone our separate ways — me to immigration and Ray over to the customs office — and Greg must've seen our truck on his way through the border and come back looking for us, although he knew he was supposed to meet us at the bank in Ferndale. Maybe he wanted to show us how easily he could turn over the those tapes to U.S. immigration. That's when he saw the customs guy and recognized him and the guy must've knocked him out or something."

Hunter nodded. "In his confession, Tom Donohue said that Greg laughed when he recognized him and said, Jackpot! Greg told him he was going to have to turn over a big piece of the action if he didn't want his secret to get out. When Greg turned to leave, Tom panicked and got him in a chokehold. Greg passed out, and Tom thought he'd killed him, so he removed all possible identification, then hoisted Greg's body in the trailer. He was too panicked to check to see if Greg was still alive."

Sharon picked up the story again. "I couldn't vouch for where Ray was all that time, 'cause I was waiting in the immigration lineup, and Ray didn't know where I was because he was waiting at the customs brokers office. It wasn't until I talked to Ray about it later that we realized that the customs guy had already locked up our trailer before either of us got back." Sharon shook her head. "But then why would we even suspect that the customs guy had anything to do with Greg? By the way, what about Greg's car? Why wasn't it found at the border? And why weren't the tapes in it – the ones he wanted me to buy off him? Where are they?"

"Tom told the police that after his shift was over, he located Greg's car parked in the customs lot, loaded his bike in the trunk and drove the car to Mount Vernon, then rode home on his bike. He threw Greg's jacket, keys and wallet into the Skagit River on the way home. I assume the tapes were in his jacket pockets. But Greg never intended to give you the only copies, anyway. Unfortunately, he'd copied all of the microcassettes onto regular tapes, and those are the ones I found taped to his speaker."

"Unfortunately?" Sharon sighed and shook her head. "I'd say, fortunately for us. It's sure lucky for Ray and me that you're so smart. C'mon." She grabbed his arm. "Ray's just walkin' the dog, but he'll meet us in the restaurant."

Hunter gently pulled his arm away, scratched his other elbow. "El told me you had good news last week."

"Yeah, sort of. Alora told me they decided not to prosecute. That poor woman who was in my cell, she's still alive, but she's practically a vegetable. I'm really sorry it happened, but I can't let it ruin my life thinking about it." She shook her head. "When you come close to losing everything that's important to you - your freedom, your husband... your dog..." Her eyes crinkled up as she grinned. "... it sure makes you appreciate it all the more. It's like we've been given a second chance at life together, Ray and me. Maybe the trouble we've been through will bring us even closer together, you know?" She sighed. "Some day."

"I'm glad you see it that way. You can't do anything about the past, so put your energy toward the future. File the bad stuff away. Learn what you can from it, then toss it out. Concentrate on the good stuff." He held the door open for her.

"Yeah. I wish I could toss out about ten years of my life." She smiled wanly. "Ray pretends he doesn't feel any different about me, but I know he does. I see it in his eyes when he looks at me. It breaks my heart to have disappointed him."

They found a good table by the window, just being wiped clean by the waitress. "Coffee?" she asked, and Hunter said, "Please". Sharon ordered one for Ray as well.

"Alora told me she's going to Vancouver after Christmas. Did she call you?"

Hunter nodded. "I told her I'd show her around if I'm in town on the same day she is. She'll be staying up at Whistler." He hadn't yet decided whether he would try to arrange his schedule around her visit, or let fate call the shots. He had lots of time to make up his mind.

"Just one day? You should take some time off and go to Whistler at the same time. She's a really nice lady, and she'll be by herself."

"You see, Sharon," he said, leaning forward with his arms crossed on the table top. "It's like this. There's this other woman I'm involved with. I just don't think she'd let me go."

"Oh!" Sharon's eyes lit up. "Tell me more."

"What's to tell? She's big and she's mean and I owe her a bundle of money, and if I don't give her every possible minute of my time, she'll take away my truck," said Hunter, and Sharon laughed.

Ray arrived, sat next to Sharon, and gave her a quick hug. Sharon squeezed his hand and smiled, a little sadly, Hunter thought.

He looked away, out the window at the setting sun glinting off the chrome of a dozen big rigs. He saw hours of aching loneliness during nights on the road, with no shining beacon to aim for in the darkness. He wished it could be different for him, but even in his imagination, he couldn't see himself anything but alone. For now.

The waitress breezed up to the table with a pot of coffee in her hand, and menus tucked under her elbow. "How are you all tonight?" she asked, turning over their coffee cups on the saucers with a clatter.

"Just tickety boo," said Hunter, with a smile. "Just tickety boo."

ACKNOWLEDGEMENTS

It's been a long road to this first printing of ICE ON THE GRAPEVINE, starting back in 1995 when the plot ideas first started taking shape, through highway drives on the I-5 to check out the Grapevine and several rewrites based on what I learned along the road. As always, I owe my late husband, Jim Donald, for getting me started and providing the inspiration for the character of Hunter Rayne. My father was an amazing supporter from the beginning, and I miss him very much. He passed away in March 2012, but a part of him survives in the character of Hunter's landlord, Gord Young.

Many thanks to my early readers, among them Californian Marc Mayfield, former long-haul trucker and author of 'In the Driver's Seat', who gave a thumbs up to the trucking depictions in my novel. I owe a great debt of gratitude to my sister, Chris, and her extremely talented husband, Steve, for taking time out of their busy schedules to create awesome covers for my novels.

I hope readers will forgive any errors I may have made in geography or description, and keep in mind that I may have taken literary license when I felt the story would be better for it. I've done my best to write a novel that mystery fans like myself will enjoy.

A huge thank you to all my readers, especially those who take the time to give me feedback or post reviews. Your enthusiasm for my mysteries gives meaning to how I spend my working days.

ABOUT THE AUTHOR

R.E. Donald is the author of the Hunter Rayne highway mystery series. Ruth worked in the transportation industry in various capacities from 1972 until 2001, and draws on her own experiences, as well as those of her late husband, Jim Donald, in creating the characters and situations in her novels.

Ruth attended the University of British Columbia in Vancouver, B.C., where she studied languages (Russian, French and German) and creative writing to obtain a Bachelor of Arts degree. She currently lives on a small farm in Langley, B.C. She and her partner, a French Canadian cowboy named Gilbert Roy, enjoy their Canadian Horses (Le Cheval Canadien) and other animals.

Also by R.E. Donald in the Hunter Rayne highway mystery series:
Slow Curve on the Coquihalla

Coming in the fall of 2012: *Sea to Sky*

For information on new releases visit
redonald.com or **proudhorsepublishiing.com**.

Printed in Great Britain
by Amazon

54316703R00169